THE
LORDS OF
THE SUMMER
SEASON

FAUX PRAISE FOR
THE LORDS OF THE SUMMER SEASON

Despite repeated requests, *The London Review of Books*, *The Financial Times*, and *The New York Review of Books* have to date resisted reviewing *The Lords of the Summer Season*. No doubt they've prioritized lesser literary efforts. So, given the absence of reputable critiques, I've cheerfully fabricated the following endorsements. I've also asked some of the novel's characters to provide their reviews.

"*The Lords of the Summer Season* is so lurid it glows in the dark. It's insane to the point of requiring the reader to be medicated. This novel is evocative enough to induce visions. And the prose is so vivid, it dances off the page in shades of purple."

—ModernUrbanFantasyFanzine(MUFF).com

"*The Lords of the Summer Season* is an amusing antidote to trope-laden fantasy novels. The hero is a magician, but he'd rather use his wits than magic to get out of trouble; there are enough ghosts to haunt a whole city full of Victorian mansions, but the specters are only nasty when provoked; there is an ancient witch, but she flies horses, not broomsticks, and rides a Triumph motorcycle like nobody's business; and there's a savage wolf, but he's so over eating people that he'd rather snack on souls."

—*The Emeryville Quarterly Literary Review*

"Despite the assertions made in this witty and fanciful book, there is no evidence whatever that Sandro Botticelli delegated painting of the face of Flora from his *Primavera* masterpiece to apprentices in his studio. What is beyond all doubt is that this work is phenomenal art."

—Maria Rubino, Ph.D., Executive Director of Curatorial Services, Le Gallerie Degli Uffizi

"A collision of the urban fantasy urtext and swashbuckling adventure . . . As in much of Blaisdell's recent work, he aims high, and here, the theme is creativity itself."

—*Haight Neighborhood Fishing and Literary Gazette*

"The author's snarky description of a southern California liberal arts college campus is scurrilous. Readers need to understand that, whatever may or may not have happened a half century ago, tolerance for the type of behavior described in *The Lords of the Summer Season* is now zero. Plus grants are a lot harder to get nowadays."

—Lucy Trellis, Media Relations and Community Outreach, Southern California Association of Collegiate Heuristic Concerns

"I wish I'd had a chance to meet Meadow. She seems really sweet. But you'll never catch me haunting a Harley."

—Connie (currently haunting Bradan's electric car)

"Let's get the band back together!"

—Jeff Dorsey, acoustic and electric bass, vocals, rhythm guitar, flute, and wind chimes for The Pillars of Creation

"I'm still keeping the beat, Bradan. They always wanted your autograph, never mine, but at least we got that royalty thing squared away. And I'm with Jeff. Let's start playing together again."

—William Constantine, drums, percussion, tambourine, vocals, and wind chimes for The Pillars of Creation

"You do time with someone, you get to know them. This Bradan guy is stand-up, but I didn't realize how old he was. He looked thirty at most."

—Edmund (Eddie) San Martin, Sergeant at Arms (ret.), MC

"Bradan, what a cool cat. Good to read his story. And I've still got the best hash in the Haight."

—George (Scarlet Zorro) Ramirez

Author's Disclaimer: All of this "praise" is as fictional as the novel itself. It was fun inventing approbation for *The Lords of the Summer Season* in which the novel's characters critique the author and the book. Also included are quotes from fake fantasy websites and nonexistent literary journals. Gentle readers can decide for themselves whether they agree with the "praise."

PRAISE FOR OTHER NOVELS
IN THIS SERIES

"Deftly written by Peter W. Blaisdell, *The Lords of Oblivion* is a simply riveting literary fantasy/magical realism novel...Impressively original and consistently entertaining from beginning to end, *The Lords of Oblivion* is especially and unreservedly recommended..."

—*The Small Press Bookwatch*
a Midwest Book Review Journal

THE
LORDS OF
THE
SUMMER
SEASON

A PSYCHEDELIC FANTASY

PETER W. BLAISDELL

This is a work of fiction. All of the characters, names, places, organizations, and events portrayed in this novel are either products of the author's vivid imagination or are used fictitiously.

Cover design by Heidi North
Interior book design by Andrea Reider

ISBN: 978-0-9992205-0-4
E-ISBN: 978-0-9992205-5-9

Library of Congress Control Number 2020919276

To my family. And to creators everywhere who let their circumstances, good, bad, or simply strange, inspire their art.

. . . for a small period of time, it was a magical thing going on and I was living it.

—Pamela Des Barres

It rained a lot during the Summer of Love.

—Anon.

THE
LORDS OF
THE SUMMER
SEASON

CHAPTER 1

The Wild Hunt

Spring Equinox, 1964, Big Sur, California

A beautiful sunset looked like the gates of Hell. Cumulus clouds fat as the sin of gluttony spewed into the sky from infernal foundries. And, high up, elongate cirrus clouds were witch's fingers reaching for a soul.

Pacific storms pushed inland erasing evening light. Bradan saw rain hit Highway 1. He rode his Harley Panhead flat out, top gear, throttle screwed back, heading south, racing the storm. No rear suspension meant every bump punched his kidneys. The old bike handled like shit even in perfect weather. On wet pavement he felt like he rode on an ice rink.

He took a corner fast and the pedals grounded on the asphalt, striking sparks. The Harley skidded and he almost lost it rolling out of the curve. Once the heavy motorcycle got out of control, there was no pulling back from a grinding crash that would abrade away skin and bone as it slid along the asphalt with the helpless rider pinned beneath it. Then the intermingled metal and flesh would smash through a guardrail and down, a long way down, to the rocks where the ocean met California.

But not tonight. He muscled the brute back into equilibrium. The acid he'd taken didn't help.

Fortunately, the ghost haunting his motorcycle kept quiet. Sheets of rain hazed his vision and the bike's anemic headlight scarcely illuminated the road.

Night fell, a headsman's ax cleanly sheering away daylight, as lightning and thunder reverberated down from the Santa Lucia Mountain gorges to his left through the redwoods. Tonight's cataclysm was well outside the norm for spring storms. It shouldn't have happened at all. Weathermen had predicted a clear March evening, good conditions to ride fast on the four-hundred-mile trek south from San Francisco to Los Angeles.

He'd pull off the road at the next overlook and endure a frigid soaking while waiting out the downpour. There'd be no shelter, but he couldn't get any wetter, and reaching LA for an unpaid gig at a Sunset Avenue club by tomorrow was a lost cause, so no sense killing himself sprinting down the coast. Also, he didn't feel remotely in control of his reflexes. A pause might clear the psychedelics bathing his neurons.

Ahead, obscured by the rain and night, Bixby Bridge's elegant concrete arches spanned a river. Bradan thought the thunder might disintegrate the regal structure. A vista point for tourists overlooked the bridge's north end. He braked gingerly and rolled his bike off the highway into the overlook, crunching over gravel, and killed the engine. Bradan smelled wet dirt from the surrounding hills and salt from the ocean. He felt unmoored without familiar visual cues. He existed in a strange purgatory, in a wild, supernatural space without tangible reference points.

Though early Spanish explorers designated the land south of Monterey *el pais grande del sur,* Big Sur was more of an attitude than a physical region and it wasn't really south of anything.

Instead, it was central to itself, self-contained, and formed a stretch of beautiful shoreline between Monterey and San Louis Obispo, which geographically and psychically connected San Francisco's dizzy environs and the vast madness of Los Angeles. Yet it was sparsely peopled and lay apart from both metropolises and was happy for that.

"I wouldn't be stopping just now." The ghost had picked the wrong moment to be argumentative.

"No choice," Bradan shouted above the storm. "I can't ride in this."

"But they can," the ghost said. "Look up."

They rode black horses. A red-bearded giant led the charge wearing chain mail and holding aloft a broadsword while clenching reins in his other hand. He headed a numberless host stretching into the sky in a long arc, all of them grasping spears, bows, and axes. Their mounts' nostrils flared red. Sweat and spittle flew off the horses; they were being ridden hard, though these stallions didn't need goading; they were as intent on chasing down prey as their riders. The army emanated from the atmosphere's very molecules, both substantial and ethereal. Some riders were robust and muscular and appeared to have leaped off a longship ready to pillage. Others were spectral and gaunt, damnation incarnate from Hieronymus Bosch art. Most were naked except for animal skins tied around their shoulders steaming behind in the wind. Amid the Dark Ages host, Bradan spotted helicopters with door guns manned by figures in fatigues. Orange tracer bullets reached out for him, splattering the asphalt and gravel. Women warriors mixed with the men, corpse-pale and nude. One, tall and lithe, hair dark as death, rode at the leader's side. She might have been his consort—or they led the pack together, co-regents of the hellish company. She stood high in her stirrups, black bush exposed to the storm, and touched her spear's tip against his sword in a collision of blue sparks, both drunk with the chase, erotic license, and inexorable momentum.

Behind the giant, rode a figure nearly as large. The rider resembled Medraut, an old enemy, but in the wretched weather, it was impossible to tell. The berserker brandished a war hammer with a head larger than a motorcycle engine. The sight should have been ludicrous, but instead it was eldritch and insane. He spotted Bradan and hurled his mad tool cartwheeling over his comrades. It struck the cliff just above Bradan like a lightning bolt, sending him toppling off the Harley to the gravel.

Big Sur, is there a better place for a cosmic ambush? he wondered.

Without thinking an instant about whether this was an acid dream or the actual Wild Hunt, Bradan stomped on the Panhead's starter.

Thank Christ the bike caught immediately despite the torrential downpour. In first gear, spinning gravel, Bradan slithered back toward Highway 1 jamming his boot on the pavement to stabilize the bike as it hit the asphalt shoulder, then lurched into second gear with a snarl audible even above the apocalyptic storm and the shrieks of his pursuers. He smelled oil, but Panheads burned oil even when they weren't being pushed through their gears in a death chase with a demon legion. Third gear now and Bradan really accelerated down the highway, hardly able to see the road save as a black, shiny serpent heading south whose spine he rode along. He pushed the pedal shifter into top gear and there was a snap as it engaged and torque and speed shoved him back on the wet seat. He had to clench the slippery handles or be yanked off the lurching brute. Bradan pushed the old engine to redline, throwing aside caution about shredding crashes in favor of saving his soul—assuming it was still his to save.

Milton couldn't have imagined more threatening agents of spiritual devastation than those he fled.

Why tonight?

He recollected that it was the spring equinox, when things were fluid, borders between different eras and realms became permeable, and, once in a great while, visions smashed into reality with uncertain consequences.

Why is this happening to me?

Perhaps he'd challenged hallowed theology or peeked behind the temple and profaned sacred rituals. His blasphemy had been noticed; a 1,500-year lifetime was long enough to offend any number of deities.

Or he was simply in the wrong place at an ungodly hour.

It was on such a night in early sixth-century Britain when gods from different pantheons—Christian, pagan, whatever— warred, and a hapless traveler alone and out too late on a muddy path through deserted fields felt the wind pick up and glanced at the sky to see he had company.

They hadn't caught him then and they wouldn't now—if he could last till dawn. It was a race to daylight. A single sunbeam could impale and vaporize the most fearsome pursuing specter.

Bradan fled south, pacing just ahead of the mad horde. Their deafening cacophony meshed seamlessly with the storm's discord. Amazingly, his bike was as fast as the pack behind him— or they simply held back savoring the hunt, after fleet prey, ready to swoop down when he became too confident he could outrun them.

Now he rode among redwoods enclosing the coast highway. He smelled trees and soil. He glanced over his shoulder to see the infernal army hindered by branches. The helicopters had to avoid conifers, and the flying, soaring mounted warriors crashed about in the tree limbs. Bradan guessed that since his pursuers had taken corporeal form, they were subject to earthly barriers and therefore liable to become entangled among the redwoods. Nonetheless, they tracked him unerringly. Another hammer strike just to his left shattered trees, sending splinters into his back. He inhaled in pain.

Despite running flat out, the Panhead's engine sounded strong.

Please don't throw a rod.

Bradan looked at his gauges.

Shit, out of gas in a few miles.

"Those guys chasing you aren't cool." Despite the tumult, Bradan heard the ghost clearly. Whatever chaos churned about him, her tone radiated serenity. And she always spoke in complete sentences.

"Can't go faster," he yelled. Big trunks blurred past, narrowing the two-lane highway to a slot ahead of him. Branches reached down. The specters had enlisted the trees to pluck him from his saddle.

"I know," she said. "I know what this bike can and can't do. I was on it when you crashed it. I'll warn you if it's about to break."

"Great."

"You're sarcastic. That's not your best quality. To the right of you, another person lost in the storm."

Far ahead and indistinct in the downpour, but closing fast, Bradan saw shapes in the road.

"I see it. A car. No, it's hunters."

Bradan couldn't help himself and instinctively locked front and rear brakes trying to avoid them dead ahead in his dim headlight. They made no effort to dodge the hurtling Harley and there was no room between redwoods and the mounted figures standing on the center line. How he kept himself upright, he didn't know. The big bike slithered past a half dozen skeletal horsemen and the spear-woman. He fishtailed wildly and barely slowed as he modulated the brakes to keep control. He rolled over pine needles and downed branches on the shoulder, just missing a redwood with a girth as big as a house. Now he was amid the marauders, a paladin without lance on a hopeless errand. However, his erratic path helped him as he evaded a sword thrust. Past them and back on the highway, he downshifted and accelerated as hard as the Panhead could move. He darted a glance back.

Behind, and distracted by his lunatic evasions, the hellish host coalesced into a massive vortex amid the trees and night and surged after him. He'd be a pagan sacrifice on an asphalt altar.

But the company was so excited by an imminent kill and another soul to collect that its movements weren't coordinated. Bradan saw in his mirrors a dozen of the foremost warriors collide to hit the tarmac in a kicking, heaving mass. More mounted warriors piled into them, somersaulting over their companions. It became a mountain of writhing beasts and men. They must be more agile in the air than on earthly roads, Bradan supposed. Just above the mess, a Huey swung its rotors into a tree, sending shrapnel and splinters in all directions. The wreckage hit the ground and exploded into flames.

Bradan heard screams and exulted. They could be hurt. But so could he.

The remaining Hueys circled after Bradan, moving in for the kill, their door gunners lining up lethal fields of fire for bursts from their guns. However, the rider with the hammer swung down to interpose himself between Bradan and the choppers. He'd take this kill for himself, but the black-haired woman barged into center stage as she landed on the road with an impact that rocked the earth, interposing herself between the horde and Bradan. She resembled the witch Morgana.

All looked to the bearded giant to adjudicate who the executioner would be, but he paid no attention, instead staring after Bradan racing south.

Bradan intended to capitalize on the heavenly discord. This was the time if ever to open up space between himself and the Wild Hunt.

Ahead of him through the redwoods, he saw a gas station with a sign cheerily illuminating the falling rain, a little frontier fort by the road surrounded by hostile wilderness out of a John Ford western.

"Gas ahead," Bradan screamed.

"They'll catch you," the ghost said.

"Running on fumes. No choice."

He rolled into the Shell station, nearly crashing into one its two pumps. The engine died in a death rattle. He truly had no more fuel. How long before his pursuers ran him to ground? How long before sunrise?

The station had no awning, dashing Bradan's hopes of avoiding the rain while the attendant gassed up his Harley. A small office sat next to the pumps, but looked more like a log cabin than a modern facility.

Stupid.

Bradan levered the Panhead's kickstand down and dashed to the door, dodging between a yellow Volkswagen Beetle and a Chevy station wagon haphazardly parked by the pumps. The cars' owners had run for the office when the deluge came without trying to fill up.

"Man, that rain hit just before you arrived," a beefy teenager with a crew cut and plastic-framed glasses behind the counter said as Bradan lunged into the office. "Hear it through the roof, whole station might blow away. Storm must be following you."

"More than you know," Bradan said. "I'm in a hurry. Can you gas up my bike?"

The attendant stared at him like he'd lost his mind. "I'm not goin' outside."

"What's the rush?" said a paunchy man in a plaid, short-sleeved sport shirt. An equally stout woman Bradan guessed was his wife in a checked woolen jacket and skirt outfit stood behind him with a little boy and girl. The kids appeared to be about seven and ten. The wagon parked outside must be the family's. They were all wet with moisture steaming out of the woman's ensemble.

"Shouldn't you wear a helmet in case you crash?" the wife asked.

"Probably," Bradan said.

"Wait it out," the stout fellow continued. "You can't ride a motorcycle in this. I can't even take my car back on the road. The storm'll blow through."

"Not while I'm here," Bradan said.

The man looked at him strangely.

"It won't last," said a diminutive young woman in a beret peering out the window of the front door. She wore black jeans and a black turtleneck sweater. It was all sodden and she looked frozen and miserable. The woman must have fabulous hair under better circumstances, Bradan thought, but the rain had turned this into a stringy mess. She smelled of damp wool and dope.

Everyone shivered in the close confines crammed between racks of candy bars, maps, and motor oil. The family's kids looked on the verge of tantrums.

The hunters would flatten the place.

An immense crash rocked the building.

"Weird light effects outside, figures dancing in the sky." The young woman peered through the front door's window. The two kids pushed over to stand beside her and stare through the window.

"You high?" the dad asked. "Don't scare the kids."

The little boy said, "No, Dad, something's out there. A lot of animals in the trees and sky."

"There's nothing there, just lightning, I think," his sister said. "Except for a wolf."

"Here's twenty," Bradan said, pulling a bill out of his wallet so sodden the money almost tore in half as he extracted it. "Unlock the pump. I'll gas it myself."

"Nothing in the register tonight," the attendant said. "Can't make change."

"Keep it all. Give me the key to the pump. I'll do the rest."

Greed was the great persuader.

Ignoring the drenching rain, Bradan jammed the pump nozzle into the Panhead's tank and poured gas in. The vanguard of the pursuing army emerged above the clearing in the redwoods surrounding the little station. Bradan flung the pump handle aside, leaving it to dangle, jumped on the Harley's starter, and blasted back onto the highway's scaly asphalt. Besides eluding the demon warriors himself, he wanted to draw them away from the gas station and the innocents inside. The hunters were fixated on Bradan, so the kids, their parents, the attendant, and the young woman were only endangered when close to him.

The hammer spiraled just over his head and ripped into old trees encircling the office, sending one of them tumbling onto the station's pumps as lightning washed over the clearing and highway. Only the torrential rain prevented the fuel from exploding and erasing the office and its inhabitants.

Bradan took his bike back up to top speed in seconds. He'd had just enough time to mostly fill its gas tank. Water was pooling in the road's depressions where it couldn't drain off to the saturated dirt shoulder. The redwoods were transitioning to coastal savannah, not good since the trees had partially masked his progress and hampered the Wild Hunters. On his right, the ocean was a gray, churning sheet whipped by the gale. Surely he hallucinated the dozens of waterspouts as sky and sea reached out to touch as lovers.

"You can barely stay ahead of them," the ghost said.

"'Barely' works for me," Bradan yelled. "And why do you care? You're dead. They can't touch you."

"They can," she said. "I haven't passed away completely. That's why I stay with the bike—and with you. They want lost souls."

"Like you?"

"Like us."

"It was an accident," Bradan said to himself, but she heard him perfectly, of course.

"I know," the ghost said. "When the bike went down, you were lucky, I wasn't."

"An accident," he said.

Bradan balanced overwhelming sadness at his culpability in her horrific death with terror at being the object of ghastly pursuit. If it were possible, the night darkened further, and then rage replaced other emotions as he worked to wring every bit of horsepower out of the motorcycle. No one, demonic or otherwise, would catch him tonight.

"You do spells," the ghost said. "Try one."

"Against them? Over my pay grade. I'm just a conjuror, party tricks. Tonight all we do is run."

"What saves us?"

"Daylight. If we stay ahead."

He flicked a look at his mirrors. The hunters weren't gaining, but they weren't falling behind. However, their clamor had died down. They must realize it was a marathon, not a sprint. The storm, their ally, pounded down unrelenting, its fury matching his own.

"Your wolf is with them," she said.

"He's in San Francisco."

However, in his mirrors, he saw she was right. Tintagel streaked along just below the Wild Hunters on Highway 1. They flew, the wolf ran. Astoundingly, the creature effortlessly paced the demons. It was integral to hunters and its eyes blazed blue. The creature appeared as intent on running Bradan to ground as the mad horde above him. Well, he was simply reverting to form. Tintagel had once been part of Gwyn's pack when that grim figure had set his animals loose among the corpses after a battle to gather dying warriors' souls. The beast had never been his pet, but did 1,500 years of companionship with Bradan mean nothing?

"Traitor," Bradan screamed. The storm ate his words.

He rode southward. The only sign of passing time was his gas gauge moving relentlessly toward empty again.

A whisper of light from the east touched the coastal mountaintops and now the riders were limned with a ruddy orange glow, backlit by a cheerful furnace just below the horizon. At the same time, he saw the wolf make a series of leaps upward at the horsemen above him, nipping at their mounts' hooves.

Tintagel appeared to be completely in his element frolicking among and distracting the demons. Then the wolf veered sharply inland away from the highway. A contingent of the Wild Hunt followed, clearly believing the animal knew a shortcut to intercept Bradan before sunrise hit. The host split to follow diverging courses.

Subtle, but inevitable, sunrise nudged the storm aside with violet-pinkish light nibbling at the thunderheads. The rain tapered off, and, high up, a charming dawn cleared the sky of riders or anything else wicked.

CHAPTER 2

Merlin's Boudoir

Early Sixth-Century CE,
Cadbury Hill Fort, Britain

In one clean motion, the big man threw a knife at Bradan. The missile just missed his head to embed itself in the timber wall behind him.

Sometimes a near miss was a warning, not intended to harm the target. Other times a miss was a blade thrown with lethal resolve but badly aimed because the thrower was drunk.

Bradan knew Medraut wanted to kill him; his musicianship must have displeased the big man, though the rest of Arthur's warriors and ladies were entertained. Arthur himself looked amused by Bradan's fluid work on a lute and creative song verses.

Faster than thought—or concern for consequences—Bradan wrenched the blade out of the wall and hurled it at Medraut's drinking horn. He threw well and shattered the vessel to spray the big man with mead.

Now it was war, though Bradan was half Medraut's age and a third his size.

Medraut upended his table, scattering boon companions, spilling food, and sending dogs running for the hall's door. Warriors and their ladies pushed back from the uproar. The big man lunged across the debris, ax in hand, coming right for Bradan who was armed with a lute. A foot appeared out of nowhere to trip Medraut and sent him sprawling onto the straw-covered floor. His ax flew up toward the rafters. As it arced back downward, Arthur deftly caught it.

"Bradan's throw was better than yours. You wanted to kill him, but couldn't; he didn't kill you, but could have."

Arthur was as large as Medraut but older, with gray streaking his beard and long brown hair. Nonetheless he moved with assurance and grace—and power. He hefted Medraut's ax thoughtfully, then hurled it the length of the dimly lit hall to bury itself in a shield over the room's main entrance. Coming through this entrance just as the ax sailed overhead, a servant carrying a platter of meat froze. If the cast had been misjudged just a little, his guts would be mixing with straw on the floor.

Medraut surged to his feet and faced his father, nose to nose. "Get my ax."

"I won't." Arthur's voice resonated throughout the hall effortlessly. "And it's my ax, not yours, just as everything in Cadbury is mine. You're just using my things; misusing them, really."

Everything stopped. Who was loyal to whom? Arthur or Medraut? Everyone must have done the same headcount. And weapons were handy if debate failed. The hall wasn't intended to be an arena, but that's what it had become.

Arthur and Medraut stood amid two dozen tables. Arthur set out a good spread, so the hall was packed with chieftains and warriors thought to be loyal to him. Even a few of the large landowners outside Cadbury's stockade had joined tonight's festivities. They still lived in Mediterranean-styled villas that were a legacy of Britain's fading Roman past. Bradan knew loyalty was a fluid notion these days, but hosting banquets built good will and let Arthur keep an eye on his followers.

It was a dangerous time and Arthur needed all the fealty he could get. Shields were hung on walls or leaned haphazardly against unused benches keeping company with every kind of weapon, close at hand if sentries shouted alarms about attacking Saxons, Jutes, Angles, Picts—their foes were numberless. Any or all of them could pick tonight to try sacking Cadbury.

Gwenhwyfar, Arthur's young blond wife, sat at the head table. They hadn't been married long. She'd paused to see how it would play out between her husband and stepson. Morgana and Merlin sat nearby intently watching the unfolding drama. Bradan knew Merlin supported Arthur; he wasn't sure who Morgana allied herself with—her own cause, most likely.

"Play on," Arthur told Bradan casually, as if his music wasn't the spark that had almost set the room afire. He addressed the hall, "Besides my son, is Bradan's music entertaining to you all?"

There was a general rumble of approval. Bradan would have been flattered at the praise, but he realized complimenting his music was a proxy for supporting Arthur over Medraut. His melodies were beside the point.

Politics, art, and music, uneasy bedfellows, Bradan thought.

"The boy sings and plays the lute well," said one of the chieftains, Ahearn, making clear where his allegiance stood.

"Bradan caresses his instrument as sweetly as a warrior strokes a maiden's cheek," Gwenhwyfar said. She was always apt to jump in with a bad simile.

Morgana sneered at her sister-in-law. Bradan wasn't sure whether this was because Morgana hated bad figures of speech or simply because she despised Gwenhwyfar.

Merlin cut in, clearly working to calm hostility between Arthur and Medraut and stifle the bad feelings eddying about the smoky hall. "My apprentice makes good music, but I'll advise him about playing with knives."

The audience laughed, even Medraut. At last they could all agree on something. Bradan was furious since Arthur's son had just tried to kill him unprovoked, but he decided he'd take the public blame to smooth troubled waters. Indeed, he should have checked his rash impulse to retaliate against the big man by making him a fool. Bradan had gained the momentary satisfaction of splattering Medraut with sticky mead at the expense of creating a vengeful enemy with a long memory. He didn't need Merlin to tell him his knife toss was stupid.

"Play on," Morgana shouted at Bradan over the general good humor the wizard struggled to create. Bradan wondered if she did this because she liked his music or to goad Medraut and counter Merlin's efforts to placate the various factions in the hall. Whatever her motives, they were sure to be murky.

Morgana blew Bradan a kiss.

Medraut turned his back on the gathering and walked toward the entrance, motioning his friends to join him. A dozen warriors grabbed shields, swords, and spears and decamped in a noisy, clanking mass. It was a loud departure in every way. As he passed through the entrance, the big man jumped high up to pull his ax out of the shield.

Apparently unperturbed, Arthur rejoined Gwenhwyfar on the head table dais. They kissed to show everyone that this was really still a festive occasion and Arthur still ruled the hill fort.

Raucous laughter and loud conversations resumed as if nothing had just happened between father and son.

Bradan took a fortifying gulp of mead and struck up a ballad with ribald lyrics and ran his fingers easily up the instrument's frets, displaying his virtuosity. Soon the entire hall sang along.

* * *

Bradan heard the sounds of sex. But it was too late. He'd already pounded on the door to Merlin's hut.

Undaunted, the activity inside went on for several moments; the flimsy hut's walls shook; then there was laughter and the sounds of bodies disentangling themselves. This took a while. Evidently, the lovers had been acrobatic. They complimented each other's sexual stamina and genitalia. While they talked, Bradan debated ambling discreetly off to a remote part of the fort, so as not to observe whoever the wizard has coupled with emerge, though he thought he knew already based on the woman's tone. It was tense enough in Cadbury without witnessing assignations he shouldn't.

"It's only the boy, my apprentice," he heard Merlin say. "He'll know to stay shut."

"Invite him in," the woman said.

"No, no, he's too young, Morgana. Off with you."

"Again, tonight?"

"Oh yes."

The hut's door opened and Morgana came out, supple and poised. She didn't bother to put her finger to her lips. She didn't need to. Bradan would "stay shut." Then she left with a swish of her long tunic.

"This is smart?" Bradan said, looking inside. The enchanter tidied up his woolen robe and pants. The smell of sex and smoke from a hearth fire permeated the confined space.

"Smart? I'm wise, not smart," Merlin said. "We have a few lessons to think on today, among them, when not to engage in knife play with warlords, so let's get on with it."

Bradan nodded at the wizard's disheveled bed. "This was also a lesson about what not to do?"

Merlin paused to stare at him. "Being clever is neither smart nor wise," he said.

Bradan strived to look contrite then said, "You know she's fucking Arthur's son, Medraut?"

"And many more besides. Should I be troubled? She makes herself available to me. That's all I concern myself about."

"She's Medraut's aunt," Bradan said. "How can she sleep with him?"

The wizard shrugged. "I wouldn't ask her if I were you."

Merlin gave his belt a final tug. "Now, if we're done pondering the caprices of sexual attraction, to the east wall then."

He was clean shaven today, probably to impress Morgana. Other times he affected a long full beard. The beard came and went at will, but even Merlin couldn't hide the gray.

They tramped through the fort avoiding groups of soldiers drilling in the mud. The mailed warriors were on horse and rode at thick, wooden posts of man height to slash at the targets with swords or gore them with lances. Bradan heard thunks as the weapons struck the timber. Medraut drilled the horsemen hard and the posts took a beating, with chips flying after each hit. Bradan believed that Saxon, Angle, or Jute foot soldiers would be slaughtered if they fought on open ground against this cavalry.

Medraut watched impassively as Bradan and Merlin gave his maneuvering men a lot of space. The war chief sat astride a massive stallion capable of carrying his weight and riding down anyone before him. Medraut was shirtless and sweating in the daytime sun and his damp hair was long and brown. Scars from all manner of weapon covered his torso. He didn't acknowledge Merlin's comradely salutation. Instead, he grabbed a lance from one of the warriors and launched himself at the nearest post, his mount picking up speed and sending clods of mud and horse shit into the air behind him. Medraut leveled his lance and struck the post, snapping it in two. The impact sent the top half of the weighty timber spinning end over end to land with a heavy thud amid his troopers, who scattered to avoid being crushed. They cheered lustily.

Bradan thought Arthur should drill the men. Ceding this role to his son let Medraut cement bonds with the warriors. Arthur's reputation still commanded enormous respect in Cadbury and neighboring Celtic lands, but the warlord frittered away goodwill, dallying all day and night with fair Gwenhwyfar rather than tending to the mundane but vital tasks keeping their hill fort secure against marauding pagan tribes from the continent.

Bradan knew what Merlin was about to tell him, so he broached the subject. "It's just a silly hobby, throwing knives. Warriors don't bother with that in battle. They use arrows, spears, and swords in a real fight. Tossing knives is a campfire trick."

"How did you learn?" Merlin asked.

"I watch our soldiers. They advise me. Then I practice endlessly. Same with swords, spears, and bows. Ahern taught me knife throwing."

"You're the complete warrior." The wizard's tone sounded disappointed. "What about the spells I've taught you?"

"I practice those more than fighting. Magic is creativity. And it's more fun than chopping a man to pieces. Last night was a mistake."

"Well said. Now let's see what you can do with your spellcraft."

Passing beyond the drills, Bradan and Merlin circled around the great hall recently built where a Roman barracks once stood. It was mostly timber, but the hall's builders had also plundered stones and a few mosaic floor tiles from a villa in the valley below to integrate into the structure. Several amphorae of wine or olive oil were propped against the walls, waiting to be stored.

Arriving atop the rude wooden ramparts, Bradan and Merlin were hundreds of feet above the surrounding countryside. It was all brilliant green from recent rains. The fort sat on a high oval hill lording it over the farmland, a huge, imposing lump on a flat expanse of plowed fields occasionally broken by stands of dense foliage. Their vantage point was godlike.

There was still extensive agriculture, though many of the once-well-tended fields had reverted to bramble and second-growth trees. Dirt roads wound between fields with several converging on the fort, working up the side of the prominence through three concentric rings of earthen defensive embankments circumscribing the hilltop, the innermost of which had a tall wooden palisade surmounting it, reinforced by rocky towers at intervals along its length. Bradan and Merlin stood on this rampart. Stone redoubts pockmarked the steep embankments below to serve as points of resistance and further hamper potential attackers. Bradan thought it impressive, though the Romans weren't impressed centuries ago when they stormed Cadbury and put the defending Celts to the sword. He wondered if today's pagan invaders would find it more of a challenge.

Directly below them, a body naked save for wool pants lay faceup in a defensive ditch abutting the rampart, his neck chopped nearly through. Deep gashes crisscrossed his chest and stomach, from a sword Bradan guessed, before the final, fatal hack to the neck. Flies coated the wounds, but there was little blood around the corpse, so Bradan assumed the man was killed elsewhere and then pitched off the wall with no attempt to conceal the body.

"It's a message," Bradan said. "But for who? And to what end?"

Merlin gazed downward. "One of Arthur's captains," he said.

"Saxons did it? They got into Canterbury?"

"No, or there would be an uproar, but activities inside go on just as usual."

Down the wall about twenty paces, a sentry glanced at the body then resumed walking his stretch of the rampart.

Fuck this place, Bradan thought. *And we're the final stronghold of civilization.*

"If not Saxons, who did it?" he asked.

"Possibly it's one of Medraut's rivals. Arthur's son is nothing if not ambitious and Arthur will have problems with him soon enough as you saw last night. Probably the fellow below—that's Ahearn—crossed Medraut. Look away, Bradan, and keep your head down."

"You should do the same."

"It's not my nature."

A villa was off to their right, in pretty good shape excepting spots where Arthur's men had commandeered building material for the fort. It was expansive with long straight sides surrounding an interior courtyard overgrown with weeds breaking through the flagstones. But more than size, Bradan reflected, what set this Roman relic apart from contemporary structures was its geometry. No builder in Britain now had the ability or vision to execute straight lines, arches, and columns on such a scale. He doubted whether builders anywhere in the world still did. Possibly in Londinium or on the continent, though he'd heard those places were also prey to tidal incursions of barbarians, so it was unlikely architects had the leisure to design anything aside from warlords' forts and walled palisades.

"Changing times," Bradan said.

"And not for the better," Merlin said. "What I miss most is heated floors in winter, much nicer for my old joints."

"How did they do that?"

"It was easier than magic. They had stone pipes running beneath the tile floors and servants boiled water and ran steam through these pipes. Even on a frigid morning, one barely needed to dress warmly inside. Long gone. Now we live with our animals, sleep on straw, and burn cow dung for heat because wood is scarce and needed for stockades."

The wizard pointed at the huts with thatched roofs behind them within the protection of the fort's walls. There were dozens already and more being built daily to the point where they hampered military drills; the dwellings housed refugees from the mayhem in the surrounding regions.

"Listen," Merlin said. Bradan saw that the enchanter's eyes were closed and he drowsed, leaning against the ramparts.

"Listen to what?" Bradan asked.

"A cohort is coming. They're cavalry. You can hear the hooves on the road. The local garrison must be marching to the coast as a show of force—and none too soon with tribes of outsiders intent on stealing anything not fastened down. Stillicho wants to use his legions to reassert control over Britain. We're on the edge of an empire, but if you can't defend the edges, the core crumbles."

Bradan thought for a moment, wondering how to pull the old man out of his fantastical reverie of times long past. Or the wizard spoke allegorically, expressing fear at shifting, fluid times and didn't mean for his apprentice to understand his plea literally.

"That was three generations ago, or four," Bradan said cautiously, trying to reel the enchanter in. "We have the same challenges at the moment—if anything, there are more trials than ever—but no legions to save us. Even on the continent, the Romans are gone." Bradan shifted from Latin to Celtic to drive home the point. Merlin was fluent in Latin, but Celtic was more visceral and would prod the wizard back to modern times.

"They were our mortal enemies, the Romans," Merlin ruminated. "Then they weren't."

"Needs change, enemies change," Bradan said.

"Times blur together if you live long enough," Merlin said.

Thinking to distract the wizard and himself from morbid thoughts, Bradan pointed to a barely discernible figure emerging from the main entrance of the distant villa.

"I didn't think it was still inhabited," Bradan said.

The man proceeded a little way from the main structure toward a well. Bradan's eyes were good and he saw the fellow was dressed in a toga, long out of fashion in these parts.

"What's he doing?"

The wizard coughed and stood straighter. "Let's find out. This can be one of today's lessons."

Merlin recited a quatrain. "Try to remember the wording and emphasis. It will be handy in the future."

A sparrow flitted overhead and angled downward away from the ramparts toward the remote figure. It took a little while for the avian to cover the distance and it became too tiny to see.

The wizard watched attentively. "Share your view," he said.

Bradan thought Merlin spoke to him, but instead they both saw what the sparrow watched. Bradan still observed with his actual eyes, but in his mind's eye, he looked at an image of the man in the toga no more than a few feet below him. The bird must be circling right over the fellow. Bradan saw him pull a leather pouch from the folds of his voluminous garment and with evident effort place this into a bucket used to draw water up from the stone well. He rushed. Coins spilled out of the pouch. The man used a partially broken winch to lower the bag slowly down the well shaft. As he did, he looked all about him, but paid the bird no mind.

Bradan intuited that the man not only interred his fortune, but also cast a way of living and thinking down the well.

"He's hiding everything," Bradan noted.

"Usually a good plan for troubled times," Merlin said. "Not always."

The view shifted as the bird flew higher. Masked from the man tending to his coins, a dozen warriors crouched behind heavy brush nearby, focused on him. No one carried shields and they weren't heavily armored, with only a few helmets among the bunch, but most carried swords and axes. Bradan guessed they were a reconnaissance party sent out from a larger Saxon band to reconnoiter Arthur's fortifications and readiness. However, they were opportunists and obviously considered seizing the hoard.

"Between being ridden like a horse by Morgana and this spell with the bird, I'm exhausted. So it's up to you. What will you do?"

Bradan froze. The wizard hadn't taught him a spell nearly powerful enough to stop the imminent robbery and murder of the villa owner below him. He couldn't simply will the marauders out of existence or spirit the toga-clad patrician beyond harm's way. So, improvise . . .

Inspired by the images evoked in Merlin's reverie of times gone by, Bradan recited eight stanzas. He needed to work quickly, but he discerned no change in the circumstances below. The Saxons were plainly ready to sprint from cover and butcher the man still struggling to lower his treasure. His toga had come partly undone and bunched at his feet, revealing a pale potbelly and arms without muscle.

"I see your plan," Merlin interjected. "I'd suggest a different emphasis on the final syllables of your first verse."

Bradan repeated his spell, making the suggested revisions on the fly.

Charging from the cover of the villa's walls, a score of Arthur's horsemen crouched over their steeds. They were mailed and their spears jutted from behind shields emblazoned with Latin inscriptions or Christian crosses as they raced toward the bushes concealing the Saxons. Bradan felt the concussive force of the troop's hooves even on the distant ramparts. The Saxons saw that they were about to be ridden down and fled helter-skelter across the fields away from the well and the approaching troop. They had enough sense to disperse, spreading out their pursuers so they couldn't be slaughtered easily in a crowd. They grew more distant, chased by groups of riders, little dots moving over the green fields.

The man in the toga stood numbed and looked ready to clamber into the well to hide, but then he let the rope loose, sending his bucket full of coins into the water below, and ran back into the villa.

"Well played," Merlin said. "You're tired, of course."

Bradan nodded wordlessly. A mountain had settled on top of him. He slid down to sit on the walkway with his feet dangling over the courtyard far below. He wondered if he'd pitch over the edge. Merlin reached down to steady him.

"Water?" the wizard asked.

Bradan shook his head. He felt marginally better and he wouldn't send his age-old mentor to fetch refreshment. He pulled himself upright, holding on to the rampart.

"You knew fatigue was coming," Merlin said. "Having practiced other enchantments."

"Worse than I thought."

"There's a cost proportional to the result. It was a complicated image you created, with sight and sound."

"I combined pieces of other spells you'd taught me like assembling blocks of stone for a building," Bradan said.

"That's where the art comes in, what to combine with what," the wizard said. "And make it all rhyme. You did it under pressure, too. I think the villa owner below would thank you if he realized what happened."

"The coins?" Bradan said.

Merlin regarded him for a beat. "You saved that fellow and his wealth. What do you think we should do?"

"Yet another test."

"Of course."

"There's no perfect answer," Bradan said. "We can leave the coins to the villa owner, but the Saxon bandits won't run from shadows forever and they'll be back to steal everything. We can recover them for ourselves and no one would be the wiser if we're careful about how we spend. Or we give them to Arthur and he buys support from Dumnonia to our west and other Celtic tribes—or he simply decorates his great hall with better style and outfits Gwenhwyfar with more jewels."

"So young to be cynical," the wizard remonstrated. "However, you're right."

"There is another option, foolish and risky," Bradan said. "We recover the treasure all by ourselves and give part of it to the local Saxon war chiefs moving westward toward Cadbury with a promise more will come if they halt their advance for a time. They've been battered by Arthur's horsemen these last several years and aren't anxious for another brawl. Their leaders save face by claiming we've bought them off. We're not in good shape, either. There's a lot of sickness among us and even our healthy soldiers want to fight each other more than the barbarians. Some like Arthur, others like Medraut. At the moment, no one needs a battle. Also, if we get into the Saxons' camp, we can gauge their strength and morale."

"What prevents them from taking the gold and slitting our throats without making a treaty?" Merlin asked.

"We give them only a taste at first and promise more monthly," Bradan said. "Also, we use a little enchantment to awe them, an image or two. They're a superstitious lot and something menacing and suitably otherworldly might give them pause. So we both bribe and threaten them. I believe a contingent of their leaders sailed round to Tintagel behind our lines and took over there. We sneak in and parlay." He paused, then added, "But first we need the gold coins."

* * *

"You made magic this morning," Morgana said.

Bradan jumped with surprise. The woman had materialized out of nowhere beside him in the little earthen-floored storeroom. His candle cast her tanned face in alternating light and shadow. She wore what she'd left Merlin's dwelling in, an ensemble evocative of mannered, aristocratic Roman Britain before the legions decamped. In muddy Cadbury, there wasn't a speck of soil on her dress's hem. The clothing's quality and elegance recalled long-gone styles and made her unique among the women in this crude hill fort beset by invasion and civil war. He knew she fancied herself above any of the locals. In fact she appeared regal, and the witch was tall enough to carry off the look. The overall impression would have been imperial and demure on another woman, but everything about Morgana's attire was figure-hugging, with the belt cinched tight to emphasize her bust and slender waist.

"I felt your enchantment," she continued. "Everyone who does a spell has their own signature. Yours is already distinctive and it carries over a long distance though you're new at the game. Do be careful. As Merlin no doubt told you, supernatural entities and other magicians can find you if you're careless about working magic. Do one spell at a time, at most two. More than that and you give away your location to any adept in these arts who cares to find you."

Restoring himself after a morning of practical magic, Bradan was discreetly helping himself to wine from Gaul by tapping an amphora in a quiet storeroom next to the great hall. The room's lock had proved no real challenge to a modest piece of enchantment he fashioned, though it tired him to do it. Merlin had wandered off to who knew where while promising to meditate on Bradan's proposed use for the stash of coins. Bradan thought they hadn't time for meditation. Someone would seize the patrician's coins soon. And now Morgana was here to further complicate matters.

She lifted a terra-cotta amphora with effort and took a long pull on the wine. The jugs were stacked five high on wooden racks. A few of the old Roman trading routes had remained open, and Arthur's garrison kept up mercantile relations with the continent despite threats of piracy and general turmoil in Britain.

Morgana set the amphora down and flipped a silver denarius into the air. Bradan caught it in flight and slapped it onto the back of his wrist. He noted the image of Septimius Severus on the coin, a Roman-Libyan emperor who died campaigning in Britain many generations ago.

"You've seen these earlier today from a distance," she said.

"You watched us," Bradan said.

"Don't be accusatory. You weren't being private. I came once I felt your spell. I was curious. You and Merlin were so busy, neither of you noticed. You constructed a very clever image to distract the Saxons."

"You want a share of the hoard." Bradan got to the point.

"I'm in on the secret, so why not? And I'm as worthy as Arthur and more so than his pretty Welsh whore Gwenhwyfar."

"And a pile of gold and silver sets it all right?"

"It buys me respect. Although I'm Arthur's sister, I don't have many supporters or much deference. Just whatever scraps he throws me. And deference has been hard to come by now that Gwenhwyfar has his ear and his bed."

Morgana moved close to Bradan pushing her breasts against his chest. "I need friends and so do you. Medraut is out for vengeance after last night at the banquet. You either kill someone like that or you eat whatever insults he aims at you."

"Should I have eaten the knife he threw at me?"

"Making a fool of him is the worst choice. Running should be your plan now. Coins make that possible."

"You know where the fortune is," Bradan said. "You have one denarius already. Go get the rest yourself."

"Using my talents to get a single coin is no feat, but retrieving the rest is impossible. I'm not yet proficient enough to know a spell that would let me salvage all of them together, and they're too heavy to physically pull out without help."

"As you're fucking Merlin, he'll teach you the right spell."

"Jealous?" Morgana asked. "Can't hide it; I can see you're jealous. I've learned enchantment from him, though nothing helpful in this case. In turn, I've taught him to last longer inside a woman, and how to please them better—including me—so we're even. Experienced with life as he supposedly is, you'd think he'd know more."

"He's wise, not smart," Bradan said, but he decided not to argue the point further.

Though he was young, he recognized the witch was insanely sensual judging by the effect she had on both men and women. Wherever she went she upset the equilibrium, and he neither liked nor trusted her. Her magical knowledge was uncertain, but surely surpassed his. Further, she was frank enough about some of her motives—the ones he'd guess, anyway—but her apparent forthrightness was a screen to keep her ultimate goals obscure. All in all, a dangerous companion to accompany on a nighttime sojourn over hostile ground to recover a vast pile of Roman coinage and then negotiate with over the division of spoils.

Where in hell is Merlin? he wondered.

However, leaving the treasure as is wasn't a good plan, either. Morgana would find other assistance sooner or later and then he'd have no say whatever in the treasure's disposition.

"We need to move," he said. "The Saxons will be back, or the villa owner himself may try to recover his wealth to put it elsewhere. He knows he was seen."

* * *

"There's someone here," Bradan breathed out.

"Merlin?" Morgana asked.

"He'd show himself."

The two of them were by the well near the villa below Cadbury Fort. He smelled manure in recently plowed fields and heard insects all around him. He felt the mass of the hill fort behind him more than he saw it. In fact, he barely saw at all. There was a bit of illumination from a crescent moon and a frosting of starlight above. He estimated it was midnight and perfect for moving about unseen, but these conditions made his own progress clumsy, slow, and hazardous. He thought he knew every game trail and tree within miles of the fort, but tonight he'd come close to spraining an ankle in slimy mud and collided with at least two stumps and several branches. Morgana glided along with eerie ease, but even she wasn't fast despite shedding aristocratic attire in favor of loose, practical, woolen pants and a nondescript forest-green shirt.

Bradan wanted Merlin to join them, but the wizard was nowhere to be found. Maybe he was putting the amorous skills Morgana had taught him to use caressing a sweaty guard captain's wife in a quiet corner of the fort.

It was just Bradan and the witch on this daft expedition.

They'd made it out of the fort through an obscure sally port, avoiding the cluster of soldiers by the east gatehouse. In troubled times, Arthur had a score of sentries patrolling the walls and main gates at night, but two shadows intimately familiar with the buildings and surrounding grounds were easy to miss. Further, thanks to a summertime contagion that infested the close confines of Cadbury, many of the men were feverish and coughing in the humid air or doubled over with stomach cramps; they were more attuned to their own misery than vigilance. The latrines stank with human waste in the hot night and Bradan breathed shallowly when he passed them. The sounds of illness also emanated from the huts within the fort. So far, Bradan had stayed healthy. He'd never seen Morgana sick.

They crouched by the well, listening. Bradan wondered if the Saxons had returned. As lifelong marauders, they wouldn't want to lose the large cache of coins despite being chased off earlier by phantom horsemen. After several minutes, he heard nothing further. Then, at a distance, he recognized a wolf's baying. The dusky world held its breath waiting for the tone to fade. It was an eldritch sound. With managed acreage reverting to wilderness, the beasts' population had leaped and they'd become bold. Come to that, Morgana was also an uncomfortable companion in the darkness; and, after retrieving the patrician's coins, a knife ripping upwards through his bowels and stomach and crunching to a stop at his sternum was a distinct possibility. No doubt it was his imagination, but he saw her eyes shimmer orange in the gloom. He did his best to watch her and his own back. For whatever good it was, he had his own steel dagger.

The woman was unconcerned by wolves and he dimly saw her pull herself to a standing position then feel around for the rope attached to the bucket of coins. Bradan stood on the opposite side of the little well and reached out to grip the rope, too. He yanked upward experimentally to see how much weight they were dealing with—a lot. Even between the two of them, he doubted they could tug up the coins along with whatever water was also in the bucket.

"You're strong for a kid," Morgana said quietly.

"Strength isn't the answer."

"Magic?"

"Leverage," he said.

"The winch is broken."

"Not completely. We need a thick branch—long, too. That may replace the handle. You've got good night vision?"

He sensed a shrug in response. "When needed." She rustled quietly through nearby underbrush then stepped near him. "Use this."

Bradan felt a large stick shoved into his hand. Exploring the well's pulley apparatus with his fingers, he jammed the branch into the cylinder where the winch handle used to fit and levered downward with his full weight. The bucket below moved upward fractionally.

"Pitch in," he said. "Two are faster than one."

A sharp point jabbed between his shoulder blades. The sword drew blood. And provided motivation.

"With leverage, one boy can pull up the coins."

Bradan recognized Medraut's voice. He stopped for a moment, but the point pushed deeper into his back and he again pulled his improvised handle, slowly drawing the bucket upward. He heard it dully smacking into the well shaft splashing water as it came. Despite the winch, he worked hard to gain even inches, and with every moment he was in danger of letting the branch slip, sending the laden bucket back to the depths.

He wondered if Medraut knew he had a dagger tucked under his tunic, not that it would matter since the big man had a sword and was a seasoned war chief. Medraut was stupider than Arthur, but he'd inherited his father's ferocity and a modicum of tactical skills and cunning useful on a battlefield. Bradan knew the man would kill him as soon as he'd dragged the riches to the surface. Then he'd dump Bradan's body down the well shaft.

Bradan's one advantage was darkness. Though Morgana seemed to have preternatural night vision, he didn't think Medraut could see any better than he could, and Bradan suspected he knew the land better than Arthur's son.

Bradan couldn't discern what had become of the witch. Had she invited this brute to come along? If so, why enlist Bradan to assist with rescuing the coins?

"Morgana, you're here," Medraut said. "I know it. You spied on the boy and Merlin on the wall. I spied on you. My hearing is good. I hear all sorts of things. Tonight you two were noisy enough leaving Cadbury to wake the dead. Now we're all here. So there are no secrets in the family. Except the boy. He's not family. He's a vexation. To his credit, he throws a knife well."

Again a wolf wailed and it was close by. Bradan was shocked into letting go of the pail, sending the branch flying off into the night. Medraut whirled around, pulling his blade away from Bradan. This was the chance he'd needed and Bradan lurched sideways, pushing sharply off the well's stonework to tumble himself into nearby weeds and brush. He felt displaced air as Medraut's blade thrashed and thrust randomly after him.

Bradan got upright, silently drew his dagger, and faded behind an oak. Based on Medraut's racket, the man was still near the well, slashing about. Bradan heard his sword clang against stone and then shear through the rope. Whatever else happened, no one would retrieve the coins tonight. Medraut realized what he'd done and cursed, then stood still, listening. Bradan could just make out his shape by the well.

With Arthur's son located, Bradan listened intently for sounds of Morgana. And then there was the wolf that appeared to be stalking them all. Bradan heard no motions or noises of a large animal, but that didn't mean much since he expected a wolf to be silent.

He was the weakest of the players near the well, but things wouldn't improve if he hid all night. It was the hardest thing to leave the oak's illusory cover, but he edged back, keeping it interposed between himself and Medraut. Then he turned and began moving toward the fort, holding his dagger in front of him, his magical talisman—or just a feeble sop to assuage his fear.

Bradan tried to recollect a bit of magic that would improve his chances. Most enchantment took too long to recite in an emergency, so he quietly uttered the first six lines of the spell he'd used to bring back the phantoms that had chased off the Saxons earlier. If he needed a distraction, that was it. The spell was now poised and ready for him to drop the last few lines into place. However, Bradan realized speaking a partial spell left him as tired as uttering all the verses, so he paused mid-verse and leaned against a tree. It would be running and luck that got him safely back into the fort tonight.

He heard Medraut thrash about again. It was frustration as much as real hope he'd hit Bradan.

Fortunately for me, he's brainless, Bradan thought. *But that still leaves the witch and a wolf.*

Morgana might try to kill him since he knew about the treasure; the wolf would eat him simply because it was hungry.

As quickly and quietly as he could, he moved across a field, struggling through wet, recently plowed furrows. He kept low to the ground but still felt exposed. He was wretchedly slow and soon covered with mud and cow shit. After interminable slogging, he cleared the farm fields and worked his way up the outermost embankment. The footing was better there, but it offered only grass and no cover since Arthur's warriors had stripped it of any camouflage for potential assault parties.

The wolf appeared next to him. Bradan heard nothing to warn of its approach. He dropped the dagger in shock. Up close and in just a trace of moonlight, the creature was bigger than Bradan had guessed and pitch black except for a dusting of silver on its fur. Its eyes were pale blue. It stared down on him from a height, inspecting him coldly, and then suddenly looked upward to howl a greeting at a frenzied and dissolute assortment of spectral warriors flocking out of the sky atop all manner of mounts, emanating from the crescent moon and the far stars—the Wild Hunt, naked, demented, and free. And intent on ripping out his heart and soul.

It was hard to see, but did he spot Morgana at the front of the pack riding a stallion? And near her rode a tall, broad warrior with scars covering his chest who resembled Medraut. They all shrieked deafeningly. Bradan knew of the hunters from campfire lore murmured during broad daylight. No one spoke of them at night for fear of summoning the apparitions.

Discarding any attempt at quiet, Bradan sprinted away from the ghastly troop toward the fort's eastern wall. He'd heard spirits couldn't cross running water and there was a brook—really an open sewer for Cadbury's effluence—at the bottom of the second ditch. He dashed down the embankment and splashed through it. His pursuers flew over the brook easily. So much for campfire lore.

He wasn't far from the sally port and considered screaming for help from the sentries, but estimated they'd either flee from the phantom hunters or shoot him with arrows before they recognized him, assuming he scouted Cadbury for a Saxon attack. He leaped up the slope of the second embankment and stopped in his tracks.

Merlin sat atop the earthen ridge close to the port. In the dim light, he looked like a demon himself.

Gazing first at Bradan, then upward at the oncoming horde, the wizard, with no great urgency, stood and faced the Wild Hunters. He held his ears against the cacophony but wasn't otherwise flustered. He was as immovable as a Druid before an altar in a stone circle.

"Gwyn, we have a deal for the wolf," he shouted. "The boy's no part of it."

As a mass, the specters screamed invective down at them and brandished their weapons. This went on for several moments, and then, amazingly, they became diaphanous and faded back into the Milky Way.

Bradan worked to catch his breath and stop shaking. "You chased them off."

"The coming morning helped," Merlin said.

"Do everyone's eyes glow in the dark except mine?"

"I didn't know my eyes glowed," the wizard said. "Amazing after all these years what you learn about yourself." He sat again and lounged back on the embankment's dewy grass, appearing to be an organic part of the defensive work.

They didn't talk while a cluster of helmeted sentries arrived on the wall above, drawn by the commotion in the ether. One had braided his gray hair, which dangled out of his helmet framing a bearded face. The old soldier peered upward and seemed relieved to see nothing. His comrades also looked thankful. The warrior crossed himself, then looked eastward out at the surrounding countryside lit by dawn. It was a long, hard gaze, but he never looked directly down. Then the soldiers moved on, talking quietly. There were no ghostly armies from on high nor waves of stealthy Saxon attackers working their way up the steep hill this early morning to launch themselves in a head-long, hacking, stabbing attack at Cadbury and Arthur's sleepy garrison. Both the sentinels' immortal souls and their worldly bodies were safe for the moment.

"How do you know your eyes don't glow, too?" Merlin asked. "Find polished metal or a still pool of water and look at your reflection at night in candlelight and tell me what you see."

"Ordinary blue eyes."

"You're sure?"

Bradan pushed hard against the heavy oaken sally port rein-forced with iron fittings. The door didn't budge. He'd left it unbolted when he exited the fort with Morgana.

"It's locked," Merlin said.

"The bitch," Bradan said.

"Morgana? She went through earlier or she may have joined the Wild Hunters. I don't know how, but she knows Gwyn. How-ever it is, don't be hard on her. It wasn't you she meant to keep outside Cadbury's walls, easy prey for the wolf or Gwyn's crew."

"Who, then? Medraut?"

"Very likely. Morgana knows you can unlock the port with a spell. You showed that skill in the wine storeroom yesterday afternoon. You'll be safe."

"So I'm to feel good about her?"

"Of course not, but try to understand her motives."

"I don't understand anything about her. She's part of the Hunt?"

"She likes a good chase now and then, keeps the juices flowing."

"How could she—why would she join that madness?"

"I don't know." Merlin was impatient at Bradan's interrogations. "I don't have answers to every question. She's a witch. She can do whatever she wants."

Bradan recited the verse he used to access the storeroom. He shook and had to repeat it thrice before he heard several heavy bolts inside slide back into the stone casement framing the portal. He leaned against the wooden rampart, taking deep breaths to mitigate the fatigue, then reached out and shoved weakly against the door. It opened inward.

He was about to stagger through but turned and said, "You should come in, too. I saw the wolf. It's still out there."

"I know," the wizard cut in smoothly. "Here he is."

Bradan lurched through the portal, staring back at Merlin. The huge beast sat nonchalantly on its haunches beside the wizard with the rising sun outlining the pair in rose-violet light.

"You made a friend—sort of," the wizard said. He looked amused. So did the wolf.

"Don't take him for granted," Merlin continued. "Ever. He'd eat your flesh in a heartbeat and do worse to your soul. He's part of Gwyn's crew."

"Gwyn?"

"A Welsh lord of the Otherworld. Not one you should meet—though you came very close tonight. Even I couldn't get you out of that mess a second time. He collects the souls of the dying after battles. Or he chases still-living men for sport; he leads the Wild Hunt. The wolf helps him. Evidently Morgana tags along too from time to time. It may even be that Medraut joins them. He's better connected to the Otherworld than one might expect."

Bradan nodded at the wolf. "It's a night for monsters. What does this one want from me?"

"He's looking for a change. Chasing down warriors' spirits is getting tedious. These days there are a lot of battles, meaning lots of chasing. Or the spirits are getting faster, more work to pursue them. Gwyn owed me a favor, so the wolf was released from service."

"You keep him."

"That won't work. He goes with you. I'm moving on from Cadbury. Whatever happens here, it's on Arthur to sort it."

Bradan was stunned. Arthur without Merlin would be like clapping one-handed. The chances of preserving even a modicum of order were immeasurably smaller if their partnership dissolved.

The wizard seemed to read his thoughts. "There's been no falling out. There are simply other things for me to do. And I'm old. Arthur will either thrive or not. Times change. It isn't in my power to make it better, worse, or different. Besides, truth to tell, I haven't felt very sagelike recently."

"And me?"

"You can go wherever, but not with me."

Bradan sat down heavily just outside the open portal, back against the wall's thick timbers. The rampart felt cold through his tunic and the wood pushed slivers into him. His world rocked. After his parents were butchered by Saxon raiders in a small village east of here a few years back, Merlin took him in, recognizing his interest in learning. Whatever else was true of the wizard, he loved pedagogical pursuits and having pupils listen to his experiences, knowledge passing between generations. Other children in Cadbury regarded Merlin as eccentric, long-winded, and possibly malevolent, but Bradan was happy to soak up what the old man had to say. He didn't know how ancient the wizard was, but he might have helped raise the blocks at Stonehenge.

Now Bradan stared at the wolf. His earlier impression of savagery incarnate was confirmed. Full morning had come, but the creature sucked up the ambient light like a vortex drawing all the illumination near him into a shadowy netherworld. Even without hearing of the creature's former vocation as a sort of ghoul chaperoning souls to the afterlife, Bradan found the wolf a fearsome entity.

"This is my new helpmate?" Bradan asked.

"It's good to have allies in disordered times. How could it harm you?"

"Well, he could tear my head off."

"Come on, pet him. He may bite, but we'll hope for the best. Based on what's he's seen so far, he's scornful of your forestry and tracking skills. You'll need to be stronger to impress him."

"He has a name?" Bradan asked.

"Gwyn named him, but it's unpronounceable even to a Welsh god. You can do better."

"Tintagel."

"Good name. Arthur's birthplace—supposedly."

"You don't know?"

"Does it matter?" Merlin asked. Again exasperation mixed with ennui shaded the enchanter's voice.

He's been around this place too long, Bradan thought.

"Arthur champions our cause wherever he came from," Merlin said.

Bradan wandered listlessly over to sit beside the wolf and wizard. If Tintagel ate him, so be it. He was tired beyond belief after floundering for hours through field and forest to unsuccessfully drag a fortune from a deep well, in the process suffering a stab wound in the back from Arthur's vicious son, being hunted by the damned, and stalked by a supernatural wolf, all the while being taunted by a scheming, sultry witch.

"I never got the coins," he said. "Didn't get close."

Merlin rummaged in the folds of his cloak and flipped a silver denarius at him. Bradan caught and examined it. Between the wizard and the witch, he'd caught many coins recently. This time the image on its front was Quintus Lollius Urbicus, a Berber from distant North Africa, who became governor of Britain at the height of the empire.

"You got the hoard," Bradan said. "After I left the well."

Merlin nodded. "I liked your idea about bribing the Saxons. If we buy them off for another few years, I think we can call that victory. It's our parting gift to Cadbury."

"This was all a test." Bradan stated it as a fact.

"Of course."

Bradan wanted to be enraged but couldn't muster the energy.

Merlin scratched behind Tintagel's ears. "No need to touch on everything you did, but I can say you showed initiative, dealt with ambiguity, and applied several of the spells I taught you. However, as you've gathered, most enchantment is campfire tricks that are hard to deploy when you need them urgently, and the spells aren't all that powerful even when you do get them out in time—and they're bloody exhausting. You can make enchantment much stronger, but you have to sacrifice a living being—with a soul—and neither of us would want to do that; it's Gwyn's thing, not ours. So, most importantly, you used ingenuity and determination. That saves you more often than magic."

"Do tell," Bradan said.

"Sarcasm doesn't become you. There is one more thing to pass along before we go our separate ways, which you'll probably think is an unmitigated delight at first, but you may come to see as a horrific curse in time—and you'll have a very long time to balance the good and bad of it."

Despite his lassitude, Bradan was intrigued. "I've been toyed with enough. Just tell me."

"We'll need to walk for a bit along this ditch here to make my point. It won't be a happy stroll. Keep your head down. The fort is finally waking up. Roosters and other farm animals will be rousing them soon enough. They may or may not recognize us before sending a spear our way."

The wolf fell in behind them as they unobtrusively moved along the bottom of the embankment before arriving at a body in the grass. This time it wasn't a warrior. A young woman lay arms akimbo before them. She was fully clothed in a woolen tunic and faded plaid dress contrasting with the greenery. The dead woman resembled a pile of discarded garments. She was beginning to bloat with rot, but Bradan saw no sign of violence.

Merlin regarded the corpse. "The sickness afflicting Cadbury is making the fort's residents miserable and the weaker ones are dying. We've lost more due to ailments than any raid. The crowding inside spreads illness quicker than usual."

Bradan stopped a distance away from the body. "We can catch what she had."

"Others might, but you won't."

"I'm not immortal."

"You're close to it."

"What?"

"I've—how can I describe this—I've transferred my longevity to you. Also to Morgana. With her it was easy. I had sex with her while saying the right spell. She'll live quite a while."

"You didn't sleep with me," Bradan said, blushing.

"No, that wouldn't have been right. You're too young. Without sex, the process was a convoluted, tiring piece of enchantment, but it worked nonetheless. You'll see small scars on your forearm that weren't there before. They're runes. To Druids they have deep significance on many levels. For you they mean you'll be around almost forever. Call it a good-bye gift. Or you may wish I hadn't bothered."

"So I won't die?" Bradan fingered the runes. They didn't hurt.

"I wouldn't say that. You can be killed as easily as anyone, sword through the gut, fall off a galloping horse, get drunk on wine and crack your skull open on a hearth. But you won't get sick and you'll measure your lifespan in generations while others measure theirs in years. You'll look about thirty years old in fifteen hundred years."

Bradan didn't know what to make of this, but it couldn't be the curse that Merlin kept hinting at.

"You'll need to be clever, smart, and wise to make it work," the enchanter said.

"First things first. Medraut, will he get back to the fort?" Bradan asked.

"I suspect he will whether the witch locked him out or not. He's not as stupid as you think, and folks as hard as him have a way of winning through. And, by his thinking, you've just cheated him of the villa owner's fortune as well as made an ass of him in front of Arthur's entire drinking hall."

"Then regardless of what you've done to make me near immortal, I'll need to avoid him to survive another day. I'll flee the fort."

"Not a pleasant choice in these troubled times, but a prudent one. Coins will ease your flight."

Merlin searched through his tunic and passed a handful of denarii to him.

"Beyond surviving," the wizard said, "just staying happy is a challenge. Pursuing learning and creativity made the years go by easily for me. Besides, exercising the mind is a bulwark against the disorder all 'round us."

Bradan felt no different from before.

"And don't be cynical," Merlin added. "You show tendencies in that direction already. You think you've seen it all, but you haven't. Life will be bleak if you don't let yourself be surprised."

Corroborating the wizard's story, Bradan remembered the rest of Cadbury had gotten sick over the last several weeks, but he hadn't even sneezed.

"Every time period is unique," Merlin said. "But one sees recurrent patterns. What doesn't change is self-interest motivating humans. Excepting a few saints and sages, it doesn't matter what people say, what they actually do usually benefits themselves. Expect it and you won't be disheartened."

"Why me?"

"For one, you've been an inquisitive pupil and good company and you work wonders with a lute. Two, I've lived a while, really as long as I've wanted, so I won't be around always. I don't wish for immortality. However, it would be nice to pass along a love of knowledge and a creative spirit, small things, but if you share that with coming generations, the world will be better, at least a little better. Call it my covenant with you. It's a mad world, so let the time and place inspire your imagination. Certain settings are more special than others, and if you find yourself living in one of those special times and places, be open to the inspiration of that moment—yes, I know, it's all hubris, not to mention hard to do, but it's my legacy."

"Why Morgana? Is she your legacy, too?"

"My motives were different with Morgana. As I said, I had sex with her—a lot. So we negotiated a quid pro quo giving her extremely long life. Perhaps she would have shared my bed even without getting anything in return."

"I doubt it," Bradan said.

The enchanter looked annoyed. "Indeed. Well, a deal's a deal; she has the same runes as you on her wrist, so she'll be around a while. Along those lines, if you should meet her again in times ahead, watch yourself. You have scruples and a conscience, but she doesn't."

"The wolf?"

"He'll live a long while too, but that was Gwyn's doing, not me. A different set of rules apply to Gwyn's pack. I never got on with that prick and his netherworld crew. Sometimes there are Norse gods among them, too. They're worse than the Welsh. However, Tintagel's a good sort once you've got his respect. You'll survive longer with him than without."

"We need to see to her." Bradan nodded at the corpse.

He tried to focus on immediate tangible activities rather than dwell on the disorder swirling through his brain. Life had rearranged itself.

"I knew her a little," he continued. "She was a Christian, so she needs to be buried with appropriate rites. I'll tell her family."

"Her family put her outside to die," the wizard said. "They didn't want to catch her malady."

"The bastards. What did you say about not being cynical?"

"They don't know better. Also, remember, thanks to me, now you won't sicken if you're near the body, so it's unfair to judge others who are vulnerable."

Bradan paused to consider, then said, "I understand. I'll bury her since the family won't touch her."

"I'm not Christian," Merlin said. "Far from it, but I'll help you dig a spot and say appropriate words."

* * *

"*I knew Arthur. You slew him.*"

"I did, my lord," Medraut said.

"My lord" might not be the proper honorific for Gwyn ap Nudd, ruler of the fairy Otherworld in these parts and leader of the Wild Hunt, but Gwyn didn't correct him. Medraut understood the Welsh god-king's free verse though the deity wasn't visibly talking. Medraut simply comprehended what Gwyn communicated to him though he wasn't truly privy to the god's private thoughts. Nevertheless, he sensed a disordered consciousness apart from human reason and rules, where any lust could be satisfied without regard for consequences. Medraut could learn from that behavior.

The red-haired god sat opposite Medraut, massive as a hill, but Gwyn's bulk was ill-defined in a way Medraut believed could make him as tall as a mountain or diminish him to human scale on impulse. His coloration was similarly fluid, with green predominating at the moment except for his hair. Currently, he was a blend of flora and fauna, merging with nearby tree trunks. Antlers and branches sprang from his head. Gwyn wore moss as a tunic. The enormous figure appeared to be carved from gray-green granite except his pose was too relaxed for stone. He'd swung an arm over his knee and propped his bearded face on the arm. He stared at Medraut with rainbow-colored eyes. Birds flew about amid the luxuriant growth of hair and whiskers.

Medraut needed to strike a bargain with this peculiar being to live. The Otherworld respected Arthur as much as Britain's earthly warriors.

And Medraut couldn't deny mortally wounding Arthur. He still wore the punctured chain-mail shirt that wasn't proof against his father's savagery toward a treasonous son, and he still bled from the deep chest wound inflicted by his father's spear, and he tasted salty metal from coughed-up blood. However, he would survive the injury, unlike Arthur, whom Medraut stabbed with a sword during battle at Camlann. It was a true thrust, getting past his father's shield; the blade ran clean through to burst out the chieftain's back, tearing away links of chain mail and part of his spine and cleaving all manner of organs. That hurt would surely be fatal despite Arthur's armor and superhumanly strong body. Over his father's long life, dozens of Saxons, Angles, and fellow Celts had tried to kill him, but only Medraut—his son—had succeeded. He was proud of that.

Oddly, just above him, Arthur's dying husk was being anointed with incense and perfumes in preparation for interment—or they'd burn the body on a pyre, Medraut wasn't sure what was planned by the sundry beauties who tended and serviced the great man just as they did when he was virile and vigorous and they straddled him in bed to ride till dawn. These included Gwen-hwyfar, Nimue, and other fair flowers of the realm.

Morgana was there, too. Medraut didn't think she rode her brother if for no other reason than Morgana hated Arthur—though one never knew with the witch. Nevertheless, she led preparations for last tributes—another sign of respect when even enemies made a pretense of honoring the chieftain's passing.

There was no love lost among the women, but they'd made common cause to conduct Arthur away to a better place untroubled by Saxons or rebellious sons. Maybe they'd set upon each other after the chief's soul was sent on its way. Medraut neither knew nor cared. He'd eliminated his father and meant to take his place, but first he needed to placate any number of earthly tribal warriors and a god.

Medraut determined to sit, though Gwyn hadn't invited him to do so, and he dropped to the ground. He'd lost blood, but he'd survive if he rested. What ground was this in Gwyn's world? Grassy, enveloping, and soft beyond the mortal kingdoms above; they were in the hill's innards, inside Avalon. He sat amid an endless forest that should have been far too expansive to be contained by the hill they lay within. It was all lit by a narrow cleft above leading to the real world, though Medraut wasn't sure he could distinguish where one dominion left off and the other began. Diffuse, sourceless light permeated his environment. It was neither entirely day nor night and he couldn't see the sun. Oak, hazel, birch, redwood, and cedar stretched away forever with a brook twisting amid the trees. Medraut knew little and cared less about forestry, but he recognized this as an odd hodgepodge of flora with some trees that didn't remotely belong in Britain. Further, for stretches the water ran uphill unconcerned by earthly logic and rules. And then there was music among the trunks with notes stretching endlessly and aimlessly from instruments he didn't recognize, but sounded like they'd come back from far in the future.

This setting was a mad god's whimsy.

Among the trees and glades, stallions cantered about and stopped to fight, hooves and teeth drawing blood. They weren't dainty creatures but huge, well-muscled equines that would do his cavalry troop proud, with nostrils flaring red. Periodically one of the creatures, impatient at ground-bound constraint, leaped high and didn't thud back to earth, but continued its trajectory upward toward the cleft above to be lost in the hazy light. Ah, so this was where Gwyn stabled his Wild Hunt mounts when they weren't running down fleeing souls.

He did his best to ignore the oddity around him and reclined, using an elbow to keep himself from collapsing completely and falling asleep on the grass. As he relaxed, a keening wail flowed out of the trees. It was feminine and as ethereal, as longing and shameless as he'd ever heard. He wondered what was among the trunks besides uncanny horses. Some of the Fair Folk were more demon than angel. Gossamer shapes flitted among the trees and up into branches and leaves. They weren't birds and moved too quickly for him to discern their character.

He could be dead and this wasn't the Otherworld, but the afterlife.

In that case he'd meet Arthur again and they'd resume their battle for the amusement of whatever gods and heroes populated the pantheon Gwyn belonged to. Medraut didn't relish the thought.

Something yowled again, more sinister than before and a lot closer. A young woman flew into view and hovered just before him a few feet off the grass. She was human size and had white-blond hair that would put even Gwenhwyfar's golden tresses to shame. Avalon's odd light suffused her mane, creating a halo, though Medraut was sure she was in no way angelic given her lascivious expression. Medraut saw no wings on the slender, white figure, but he believed she was one of Faerie's denizens. Pointed ears poked through her hair and gravity didn't limit her movement. She a wore a cape draped over one shoulder and copper-colored chain mail from head to toe, but it was no proper warrior's armor. Instead it was an artistic confection and a mockery of the recent savagery in Camlann where human soldiers hacked at each other to leave cut-up meat and metal for Gwyn's Wild Hunters to pilfer the souls of and ravens to pick the flesh from. This bitch meant to have his soul.

Did she read his mind? Her wail mutated into sinister laughter and then transformed into the vocalizations of sensual ecstasy. The elfin woman somersaulted over his head with a metallic shimmer and righted herself behind him. She was incredibly fast. He pivoted to keep her in sight. The dappled illumination coming through the forest painted stripes on the maiden like a tiger's. She was dangerous, but Medraut lusted after this feminine vision as he'd never desired a woman before, except Morgana. After battle—assuming a warrior survived—overwhelming terror and blood madness transformed itself into a driving need for erotic release.

But it wouldn't be consummated on this day.

Gwyn cocked his enormous head, watching Medraut's reaction to their visitor, then raised his hand. She was acutely attuned to his signals. The damsel's vocalizations trailed away and she vanished with a disappointed smirk. Gwyn raised his other hand and a chalice appeared in Medraut's hands containing an effervescent elixir. It was compensation for denying him a bout or two or three with the Faerie woman, or it was poison, but Medraut was so parched he'd risk heaven, hell, or the new kingdom he'd inherited from his father for a gulp. He drained the vessel and felt refreshed. He'd kill for another drink.

Medraut set aside the chalice and his helmet and unstrapped the shredded and bloody mail-armor hauberk and padded under-jacket. With painful effort he pulled these off over his head and pushed them aside into a sweaty, crimson-stained pile and sat before Gwyn in a thin shirt and britches.

Medraut didn't know whether he had just an instant to make his case or until the end of time. Best get started.

"We've ridden together before," he said. "I promise you souls to usher into the next life from battles that are in the offing if I lead the Celtic tribes, more battles than Arthur fought."

"*We hunted together. What does that signify? Arthur was known to me. You are not. I can bring Arthur back, and put you on a pyre.*"

Was this a declaration of intent to kill him or was Gwyn musing about possibilities? Medraut intuited it was best to get on with his entreaty before it became a statement of fact.

"I'm an enemy of Merlin," he said.

There was no obvious reaction, but Medraut sensed a godlike pause for consideration.

"I will make Merlin nothingness. That is my match with him. You cannot contend against him."

"But I can help. He has weaknesses, but especially he desires Morgana. Use the witch to bring down the wizard."

Medraut wondered if this thrust hit home.

"I did not get the boy I hunted. He is minor. Howbeit, because Merlin helped him, he cannot live."

Medraut guessed Gwyn meant Merlin's apprentice and Arthur's bard and minstrel, Bradan. That boy was inconsequential. However, Bradan had made a fool of Medraut in Cadbury's mead hall. Further, he'd cheated Medraut out of a Roman treasure beyond counting, coins that would have gone a long way toward easing the assumption of his father's lands and rights, Celtic chieftains that could have been persuaded—with enough of the old empire's coins—that a son's treason was actually a ritualized killing of the king and a necessary changing of the guard, and Christian priests might have been induced—with contributions to new, sturdy, stone churches—to sanctify even the sin of patricide. Maybe Bradan wasn't so inconsequential after all. There was cause enough to execute the minstrel. All the better that Bradan had earned the ire of the Otherworld.

"Odin would lead the Hunt in my place. Losing the boy is my weakness. Merlin did that to me."

"Why not kill Bradan with a wave of your hand?" Medraut asked.

"That way is weak. Instead my hunters must seize his soul. You can help."

Fair enough, Medraut decided. It would be easy to find and murder Bradan by mobilizing the Wild Hunt and putting them onto his scent. Or Medraut would kill the kid himself.

Medraut believed he actually bargained with Gwyn. How did negotiating with a Welsh god work? Medraut determined to act the bluff, open warrior and not display subtlety that might make the god conclude he was being played. There was competition among deities over leading the Hunt. The Norse gods wanted to displace Gwyn. That worked in Medraut's favor; Gwyn needed allies. At the risk of totally misjudging his relation with the hulking green figure, he'd make a proposal.

"So, a deal," he said. "I continue to fly across the night sky with your fellows. Also, I live as long as the demons that accompany you on your grand hunts. In return, over a long life, I encourage bloodshed and disorder. People die. That gives you many souls. And I convince Morgana to ensnare Merlin. Further, I find the boy, kill him, and his soul will be yours to rip apart."

Men were quick to war on each other; it was easier than thinking. He could imagine no nobler vocation. So under his leadership, the tribes he ruled would expand his domain apace, sowing bloodshed in their wake. Further, he knew his aunt was already well on her way to ridding Cadbury of Merlin; perhaps the wizard would simply die of exhaustion brought on by the witch's sexual appetites.

With an indefinite lifespan, Medraut would be free to love and bed Morgana himself. And he'd love her well. Certainly he wouldn't tire as easily as the old shit Merlin. Already the witch had favored Medraut with more pleasurable nights than he could count and those could continue over coming centuries. She was prettier and more sensual than even the blond elf maiden attending Gwyn or, for that matter, any other woman, mortal or supernatural.

And how hard could it be to locate and kill Bradan? The boy was an afterthought.

CHAPTER 3

Free Speech, Free Love, Free Bradan

Fall Semester, 1964, University of California, Berkeley

"Were you ever in a war?" Gail Halpern asked.

"Which one?" Bradan responded.

"You were in several?"

Recovering, Bradan said, "World War II. I flew in the European Theater. Mine's not a particularly heroic story, but I remember the guys I flew with. A lot of them made it look effortless. For me, it was tense during the missions over France and Germany and there were truly god-awful times when I was sure my plane would go down."

"Don't talk about it if you don't want."

"A lot of guys don't, but I'm all right with it—most of the time."

His recollections had developed their own momentum. "Oddly, when I dream about it, I don't remember those bad moments as much as flying back to my air base in England, looking down and seeing the breakers hit the coast of Norfolk and knowing I was okay for another day. I haven't thought about it recently."

That was two decades back. Of course he couldn't tell her about the earlier wars he'd fought in over 1,500 years. As much as he'd tried to spend his time on creative endeavors, meaningful artistry, he'd seen conflict. When he'd survived those earlier battles, he'd felt exhilarated just as he had when he'd flown a shot-up plane and made it back in one piece to the air base.

That part of his life felt a world apart from being a guest instructor in folklore at Berkeley for a couple of semesters. However, this term had turned out to have tension of a different sort, less warlike and more of an insurrection.

"Sorry to remind you. I always step in it." Gail touched his hand. "That's twenty years ago. Except for the eyes, you don't look that old."

"Thanks. Clean living. I'm too old to be drafted when this Vietnam thing heats up, unlike the kids out there."

They stood on the top steps of Sproul Hall on Berkeley's campus watching an ocean of students on the plaza below them all staring up at Mario Savio standing poised near a microphone ready for his moment. He was about to address the crowd.

Bradan and Gail wore Free Speech Movement armbands. Tintagel had grudgingly allowed Bradan to enlist him into the cause and tie an armband around his neck. Now the wolf resembled a political version of Rin Tin Tin, though enormously more sinister than the TV animal actor.

For Gail, the band emblemized a heartfelt expression of solidarity with the movement. Bradan supported free speech on campus and bridled at the university administration's heavy-handed attempts to squash it, but he couldn't decide how he felt about the armbands; he'd seen them in other contexts, and by the time people started wearing them, room for nuance was gone. In nuance there was truth; verity in the interstitial spaces between extremes. Today's crusade admitted to no shades of gray, but then movements never did in his experience. Absolutes and stark contrasts were easy to explain to a crowd, but not gray tones—Merlin would have chided him for cynicism.

Savio followed other speaker-activists reporting on failed negotiations with the university administration. Despite this—because of it—the mood among the students was exuberant. No one knew what would happen next, but they anticipated something momentous. And the individuals below on the plaza were ready to cohere into a unified entity. Bradan understood the feeling, a crowd waiting for direction, a charismatic leader with a clear sense of goals and enemies, the forces of authority—in this case campus cops—waiting in the wings wondering if they could contain the potential chaos, but ready to bust heads if it came to that.

People began to make way for Savio, the tall, thin graduate student who mixed passion, gravitas, and a rumpled manner as he headed to the microphone. A dozen recording devices materialized in his face. News organizations eavesdropped on a movement and Savio was at once good for a quote, alarming to university administrators—and older TV viewers—and inspiring for students.

Bradan and Gail jammed themselves close to Savio amid earnest students and newsmen, most of whom seemed to be wearing horn-rimmed glasses. An older cop with his stomach stretching his tan jacket stood next to them watching Savio. Bradan noticed his bristly crew cut beneath the policeman's hat, and the cop's hand rested on the butt of his holstered service pistol. He had a tattoo of an army divisional insignia on the back of his gun hand in faded red ink. The gun belt wrapped tightly enough around his middle to indent his stomach.

Savio took a while to get to the meat of his speech, but, when he did, he became memorable and poetic. The performance looked impromptu, as if he'd made it up as he went along complete with stumbles, but the passion was there and the cadences accelerated toward the final declamations encouraging the assembled students to throw their bodies upon the gears and machinery of oppression. Sproul Hall made the perfect architectural backdrop, imposingly academic, architecturally unmemorable—and about to be occupied.

"He's a natural, great imagery," Bradan said. "The university played right into his hands by banning a few students from setting up tables and handing out pamphlets on Bancroft and Telegraph and then sending in police to arrest one of them. Revolutions have started with less."

He remembered past revolts he'd lived through. "Or they've been stamped out by the powers that be. They can just lose steam on their own and get forgotten."

"This has way too much impetus," Gail said.

"Let's find out," he said. "We'll join the rest and take over Sproul."

"We'll both have trouble if the university identifies us." Her words rushed out; she'd lose her determination if her momentum faltered. "They could throw us out. If they play hardball, you'd be fired from your instructor's position in Folklore and, for me, there goes my history Ph.D. and academic career. That's the most important thing in the world to me—but I'm game. It's vital to take a stand."

Other students seemed to weigh similar choices if they occupied the administration building, but most surged forward and, with Savio and other Free Speech leaders orchestrating the movement, the crowd began an inexorable but orderly flow up the building's steps and through the main entrance. It would be their building today.

The cop next to Bradan was fixing to intervene and plant himself before the crowd to block the press of kids pushing toward the doors, but he realized no fellow officers were nearby, and he was hugely outnumbered. His pistol would be the only equalizer. Bradan sensed emotions teetering between self-control and bottled-up resentment at authority flouted.

"It wouldn't be good to fire the first shot, officer," Bradan said as he and Gail slid past the cop. "There are cameras and press everywhere. Your brass wouldn't back you."

Bradan gestured at the students. "All this theater, it's nothing to lose a career and pension over. Or your mortgage. Let them talk it out between the administration and the students."

"That's all they do, talk. Don't come to nothing."

"Then it doesn't come to anything. Who cares? People making a lot more than either of us get to take the credit or blame for the commotion. For both sides, it's their day in the sun, the only time in their lives they'll be important."

Students shoved past them. The policeman's hand was still on his gun.

Bradan realized he was bargaining with the cop. How did negotiating work here? And what could he offer up? Perhaps the appearance of respect.

"Your division could have taken France single-handedly," Bradan said.

A switch flipped. The cop now looked puzzled. "You were in the division?"

"Nope. Fighter Group, Eighth Air Force. Flying right over you. P-51, escorting bombers."

"Fly-boy. You don't look that old." He took his hand off the gun.

"Pilot, not fly-boy," Bradan corrected. "I keep hearing about my age."

"You two going in? And the dog, too?"

"Yep. Why not? We troop in and sit around on the floor for a day or two. My dog is house-trained. I teach a folklore class to whoever wants to hear it—probably no one. Other folks lecture about the Constitution and whatever. We sing songs and feel committed to our principles. People make more speeches."

"The governor has to take a stand or he looks weak."

Bradan nodded. "Reagan will use this as a club to smack Pat Brown."

"We'll drag you out," the cop said. "They're assembling a bunch of us to do just that."

"Won't be the first time I've been dragged out of a building."

"They'll shoot your dog."

"People have tried, but he's a bad target."

The cop looked him over. "Keep your head down."

"I've heard that before. I'll try, officer."

He, Gail, and the wolf joined the throng moving into the building. Joan Baez led them in singing "We Shall Overcome."

"That police guy might have shot us," Gail said.

"Probably not," Bradan said. "But I wanted to be sure, so I gave him a moment to process consequences."

"You had it figured out. Have you been in this situation before?"

"Sort of."

"What you said to the cop, you're totally skeptical about everyone's motives," Gail said. "Don't you believe in the ideals behind this?"

"I very much believe in them, but I'm also a realist about human nature. People say all sorts of things, but self-interest usually dictates how they actually behave."

He flashed back to Paris during the Terror. They'd done more than occupy buildings, and the consequences were worse than arrest for disorderly conduct. There had been dozens of factions, led by hundreds of charismatics, each more rapacious than the next, and the border between idealistic principle and self-aggrandizement was hazy. He hadn't been sure whom to support, but he'd chosen badly and, after waiting in a holding cell for the guillotine, he'd been lucky to escape with his head on his shoulders.

Intellectuals often troubled society more than warriors.

Florence under Medici rule five centuries before had been even more volatile. Mobs and mercenaries vied for control of the streets and merchant princes plotted against the Pope to settle the city-state's fate. Bradan had tried to sit out the turmoil in an artist's studio painting an exceptional woman, but instead he'd been dragged into a duel and internecine strife. Whose principles had he pledged himself to then? In the end, he'd focused on survival.

Today they all moved into Sproul in a mass surging up the flights of stairs to completely fill the building. The moment's unpredictable energy felt familiar.

"This is for a good cause," he said to Gail. "It's important that we're here. Doing this. I'll check my cynicism at the door."

"Hey Bradan, I should have known you'd be at Sproul," Joan called to him over the mass of students. "You still singing in coffeehouses and playing twelve-string?"

Bradan waved back at her. "Starting a band," he shouted above the hubbub. "If Jim McGuinn and David Crosby can do it, so can I. It's all about timing. Join my group. We need a great voice like yours."

"Being in a band is a perfect way to kill friendships," she yelled back.

He nodded. "Then I'll find enemies to join me instead."

"You know her?" Gail said, sounding impressed. "And you sing? You've got a whole other life."

"It's just a side thing at the moment. Academic research, getting grants, and finding a college to get tenured at are my focus. Let's locate a comfortable spot to sit," he said. "My back hurts. I need a wall to lean against."

* * *

Bradan and Gail looked out the front windows of Sproul Hall. It was night. A few students not committed enough to follow Savio into the administration building still milled about on the plaza below. Journalists lingered, too. Streetlights cast them in shadow. Several buses from the Alameda County sheriff's department had rolled onto campus near the plaza. They had barred windows and Bradan guessed when the cops arrested students, this is where they'd put them to be driven over to county lockup. Probably their fate would be a cold few hours in a cell before being bailed out or released on their own recognizance—if the judicial apparatus was feeling generous. A contingent of police forty strong and growing faced Sproul, and a dozen more circled around to the side flanking the main entrance. They wore helmets. Bradan saw nightsticks and guns. In the dim light, they appeared to be specters assembling.

He and Gail stood near the main stairwell and next to an administrator's office. Tintagel, looking like a huge rug that had been wadded up and stuffed under the stairs, snored blithely. The wolf had seen worse circumstances. He'd torn off the armband.

"Well, let's give them a vision to look at," Bradan said.

"What?" Gail asked.

"Talking to myself," he said. "I need to go to the bathroom. Be right back."

"They're pretty well used," she said. "Cops tried to lock them, but we scared them off by saying that we'd piss in the hallway if they prevented us from using the bathrooms."

"Brilliant."

The men's bathroom was packed, but he found an empty stall, closed the door, and quietly mouthed a twelve-stanza spell. Bradan had tried a similar enchantment in the past, but he had no idea if it would work in this setting and with the particular vision he conceptualized. It would be easy to check. He hoped no one heard his mumbling, but in the echoing lavatory full of boisterous, anxious students that wasn't likely. He knew it was working as he experienced the familiar heavy blanket of lethargy settle over him while the enchantment sucked intellectual and physical energy out of him. Bradan held himself upright using the stall door for support. Time to see what effect, if any, he'd elicited from whatever wellspring birthed his magic.

Trying not to stagger, he exited the bathroom.

"Tired," he confided to a guy by a washbasin who reached out to steady him. "Can't sleep on these marble floors."

The young man gave him a thumbs-up and told him they were doing righteous work.

Back beside Gail, she said, "Look out the window. It's strange. A student must have gotten up on the roof with floodlights and stencils, really powerful floodlights."

Bradan looked at the plaza below. The flagstones were emblazoned with an enormous "FSM." The individual letters were a hundred feet long and stretched halfway across the plaza to the student union on the far side. Despite the scale, the image had crystalline clarity. The *F* and *M* were gold and flanked the blue *S* in the middle. The cops beneath them stared at their feet dumbfounded by the sudden, vivid image that they now stood atop.

"I got the colors right," Bradan said.

"Were you on the roof?"

"No, I meant the student leaders got the colors right, Cal's colors. I like that image down there better than the armbands."

Other students clustered by the window and called over friends to laugh at this piece of political theater. Gradually the vision faded away to nothing. Concurrently, Bradan's energy slowly recovered. Amused, he saw one cop below shake his shoes as if the ephemeral image stuck to his soles like gum on a hot sidewalk.

"You could use food," Gail said.

"I saw them making sandwiches down the hall," he said. "They're pretty organized, but I'm not hungry. They're teaching informal classes in corners, too. Even the floors have been divided up for different purposes. I'll see if anyone wants to hear about folklore, but let's sit down first. I'm beat."

"God, my parents would be so proud," she said.

"About their daughter lounging on a dirty floor waiting to be arrested?"

"You bet. My mom was a labor organizer in Brooklyn during the Depression."

"You're the classic red diaper baby," he said.

"So you know the term. It fits me. Pops taught at a New York City teachers college until they fired him for being a communist party member. He's on every FBI watch list there is. He fought in Spain, too."

"Abraham Lincoln Brigade?"

"Were you with them?"

"Christ, do I look that old?"

"No. You look pretty young, actually."

Gail's curly reddish hair spilled over a disheveled overcoat and scarf. The woman had dressed for a siege. She rummaged in a pocket, found what she was looking for, and put her glasses on. Was it vanity that kept them off while she stood near the microphones and speakers at the top of Sproul's stairs in full view of thousands?

The color of her eyes looked like tea that had steeped for a long while.

She cuddled up to him. Her hair bunched up on the coat collar and tumbled down her shoulders. He felt curls brush his face. She awkwardly positioned her legs under herself and tugged a gray, wool skirt over her knees. The skirt wasn't meant for modesty while sitting on a floor.

Completely inappropriately, he wanted to put one hand up her skirt while caressing her breasts under the sweater with the other, but Gail was the epitome of earnest propriety. Further, the police were about to launch a frontal assault on Sproul, and Bradan and Gail sat jammed in among hundreds of students in a noisy corridor. If there was a nonsensual setting, this was it, and he still thought about sex.

He wondered if a lustful thought about him had ever crossed her mind during their many discussions about politics and public policy.

Bradan looked about. Students lined the hall as far as he could see. For a while during the afternoon, the police had allowed occupying students to come and go from Sproul as they pleased. Bradan guessed they expected many would get bored with the cramped conditions and not return, but by the evening, access to the building was halted and the message got round from the strike leaders that no one was getting back in; reinforcements had been cut off. He heard a siren close by outside the building and a dispatcher on a police radio.

"You guys need any instruction on how to be arrested?" A woman Bradan recognized as one of the student floor captains stood over them.

"Hey, I know you," she said. "You're Dr. Bradan Badon. I took your graduate folklore seminar last year. I wasn't expecting much, but you connected old belief systems to modern culture really well. I hope they bring you on tenure track."

Bradan nodded thanks. He loved it when his message got across.

"You also do guest spots on KMPX, talking about social changes happening now for a popular audience, 'Culture for the Cool Set.' You're kinda famous."

"Kinda. It's an idiotic show, but it's extra cash."

"So, when the police come in—" the floor captain started.

"—hopefully, if we go limp when they drag us out, we avoid getting smacked around with clubs," Bradan finished.

"That's pretty much it. We won't make it easy for them. They'll go after the leaders first, then the rest. We're stuffed in here so they'll have to climb over lots of passive bodies to haul the floor captains out. They'll pull you up by your arms and twist them behind you. They won't go easy on any of us."

"Just instinct, but I'd say they'll be moving in to make arrests," he said. "The party will be over soon."

"Yep," the leader replied. "They'll take most of us to Santa Rita or another county lockup. Or Corvalle Mesa if there's overflow at the other places. It's supposed to be the worst."

"How long will we be in prison?" Gail asked.

"Until you can make bail or there are so many of us they begin to let us go because we're not really flight risks," the captain said. "Also, people on the outside will try to find where they send us and set up lawyers and negotiate about what bail they set."

Bradan couldn't tell how well this bit had been planned. He thought once they'd occupied Sproul, the next steps were being improvised based on the administration's and the cops' response. That would be predictably blundering, but aggressive.

"Will they put us in with real prisoners?" Gail asked.

She didn't sound panicked, but her tone wasn't as confident as it had been a few minutes ago.

"They'll be a lot of us for company," Bradan said. "Stay as calm as you can. I've got money enough to get us both released if they demand bail."

"I've saved up a little money, too," Gail said. She smiled, but it came out as a grimace. "I was going to buy a new coat as a reward after my dissertation defense, but leaving jail takes priority."

She put her head on his shoulder.

"While we're waiting for whatever happens next," he said, "there's a utilities closet on the fourth floor."

She looked at him. "You're suggesting we pull out mops and clean up, show the chancellor we're all solid citizens despite the occupation?"

Irony drenched his words. "The public will be impressed that we've left the place spotless."

He continued, "What I really was thinking was the closet would be private enough for the two of us to be romantic. I checked earlier this afternoon and it's not locked. And there aren't that many people on the fourth floor."

"Wasn't that farsighted of you, doing a reconnaissance mission?" She was sarcastic, but didn't sound apprehensive any longer.

"Close confines in the closet," he admitted. "And we'd have to avoid the Clorox and paper towels."

Her commitment to causes and her intelligence made her admirable. She'd make a great history teacher. Yet all Bradan thought about was Gail with her legs spread apart. She was cute beyond belief. It had to be the anxiety of an imminent clash heightening animal lust.

Shit, how was she going to react to his overture? Not with animal lust. Instead she'd get up and march to the far end of the hall without a backward glance at him. He had to admit cleaning supplies didn't sound very mood-setting, but the paper towels would come in handy.

Gail regarded him for a moment. "Love in a time of protest?"

"Why not? Life isn't on hold. You don't think other couples in this crowd haven't found quiet spots to do it?"

"We're a couple?"

"I'd hoped so."

"A closet isn't exactly wine and candles. You really know how to win a girl over."

"You're right," he said. "It's a silly idea."

Sometimes one was right in tune with the other person about sex, sometimes not. Tonight was clearly in the "not the right time" category. Maybe she'd never be interested in him under any circumstance. So be it. Keeping things platonic and rational was in Gail's character, frantic fucking a lot less so.

"We'd have to work around brooms and whatnot," she said.

"Crazy idea."

"Yeah, crazy. Let's talk about how your dissertation is coming along."

"Anything but that."

She looked up and down the hall. It was crowded, but nobody paid them any attention. Many students looked to be asleep. Discreetly, she pulled his hand under her coat and over her breasts. Even through her sweater, Bradan thought they felt fantastic.

"I didn't say no," she said. "I just hadn't thought of it tonight, in Sproul, and, for sure, not in a broom closet, but I think we can make it work. Is there a place to hang my coat and can you lock the door from the inside so no one walks in? It would be our first time and a good story to tell people later."

"A lot of great sex happens during revolutions," Bradan agreed. He spoke from experience.

"Can we be done before the cops break in?" she asked.

"Depends on how often we do it, but let's try."

He stood first and extended an arm to pull her to her feet. Gail was normally decorous, but her skirt hiked up past her panties and she didn't hurry to pull it down.

"No one's watching," she said.

Leaving a pile of his class lecture notes and her books on the floor, they climbed up two flights of stairs.

On the fourth floor, Bradan held Gail's hand and led them halfway down the corridor. It was less crowded than the lower floors so he was surprised to see the closet door wide open and several strike leaders caucusing. As he approached, he overheard the gist of it: They felt it wouldn't represent the Free Speech Movement well if they left Sproul a wreck. So they were going to issue brooms and tidy the halls and bathrooms.

"Goddamn," Bradan said with feeling. "Just goddamn."

"What about an office?" Gail asked.

There were several offices along the corridor. He'd heard they'd been broken into in search of embarrassing documents to shame the campus administrators. At the far end of the hall, Bradan discreetly examined the handle of a door with a frosted-glass pane labeled "Curriculum Planning and Development." It looked undisturbed. Either no FSM folks had forced entry or they'd been better than professional burglars at covering their tracks.

He twisted the handle. *Locked. Son of a bitch.*

"We can wait till this is over," Gail said. "My apartment is private and comfortable. I've got a king bed. After we're out of jail or wherever they take us, we'll go there."

"The mood is cool right now, right here," he said. All he felt was headlong urgency. "Don't give up yet. We're making a statement if we do it here. Be right back, washing hands."

"You're spending lots of time in the bathroom."

"Powdering my nose. Got to look good for the mug shot."

In a deserted stall, he mouthed a sixteen-line poem. Locks were never his specialty, but he remembered getting into Cadbury Fort fifteen centuries earlier as he fled the Wild Hunt. Tonight Bradan sensed tumblers rearranging themselves favorably. Drained, he leaned against the side of the stall breathing heavily for several minutes, but Gail wouldn't wait.

"It's open," she said as he returned to her by the office he'd tried to access. "This office and every other door handle I tried, they're all open. Didn't you twist the door handles hard enough?"

"Evidently not," he said. His enchantment had worked, albeit nonspecifically. Magic could be glitchy. "Let's slip inside before anyone notices."

Now the woman was on a mission. With the frosted-glass door closed behind them, she had her coat off in a flash and carefully folded it on an armchair behind an expansive wooden desk strewn with folders and letters emblazoned with the university's letterhead. Whoever used the desk when Sproul wasn't occupied was both busy and none too tidy. Two big metal file cabinets flanked the door—they could have held half of Berkeley's confidential student files—and three chairs faced the desk, but that was the only furniture. Bradan and Gail regarded the desk for a moment and nodded agreement.

"Let's leave the papers and documents where they are," she said.

This saved a lot of arranging and moreover screwing on official forms showed a calculated contempt for authority, a libido enhancer if ever there was one tonight in occupied Sproul.

Without the overcoat, Gail's curves became apparent. He moved behind her and pulled her sweater over her head. She extended her arms straight up to make it easier for the garment to get past her mane of curls. She shook her hair free and reached back to unhook her bra, but kept her glasses on. Still behind her, Bradan cupped her breasts. He always noticed nipples and Gail's were soft, then firmed under his fingers.

The room was dim with crepuscular light coming through the frosted glass from the hall fluorescents. It patterned her skin like a leopard. The only other light filtered through a small window looking down on the nighttime plaza. Their top-floor office was just under the building's eaves with a low ceiling and warm from rising heat. He sweated and she did, too.

Keeping a hand on Gail's breast, he let his other drift down to her wool skirt and unzipped it from behind and pushed it down her hips and legs. She shimmied out of it and he moved his hand down her belly and into her panties and his fingers slid into her. She spread her legs as he stroked gently, persistently.

The rest of their clothing came off and got piled atop Gail's coat.

Bradan heard a commotion on the floors below as an authority figure speaking through a megaphone ordered students to vacate the building immediately. Bradan also noticed sirens out on the plaza.

"Now or never," he said and lay down on the desk. He was very ready.

Gail also climbed on the desk and swung her leg over to straddle him. She pushed him inside her, no preliminaries, and aligned herself comfortably, shifting her hips, taking time, then slid herself all the way down on him. His back felt cold against the desktop contrasting with the woman's warmth on top of him. Gail and Bradan moved together as he held her hips and pulled himself almost out and then pushed way into her.

She looked down at him through her glasses.

"That works," she said and off they went.

"Get ready. They're here, coming up the floors," a floor captain shouted outside in the hall not far from their office. "Remember to go limp."

"Don't take that limp bit literally," Gail whispered, leaning down over him so that her breasts pushed into his chest.

"Not likely," Bradan grunted. "Keep doing what you're doing."

And she continued to ride him, at first, looking very aware of her circumstances, running her hands through her hair, pushing her glasses up her sweaty nose, glancing at her piled clothing, checking the translucent window in the door, scrutinizing his reactions as she moved up and down on him with increasing pace, then looking ever more distracted and focused on her own sensations, moving herself about on him, trying different angles, absorbed by what her body was feeling, making the moment stretch, police be damned. This went on for several minutes.

"I'm on the pill."

"Good to know." Bradan came buckets. She was tight. He felt her muscles inside contract. And then quickly several more times.

Gail leaned down on his chest breathing hard. "That doesn't happen for me the first time with anyone."

"Revolutions and sex," breathed Bradan. "Unusual times."

In the hallway, young men and women yelled and swore. Police argued over who to drag out first and where the hell were the leaders so they could get to them? Evidently, extracting a host of passively resisting students had turned into a major chore and no fun.

"Again," Gail said. "Can you go a second round?"

"That would be pretty quick," he said.

"Revolutions and sex," she said. "Unique times. Can you accelerate things? I can help."

He felt her muscles inside contract, urging him on.

"We're going to have company any second," Bradan said. "They'll not only get us for breaking and entering, but indecent behavior and public lewdness."

"They're going to make arrests, anyway," she said. "Now they can throw the book at us."

"Let's go," he said. Fear and excitement supercharged every feeling.

Bradan reached around Gail's waist and flipped her over so she was under him on the desk. He pulled her legs up to rest on his shoulders and got between her thighs and pushed himself all the way into her. At first they were measured, getting used to the new position, stirring the cream from their first bout, then it was hell for leather, plunging and getting just as close as physically possible before a tsunami of wetness rushed out everywhere.

Lying together, they breathed for a moment. He wanted to stay inside her for a time.

A fist hammered on the door and wrenched at the handle and hammered again.

"Locked," he said, pulling himself out and standing.

Postcoital, he'd rather have slept on the desk awhile.

"I locked the door coming in."

"Good thinking." She rolled off the desk to stand beside him unsteadily. "Let me hold on to you for a second."

They kissed.

"I assume I can go limp now?" he said.

She looked at him. "Down, big boy. Not a good idea to be arrested in that condition."

"They'll find a master key or break it in," he said. "We made noise. They know we're in here. Clothes." He guided her over to the desk chair.

As she pulled her clothing on, she bent over to inspect the desk and giggled. "We were after maximum mess. Mission accomplished."

Bradan looked at the desk, too. "There's a memo on top about faculty salaries."

* * *

Getting yanked out of the building was every bit as unpleasant as they'd been warned. At least they were fully clothed when

Bradan unlocked the door and he and Gail moved into the hallway. Gail even had her overcoat draped over one shoulder like a cavalry hussar. However, Bradan and Gail had obviously accessed an office for God knew what nefarious purpose, unlike the rest of Sproul's student occupants, who simply lay or sat clustered in the hall, many in the process of being bodily hauled to the staircase and half pushed, half carried down the stairs.

A police lieutenant shoved them aside and marched into the office flipping on the lights. Bradan could see mental wheels turning—ransacking the office and trying to pry open file cabinets for confidential documents? The cop paid no attention to the soaked desk and yanked at the drawers in the file cabinets. Every file drawer was locked. Then he inspected the cabinet locks looking for any sign of forced entry. He checked the door handle again. Everything looked kosher.

Evidently political orgasms hadn't been included as part of standard counter-civil-disobedience training.

"Just looking for a quiet place to sleep," Bradan said to the lieutenant. "Noisy as hell in the hall. We didn't touch the cabinets."

"How'd you get in?" the cop asked. He seemed genuinely puzzled. "The college administrators locked everything before you jerks moved in."

"It was unlocked," Gail said. "They forgot this office."

Another cop approached the lieutenant. "The whole floor is unlocked. Nothing was secure."

"We didn't do it," Bradan said. "How could we have unlocked a whole floor's worth of doors with no forced entry? Magic? The administrators blew it and didn't secure the place before we showed up."

"I'll follow up with the university," the lieutenant finally said. "Meantime, get these two out of here and onto the buses." Several cops responded by grabbing Bradan and Gail. Bradan was happy to see that Gail appeared unconcerned and defiant in their grip. Apparently vigorous coupling agreed with her.

Two helmeted highway patrolmen dragged the floor captain past. She winked. Bradan guessed she'd been among the students who had heard him and Gail going at it.

"See you in lockup," she said.

Bradan wondered what the bureaucrat whose office they'd misused would make of the sopping-wet documents on his desk. Likely they'd just be refiled after air drying.

* * *

The cop with the army divisional tattoo on his hand intercepted Bradan as three other policemen half dragged, half carried him down the final flight of stairs en route to the basement for processing. After being bounced down dozens of stone steps, Bradan's back hurt like hell. He could have actively fought back, but the whole point of the Sproul occupation was nonviolent civil disobedience. Turning his arrest into a brawl contravened that ethic.

"I've got this one," Tattoo told his fellow cops. "He's going to preliminary booking below."

"Good riddance. He looks thin, but he's all muscle and weighs a ton." The trio of highway patrolman marched back up the stairs for more students. The forces of law and order had turned the process into an assembly line: Cops trudged up the stairs empty-handed and returned pushing and dragging students.

Most stayed limp per their training, others struggled ineffectually with their arms jammed up into the small of their backs.

Bradan stood up on his own feet. He'd made his point with passive resistance. He flashed a *V* for victory sign at several newsmen near the main entrance.

"Listen, you've pissed someone off real good," the cop told him. "A congressman, Van Newman, wants you pulled away from the others when you get to Corvalle Mesa lockup. The guy's on the House Un-American Activities Committee or some such thing and he's saying you're a known communist with ties to the Soviet Union. You're here to stir up the situation. They've got an isolation cell for you separated from other detainees."

Bradan was baffled. "I don't know anyone in congress. I'm just a campus folklore instructor." He wondered if breaking into the fourth floor office so he and Gail could have sex qualified him for special attention. Or it was it those damned radio guest spots which had created unsuspected notoriety for him. That didn't seem possible. He got fan mail and no one ever was offended by his platitudes about society and culture.

"Does folklore have to do with communism?" the cop asked.

Bradan stood dumbfounded. "It's about a culture's traditions and how those get passed along generation to generation. Usually, that's through storytelling—"

"Spare me. You're to be separated from the rest in Corvalle. You won't be prebooked here, either. I'm to escort you directly to a bus. I was you, I'd get a good lawyer, keep the culture stuff to yourself if you get in front of a judge."

"Good advice," Bradan said dryly.

"By the way, where's your doggy?"

"He's not a communist as far as I know. He'll find his own way out of Sproul. He's good at fending for himself."

* * *

Bradan found himself in "the hole," a windowless cell the size of a closet with a drain in the middle of the floor and no furniture. He tried not to look at the drain. The room smelled of piss. A trail of ants led from it to a solid metal door that was the only exit. Bradan had seen any number of prisons in his long life and this one was more benign than many—until he'd been brought here. There wasn't even a peephole. He didn't think American prisons had such places. This was a Russian gulag. He'd laugh if it didn't stink.

Who wants me here? he thought. *Where's Gail?*

As far as he could tell, the rest of the Sproul students were being processed in a chaotic open yard beyond the main gate with some being detained while others were released. Personal belongings were seized, then returned with no rhyme or reason. Gigantic as it was, the Corvalle Mesa County Correctional and Rehabilitation facility was now swamped with college kids as well as regular criminals, the less dangerous of whom were set loose to make room for the students. A quartet of guards pulled him aside from the confusion and marched him to the hole. En route, his impression was of badly molded concrete, metal bars, and a barren exercise yard.

What am I charged with?

He still wore his civilian clothing. Maybe he wouldn't be here long. From past incarcerations, Bradan knew his first challenge was mastering helplessness and uncertainty about what happened next. A tactic to confront this fear was inventorying every feature of his setting and whatever they'd left on his person.

They've taken my belt so hanging myself isn't an option, he thought sardonically.

He patted himself down. In the rush to process him, they'd removed his shoelaces, but left a plastic pen in his slacks' back pocket, not a real oversight since it wasn't much of a weapon, but one never knew. He'd made do with less. Even if the pen wasn't very dangerous, he could scrawl his name on the wall in as many scripts as he could remember. The ink barely showed on the institutional paint, but he'd nonetheless altered his environment; he had a miniscule bit of control over his surroundings. His name in classical Arabic looked pretty. He stuffed the pen back into a pocket.

The light was so dim he couldn't tell what color the paint was; aesthetics hadn't been top of mind when they'd designed the place. Incredibly, the adamantine door had gouges and scratches on it. Past occupants had been desperate to get out or, like Bradan, they'd just wanted to leave their mark. He looked around the tiny enclosure and then up at the ceiling; it was all featureless except for a fixture far out of reach emitting watery light.

Why can't I call a lawyer?

Well, he was a magician, and his bag of tricks included manipulating locks so he had a leg up on the average inmate—though the spell worked unpredictably as he'd seen at Sproul in his desperate haste to access an office and get inside Gail's pussy. However, he remembered a room full of deputies and shotguns down the corridor from the hole. If he worked a spell to escape, he'd be spotted instantly. The guards could observe his steel door as well as a dozen other cells near Bradan's.

The neighboring enclosures were barred and arranged along an endless corridor leading from the guard station to the hole.

Diffuse light permeated the environment, neither day nor night. The cells housed an assortment of men who must be the hardcases deemed too dangerous for general lockup. Bradan's fleeting impression of them as he'd been hustled into the hole at the remote end of the corridor was that they were of all races, big and ugly, emerging as apparitions from the ill-lit reaches of their cages to check out the newcomer. They were bare chested and tattooed with an assortment of gang affiliations and religious symbols that would have done sixth-century Celtic warriors proud. On the way to his cell, Bradan expected a volley of taunts, but the inmates seemed flabbergasted to see an academic type hauled down to the nether reaches of their world.

They were silent. However, Bradan felt insensate hatred emanating from the cells. It wasn't directed at him. Instead, it was focused on the guards. While the students might be outraged at the university administration and a society unmoved by their demands, theirs was a principled, abstract stand against broad cultural forces; the inmates had a visceral rage laser focused on their jailers.

In the hole, Bradan lost his sense of time. He expected this, but felt disoriented nonetheless. He hammered the door with his fist, eliciting muted thuds from the steel. This didn't change his circumstances one iota. The portal deadened every punch he threw at it. This made him feel more powerless, not less, so he stopped.

Have they forgotten me?

After an indeterminate period, his door was pulled open. First Bradan saw two deputies. Hulking behind them was a huge man in a suit. He'd taken his tie off.

"I've got it from here, officers," he said. Bradan heard a familiar accent.

"Congressman, he's been demanding a call, a lawyer," one of the guards said. "We hustled him straight here from the bus, but we gotta give him that sooner or later. And he's not booked yet."

"Let me talk to him before processing."

"You want in there alone with him?" the guard asked. He sounded dubious. "If he's as bad as you say, how about we stay here?"

"How about you leave him to me," the big man said. It was an order, not a question. "Come back in ten minutes."

"We close that door, no one can hear you." The cop kicked at the steel door hard to make the point. The metal muffled his shoe's impact to inaudibility.

"Then no one hears us, officer. Come back in ten."

They eased the heavy door shut.

"Medraut," Bradan said. He hadn't seen the son of a bitch in centuries and he'd hoped never to meet him again. Now he was locked in, mano a mano, a hair's breadth from his face.

"Congressman Van Newman. I don't use Medraut anymore."

"Will 'traitor' suit?"

Bradan smelled peppermint toothpaste on the other man. It didn't go with the cell's piss odor.

Bradan was as tall as Van, but the other man outweighed him by at least seventy-five pounds. And it was all muscle hardened by endless centuries of killing starting in Arthur's sixth-century fort. The hole barely contained both of them; an intimate space for murder. For a blood feud, nothing else would do but for Van to kill him personally, the Celtic way. Of course, Van strangling or stabbing him here would raise a dozen questions from the police and judicial system, but the big man must figure that his political stature, a crack legal team, and a public relations agency would shield him from prosecution. In fact, this might burnish his reputation with the public if he swore under oath he'd planned to question Bradan, a reputed agent of the Soviets and participant in a leftist insurrection at UC Berkeley, and Bradan had attacked him.

Van's switchblade came out in a flash, but Bradan hadn't waited. He hit Van as hard as he could in the neck given the limited space in the cell while jerking his knee up into the congressman's crotch. If you couldn't avoid a fight, strike first. "Good guys" died playing by the rules while "bad guys" not only survived but flourished. Besides, what rules was he supposed to play by? And was he the good guy here? Shades of gray, he'd lived in that space before. Besides making art and music, he'd fought as often as Van and for causes nearly as murky.

The big man gasped and fell into Bradan as his knife slashed Bradan's forearm. A thin dress shirt didn't protect flesh like armor from a sharp blade, and Van's reflexes allowed him to stab again at Bradan after the first slash despite two hard hits. However, the tiny space they struggled within hampered the congressman as much as Bradan. Bradan had expected Van's movements so he'd been able to pivot away a fraction of a second before the blade sliced him. The cut was deep, but could have been worse. Bradan clawed at Van's eyes. Another stab from Van missed his jugular and caught his deltoid.

"You picked the wrong side in Florence," Bradan snarled. "You didn't kill me then and you won't now."

Keep moving sideways away from the weapon, he thought. *But there's no room to move in this cage.*

Then Bradan's feet slid out from under him, leaving him on the greasy drain with Van on top of him. Now Bradan's face was right on the floor grate. He retched.

Wherever I die, it won't be with my cheek on a pisshole.

Bradan's revulsion launched him upward despite Van's weight. Bradan ripped the pen from his back pocket. His opponent had survived Arthur's lance so a plastic pen wouldn't do much damage, but it could distract the big man. Struggling upright, Bradan blindly jammed the pen backward holding his thumb over one end to maximize penetrating force and felt it hit a thigh, a bicep, Van's torso? Van exhaled in pain. The man's suit coat protected him, but not completely, and yet another stab from Van's knife went wide. Bradan grabbed the big man's knife hand and slammed it into the cell door, breaking the switchblade's lockout and folding the blade back into the handle. This gashed Bradan's forefinger, but chopped deeply into all of Van's fingers. The congressman would have screamed, but Bradan rammed an elbow into his solar plexus. Bradan now was on top.

Don't let up when you're ahead.

Bradan stamped downward at the big man's stomach and again at his face, blocked by Van's forearm instinctively coming up to protect himself. Bradan saw the end of his pen broken off in Van's shoulder. Bradan danced about in the hole looking to connect with his shoe again, but the congressman was quick despite the damage he'd sustained.

I won't win this way, Bradan thought.

He remembered the spell for locks. Reciting it recently in Sproul meant that the stanzas fell right into place, commensurate with crushing fatigue. He was weak and at his attacker's mercy now. Bradan fell backward into the door and out into the corridor as the now unlocked barrier burst open under his weight. Van on hands and knees tried to scramble after him, but slipped on blood and piss and collapsed half in, half out of the cell.

The two cops who let Van into Bradan's cell loitered just down the corridor clearly skeptical about the congressman's safety. Their worst suspicions confirmed, they rushed at the two struggling combatants on the floor, reaching to pull them apart.

"They're open," Bradan wheezed at inmates in the nearest cells. "Doors unlocked. Get out."

And then he wasn't alone.

They heard him, and the corridor filled with prisoners who'd experimentally tried their cell doors and, finding them open, erupted out into the corridor in a confused, violent mass. Two prisoners attacked each other. Several launched themselves at the deputies' station at the corridor's far end while others tackled the cops who were wrenching Bradan apart from Van. Bradan found himself in a rugby scrum. The inmates ignored him and tore at the two guards, grabbing for their sidearms and batons. Van looked to be an authority figure, and one wiry inmate with a tattoo of Jesus on the cross punched the congressman repeatedly.

Bradan lurched to his feet, clumsily extricating himself from the writhing figures. He glanced at his arm. Van had slashed him from his wrist to elbow. It bled profusely, but it wasn't deep. His shoulder hurt, too. It was an in-and-out puncture, bad but not life-threatening.

"Give me room," Bradan yelled at the inmate battering Van. "I want at him." He intended to kick the congressman, but instead lost his balance, reeling from the spell's exertion and his fight.

"What's your name?" he yelled at the inmate.

"Eddie. I pounded the guy. Now he's yours."

The tattooed inmate followed the rest of the prisoners mobbing the guard station. The onslaught had been so precipitous and overwhelming that the deputies hadn't been able to rip shotguns from racks and, without firepower, it became a pitched battle with fists and batons and whatever sidearms could be drawn from holsters in time to get off a shot. Bradan heard a pistol's deafening boom reverberate down the corridor of cells, but couldn't tell who'd fired at whom. He wondered if anyone had gotten an alarm off.

He regained his feet. The pen was still lodged in his opponent's shoulder, and Bradan wanted to rip it out and hammer it through Van's eye socket into his brain.

What side of the white-to-black spectrum was he on now? A shade of dark gray.

However, murdering Van with a pen would take time. Bradan didn't have time before guards arrived in force to quell the insurrection.

Bradan backed out of the cell and shut the door. He could relock it with a spell, but that would exhaust him further and flight was imperative. Regardless of the irregularity of his incarceration, if they caught him again, no lawyer could get him out of an attempted murder charge after his fight with a congressman. However, he wasn't booked, so no one knew his name; his anonymity might let him leave.

He looked at the two deputies who'd escorted Van to his cell. They were meat piled one atop the other in the hall after the inmates' ministrations. He'd unleashed this maelstrom and orchestrated his own Wild Hunt.

The deputies' guns and batons had been ripped out of their hands, but one had two key rings still attached to his belt. The inmates wouldn't have bothered with keys since they were now loose anyway, and main strength coupled with speed would win them through the prison's outer enclosures, or not.

However, Bradan wanted a particular key. He stooped. One ring contained many keys, the other, just one. Guessing that this was to the hole, Bradan ripped it off the cop's belt and jammed it into the steel door's lock. It fit. He locked the barrier, then snapped off the key and hurled the empty ring into a nearby cell. Van could rot in the hole until guards finally thought to look for him many hours from now. And then it would take still more hours to free him by burning through the blocked lock with a torch.

Bradan bent again and checked the two deputies. They breathed. He paused for a beat, considering, then pulled off one of their jackets and grabbed a cap. He wiped blood off the brim and stuffed the clothing under his arm. He also took the bigger key ring. The keys made his disguise real.

From the sounds, the battle down the corridor wasn't going well for the outnumbered deputies, but eventually the rest of the prison guards would mobilize to rescue them. Meantime, he'd capitalize on the chaos. Getting out depended on how broadly his spell had worked. It had gotten him out of the hole, but what other barriers were unlocked?

He tottered down the corridor toward the guard station, where three deputies were lined up by inmates with leveled shotguns, hostages. A prisoner was draped over a desk bleeding profusely. Maybe he'd been shot. A dozen screaming inmates beat and kicked two other guards—perhaps the shooters—who were on the floor. Tables turned, the former prisoners were striking at the helpless cops with all their strength. Fountains of blood arced upward to splatter the walls and desks.

"Leave them," Bradan yelled.

Is Eddie their leader? Is anyone?

"Eddie, call them off. You want out? Now's your chance."

For the moment he was one of them, proven by the fact that they'd seen him marched into the hole. Bradan pushed into the station interposing himself between the prisoners and the two guards on the floor.

They'll go after me for interrupting reprisals. Don't let them think or their hatred comes at me.

"How long before they hit you with more guns than you've got?" he shouted. "I'm going out into the yard."

"Can't get past the gate for this building," an inmate said. "You're trapped. With us."

"The locks in the building and the yard are busted," Bradan said.

"You know that for sure?" Eddie said.

"No. I'm about to find out."

"They'll see you," Eddie said. "You look like us now."

"I'll look like them when I cross the yard." He held up the guard's jacket and hat. "See what happens to me. If it works, do the same. Use their clothes." He nodded toward the cops.

Let them work it out. I'm leaving.

He pushed through the prisoners, out of the station to a barred, sliding door leading to the exercise yard. He tried to slide it open. It didn't budge.

Stuck or still locked?

Bradan pulled harder and the barrier rolled aside. He looked across the expansive yard to yet another gate in the distance accessing an open-air area where officials booked and processed multitudes of arriving students. This was his path out of the prison if he could make it that far, but first the yard.

Before him, groups of inmates exercised or strolled aimlessly. The open space was just dust and scuffling prisoners with a few rusting barbells in one corner. The prisoners didn't appear as vicious as the group he'd just released, but they didn't look friendly. He placed the deputy's cap on his head, pushing as much of his nonregulation shaggy hair under it as possible. Stifling pain, he stretched his arms into the lawman's jacket.

The fit was bad, but it covered his wounded arm and shoulder. He'd have to hope no one paid particular attention to his cut finger visible outside the sleeve. His collared dress shirt could pass muster, but his pants were nonstandard issue. Projecting confidence he didn't feel, Bradan strode across the yard.

At any moment, the inmates in the cell block behind him would burst forth, or if they had any brains, they'd take his suggestion, handcuff the deputies inside, don their uniforms, rip out the phone lines, and filter out into the yard, then coalesce by the main gate and attempt to overpower the guards there.

Will this work? he wondered.

It was complex chorography to shift appearance and allegiances as he moved from inmate-controlled parts of the prison to areas under the jailers' oversight. In the yard, inmates stared at him and swung by close. He must look enough like a guard to elicit their animus, so the jacket and hat gave him credibility. Guards didn't walk alone here during exercise periods. Experience in other jails told him whose stare to meet and whose to ignore. When they stepped into his path, he moved aside slightly, but not too much, like he could face them down if it came to that. He'd molt out of the lawman's cap and jacket as soon as he crossed the last gate ahead where he could became an academic again.

He walked slowly, stalling. Would his cobbled-together disguise let him through? Why hadn't hell broken loose behind him in the cell block? He needed the ensuing disorder to bluff his way out.

The facility was big enough so that he hoped his unfamiliar face wouldn't give him away to other guards. He'd find out very soon. His shoes flopped about loosely.

Shoelaces—I don't have any.

He shuffled along trying to keep his pant cuffs over the shoes. There was a guard station immediately flanking a sliding main gate built into a stockade fence topped with rolls of barbed wire. The gate was open and guards clustered about it. Two of them slammed it shut with a clang.

"Won't stay locked," a deputy said. "Shuts, but won't latch."

One of the others laughed. "We ain't much of a prison if we can't lock our own doors."

"Must be a relay shorted out in the gate control panel," the first deputy said. "I hear they had lock trouble elsewhere in the facility. I'll call maintenance and also the super. Meantime, we use keys to manually secure it. So whose got the keys?"

"They're secured in the lockbox by the gun rack inside." The guard nodded to their station. "Anyone got a key to that?"

"Would these work?" Bradan asked. He worked to control his breathing, but he'd decided he couldn't loiter indefinitely without obvious purpose waiting for the cell block behind him to explode, so he confidently walked up to the gate. He jangled the key ring he'd pulled off the deputy whose jacket he wore. Now he needed to ease his way past this cluster of deputies. With his good hand, he tossed the ring to a sergeant.

"They issued to you?"

"They were checked out to me. I escorted the big guy from congress or California Prisons. He was seeing some inmate in the hole."

Bradan pointed toward the cell block he'd just vacated. He shrugged, just a wage slave like the rest of them, uninformed and unconcerned with senior-level visitors.

A phone in the station went off.

"Get it, will you?"

Bradan wandered inside, keeping things casual. It was the central guardroom on the phone with garbled information about a break-out from the cells by the hole.

"Trouble," he shouted through the open station door to the deputies. "Trouble in the hole. They don't know much, but a prisoner's out. Or a bunch of them."

"Oh shit," a deputy said. "And we're short-staffed 'cause of the Berkeley kids."

"Get the shotguns and clear the yard," the sergeant yelled. "Any students here gets escorted back to processing. The regulars go back to their cells. The rest of us go to the block—with the shotguns—and see what in hell's happening."

Emphasizing the point, the phone rang again.

"I'll get it," the sergeant said. "That'll be next steps to contain this. You, hustle the students back to processing." He pointed at Bradan.

Escorting students through the gate, Bradan recognized a few from sitting near him in Sproul. One had been in his modern folklore seminar last year, but none saw past the uniform. He embodied faceless authority. Clearly, their focus was on getting out of Corvalle Mesa. They'd taken a stand. Now it was time to return to their university lives. He thought of Gail. Christ, he hoped she'd gone to another lockup.

Buses still pulled up to discharge loads of students, but the processing was perfunctory and more left than entered. Evidently FSM had lobbied to convince a judge to lower or waive bail entirely for late arrivals. Bradan angled away from the students toward an administrative building with little foot traffic. He flipped his hat into bushes that flanked the structure, then, as quickly as he could, shed his uniform jacket and left it on the path, simply dropping it. Gasping in pain from his injured finger and shoulder, he ran his hands through his hair, intentionally disheveling it and completing his resumption of the role of a visiting instructor at UC Berkeley.

Confusion was his cover. As Bradan moved back into the mass of students, he took inventory. He was bloody and unkempt, but so were a couple of the students who'd fallen or been pushed down stairs as Sproul was cleared. A few people nodded sympathetically at him.

"Any possessions to reclaim?" a balding prison administrator at a long table asked him. "You'll need to sign for them."

Bradan shook his head. Let them keep his belt, shoelaces, and the few dollars he'd carried in his pants. He hadn't brought his wallet when he'd entered Sproul yesterday, vaguely guessing that the less of value he had on his person, the better. That instinct had proven correct.

"When were you booked?" the administrator asked.

Bradan thought for a moment trying to remember. "I wasn't booked, didn't happen."

"We missed you?"

Bradan feigned disinterest. "Not my fault. Do you want to do it now? I honestly don't care."

"Name?"

Bradan gave it to him. The administrator checked a hand-tallied list.

"You're not on the list. So you don't exist as far as we're concerned. They didn't do it for the last couple of batches if they weren't going to charge you."

"I think they got my name at the prebooking in Sproul," Bradan said wearily. Actually, no one had taken any information about him in Sproul's basement where the other students were registered and briefly questioned before being escorted onto buses. He'd been hustled right onto a bus for Corvalle with the cops no doubt thinking that they did the bidding of higher-ups in police echelons by getting Bradan to prison posthaste.

He watched a squad of shotgun-toting guards sprint past, heading for the block containing the hole. The alarm had finally gotten out, but he didn't think they'd miss him, since he wasn't officially at Corvalle—courtesy of Van. No one even knew his name. Eventually they'd stumble on the congressman himself in the hole—after using a blowtorch to burn through the locked steel door Bradan had thoroughly jammed—but Van wouldn't say much except that he'd been at Corvalle to check on how the student miscreants from Berkeley were being processed and he'd gotten caught up in a prison riot. He'd praise the prison staff's response and his aides would spin the story to flatter Newman. After they'd patched him up.

Bradan sensed that his spell had worn off. Locks would work again, a good thing for a prison. However, it would be tricky to explain how two dozen of the prison's most violent felons had suddenly gotten loose. Officialdom would quietly bury this awkward and mysterious situation. In time Van would come after Bradan again, but no one else knew enough to identify and prosecute him.

"Did my friend Gail Halpern get processed here?" Bradan asked the administrator.

"On the women's side? I don't know. Listen, in case you hadn't noticed, we got a million of you kids here and we've got other issues, too. I can't chase down your friend. See if she's outside or have a lawyer look into it for you. She might not even be here."

The official motioned for him to join a group of students leaving the prison. Many embraced parents or friends. Jubilation mixed with fatigue from sleepless nights in Sproul as they moved out of the prison to dozens of cars parked outside.

"Have your doctor look at that cut," the administrator said in parting. Plainly, he stretched his ability to sympathize with the protesters to the maximum. "Or the campus infirmary when you get back to Berkeley. You don't want an infection. Get shoelaces, too. No one teaches you how to dress at university? A degree ain't what it should be."

Bradan nodded. "Infection's never been a problem for me. And I'll get laces."

CHAPTER 4

Canyons Near and Far

January 1967, Los Angeles

"Hey Bradan, I caught your band in West Holly-wood last Friday," Cass said. "You guys were good, pretty lyrics, strong solos, but I can make you better. There's a person you should meet. Just don't call her a chick singer."

"Always the matchmaker," Bradan said. "Thanks, but I don't need another singer for my band, chick or otherwise."

"At least talk to her," Cass said. "She can really play guitar and sing. I just harmonized with her by the pool, David joined in too, fooling around, but she has wonderful vocal timbre, from a different world. Her accent sounds kind of like yours. She accompanied us on her Martin guitar. She's the complete package. She writes her own stuff, too."

"I play guitar and sing—I hope pretty well. The whole band writes the songs. Let's not play with that chemistry. I've already got what I need to take the Pillars beyond where we are now—"

Bradan stopped, seeing the earnest helpfulness on Cass's face. Her informal salon was a unique place to make musical connections and share creative ideas. He didn't have many industry friends in LA, so ignoring her well-intentioned advice without setting eyes on the prodigy would be stupid. Besides, the prodigy could be cute.

"—let's meet her," he said unenthusiastically.

They walked over to the pool and a buffet table stacked with deli items from Canter's. People stood gobbling down food; the instincts of itinerant musicians died hard; one didn't know when the next meal would come along. Bradan sensed they were in local bands. He recognized most of the San Francisco music crowd, but he only knew the LA folks by reputation. He needed to make more friends. Cass was his entrée into this world.

Her Laurel Canyon house sat near the top of one of the region's innumerable hills covered with stands of trees that were integral to the neighborhood and abutted homes built into steep slopes to form a man-made and natural tapestry. However, all the magnificence didn't make it easy to navigate. Every road through the area twisted in haphazard, mazelike patterns; riding his Harley to Cass's place, he'd had to deploy his path-finding magic three times to locate his destination. He'd arrived exhausted from the spell-craft.

As far as his eye could see, the setting had a rustic look; beyond what he could see, he knew urban Los Angeles stretched seemingly forever. They existed in a bucolic island beset by a bland asphalt plain.

Musicians from the burgeoning LA rock scene were colonizing funky, old homes in the neighborhood. Ostentation came easily to performers armed with fat royalty checks and spectacular recording contracts, heady stuff indeed to strolling minstrels who'd only recently played for tips in coffeehouses. Members of The Byrds, Buffalo Springfield, The Doors, and a dozen other bands resided throughout the Canyon racing late-model Porsches and Jaguars on the hills' hairpin turns. Bradan lusted after the money they pulled in.

Beyond the pool, the view was eastward facing, away from the Pacific, over eucalyptus, pines, and rooftops. An ocean view would have made things perfect, but it was still a superb vista and the air felt soft. Everything was muted by evening coming on, and it was easy to imagine the Native Americans who'd once tended the land filtering back to their homes as the sun set after a day fishing in the river that had once run through the area.

Depending on the vantage point, every LA sunset was unique, subtly different colors, variations in how the shadows fell, what smells nature chose to throw into the air. Tonight Bradan inhaled jasmine and acacia. He was a million miles and a billion years from dank, hard Cadbury.

The fairyland setting made Bradan want to compose music with his feet in the pool's water. He'd write a tune with an LA vibe, but edged with acid rock guitars from San Francisco, the perfect blend of northern and southern California circa 1967. He could do it, too. He'd brought his twelve-string and a notepad. He'd scrawl lyrics and music as the song evolved in his mind. However, first he had to meet the woman Cass was pushing.

She sat with her jeans rolled up mid-calf, feet in the water, regarding him across the pool. He wondered if she was compos-ing a song of her own with a half-smile on her face. The woman seemed to peek into his mind, borrowing images and melo-dies for her own work. She had black shoulder-length hair that brushed over the collar of a flowy, paisley-patterned shirt. The shirt looked like silk, so smooth it invited a touch and matched a scarf around her neck. He couldn't see her eyes behind Ray-Ban sunglasses, which she wore despite the gathering night. It struck him that it could have been 1935 and she was a starlet under contract with Paramount. The clothing was up-to-the-minute Melrose Avenue, but the attitude was the incandescent, cool glamour of golden-era Hollywood that burned right off the big screen. Paradoxically, her manner was also timeless, of no particular era or place.

She plays guitar? he thought. *Well, let's see if that's true.*

"Bradan, this is Taryn. Taryn, Bradan."

On the other side of the pool, a fully clothed man fell in with a big splash, leaving his Borsalino hat floating on top of the water. A ripple of laughter met the fellow's furious cursing when he surfaced. A woman fished his hat from water, but didn't offer to pull the man out. The interpersonal politics in the Canyon rivaled Renaissance Florence's court life.

"Let me rescue him," Cass said. "Too bad about the hat. What a style sense he's got."

She swept away to manage the crisis.

"It's clichéd, but you look familiar," Bradan said to the woman.

His banalities froze. She *did indeed* look familiar, resembling the alabaster-pale, wind-blown specter who'd chased him during the Wild Hunt three years back on Highway 1. However, back then his pursuer had been too far off and storm-tossed to make out facial features clearly. Anyway, the woman before him looked real enough, and she was deeply tanned like she hung out on a Malibu beach in a bikini rather than chased lost souls.

Bradan worked to expel chilling memories of past demons from his psyche by focusing on tangible, in-the-moment sensations. Her high cheekbones looked spectacular, and though the shades masked her eyes, he guessed their color would be intriguing if she took them off. Her half-smile was still there, but now hinted at a deep perception of him he found discomforting.

"People don't usually say they've seen me before unless they're trying to pick me up," she said. *"Are* you trying to pick me up?"

"Nope. Cass said come over and chat. That's what I'm doing."

"So I'm an obligation?"

Pretty or not, this conversation was going nowhere fast.

Okay, one last effort, he thought. *Start over.*

"I'm Bradan."

"I know. You have a band, The Pillars of Creation. Cass told me. I'm Taryn. Taryn Valente."

"You brought a guitar?" he asked. *Get right to it.* "I have mine, too. Let's strum a few chords, see what comes of it."

What came of it was a duet that started with a simple chord progression and evolved into elaborate melodies and runs up the fretboard. They traded leads seamlessly and shifted between major and minor keys to give the nascent song texture. The instrumental exchanges all came naturally, so words came next. Bradan contributed a couple of rhyming stanzas and Taryn paired them with verses of her own. It was magic. He thought of fairies mingling and mating among the eucalyptus and added those images to the improvised song. It was all acoustic and not very loud, but the notes nonetheless carried over the grounds, into the trees, and tumbled down the hillside. The verses would be audible all the way to Faerie.

The imbroglio at the pool's far end had finally resolved itself, and the rest of the party shifted attention to Bradan and Taryn's impromptu jam session. At first the listeners were disdainful and standoffish, like they could have dashed off an even better tune if they'd had half a mind, but then the song pulled them in and they stood in a half-circle around the duo as wine and a joint made the rounds.

When it was done, the spectators clapped.

"I don't know how you two just came up with that, but it belongs on your next album," Cass said. "Add a second bridge and arrange it to include the rest of your band, but don't lose your harmonies together. In fact, push those up in the mix. That part makes it enchanting."

With the song demonstrating his musicianship and song-writing capabilities, Bradan considered petitioning the crowd for an exec's phone number who could green-light a record deal for them. However, he'd look like a rank amateur begging for an introduction from this crowd. There would be other times.

A long-haired man had a guitar, and Bradan and Taryn stepped back to give him his chance to be the focus of attention. In a business where Bradan was a nobody, there was no point stepping on egos tonight by hogging center stage from all the somebodies.

"Was that an audition?" Taryn asked. She slung her guitar over her back like a gunslinger.

"Did you want it to be? You know the Pillars' material? We've only got one record out, which we mixed and produced ourselves. It gets zero airplay even on the coolest stations—few of those that there are."

During their duet he'd decided Taryn would be a great addition to his band if she wanted to join. She was a superb mezzo-soprano and her guitar playing on the Martin was outstanding. If she could also play electric guitar, she'd contribute to the musical alchemy he wanted to create.

"Where'd you learn your chops?" he asked.

"I've played music off and on over the years," she said. "The instruments and styles change, but quality is what I'm after. You have a really sound grasp of song structure. Your lyrics just sort of dropped into place fully formed when we improvised."

"Let's see if I can turn that into any kind of success," he said. "We're getting press thanks to relentless playing. We did a free concert last month up in Golden Gate Park that got covered by the *L.A. Times* and the *San Francisco Chronicle*, drew five thousand people."

"Yeah, I was there," she said. "I've also heard your record. It's great and totally underrated, but you're right, your gigs are getting you noticed. Word of mouth is strong. That's how I found out about you. I knew Cass a little and asked to drop by when I heard you might be here tonight. Where do you want the band to go?"

"As far as we can commercially, but we're never going to become pablum. I want to keep the music's integrity and blend different genres, but make tons of money, too. I'm going to see if my art and the record companies' lucre are compatible."

"I'm in if you want me."

"We play in both LA and San Francisco," Bradan said. "Our sound kind of bridges the two tribes, SoCal folk-rock and sunshine, and Bay Area acid and psychedelia. I have a house up in the Haight. You can crash there when you're up that way. We're playing the Fillmore next month. You're great on an acoustic guitar; do you play electric?"

"Of course." Her tone hardened. "I'm not just a chick singer from the coffeehouses. I get loud."

"Groovy," he said dryly.

"Do you think only guys know how to use those phallic symbols?"

"I'm not sure about other guys in this biz, but I use my Gibson to make music."

"Fair enough," Taryn said. "I've got a Fender Strat. Their sounds should marry up well when we trade leads. Let's split. Half the partiers are comatose. Can we work up this new thing that we just did? I saw you roll up on a motorcycle."

"My Harley's out in the driveway." Bradan wondered what Meadow would make of Taryn. "It's parked next to a Porsche and the Triumph bike. Want a lift home? Might be crowded with both of us and two guitars. We can leave the instruments here and pick them up tomorrow."

"One of the guys offered to take me to his home." She nodded in the direction of the group haphazardly making music by the pool. They'd become sloppy as ethanol, weed, and who knew what took hold. Several had wandered inside to lounge on couches, one with a wineglass prominently dangling in his hand. To Bradan they seemed to be posing in attitudes they assumed would be expected of dissolute rock stars.

"He's with one of the LA bands," Taryn continued. "They're signed, so he's a god in his pea brain like he's doing a favor by bestowing himself on me, but he can't carry a tune and he isn't cool enough to sleep with. Two strikes and you're out. I'll go home in a cab. I have a place off Sunset. Ride your bike on down. I've got two amplifiers and a spare Fender. If you can live without your Gibson, use my Strat and we'll work on that song, then spend the night."

"I have a girlfriend," Bradan said.

"I won't tell," Taryn said.

It was dusk now. Bradan heard wind flit past the canyon's trees and homes. He felt it touch the back of his neck, frigid as a meat locker. He looked upward. Far to the north, but coming fast, two airborne figures grew from specks to Dark Ages warriors astride destriers, muscular horses bred for mounted warfare. Bradan hadn't seen one in six centuries. He recognized the Welsh god, Gwyn, from the chase on the coast accompanied by Medraut, who Bradan now knew to be one and the same with Congressman Van Newman. As on Highway 1 three years ago, they looked utterly malevolent, organic to the twilight, and the heavens made room for their passage.

They were relentless in their intent and they'd found him again.

"The stupid prick," Bradan heard Taryn hiss. She looked angry, but not surprised.

Bradan was both angry and surprised. After miserable failures in a prison holding cell and on Highway 1, Van was here to finish the business. How had the big man tracked him to a party in Laurel Canyon? Bradan remembered using several spells to find Cass's home. They were minor incantations, but repetition must have broadcast his magical signature to Faerie realms, allowing Dark Ages wraiths on search-and-destroy missions to locate him. Or had the talented and mysterious Taryn fingered him? Her presence had barely preceded the hunters' arrival.

Discretion seemed the order of the night, as his pursuers had left their numberless army behind to fly over heavily populated LA. However, they didn't need an army. The two of them were enough to murder him and wrench away his soul.

Bradan sprinted down the driveway to his bike. He should feel flattered. Van had forgone mano-a-mano fights and enlisted the Welsh god of the Otherworld for tonight's manslaughter.

Tintagel, contentedly snoozing next to the motorcycle, looked up at the approaching hunters and seemed momentarily torn between ecstatically greeting the phantoms and loyally defending Bradan. The beast settled on jumping up and heading down to the road.

"Get on," Bradan shouted at Taryn. He started the Harley with a blast of engine noise.

She glanced at him but ran for the Triumph, reciting a poem. When she jumped on the starter, it caught immediately. The key must have been in the bike's ignition. She beat him out of the driveway and raced down the twisty road heading toward Mulholland Drive and then Laurel Canyon Boulevard. Maybe she assumed a moving target would be harder to catch or the crowds in West Hollywood would inhibit open slaughter. He didn't have a better plan. Sunrise was hours away. Friendly daylight wouldn't save him this time.

Behind him on the driveway, Bradan heard a man shouting that the Triumph had been a gift from Peter Fonda. Well, Taryn could give it back later—if they survived the night.

The partiers must have seen the specters. Not his problem. They could rationalize the visions any way they wanted.

The wonderful thing about an era of license and debauchery was that no one believed their senses the next morning.

Christ, she can ride, he thought. *Her bike handles way better than mine, but it's not just the motorcycle, she's lightning.*

Bradan and Taryn sped crazily through lethargic traffic that didn't feel any urgency to clear a path. No one knew he fled for his soul. This was LA, so they wouldn't have cared, anyway. Tintagel howled and snarled at laggard cars to goad them out of the way, but this had the opposite effect as terrified drivers veered wildly about to careen into the ditch or crash into one another.

Sometimes Bradan and Taryn were masked from the flying specters by trees overhanging the road, sometimes not, but Bradan saw them getting inexorably closer. Ahead of him, Taryn took corners brilliantly, but tarried on the straightaways. Was she letting him keep up? Or was she trying to catch the attention of their pursuers like a bird trying to draw a cat away from her nest? Regardless, they focused on him and ignored Taryn.

"Trouble again?" Meadow asked.

"Again," he shouted over the engine.

"What works this time?"

He was a folklorist. What wisdom could he deploy?

Running water, a barrier to pursuing phantoms.

It hadn't worked fifteen centuries before, but Cadbury's moat had probably been too stagnant to qualify as a flowing stream. Further, the entire Wild Hunt had chased him then, but it was only Gwyn and Medraut tonight. Perhaps the hunters' ability to surmount supernatural obstacles diminished with their number.

Worth a try, but was there running water anywhere in Laurel Canyon besides lawn sprinklers?

Bradan was no hydrologist, but in researching local Native American folklore, he'd stumbled on references to a nearly forgotten river that once flowed down the hills, beneath what was now Laurel Canyon Boulevard, through ravines, and ultimately made its way to the ocean. The flowing water had long since been entombed by the growing metropolis, but the river occasionally burst from its civilized crypt to surface in backyards and undeveloped forest spaces before being pulled underground again.

"Tintagel, find running water," Bradan shouted. The wolf's nose could locate anything.

"Meadow, I'll cross water. There's a stream around. Maybe it works, maybe it doesn't. You're a spirit. Will you survive?"

"Is there another way?" she asked.

"No. They're on top of me. I could jump off and try to escape with Taryn. Or run across the water on foot. That gets you out of the picture."

"Do the water. I may be okay. I'm not chasing you. They are."

"That's important?"

"I think so," she said.

The wolf vaulted off the boulevard and charged into trees in yards flanking the road. Bradan gestured hugely to attract Taryn's attention and turned sharply right, following the creature up a steep hill, gunning the Harley's engine to make the climb. The big tank wasn't a dirt bike, so his rear tire spun madly, grasping for traction over loose dirt and branches to climb the steep embankment. No doubt he uprooted any number of endangered plant species in the process.

He bounced through a eucalyptus grove narrowly weaving his ungainly bike through the trees, and crashed into a back-yard scattering stone ornamental lawn gnomes and garden fairies.

Behind him, he heard Taryn on the Triumph. She'd seen his sudden departure from Laurel Canyon Boulevard and followed, no doubt wondering what in hell he intended. A glimpse in his mirror showed that she duplicated his route with more aplomb than he'd managed. She kicked a stone fairy aside as she skidded through the yard.

And ahead, led by the wolf's preternaturally acute nose, a spring erupted into the backyard and rushed over rocks down the hill through a dozen yards. The narrow stream bed channeled the water, creating a rushing torrent. Homeowners had designed their yards around wild nature's intrusion into their otherwise well-mannered lawns by placing all manner of outdoor furniture and gazebos around the rushing water to tame it. But it wasn't tame.

Moonlight slithered along the water's roiling surface allowing Bradan to see the river's terminus several lots down, where it grudgingly tunneled back underground.

He accelerated his Harley down the slope heading for the ribbon of silver below. The steep incline looked like he was going down Everest. How did the risk of a devastating crash weigh against whatever horrific fate the hunters had in store him?

Can the motorcycle take the shock? Is the water deep?

No time for doubts; he rushed into the whitewater. Things happened fast—the deep creek splashing the frame, submerging the wheels, and soaking him through. Unseen rocks knocked the Harley this way and that, adding to the buffeting the current gave him. Meadow gasped in pain. The bike lurched sideways as forward momentum slammed him into the steep opposite slope. He feathered the throttle to gain traction going up mud and slippery grass, but didn't give the bike too much power or he'd lose grip and fall over backward into the water with the Harley on top of him. Then he was up and over and sliding to a stop, leaving a giant gouge in the lawn. With a happy yelp, Tintagel leaped from one bank to the other in a single bound.

Did it work?

He looked above him. Medraut, Gwyn, and their eerie horses were gone, leaving a purple haze of smoke dissipating in the night air on the far side of the stream. They would come again: a duel across history delayed tonight.

"Meadow?" Bradan asked.

"I'm here, but not completely. The crossing ripped something out of me. I'll be whole again in a few minutes, but don't do that again for a while."

Taryn careened toward him from the opposite bank, duplicating his path. Just before she hit the water, she called out verses. Her lighter bike gracefully swept down one slope and up the other, though she also got drenched head to toe as she sliced through the stream.

Rolling to a stop beside him, she said, "My suede boots are ruined, but you sure know how to show a girl a good time."

Her Ray-Bans had stayed in place the entire time.

"Who were you talking to?" she asked looking at his motorcycle.

Bradan got out of his saddle and checked himself and the bike for damage. He sat down on the grass. Tintagel sauntered away to pee on a lawn gnome then came back to stretch out beside him.

"Just babbling," Bradan said. "I'll ask you the same thing. What did you say just before you hit the stream?"

"I don't do flowing water very well," she said. "I guess you could call it a prayer to buck up my confidence. It's been a thing with me since I was young. Once I'm actually in the water, I'm fine, swim better than a fish. It's getting in that's the problem."

"It rhymed," he said.

Taryn wrung water out of her hair. "I'm apt to rhyme at odd moments, the soul of a poet, like you. It helps me write songs." Both boots came off. She upended them to drain out water and settled down beside him.

"You're shivering," Taryn said.

"Seems appropriate after what we've been through."

"Know anything about what we just saw?" she asked.

"Why would I?" he asked. "I figured it was all the dope and wine. Or the Coke was spiked with windowpane at the party."

Fifteen hundred years spent in every imaginable circumstance made him watch expressions closely. The shades masked her eyes, making it hard to read the woman, but her nonchalant innocence appeared to be calculated. And she'd kept her poise when anyone else would have been catatonic. Indeed, she'd ridden the Triumph like she raced motorcycles for a living, easily pacing him and the demons. Now she sat with him chatting about the death race as if it were a thoughtful classroom debate.

Was she the sixth-century witch who'd haunted Cadbury? Why show up now? He tried to remember the Morgana he'd known fifteen centuries before, but his mind's eye distorted her image after all the elapsed time. However, the real truth was that he wanted to find reasons why she couldn't be the witch. He liked making music with her; how would that be possible with an entity that hunted souls?

"Pretty realistic visions," she said. "Horsemen flying through the air, how did we share the same sighting? I wasn't doing much drinking or smoking reefer at Cass's and neither were you. And I don't think anyone slipped us acid."

"Well then, what else would explain what just happened?" Bradan asked. "Also, how do you ride motorcycles so well?"

"I like riding fast things. I'll show you one day."

* * *

"What's the Wild Hunt?" Bradan asked.

The students stared at him. The silence was tangible. At such moments, he knew teaching undergraduates was hard. They didn't always respond to spontaneous lines of questioning. So much for the Socratic method.

However, Bradan had to tell someone about last night. The adrenaline remained and he couldn't keep the chase bottled up. He remembered a savage god over Laurel Canyon and his nemesis, Van, skipping with supernatural ease through the clouds to visit their wrath on him. The trick would be integrating his eldritch adventure into regular classroom discourse on folklore's tropes without raving.

Bradan glanced at his hands and realized he gripped the lectern with crushing force. He willed himself to relax his hold on the wooden stand. He was still damp, but thankfully he couldn't catch pneumonia—that was Merlin's gift to him. There'd been no time to change into dry clothing before class. He must present an unkempt sight to his morning seminar. Whatever their political leanings, the students expected their professors to adhere to traditional sartorial standards. Stodgy was okay. Scruffy and dirty wasn't.

The students weren't quite as intimidating as the warrior demons he'd fled hours ago, but almost. And today they seemed to have about the same humanity and intellect as his nocturnal pursuers.

Gail, sitting in on his class, watched from the back of the small room and didn't hide her smirk at his discomfort as he stood before the impassive students.

The setting contrasted completely with last night's desperate flight. Warm, early-spring zephyrs swept down from the San Gabriel Mountains through open windows, distributing the academic odors of chalk and textbooks among the undergraduates. Faintly, outside, voices from students and faculty carried into the classroom, conversations sounding measured and thoughtful, important issues carefully considered. The campus scenery could have formed the subject for a Constable pastoral landscape with forest-green vegetation and Spanish Revival buildings in muted browns. He worked at rebalancing himself with the university's deliberate pace.

To inject political irony into his class, Bradan had scrawled, "Clean up the mess at Berkeley" on the chalkboard behind him. The quote came courtesy of California's new governor, Ronald Reagan, who'd run a supremely successful election campaign partly by capitalizing on working-class and older voters' fear of systemic changes swirling about the country. Well-publicized campus protests were emblematic of this change and made a big, fat target for ambitious politicians, stirring up contempt and fear among wide swaths of the population and promising to squash campus protesters' efforts to speak out of turn.

To Bradan's disappointment, the class didn't see the mockery. They probably thought it was their next assignment.

The wolf snoozed unconcernedly on a side table beneath the windows occasionally baring his fangs, facing down opponents in dreamland, Wild Hunters on surreal highways. Bradan smelled Tintagel's rank, damp fur. There was something else in his smell. Sporting with the damned had rubbed off on the beast, leaving a charnel house residue. Everyone assumed the creature was just a very big German shepherd, but the wolf brought an atavistic quality into the classroom, folklore made real—and not altogether welcome. None of Bradan's class sat near the animal.

Finally, a young brunette in the first row with hair pulled perfectly into place responded, "Why is the Wild Hunt relevant to last week's lecture about critiquing folklore's tropes? That's what you said to prepare ourselves to talk more about today."

"Good question, Amy," Bradan said. "The Wild Hunt is one of the oldest folkloric motifs; so, it fits neatly into our discussions today. Do any of the rest of you want to respond by hazarding a guess at, first, what the Wild Hunt was—or is—and, two, why it's relevant to anything we've talked about so far?"

The college prided itself on small class sizes and intimate contact between professor and student in furtherance of scholastic quality, especially for upper-division courses, so he knew all the students at least by name. Amy Allen was one of five women among nineteen juniors and seniors. His Folklore and Modern Culture class was an uneasy mix of what seemed like the *Leave It to Beaver* TV show cast and the Grateful Dead. A few of the guys wore suits and a few more were in ROTC uniforms. A well-trimmed fellow in a navy-blue sport coat sitting next to Amy set his pipe atop a pile of textbooks, evidently working for the Hugh Hefner, big-man-on-campus look. Bradan remembered he was a trust-fund kid from out east named Todd. Three of the girls including Amy wore white shirts tucked into calf-length plaid skirts, quite prim and proper, legs crossed tightly beneath the dresses. Bradan guessed they were in the same sorority and wore matching wide cloth headbands. However, based on attire, other students were on the cusp of rethinking who they were—or at least what appropriate student raiment should be. In the space of just a few months, the men's hair had grown to shoulder length. This second group could just have strolled into class after a night at the London Fog or the Whisky a Go Go on the Strip, ears still ringing from listening to The Doors or Love, dressed from a West Hollywood Salvation Army store. He hoped a few of them had heard The Pillars of Creation now that the band was getting LA club dates.

Nobody responded to his challenge, so Bradan decided to seed the discussion.

"We can use the Wild Hunt as a case study. No, make that a metaphor for our modern, chaotic times. The hunters are supernatural forces unleashed, demons or gods presaging worldly disaster. And that shows up in stories across cultures, so obviously other times and places faced the same challenges we see today and used folklore, tribal myths, childhood tales to, if not explain, at least comfort themselves in strange times."

The room was cramped so Bradan stood virtually on top of them. He moved away from the lectern and his prepared notes, since he disliked being tethered to a single spot and preferred to stroll about amid the students in their closely spaced chairs, though that made them visibly uncomfortable. For budding Marxists and free-thinkers, they could be remarkably comfortable with structure. Professors should keep a podium between themselves and undergraduates. Everyone—especially authority figures—should stay in their allotted roles, but this morning he was overwrought and couldn't stand still. He also urgently wanted brandy.

"I know, it seems remote from current issues, but it's not, and we need to see connections between past traditions and right now."

Gavin Chaffee, the department chair, entered the classroom, nodded collegially at Bradan, and sat down beside Gail, swinging his arm over the back of her chair possessively.

Why is he here? Bradan wondered.

Normally Chaffee wouldn't have sat in on any of his faculty's lectures and certainly not a junior academic like Bradan. This must concern Bradan's upcoming tenure hearing.

I don't need this scrutiny today.

Tintagel choose that moment to wake suddenly, half rise, and energetically lick his crotch. Then, satisfied, the wolf collapsed back on the side table with a contented groan.

"Jesus Christ," one of the students muttered. The whole classroom unobtrusively crowded further away from the creature, pushing their desks flush with the room's back wall. Even Chaffee, fond of affecting sangfroid under any circumstance, looked nonplussed.

"So, what is the Wild Hunt?" Todd asked, gesturing with his pipe stem to make the point.

"I can show you," Bradan said. "Gail, can you kill the room lights?"

He pivoted toward an overhead projector that occupied the center of the classroom like an Aztec sacrificial altar. The device's one virtue was that it projected a huge image on the roll-up screen behind him. Bradan toggled the projector on. It started with the sound of a fighter jet taking flight off a Navy carrier accompanied by a blast of hot air from its fan that engulfed the nearest students. He quickly sorted through his plastic slides before finding a blank one and flicked this onto the projector's lit glass plate. Masking his voice with the projector's racket, he turned away from the class momentarily and softly spoke a quatrain.

Before him materialized a three-dimensional replica of the chase he'd experienced three years ago on Highway 1 complete with a horde of gods, demons, and Hueys exploding out of the projector's screen and seemingly ready to trample the classroom into bloody shreds. Steel-shod hooves reached out to crush the front row of students' skulls. The images looked real. Bradan even sensed rain on his face and heard the hunters' mindless rage over the projector's roar.

Several of the students fell off their chairs, Amy shrieked, and Todd's pipe sailed through the air. Others yelled or swore. Bradan snapped the projector off. The Wild Hunters vanished.

His spell had worked too well. Bradan regretted giving in to his urge to show off. He breathed heavily, recovering from the exertion of making magic. Even a minor piece of enchantment like the image he'd just fashioned sucked him dry for several moments. He backed over to the lectern and leaned against it.

"Sorry, that was more theater than I expected," he said weakly. "I pulled the illustration from German eighteenth-century source material, which in turn is a copy of much older drawings. The depiction was way too vivid."

The instant the words left his mouth, he realized the image he'd created had contained helicopters, which certainly hadn't been part of centuries-old depictions of folklore. However, there was so much confusion in the class he doubted anyone noticed the anachronism.

At least he had their attention. Amazing what a simple, lurid image could do. The class gradually regained its composure.

He heard Kay Liu cut through the tumult. "Professor Badon, your overhead showed a nuclear apocalypse. The sky behind the riders was red."

"Sucking up to the prof," Bradan heard Amy say.

"That's observant, Kay," Bradan said. "Not an apocalypse, but close."

"So these medieval images warn us about 1967 issues," Kay continued, unfazed by Amy's catty remark.

Kay was one of his smarter, more intuitive students. She had also aligned herself with the hipper, overtly political elements in class and wore a poncho over bell-bottom jeans. Maybe she appreciated his chalkboard quote from Reagan.

"Precisely," Bradan responded. "Folklore can alert us to present-day threats. In the modern world, we've separated our-selves from magic and nature to our detriment. Historically, the boundaries weren't as clear. I showed a world where magic and the regular world coexist."

"Trying to make this relevant is a stretch," Todd said.

Bradan guessed he wanted to impress Amy by engaging with the professor. However, he hadn't done much else to contribute to classroom discourse, and the papers he'd seen from Todd over the semester were total shit. In this regard the fellow was emblematic of much of the class. Bradan's passion for the touch point between vision and reality bounced off of their indifference like a .22 bullet off a tank.

Taking Todd's remark as a gauntlet thrown before him, Bradan spent the remainder of the period orchestrating a freewheeling discussion about Jungian archetypes, primordial images, and the monomyth. He wanted to synthesize it all. At the end of the class, Gail applauded loudly, Chaffee clapped politely, and a few students joined in tepid support before exiting the class. They looked shell-shocked. Anyone who had survived today's class deserved a medal, Bradan reflected.

"I took folklore to satisfy a distribution requirement," Bradan heard one of them say. "What did I get into?"

Talking and laughing, Gail and Chaffee ambled out of the classroom trailing the press of disoriented students.

"Where's the accent from, Professor Badon?" It was Amy. She and Todd had followed him as he left the room with the other students. Bradan hadn't decided whether she was genuinely intrigued by his approach to the material or simply better at masking boredom than the rest of the students.

"Sorry to pry," she said. "I was just interested. Don't answer if you don't want to."

"It's fine," he said. "I lived in Britain at various times in my life. That's what you're hearing."

"I took a semester abroad last year at the University of Birmingham. Your accent doesn't sound exactly English, nothing like any of my teachers over there."

"Thanks," Bradan said dryly. "My graduate work was in Germany. That also influenced how I sound." He had indeed studied in Heidelberg with Max Weber, among others, but explaining that his studies had occurred in the years around the turn of the century would immediately date him and raise uncomfortable questions about his age. One could pick up a lot of accents in fifteen centuries of hard living.

"Loved your Reagan quote," Kay called over to him. One person got it, at least.

"Super-neat bike," a long-haired guy in his class said. He and Kay looked to be a couple.

Bradan nodded acknowledgment. His mode of transportation might help his credibility with hipper students. In a rush to get to his seminar this morning after his dash through Laurel Canyon and a night with Taryn recovering from the terror, Bradan had parked the Harley on a sidewalk directly in front of the classroom building. The machine stood as an anarchic affront to organized learning and decorum. Oil leaked onto the concrete. Normally he'd have hidden it in a distant campus lot.

"You covered a lot of territory today, Professor Badon," Amy said. "And that was a weird illustration you flashed of the Wild Hunt. I about fainted."

"Thought I was seeing things," Todd said. He lit his pipe. "It jumped right out of the overhead. How are you going to test for that on the midterm?"

"Don't worry much about today's discussions. We got off on a tangent—though it was an important tangent. I challenge my classes periodically, but this stuff won't be on my test."

Amy and Todd looked relieved. As they turned to go, Amy noticed the department chair.

"Oh, hi, Professor Chaffee. I'll be by for your office hours at 4:00. Is that okay?"

"There's always time for you, Amy. Your last test for my seminar didn't go so well, but we can sort it out before the final grade."

Amy nodded thanks, waved at all of them, and then she and Todd wandered off, dispersing along with the rest of the kids, leaving Bradan, Gail, and Chaffee to chat.

"Ah, youth," Chaffee said. "Wasted on youth." He looked after Amy for a bit.

The department chair had always struck Bradan as a bureaucrat for whom mindless conversation came easily, important for keeping the dean happy and massaging the egos of the history department's senior faculty. His tone was perfectly modulated, warm and smooth. Complementing his easy loquaciousness, Chaffee liked to portray himself as the understanding paterfamilias presiding over his expansive fiefdom, at once understanding of his staff's foibles and able to rise above them to mediate squabbles. However, Bradan knew the chairman had sharp elbows when overseeing the departmental budget. He wasn't aware of anything peer reviewed that Chaffee had published recently.

They all stood next to the Harley. Worse than looking rebellious, Bradan reflected, it looked blue-collar. While academics expressed solidarity with the proletariat, they preferred to keep the masses at a comfortable remove.

"Yours?" Chaffee asked.

Bradan barely nodded, reluctant to claim ownership. "Saves on gas."

"Never ridden one," Chaffee said. He turned his back on the machine.

"He's not a good person." It was Meadow providing a shadow commentary on proceedings with whispers in Bradan's ear. He hoped to hell she was inaudible to Chaffee. Subtly, he tried to edge away from his motorcycle.

"Interesting points you raised today in class," Chaffee said. "You laid out a grand unified theory of folklore and ethnography. Ambitious. I wouldn't have thought to link Chomsky's perspectives on semiotics and analytical philosophy with folkloric tropes, but it was clever, a bit beyond most of your students. Were you trying to spice up the discussion with your Wild Hunt digression? You had real passion about that. And how did you get your overhead to look so real? It popped right out at us, took up half the class. I'll have to sit in on more of your lectures."

"Just a trick of the light. It's a bad projector. And I needed to put the Hunt into play, get the kids to focus on a specific example. Otherwise it's all too abstract. It's just one of many leitmotifs I could have chosen. I don't know why I thought of that one."

"You got a respectable article published last month in *Journal of American Folklore*, 'Magic as Cultural Appropriation in Ancient Britain.'"

Bradan was surprised Chaffee remembered his paper's title. Bradan had circulated several of his recent publications to the tenure committee ahead of his hearing and wondered if the chairman had actually read any of them.

"Thanks," he said. "I had another one in *Asian Folklore Studies* early this year. Gail saw the galley proofs."

"Even reading it with a historian's eye," Gail said. "It was pretty fascinating."

"Folklore *is* fascinating," Chaffee said. "And important academically. That's why you're part of my group, but, speaking honestly, your area is a little intangible to me. Historians like myself and Gail look toward facts. Granted the record is usually imperfect, but written material and touchable artifacts give me a lot more confidence about illuminating past events than the oral tradition and bedtime stories."

"He's so pompous," Meadow breathed into Bradan's ear. Chaffee was oblivious, but Gail looked about. Had she heard?

Bradan felt himself getting angry with Meadow's Greek chorus running commentary and Chaffee's condescending characterization of his field. He wanted to articulate a firm defense of his research while not letting Chaffee sense his distaste for him.

"In historical writing, you're still stuck with biases, gaps, and uncertainties," Bradan said. "For example, the King Arthur story—widely distributed throughout medieval times—is it legend or is there a kernel of historical reality? The written record is fragmentary, to put it mildly, so it's quite difficult to come to conclusions." He could have added that having lived this part of history, he knew later writings wildly distorted the past.

Chaffee nodded noncommittally, clearly not interested in being drawn into an extended discussion with a junior academic on the potential for fallacy in historical interpretation.

"Folklore is an odd fit in History," he said. "I think they stuck you in my department because there was nowhere else to put you except anthropology—and they weren't interested."

"I'm happy to be part of your group." Bradan kept it neutral and affable.

"You really need to be careful with this guy," Meadow murmured.

"Have to run," Chaffee said. "Consider getting a haircut before showing up in front of us for your tenure hearing. That makes you more relatable to our older faculty. I guess casual dress standards are to be expected, given that you taught at Berkeley for a while, but on this campus they can be off-putting."

"I'll get a jacket, tie, and better slacks."

"Can't hurt. You were up north, too, Gail. Did you overlap with Bradan?"

"For a couple of semesters," Gail said. "I was finishing up my dissertation and Bradan was teaching folklore as a guest lecturer. We met on campus."

"So that's how you know each other. It's good to see affection among our younger faculty. Makes old codgers like me jealous." He chuckled. The wrinkles around his eyes scrunched engagingly. "I'll catch one of your classes, Gail. You've got tenure review coming up, too. It makes me wonder whether this department can give two junior faculty tenure at the same time. I'll confer with the other committee members. I'd hate to see this become an either-or situation."

As Chaffee turned to go, he patted Gail's butt and caressed it for a lingering moment through her skirt, then strolled off toward his office. She glanced after him, then away.

"That son of a bitch," Bradan said.

Gail put her hand on his shoulder. "Leave it. I don't want a Galahad defending my honor. I'm not making waves ahead of tenure. We both need to stay on his good side, jerk that he is."

"That deserves breakfast."

"Getting my ass fondled?"

"Having to tolerate a potbellied creep to get a position," he said.

"I need a tenured slot. My parents were totally committed to their ideals, but they stayed dead broke, lifelong. I only got through undergrad at Brown and then grad school at Berkeley on scholarships and a teaching assistant stipend with no help from them. I can't eat ideals."

Gail smiled to herself. "Three years ago, I was proud to march into Sproul with you, take a stand. Today I really don't know what I'd do if given the same choice. Probably just clap politely at the speeches and head back to my office. I can't believe I'm desperate enough to say that. My parents would roll over in their graves."

"I'm desperate, too," he said. "You can beat yourself up for not being pure, but I think I'm old enough to say I don't know what 'pure' is. I do know I don't put faith in folks who claim to know purity."

"I've never said I was pure," she said. A little of her Brooklyn accent came through. Usually she hid traces of her working-class background in New York's boroughs.

"We're all playing games to get what we want," she added.

"If you make tenure, teach your ideals in class. That's ultimately more influential than attending a rally. There are so many rallies, people lose count."

"You always say the comforting thing."

"I like her," Meadow said. "She's genuine, but you can't trust her completely."

He needed to move away from the Harley. He reached out for Gail's hand. "We can't eat ideals, but do you have forty-five minutes to dine on the cafeteria's toxic grub?"

"I think Chaffee's sleeping with Amy," Gail said. It came out of the blue as they walked through the campus commons.

"Why say that?" he asked, startled.

"Intuition. She's taking one of his upper-division classes. She's young for that class and having trouble keeping up. She can't be more than nineteen. I'm the student adviser for history undergrads, so she confides in me. She isn't explicit, but you can tell she's got something going on with him. And you can see the way he looks at her. He's got such a reputation for having sex with undergraduate girls. So do other faculty members."

"I wouldn't put it past him, but do you have proof? Let's talk to the dean."

"No. Nothing. Nada. Forget I said anything."

Gail waved at someone across the commons.

"It's the way it works here," she added. "Things look superficially pretty, but there's always subtext."

"You can be cynical about universities," Bradan said. "I am. Of all institutions, they're the furthest from living up to their ideals. If you hear more about Amy's situation, let me know. Two junior faculty will carry more weight than one."

He burst out laughing, startling students strolling past. "What am I saying? Neither of us has any pull with administration here whatsoever."

Tintagel splashed about among cascades of lawn sprinkler water that flanked the paths they walked along, chasing the little rainbows in the spray. Unusually among History's conservative faculty, the wolf's behavior and appearance didn't perturb Gail.

"I kept thinking someone was eavesdropping back there with Chaffee," she said. "But I'd look around and not see anyone."

"It was just the three of us," he said. He turned around. The Harley was in the distance across campus. "We're both under huge stress, this tenure thing. That's made you jumpy."

He needed to change the topic right now.

"The glasses," he said. "I've wondered since I first met you, there's no rhyme or reason about when you wear them. Are you near- or farsighted?"

"Neither. They're fake. I figured they fit the image of an intellectual academic. It's superficial as hell, but it impresses the older faculty."

Bradan laughed. "A little image manipulation never hurts."

"They're hideous, frankly, but whatever it takes to get tenure."

She dressed that intent with a conservative skirt and navy-blue sweater pulled over a light-blue, collared blouse, the outfit a bit disheveled. Makeup barely touched her face and, what there was, she'd applied haphazardly. The combination sent the message she wouldn't be inordinately bothered with impressing the world with appearances; she'd let her learning and intelligence make her reputation.

"Need to change?" she asked. "You're shivering with cold."

"I'll buy a sweatshirt and sweatpants at the union—something with the college's colors. The day is warming up, anyway." He pulled off his damp jacket and threw it in a trash container.

"It was cheap," Bradan said. That left him wearing jeans, motorcycle boots, and a T-shirt. "Very professorial, I could be an extra from *The Wild One*, one of Brando's buddies."

"How'd you get wet? Fall in a pool?"

"I was up in Laurel Canyon last night. Ran into a huge puddle of water going home along Mulholland. A main burst and flooded the street." Lies came easily, but this one avoided him explaining fleeing lethal phantoms to the ever-rational Gail.

"Laurel Canyon. Seeing someone?" It came out too casually, with the light disinterested inflections that Bradan recognized as Gail covering possessiveness.

"Music stuff," he said. "I'm trying to get my band's name into the right ears. There were a bunch of musicians, so I jammed with them into the small hours. Coming home wasn't supposed to be a cosmic road trip—I nearly crashed the bike—but that's how it turned out, sort of a slice from a Jack Kerouac novel."

"Sounds crazy. You need to tell me when you feel like it," Gail said.

"She thinks you're being evasive." Despite his growing distance from the bike, he heard Meadow.

"I'm sure Chaffee noticed I looked messed up," Bradan said to Gail. "Hell, he sat in today, so I'm being watched. As you say, try not to make waves. I'm enough of an outlier in History as is. I'm not giving them more reasons to deny tenure."

"Why divide your time between music and teaching?"

"Inconvenient as it is, I've got a life in both worlds. What's the German phrase? *Dichter und denker,* poets and thinkers. Part time, I compose music. Other times, I'm here, at the college, in my thinker role. A nice balance, but I'm happy the worlds don't cross. I can't imagine what History would say if they found out I front an acid rock band."

"You had that thing in San Francisco and now it sounds like in LA, too?"

"Don't be superior. It's my band 'thing,' I'm still doing it, The Pillars of Creation. We played a club in West Hollywood last Friday and in Golden Gate Park last month. The city hadn't permitted the concert, so we got shut down mid-set, but that actually helped our reputation, though we may be stuck with a fine, depends on the judge. The *San Francisco Chronicle* did a piece on it."

"What an outlaw," she said.

"You're being sarcastic. We play the Fillmore next month, so there's accomplishment in doing 'my music thing.' The scene's growing and getting more profitable. That's not a totally good thing, but bands are making real money. I want to be successful in both spaces, music and academics."

"You'll have to prioritize which path to follow. In academics you can be creative, and you've got a predictable career ahead of you." She shrugged. "With music, who knows?"

"Like either of us has lots of predictability in this college? We're both beholden to Chaffee. Also, Reagan hates California's universities. To him we're all a bunch of Berkeley free-speech radicals. This place is private, but the political environment isn't friendly to academics at any type of college, so we're vulnerable."

They'd arrived at the student union's shop devoted mostly to textbooks, but with a collection of clothing, too. Overcoming his distaste at the limited selection and goofy styles, Bradan grabbed the thickest sweatshirt he could find along with sweatpants. He felt ludicrous, but warm.

"How about investing in a comb while you're at it," Gail said.

"So," she continued as they walked toward the union's cafe. "I was watching when you did your projector trick in class—by the way, impressive. You turned away, but I heard you reciting a rhyme. Is that your poetic side coming out?"

"I love verses, but no, I was just talking to myself. Last night was a fever dream and I'm still recovering. A little ranting and raving is therapy." He smiled. "And it fits my eccentric reputation with the undergrads, staying in character."

"The image you showed of the hunt, sort of *Götterdämmerung*."

"The Wild Hunt isn't really Wagnerian. This isn't the fate of the gods; it's the gods hunting humans for sport and to foreshadow pending disaster."

"There must be more cheerful myths you can study," she said.

"A lot of folk myths are gloomy. Those are the scariest stories, the best lessons; it's the psychological insight you need for what's occurring in the world right now."

Gail shook her head. "I prefer fairy tales. We all need a Camelot, a bright castle on a hill to aspire to. Especially in modern times."

"Suppose the place that inspired all the legends and folklore was just a pisshole full of vile, violent people?"

"Immoral people?"

"Amoral people—morality as we think of it today would have been meaningless to them."

"Remind me not to go on a motorcycle trip to Laurel Canyon with you. It makes you nihilistic."

After breakfast, they kissed on the union steps.

"You cut quite a figure in track attire," she said.

"More sarcasm? As soon as I can, I'll change."

"In your office?" she asked. "I'll come along, watch you change. You're so shy. You've got a desk and we've used desks before to screw. It's not as civilized as your apartment's mattress, but it brings back memories. Remember Sproul? Does your office door lock for privacy? Is there time today?"

"If only. I'm going to the Admin building instead. Chaffee stuck me on two cross-campus committees no one else wants. One looks at departmental budgeting, so Clara and I represent History."

"Christ, that sounds tedious. Clara, she's History's bookkeeper? And the department administrator too? She's the woman with the weird bouffant hairdo?"

"Yep. She's a complete bureaucrat, totally compulsive down to the last penny spent on pens. The second thing is even more deadening. You mentioned privacy in my office. Well, I'm on a faculty committee reviewing curfews and dorm visitation rules for undergrads. It's more in loco parentis crap. This year the big debate is what to do if an undergrad gets a visit from the opposite sex. Currently the dorm-room door has to stay open at least three feet. We're also considering whether to allow female students to visit men off-campus. Honestly, there are wars, riots, and chaos all over the world and the great minds of our august institution are focused on this? Fifty years from now, no one will worry about guidelines for dating behavior."

CHAPTER 5

A Ten-Penny Nail
Stretched Six Ways

February 1967, San Francisco

*A*rpeggios are magical. Shift a few fingers on the guitar and you sound like God—if the amplifiers are set at infinity, their red lights as bright as demons' eyes.

He improvised over The Pillars of Creation's thunderous rhythms, shaping what was in his mind into melodies, painting solos from his guitar's fretboard like a Renaissance artist. Vaguely he noticed people filtering into the Fillmore. The auditorium looked cavernous with murky reaches resembling a fifteenth-century Italian cathedral, challenging the bands to saturate the hall with music; but as the auditorium filled, it transformed into a more intimate and communal space where strangers shared cigarettes or joints and recognized a tribal affiliation and a collective interest in the music, their music.

He remembered other times, other places, feeling connections between tonight's Fillmore scene and long-haired warriors and witches in Arthur's smoky, dimly lit great hall listening to Bradan playing a lute and singing surreal epics of lost kingdoms. He'd also composed sacred and secular music for churchmen and merchant princes in Renaissance Florence. Those febrile times had seeded vaunting ambition and stimulated artists to surpass themselves and their peers' creative achievements, threatened only by Florence's incessant political violence.

Tonight the Fillmore was cold. There were no seats, so people sat on the floor or stood beneath antique balconies. The crowd was at first aloof and ambivalent about his little-known band with only one album out. However, soon the Pillars' songs drew them closer. Amazingly to Bradan, they weren't picked up bodily and hurled to the hall's back wall, leaves in a wild storm, under the sonic impact from stacks of hundred-watt Marshall amplifiers driving piles of speaker cabinets haphazardly arranged on the stage, the music's sheer volume commanding attention.

I'm swimming in an ocean of sound, Bradan thought. *And light.*

The scrim behind them had a huge logo of the band's name, which periodically melted into a Salvador Dali pool of viscous liquid only to reemerge fully formed with crystalline definition. An ever-changing mélange of hues drowned everyone in blobs of purple, green, and red.

The Pillars opened for two other acts. One was a venerable blues performer, the other a preeminent acid rock band that played meandering solos and sang opaque, flowery lyrics, sometimes in the right key, a snapshot of current San Francisco psychedelia. They were earnest, but not always proficient with their instruments, so Bradan hoped the Pillars would blow them off the stage. Indeed, despite the chemicals, his band was firing on all cylinders and there was subtlety amid the echo, reverb, and other effects distorting their instruments' tones crazily, bouncing aural energy everywhere.

The band's anthems started with simple chord progressions. Then the song's structure extended like taffy in instrumental jams that drifted off to the far ends of the universe. Eventually—however untethered it all got during the middle stretch—the band wrestled the piece back to the concluding climax. Bradan felt it was like doing enchantment. And the crowd came along for the ride with many of them dancing, the young women cajoling hesitant male partners to join.

Bradan looked about him onstage. The Pillars' musicians were the creative amalgam pulling people into the maelstrom. Constantine hammered his kit so hard the sticks splintered; Jeff Dorsey on bass, challenged Bradan's guitar for attention and locked in with Constantine; Kenny Salazar played a Hammond B3 organ and tripped on Owsley Stanley's finest acid—absorbed through his eyeball before the show—periodically stopping in the middle of a riff to stare in wonder at his fingers and the notes they coaxed from the B3; and Taryn, the new co-lead guitarist with Bradan. She was one of the few women in the Bay Area rock scene who played electric guitar and cranked the volume, ignoring expectations that she strum warm, subdued notes on an acoustic instrument.

And everyone handled vocals to create pure harmonies; on this front, the band was a delicate democracy.

Then it was over. The crowd called for an encore, but the promoter holding a clipboard ran a tight ship and the Pillars were ushered briskly offstage to make way for the next band.

"Hey Bradan, your set was magic, better than real," Janis Joplin said as she threaded her way through the crowd of roadies, hangers-on, and musicians in her sequins and feather boas. She pushed rose-colored glasses up her nose and blew him a kiss.

He nodded thanks, elated at the validation. He wanted to make love to her fueled by whatever cocktail of drugs enhanced lust until morning.

As the Fillmore's staff manhandled the Pillars' gear out of the way and replaced it with the headliner's speakers and amps, their lean, long-haired lead guitarist approached Bradan to explain that his instrument had been stolen from the back of the band's VW Microbus parked in the Haight just before their Fillmore gig tonight and could he borrow Bradan's Gibson Les Paul?

Bradan snapped open his guitar case, gently lifted the instrument out, and handed it over.

"Don't drop it," he said with mock gravity, but he meant it, too. The Les Paul was his talisman.

"This saves my ass," the musician said, sweeping his hair out of the way to attach the shoulder strap. "I owe you a baggie of primo or a couple of tabs of windowpane."

"No need, man," Bradan said. "Just give me my instrument back in good condition. The bridge pickup was cutting out during my set. You may have just the neck pickup."

"Didn't hear it in your playing, Bradan. You soared, the rest of the band, too. And who is that splendid chick with the Strat playing second lead? You two were bouncing off each other, trading runs like you'd been doing it for centuries. She looked cool as hell in the shades, completely righteous."

"That's Taryn Valente. We've known each other off and on for quite a while."

"She's your girl?"

"We're together, but she's her own girl. She's around. Go over and say hi if you want."

"Later. I'm on now. Also, I got to warn you, a really big dude was looking for you backstage. Don't see him now, but he was kind of hostile. Could have been a plainclothes cop or a bill collector. Watch yourself."

Bradan looked about, but didn't see anyone fitting this description. "Thanks. I don't know what his trip is. I'm not dealing and I don't owe anyone money. Take care of my guitar."

"It's in good hands." The musician strode onto the stage to join the rest of his band as the promoter screamed at him to get a move on. They lurched haphazardly into a cacophonous start before their drummer finally corralled them into a semblance of cohesion. Bradan watched his Gibson protectively from side-stage.

"Setting me up on a date?" Taryn appeared at his shoulder.

"Not unless you're lowering your standards," he shouted over the volume.

"I hang out with you, so I'm used to slumming."

"At least I take showers. He couldn't believe your playing tonight."

"He wants to touch me to see if I'm real?"

"I'm sure touching you is the plan."

They observed the other band. "Your guitar?" she yelled. "You shouldn't have loaned it out. What key's he in? He can't play for shit."

"So you do have standards. With enough echo and wah pedal, no one will notice."

"Bill said a rep from ATCO or Elektra was scouting us from out in the crowd," she said.

"They picked a good night. We were on fire. Let's find him and pitch the Pillars. We put out *A Ten-Penny Nail Stretched Six Ways* ourselves. The material is great, but it would retail a hell of a lot better with a big company pushing it. We'll have to convince the rest of the band we're not selling out if we want to do a deal with a label but I don't think that will be hard; in the last few months, they've gone from holding tight to their ideals to being super willing to cash in."

"I'm happy to sell out."

"Other bands have," he said. "Guess they sorted out their moral quandaries."

Bradan heard his name called from the crowd. It was a woman, barely discernible over the avalanche of noise. He was side-stage, but visible to the crowd behind the headlining band.

"A friend?" Taryn asked. "You've got an admirer. See her over to the right? She's pretty in a studious way, doesn't fit the Fillmore scene. Doing her hair differently might help."

Staring into the spotlights, Bradan still couldn't see who yelled at him from out amid the amorphous, seething crowd. Then the band paused between songs, giving him a chance to recognize Gail's voice. And see her, too.

"Fuck me."

"Is it a good or bad thing she's here?" Taryn looked at him sardonically.

"A surprising thing."

"So, this has got to be related to your college gig in LA."

"Yeah, my 'college gig.'" He paused, then said, "I'll introduce you."

"Groovy," Taryn said archly. "No way out of it. Can't wait to meet her."

"I'll bet."

* * *

"Taryn, Gail," Bradan said. "Gail, Taryn."

It felt awkward as hell.

God, where is Gail going to sleep? he wondered. He had an outré image of all three of them in bed together at his house in the Haight. Janis could join them.

They stood in the Fillmore's downstairs lobby sheltered from the berserk volume above. Periodically the main hall's doors on the second floor popped open, letting out a blast of music while allowing in more concertgoers.

"I'd never seen your band," Gail said to Bradan. "You said you were playing the Fillmore. I'm not teaching this week, so I decided to come up to the Bay and see for myself."

"Just like that, spur of the moment," Taryn said.

"I was curious," Gail said earnestly.

The women were a study in contrasts starting with clothing. Gail dressed exactly as she did on campus, knee-length skirt, shapeless department-store sweater, collared shirt overlaid with a tan raincoat, slightly rumpled against San Francisco's damp. The exceptional item was a long, flowy, paisley scarf loosely draped around her throat. He wondered if she'd spent time in front of a mirror taking off, trying on, taking off the scarf before finally deciding she couldn't just arrive at a concert with psychedelic bands and their bell-bottomed, mini-skirted devotees looking like an assistant professor. So the scarf finally stayed. Ironically, the Fillmore's crowd was every bit as disheveled and nondescript as she was with nary a Carnaby Street fashion model among them. Except for Grace Slick or Janis, even the bands were ostentatiously unkempt.

Taryn was anything but unkempt. Bradan thought she wasn't pretty because she was young; she was striking because she was ageless and looked exuberant enough to party all night and jam with the Pillars all day and not show any smudges under her eyes or sagging skin. Her tight jeans tucked into calf-high, chocolate-brown, suede boots. More leather: She wore a buck-skin vest over a V-necked white T-shirt. The singular point of overlap between the two women style-wise was a silk scarf. Taryn wore hers tied around her hair. During a set she wrapped the scarf around her guitar strap out of the way. Bradan had to admire the woman's look; what should have been too flamboyant for the Fillmore scene tiptoed right up to the edge of patronizing the crowd, and then stepped back, rescued by her chilly grace and immaculate guitar work.

"You look different up here in San Francisco," Gail told Bradan. "You're wearing a bowler hat, of all things, and your hair's shaggier."

"I got the hat from a secondhand store. It's quaint. I'm away from campus, so there are different expectations. Did you like the music?"

He couldn't think of what else to say. He had a million things to talk to Gail about in an academic setting, but in the Fillmore he struggled with the long silences of a first date. She'd never expressed more than passing interest in this side of his life.

"I don't know much about popular music—I like Chopin, Franz Liszt, piano pieces—but your material was good, more complicated than I'd expected." She turned to address Taryn. "You play guitar really well." Bradan thought she was uncharacteristically tentative because she was totally out of her element.

"It was so loud, but you really know your way around the instrument," Gail continued.

"Thanks," Taryn said blandly. She'd left her aviator sunglasses on after the Pillars' set, giving her an opaque, intimidating visage. The charisma she exuded onstage still adhered to her—or it was always there, an inherent component of her terminally cool character.

"And you sing well, too," Gail said. "You sound good together."

"The volume feeds the crowd's energy," Bradan said. "Everyone expects it. We channel the energy so it's not just noise. That's a thousand hours of practicing and working on lyrics. And listening to what other bands are doing so we can play better than them."

Gail looked at Bradan and Taryn. "Hearing you side by side, you must be from the same place and it's nowhere near 1967 San Francisco."

"Not a bad guess," Bradan said.

"Mysterious. So, where are your accents from?" Gail asked.

"I can't speak for Bradan, but I've bounced around a bit," Taryn said. "I've picked up a half dozen different intonations over the years. It works for my singing. It gives the songs kind of a mystical, spiritual vibe."

Gail reached out and deftly removed Taryn's Ray-Ban Aviators and put them on herself.

For an instant Taryn looked startled, and then she smiled indulgently, as if this was an act of lèse-majesté, but she would ignore the affront for the moment since she didn't face a true opponent. Bradan saw Taryn's eyes flicker then revert to mocha brown.

"The shades give you a new look," Bradan told Gail. He kept his voice mild. "Why don't you make it a trade and loan your glasses to Taryn?"

For the hell of it, he wanted to see how Taryn would react. The night couldn't get any more strained. He might as well stir the pot.

Gail pulled her cheap, plastic-framed glasses from a purse. They had a vaguely cat-eyed shape.

"They won't hurt your eyes," Gail told Taryn. "They're not prescription."

"They hurt," Taryn said. "Even without putting them on."

CHAPTER 6

The Cardinal's Daughter

1478–1482, Florence, Italy

Bradan heard music fill the enormous building. Florence's cathedral created the perfect acoustic environment for the polyphonic choir's voices to echo up to the heavens. One day, he vowed, he'd create melodies to serenade angels and entrance a crowd in a big space.

He smelled perfume and sweat from the Easter high mass congregants, and dead saints' bones buried in vaults, a beatific blend of sacred and profane scents. There had been plenty of time to accumulate hallowed bones. A church had been on this spot for eleven centuries, a bit longer than he'd lived. However, the edifice had been completed only recently, capped by Brunelleschi's monumental dome reaching up to shake hands with the heavens, surpassing even Rome's Parthenon. Inspired by classical monuments, moderns had taken up the gauntlet and determined to surpass the ancients by blending pagan simplicity with Christian architectural ambition.

The whole city attended mass, many out of piety, others for the spectacle. What better time to see Florence's merchant princes and their families in splendid raiment? Regardless of motives, the cathedral's confines engulfed the holiday multitude. Bradan looked upward to see eight circular windows illuminating the proceedings below, but even supplemented with candles, the cavernous room was dimly lit, the better for the crowd to listen to holy music, contemplate spiritual redemption, or bring on a nap lulled by the priest's sonorous Latin.

Indeed, despite the cold dampness of the morning, Bradan wanted to recline back in his wooden chair except that it had been expressly designed to be too uncomfortable to allow slumber. And he sat only two seats away from Lorenzo de' Medici, the Magnificent, and Bradan's patron. Though he was grateful for the merchant prince's sponsorship, it obligated him to sit through the service. Bradan doubted de' Medici cared a whit more for religious formalities than he did, but the man did respect the power of appearances. Appearances kept the public's esteem. Lorenzo pulled the strings in Florence, but he'd adopted Augustus Caesar's approach to rule by accepting few titles and leading the fractious city-state through surrogates while trying not to antagonize Florence's other power centers. Nonetheless, both within the city and in Rome, Lorenzo had stepped on toes.

Bradan, Lorenzo, and a few other family friends including his children's tutor, Poliziano, sat in the front row near the priest even now preparing to raise the host. Behind them were the rest of the Medici clan, several children and a good dozen extended family members, and Clarice Orsini, the great man's wife and scion of a noble Roman family, their marriage cementing a formidable alliance of families.

Despite the assembled splendor, Bradan had eyes only for Veronica Varano, a friend of Clarice. She sat next to her husband, white-haired, at least twice her age and dozing slumped forward despite the hard chair. Veronica sat erect, young, and alert and looked angelic with blond hair darkened by touches of brown. He wasn't close enough to see the color of her eyes, but he would kill for a better look—especially at her supple form. She was tall and perfectly proportioned.

A better look at a wealthy noblewoman was next to impossible in hierarchical Florence for Bradan, a man of limited means. At the moment he was an itinerant artist and scholar brought to the city on a modest stipend from Lorenzo to join an established collection of classicists, philosophers, and creators who made the city preeminent in Christian Europe for culture and artistic ambition. Besides political machinations, the merchant prince could rightly claim to be a patron of the arts rivaling the Pope. Bradan also performed diplomatic and business duties that sent him throughout Italy on behalf of Lorenzo, allowing him to begin accumulating a pile of florins. Heady as all this was, he wasn't rich and none of it brought Bradan any closer to Veronica. Well, best to stick to women of his own modest circumstances.

Despite the crowd of people in the cathedral, Lorenzo had no guards. Bradan believed this was a calculated show of nonchalance. By not acknowledging potential threats, he made the point not just that he *couldn't* be harmed, but that he *wouldn't* be harmed, secure among a populace well disposed toward him.

As the priest raised the sacramental bread, radiance from the dome above washed his hands. Simultaneously, Bradan heard cries of agony behind him and the sounds of a butcher shop. He'd seen enough battles to know the thud of knives puncturing flesh driven by lethal force.

A second priest attending the holder of the host suddenly lunged at Lorenzo, drawing a dagger from the folds of his robes.

Another man swung a knife at the merchant prince's head, hitting his shoulder. He drew blood, but the blow didn't cleanly slice through Lorenzo's heavy cloak. The entire cathedral resounded with shrieks and shouts.

Carnage on Easter, Bradan thought.

Bradan launched himself off the chair, grabbing at the murderous priest with one hand and the second attacker with the other and missing both in the press of colliding bodies. The priest slashed at Bradan, but he was no warrior and hit a chair, sending his blade clanging to the floor and himself caroming into Bradan, entangling them both in his robe. However, the second assassin was more skilled and charged over intervening bodies to dispense with Bradan and then move after the merchant prince.

I'm not dying in another's fight. But this is my fight now. So stupid, I left Tintagel in my room. I could use him.

The assailant knew what he was about, stabbing straight forward, using the dagger as an extension of his arm rather than slashing blindly.

Give me a sword and he'll be a piece of meat when I'm done, Bradan thought.

Instead he powerfully pushed the flailing priest into the attacker, sending them tumbling to the floor amid overturned chairs. Poliziano frantically yanked Lorenzo away from his two would-be assassins and forced his way through the mass of congregants to the front of the nave and whatever protection the sacristy offered. Bradan grabbed the merchant's other arm and pulled him along. He looked about. He'd lost sight of the priest and the other murderer, but they'd be on his back momentarily. He stared at the surrounding faces. He didn't know who else in the crowd was intent on assassinating de' Medici. If a dagger-armed priest could partake in murder, everyone was a potential killer.

"What of Giuliano?" de' Medici wheezed, dabbing his bleeding neck with a sleeve. "My brother, I heard his cry?"

They were at the sacristy door. Bradan shouldered it open.

"I saw him fall," Bradan said.

Lorenzo lurched back toward the nave. Bradan and Poliziano restrained him and bodily shoved him into the sacristy.

"Your people were with your brother," Bradan said. "Your wife and other family members made it out of the cathedral through a side door, though in the confusion, I'm not certain."

Three others Bradan recognized as part of Lorenzo's retinue forced themselves in after them and then pushed the heavy door shut. Poliziano slammed a deadbolt into place. None of them were armed and the room contained candles and vestments, but nothing remotely useful as a weapon.

Lorenzo de' Medici collapsed on a chair. Bradan pulled aside his cloak. The wound on his neck and shoulder looked painful, but not deadly. The great man was shocked; his sense of civic order and his invulnerability had been upended.

Dully, the sounds of tumult from the main portion of the cathedral quieted and the screaming faded to silence. For many moments the six of them breathed deeply, trying to recover their breath and their wits. Then fists pounded on the door. Were they now in a trap, easy prey for the assassins returning with reinforcements to finish the job? Bradan saw a narrow circular staircase at the back of the sacristy leading to floors above.

"I'll go up and see who's on the other side," he said.

"This door won't hold," Poliziano said. "Hurry."

Bradan vaulted up the corkscrew steps emerging onto a second-floor balcony overlooking the nave. Chaos. Articles of clothing lay strewn on the floor. Broken chairs were scattered about along with overturned, floor-standing, iron candle holders—fleetingly he registered that it was a miracle the entire edifice hadn't caught fire. Otherwise the cathedral was deserted except for a few stragglers still trying to cram themselves through doors and flee the carnage. And there was a huge smear of blood by the cathedral's main entrance where he'd seen Lorenzo's brother fall under a shower of dagger strikes. A body contained a lot of blood. The body was gone. So was the murderous priest and his accomplice.

Bradan slid over to the balcony railing and looked over. The vantage point allowed him to see who hammered at the sacristy door.

"He's not badly hurt," Bradan shouted down. "I'll let you in." Two dozen Medici retainers clustered around the door below. He saw swords, spears, and axes. The tide had turned.

Back in the sacristy, now jammed with his frenzied supporters, Lorenzo convened a council of war. Where was his brother? Who was behind the attack? Where was his family? His wife, Clarice, and other family members needed to be escorted out of town immediately if civil war broke out. Who would the populace support?

"The Palazzo della Signoria," Bradan shouted. "The civic center."

"What of it?" someone responded.

"To seize Florence, they'll go there next."

Lorenzo's voice rose over the ensuing tumult. "The fellow's right. We don't know how many of them there are, so we'll mobilize more of us." He looked at Bradan. "You seem young and fast. No one will notice one person. Run ahead to alert the city officials that they may be attacked and to defend themselves and dispense justice as they see fit until I arrive."

Bradan shoved through the crowd, out of the sacristy, and sprinted down the empty nave leaping over debris and giving the bloody floor by the door a wide berth. Exiting the cathedral, he burst out into bright daylight onto a square in front of the cathedral. After the dim interior, the sun blinded him, but he made out groups of citizens milling about uncertain who had attacked whom or why.

A troop of horsemen cantered into the square as if they owned it, heading toward the Palazzo della Signoria. They moved purposefully, letting their stallions bully the people aside. A small figure in archbishop's robes rode at their head. The rest of the horsemen belonged to a free company. They were heavily armed mercenaries bearing no city's insignia and available to be hired by whoever could pay them. These soldiers enabled the endless wars on the Italian boot between city-states. They weren't local to Florence; in foreign accents, they shouted for the crowd to mobilize for freedom and throw off the yoke of Medici tyranny. But despite the archbishop's presence, the horsemen didn't look like liberators to Bradan. Their threatening appearance crystallized popular sentiment against the prelate and his soldiers. Small family groups of citizenry just out of the cathedral of all ages and genders coalesced into a dense crowd and hurled invective at them. Children threw stones.

Incredibly, Veronica and her husband stood among the crowd unattended. Bradan guessed they'd become separated from the rest of the Medici extended family group during the panicked exodus from the cathedral. However, Veronica, in a fine red dress for Easter Sunday mass when all of Florence would be watching one another, seemed inspired and joined the rest to shout insults at the mercenaries, exhilarated to be part of an out-of-control situation. Bradan guessed this was a new sensation for the noblewoman, as she only emerged from behind stone walls for Sunday mass or city holidays, cosseted by household staff. He'd never seen women from wealthy families roam freely. This was a volatile day to start.

The old man held Veronica's arm and tried to steer her toward the periphery of the gathering fight and back in the direction of the Medici's fortified palace. He'd seen rebellions before and knew what savagery looked like. He wore a decorative dagger—not at all like the weapons that had just punched bloody holes in Lorenzo's brother. The trinket would be useless if things got out of hand. They were in deep waters. Surely, Bradan thought, the best destination for them would be in the Palazzo Medici with stone walls many feet thick and dozens of armed men to secure their personages.

Bradan watched the brewing storm. He needed to alert Florence's officials, but he also needed to move Veronica—and incidentally her husband—to safety. He pushed down the front steps into the crowd toward her.

"Who are you?" Veronica's husband started at Bradan's sudden presence and interposed himself between Bradan and his wife. He drew his knife.

"I'm a friend and that's a toy," Bradan said. "Leave it sheathed or someone will think you want a fight."

"Are you with the Medici?" Veronica asked. "You're the new artist Lorenzo has added to his court?"

He nodded. She didn't know him from Adam despite sitting near him in church just minutes before and seeing him in Lorenzo's company. He now saw her eyes were slightly different colors of blue, violet, and amber. The blend of hues tilted toward violet for one eye and blue for the other. He was both enchanted and disconcerted.

"Does Lorenzo live?" she asked. "And what of the rest of the family?"

"Lorenzo lives. Giuliano does not."

Veronica and her husband looked stunned.

"What does this mean?" the man asked.

"I'm new to Florence, but another family—I don't know city rivalries well enough yet to say who—means to take power away from the Medicis. I'm going to the Palazzo della Signoria to alert the city council of how things stand. I need to move on that errand and you have to depart this square. There's no telling what happens here."

The crowd vastly outnumbered the mercenaries and grew by the minute, but the soldiers maneuvered as a cohesive unit and now drew their weapons. There were even crossbows among them. In Bradan's assessment, they could slaughter dozens, hundreds, with a simple charge across the square slashing with their swords, shooting crossbow bolts, and trampling individuals under their mounts' hooves. They would be indiscriminate, riding down men, women, and children. Bradan knew that if your life was war as a business, massacre came easily.

"You need to go to the Palazzo Medici," he said. "Now. I can point you in that direction."

"I know how to get there, artist," the old man said tartly.

"Why go?" Veronica asked. "We'll display our anger at the plotters as everyone else does."

"Everyone else may die," Bradan said.

At the head of the free company, their condottiero, a huge man armored for battle, shouted orders in accented Tuscan. He'd slung his shield over his back and held a sword in one hand, reins in the other. He, not the archbishop, was the clear commander of the mercenaries and citizens fell back from his prancing charger.

Bradan froze. Medraut. He hadn't seen him in centuries, but there was no mistaking his visage beneath a steel helmet with the visor up. His hair was as long as Bradan remembered it from Celtic times a millennium back or in Córdoba four centuries ago. Bradan had hoped he'd been killed, but he seemed as indestructible as ever and he'd picked a vocation that matched his skills and inclinations. Acting as a Celtic warlord was excellent preparation for leading a band of mercenaries. And times were good for a man without scruple and with an unerring sense of who had the power in circumstances where half of Italy fought with the other half or feared an invasion from the French or the Turks.

The big man didn't appear to see him across the intervening soldiers and citizens.

"If you won't go to the Palazzo Medici," Bradan said urgently, "then follow me to the civic center. That's your best way to support the family and Florence. And stay alive."

Using his hand to shepherd the couple through the buffeting mass of people, Bradan circled the volatile assembly keeping close to building walls and out of the way, moving in the direction of a street on the other side of the plaza leading toward the government center. He saw its tower above intervening buildings.

Veronica moved slowly, encumbered by her long heavy dress. Probably, joining civic unrest seemed less appealing now, but she gamely strode along behind Bradan, occasionally tripping, grabbing the garment to pull the hem away from the filthy street and her shoes. Her husband moved only slightly faster. He still held his ridiculous weapon. Bradan needed to get to the Palazzo without being seen and ridden down, but he wanted a blade of his own, a sword or at least a dagger.

"Forgive me while I pray," he shouted over the din. Keeping walking, he turned toward the wall away from the couple.

Remembering one of Merlin's lessons, Bradan intoned a spell in Celtic British. He had no desire to be burned for sorcery, but no one would understand what he said. A paintbrush materialized in his hand. Useless. Disgusted, he let it drop and stumbled onward, his movement masked by the surrounding commotion. He could try a second time to create a weapon, but the spell might fail again and further sap him of energy. Bradan pressed forward using the wall for support. Now, besides being defenseless, he was fatigued by the worthless spell and his progress slowed to a crone's shuffle.

Before he'd gotten a block, he heard the smack of hooves on flagstones behind him.

"Run," he shouted at Veronica and her husband. Despite the danger of their circumstances, they moved deliberately, thinking their stature protected them, not recognizing that they should flee for their lives to avoid being trampled by the crowd or hacked to pieces by the soldiers. He fell back a step and pushed both of them forward, no time for etiquette. He glanced over his shoulder. Medraut led the charge with the archbishop at his side and the whole mercenary troop following, struggling through the citizenry and hemmed in by buildings. Suddenly it seemed that everyone, free company soldiers and citizen alike, realized the issue would be decided at the Palazzo della Signoria and the entire mass flowed down the few blocks separating the two plazas, with the horsemen bobbing like corks amid the citizens, everyone channeled by the narrow street and the tall stone buildings on either side. This fast-flowing river would determine Florence's future.

Looking back, Bradan saw the mercenary chief recognize him over the crowd. Medraut sheathed his sword and wrested a crossbow from a soldier. Medraut forced his brown charger ahead of the troop, sending citizens sprawling to the pavement beneath his hooves. Bradan zigzagged. A crossbow bolt zipped past his head to thud home in the neck of a man as tall as he was running next to him. His height had been the fellow's final mistake. Bradan knew crossbows couldn't be reloaded on a galloping destrier, but Medraut still had his sword.

Gwyn must have granted the big man longevity in return for tracking Bradan, since the god hadn't been able to seize Bradan at Cadbury. Once you were marked as fair game by that horde, nothing could commute the sentence, and a thousand years of Medraut's failure to kill Bradan would enrage Gwyn.

"Down!" Bradan shouted at Veronica and her husband. A second bolt flashed overhead, shattering itself on a stone wall. Medraut had grabbed another loaded crossbow from a soldier to send this second bolt their way.

The old man fell headlong. Without missing a step, Bradan seized a handful of the lord's tunic and hauled him bodily forward. Veronica turned to help her husband.

"Go," Bradan yelled. "I have him."

Bradan and his charges just beat the mercenaries and the archbishop to the civic center and ran inside and up a broad marble staircase to the second floor. Both Veronica and her husband were gasping and winded and tumbled into the expansive council chamber at the top of the flight, pushing through an open, heavy double door. No guards defended the portal.

The lord mayor and a dozen council members stood by the windows looking down to the square below and the growing group of horsemen. Citizens filtered onto the large open space, too.

"What news?" the mayor shouted at Bradan. The stout civic leader looked to be a man of gravitas and prosperity dressed in robes that displayed his stature to the rest of Florence. He didn't look like any sort of military leader.

"An attack in the cathedral against the Medicis," Bradan yelled. "The men below are here to take over, probably kill you."

"On Easter! Does Lorenzo live?"

"Wounded, but, yes, he'll live. I just left him. He'll arrive shortly with his own men, but what to do in the meantime? You have a hundred mercenaries and an archbishop at your doorstep."

Emphasizing the point, raucous threats came from below. Bradan heard horses clatter on the marble ground floor as soldiers rode their mounts directly inside the palazzo, indicating their contempt for Florence's current government.

"Stay here," the prelate ordered from below. "I'll deal with the council. Come up on my command."

"Council be damned," Medraut shouted. "One of those that fled is mine to kill."

"That's minor. He's yours once they've agreed to terms. Meantime, stay here. I pay you and your men, so that's how it is."

The archbishop accompanied by three attending churchmen stomped up the stairs and arrived through the double doors. The prelate wore the accoutrements of his office including a cassock and carried a staff. Bradan guessed the regalia was to intimidate Florence's civil authorities, but looking at the angry expressions on the mayor and councilmen, they saw only usurpers bent on seizing their power.

The mercenaries including Medraut stayed below to preserve the illusion that there would be polite negotiations as equals between the council and the archbishop, but with the threat of crushing force if need be.

However things turned out between the archbishop and Florence's civic leaders, Bradan knew Medraut would come after him to run him through with a sword.

"Would you believe this fellow?" the archbishop addressed the mayor and councilmen, pointing at Bradan. "We won't kill you. He's a foreigner. You can hear his accent. Throw him out the window. He deserves no better."

"Your soldiers below are foreign, too," Bradan yelled back.

"And they're armed," Veronica cut in.

"We mean no harm," the archbishop shouted to the council members. "Yes, we're armed, but by necessity. We're here to depose the so-called 'magnificent' Lorenzo and his cabal of thieves who run the city for their own aggrandizement. Join us. This is liberty for Florence with the Pope's blessing. Do you see any soldiers with us? They're downstairs waiting in your antechamber and taking their morning repast with wine and cheese. We've no intention of storming the palazzo. However, they are available if you see fit to stand in the way of justice and virtue for Florence."

Bradan saw how things were going. A hundred war-hardened soldiers acting with calculated brutality would tip the balance of power in the conspirators' favor over a collection of unarmed city officials and an enormous, potentially violent but leaderless pro-Medici mob gathering in the square below. Nonetheless, the mayor stood his ground and demanded the archbishop retreat along with the mercenaries. Bradan had stiffened his spine by promising Medici forces arriving shortly.

Bradan moved back toward the double doors and looked down the grand staircase. No one noticed him. The mercenaries he'd just seen outside the cathedral had moved en masse into the palazzo's ground floor with Medraut at their head. The big man kicked at a marble statue, sending it falling to the flagstones. His men took the cue and began ripping hangings from walls and toppling vases and decorations. Several lounged on the staircase's lower steps. One fellow on horseback threw a sausage and wine flagon to Medraut, who caught them and planted himself on the stone balustrade with his sword unsheathed across his legs. If this crew came up the stairs, Bradan, the mayor, Veronica's husband, and the council members would be cut to pieces with swords and axes. Veronica would be raped, then thrown out the window.

As discreetly as he could, Bradan pushed the doors to the council chambers shut. Peeking through the closing doors, he saw Medraut bolt to his feet and leap up the stairs with dozens of his men at his heels sensing Bradan intended to block the door.

The door had a broken lock mechanism, so Bradan whispered a simple eight-line spell, careful of the emphasis and meter. This was among the first of the spells he'd learned and he'd performed them at Cadbury and occasionally in the centuries since.

Do I remember it now?

"It doesn't bolt," the lord mayor yelled at Bradan. "It was broken during the last civic disturbance."

Bradan bent over gasping as the last stanza fell into place.

"I fixed it," Bradan said.

His physical exhaustion was balanced by the satisfaction of intellectual accomplishment. He squatted by the double door.

From outside the chambers, he heard Medraut screaming curses, and sword pommels and axes smashing into the door, but the barrier was built to withstand assault and didn't budge. The archbishop shoved Bradan aside and tugged and kicked at the door trying to open it to no avail. From either side, the spell made the portal more immovable than any lock.

"Lorenzo's retainers and soldiers are arriving, several score, on the plaza below," a councilman by the window shouted back into the room. "They join with the crowd to come this way."

Bradan stood up, regaining his strength, and staggered over to the windows. A gigantic throng packed the square three times the original size. He also saw armed, liveried retainers. Medraut and his mercenaries were effectively trapped between an unyielding barrier into the council chambers and an over-whelming force of Medici men and general citizenry about to burst into the ground floor.

The lord mayor marched over to the archbishop and grabbed him. Other councilmen, seeing which way the wind blew, and gaining valor by the second, followed suit and tackled the prelate's three followers. All four were dragged over to the open windows. The crowd observing from below saw the figures and roared with anticipation and cursed the conspirators and Pope Sixtus.

Screaming for mercy and threatening excommunication, the archbishop found himself with a cord around his neck and pushed over to the windowsill. Bradan noted iron hooks sunk into the casement surrounding the window. Evidently this wasn't the first time enemies of the city-state were summarily dealt with using a rope looped through a hook. Florence's high officials could serve as the final court and executioner without leaving the grand council chamber. The dangling corpses would amuse and edify city inhabitants who strolled across the square and chanced to glance upward at cadavers hanging from the stately civic center.

"I knew this happened," Veronica said. She stood beside Bradan. "But I hadn't seen it."

Her husband aloofly watched proceedings by the window. He still held his dagger.

"Civic justice," Bradan said. "Florentine style. That's one advantage to living life behind high walls. The city conducts its affairs without troubling you. You've never witnessed an execution before. There's no reason to see it now. Turn away."

"Can you delay them so a proper hearing can be organized?"

"I can't help the prelate. Emotions have taken over. He's an agent of the papacy against the city's political interests and he threw down a gauntlet to the council just now. They won't let that go. I can ask for a delay for the other three, though I have no standing in this city."

"As a woman, I don't have any standing, either, despite living in Florence for years as a member of a powerful family."

Veronica crossed herself and turned away from the execution.

The archbishop wriggled and kicked desperately, but he was small and held by a half dozen men moving him inexorably toward destruction. The churchman's fingernails raked the sill with enough force to rip out his nails, leaving ten thin trails of blood marking his final earthly progress before the pending drop. After a lifetime of scrawling church directives in ornate Latin, these gory traces would be the last inscriptions he'd ever make.

"Loop the rope through the hook here," the mayor said. "Tie his hands behind him. Then let him over the edge gradually. Don't snap his neck with the drop; let him gasp out his life slowly."

"That's what he planned for us," a council member said. "Should we gag him?"

"Why? His screams won't disturb us long. The rope will choke them off."

And with that, the men holding the archbishop gently lowered him out the window, carefully playing out the rope until it reached its full extension with the archbishop suspended far above the flagstones and baying crowd below. Bradan saw the churchman kick and buck crazily, his terminal exertions sending his body swinging in a pendulum arc bouncing off the building's stone wall.

In a sadistic inspiration, the council members forced the prelate's three associates to peer out the window to observe their leader's final agonized moments against a glorious view of Florence before them and blue skies and cumulous clouds above.

"Before killing the others, shouldn't we wait for Lord Medici?" Bradan addressed the mayor. "He'll want a say in their disposition. I just came from him in the cathedral."

The last part was theater. He'd been delegated no special authority on the merchant prince's behalf, but he guessed Lorenzo would want to take a measured approach to reprisals despite losing his brother.

"Young man, that would be the civilized action, but we're not feeling civil." The mayor nodded to his fellow council members.

"No, don't bother with hanging them, out they go."

Rage swamped sadistic patience and the other three conspirators were tossed out the windows sequentially with no time to contemplate their fate.

Bradan heard three squishy plops on the plaza below and turned away. Whether or not the men were dead from the fall, he didn't need to observe the crowd tearing the bodies apart.

How would he keep those images out of his nightmares and his art?

* * *

"The bodies float."

"That is my intention," Sandro Botticelli said. *"Primavera's* figures are mythical. And mystical, too. I focus on their faces, their essences. And I look to how the pieces fit together and flow, the balance, and the linearity that integrates it all together. Who cares about their feet?"

"Having their forms anchored to terra firma seems a nice counterpoint to all that divinity."

"Dear Bradan, who is the maestro of this little studio and who is the apprentice? You would give the figures gravitas they don't require and, anyway, this solidity of form you're proposing goes against the intention of the composition."

Bradan didn't agree, but he bowed slightly acknowledging the master artist's suzerainty in his empire.

The rustic, high-ceilinged workshop was perfect for creative endeavors, a place for transmuting inspiration into divinity. And the city didn't disturb the magic. Florence was at their doorstep, but kept at bay by thick walls that admitted muted noise from a busy neighborhood of craftsmen and street hawkers going about quotidian life. Amid this, the expansive studio was a well-lit island with large openings far above eye level for privacy that allowed in floods of light from daybreak until dusk so Botticelli and his disciples could achieve their chiaroscuro effects with shading, color, and line.

Creativity was strewn about the studio with the supremely ambitious *Primavera* occupying a place of honor in the room's center and three smaller, half-finished pieces in the corners including one of Bradan's own. He smelled poplar wood from the newly sanded panels, abraded to a satiny-smooth surface, several with the gesso applied to prime them for the tempera paint the artists would soon work their enchantment with.

Bradan had propped his lute against a wall in a little-used area of the workshop. He had almost no time to pluck it and when he did, Botticelli told him he wasted his time, but Bradan found it stimulating. Painting and composing music both used his creative energies and switching from one to the other was good counterpoint. After the master painter left the studio at night, Bradan would put down his brush to pick up the instrument and amuse himself and the apprentices with airs and melodies. He'd even managed to teach the lute's rudiments to several of the youths.

Today two boys sat on a long wooden bench next to a huge basket of eggs, hunched over mortars assiduously grinding cinnabar for red hues and crocus flowers for yellow. One of them worked on the crocus, his long blond hair nearly falling into the mortar, and his hair color matching the flowers. The dark-haired boy labored over cinnabar. The pulverized colors would be added to egg yolk as the concluding step in creating the tempera. Botticelli periodically looked over to ensure that none of the expensive ingredients were spilled. However, prompted by this surveillance, the dark-haired youth inadvertently nudged a bowl of bloodred paint off the bench to shatter on the straw-covered floor. An egg followed to land atop the spreading paint stain, creating a yolky, viscous mess. The maestro frowned.

"Ho, Luca, how can you learn to be a painter of subtle detail like Bradan with two left hands?"

This rebuke provoked a flood of excuses accompanied by gestures energetic enough to send more eggs skittering out of the basket to smack on the floor.

"Out with both of you," Botticelli stormed. "Out of my workshop. Back to your farms or wherever you came from. You're as clumsy as pigs."

Bradan knew the youths were indeed inept and neither had the talent to develop into painters of any repute. Botticelli, ever a slave to his sense of aesthetics, only allowed the handsome boys to apprentice in his workshop as an inspiration for the visages of young Saint John or other saints in his paintings. However, Bradan thought they were good company and lightened the otherwise intense mood in the studio, particularly important now with several commissioned works well behind schedule.

"Maestro, it was an accident," Bradan said. "They'll clean up the mess and have the tempera ready shortly. Without them, you and I would need to prepare our own paint, and tend to the studio, and these works—these great works—would never get done."

Botticelli walked over to the red splotch on the floor. "Address this immediately. And don't track it over my workshop."

Obviously relieved, Luca and Biagio hopped off the bench to find mops and water. Disturbed by the wobbling bench, still another egg teetering on top of the pile in the basket splattered onto the floor.

With the goals of distracting Botticelli from the maladroit apprentices and furthering his own desire to contribute significantly to *Primavera*, Bradan said, "Give me a token for my effort on this work you have had me laboring away on while you were off in Rome catering to our illustrious Holy Father."

"You want to improve their feet so they won't 'float'?" Botticelli smirked.

"Spare me that," Bradan said. "We'll leave them floating in the ether. As you say, it's your studio. Instead, I'd like to choose a model for one of the faces."

"I'm halfway through with the piece and we're behind my promised schedule. This is no training artwork. Also, I never compromise on the faces—of the women in particular. However, I'll listen because you're always full of amusing recommendations and, unlike with his revered holiness, Pope Sixtus, I'm free to laugh at your input."

"You're not done with Flora, your lady of the flowers. She's a charcoal outline and I'd like to propose a model for her. You've put in no detail yet, so it won't change the overall composition."

"I didn't leave her blank for your tender touch! However, let me guess, you want la Veronica that you so lust after as your model. She's the friend of Clarice Orsini? I see her at Sunday mass. She *is* an interesting creature, I'll give you that, but better observed from a distance. The woman is forbidding, all that piety. Don't get close to the flame. She is more to be admired than held in your arms. You know, unlike you, I don't have to be near them; I idolize women, but I don't love them."

"I love them, but don't idolize them."

"You're not so old you can speak from a vast body of experience," Botticelli said. "Though you're taller, you look as young as any of my apprentices, a new man to Florence without name or family. You're fortunate to be in my hire."

"I'm richer than I look and older," Bradan said. "I've lived long enough to understand a little about people and art so you're lucky to have such a talented apprentice who rises with the morning church bell, unlike the rest of your crew who come late if they come at all."

He saw the maestro pout. Botticelli had a voluptuary's lips that displayed every mood.

Careful, Bradan thought. *I shouldn't beard this sensitive lion in his own den. I'll turn the talk back to the painting.*

"So, let's see which perspective produces better painting," Bradan said. "Idolization or love."

Botticelli snorted and stepped back to take in the work currently consuming his workshop's efforts. Bradan also moved away from the details he worked on. He was out of paint, anyway.

Bradan had to admit, the whole of it was masterful, showing the arrival of spring personified by a collection of sometimes amorous, sometimes reflective gods, goddesses, and nymphs. The enormous work emerged from the master's sensuous, egotistical brilliance, barely contained by the workshop's main room. Given inspiration and direction from Poliziano, the most learned of Lord Medici's classical scholars, Botticelli's fecund imagination could lift a Roman allegory with Venus, Mercury, Flora, and various graces to heights the ancients couldn't have conceived. Even half finished, with more background white than color and with the eight figures only partially detailed, this was a remarkable work. And he, Bradan, contributed in his own small way. Yes, he was lucky to be working under Botticelli's tutelage. Even the wolf had been grudgingly given a spot to snooze in a little-used corner once the master artist realized having the beast in residence rid his workshop completely of rats. Local ruffians also steered clear of the workshop. Everyone assumed Tintagel was simply a very large dog and Bradan didn't enlighten them. Even the apprentices got on well with the wolf.

The studio was a discreet refuge in turbulent times when one could get a knife in the back without even looking for it, just by strolling about on Florence's streets anytime, day or night. And there *were* men looking for Bradan. Taking sides five years ago by blocking a dagger thrust aimed at Lorenzo de' Medici had cast his lot irrevocably with the currently ascendant faction in the city, but for how long? Lorenzo had more than his share of vengeful rivals—open and hidden—as well as an imperialistic pope in Rome anxious to expel the merchant prince and willing to turn a blind eye at assassination attempts against him. Playing the artist's apprentice to an opinionated genius like Botticelli in this laboring-class, out-of-the-way side street satisfied both Bradan's creative inclinations as well as his need for a lair.

"Veronica Varano will never sit for you," the maestro said. "The picture is too big to go to her, so she would have to come to my studio. That would be improper and la Veronica is the soul of propriety."

Botticelli turned and shouted over at the youths finally finished with the colors and cleaning egg yolk off the floor. "Ha! Luca, Biagio. How would you like to have a noble lady and her retinue join us in the workshop? That is what our dear Bradan proposes."

"Wouldn't their dresses get paint on them?" Luca asked, uncertain whether the master joked or this was a serious proposal to bring more verisimilitude to the studio's art.

"Besides their clothing, their reputations would be stained, as well," the master artist said.

Bradan stood arms folded, letting this play out. Interrupting the merriment wouldn't work to his advantage. Botticelli, at the height of his powers, was ever ready to mock his apprentices. And he was already becoming set in his ways about technique concurrently with becoming stouter, softer, and less energetic. Bradan doubted he had the stamina to mount two flights of stairs. His once blond-brown hair that had flowed easily down to his shoulders was now gray-streaked and thinner, though the old backward tilt of his head remained along with the arrogance it conveyed about his gifts. However, Leonardo was passing him. Still, Botticelli was right about access to well-born women by humble artist's apprentices: It didn't happen.

Fortunately, Bradan was more than a mere apprentice. And he didn't think of himself as humble. Before joining the studio, he'd performed diplomatic and merchant banking missions for Lorenzo and prospered from the effort. Unbeknown to Botticelli, he still undertook such missions from time to time when the master artist was in Rome working on the Sistine Chapel. However, whether his circumstances were august enough to gain him access to Veronica Varano had yet to be ascertained. At least her wretched husband had died and wouldn't intervene.

"It would be better if she did sit for me, but she doesn't have to," Bradan finally said.

"So you'll use a servant or shop girl for a model?" Botticelli asked. "A whore? But no one of such low station will convey the complexity and refinement needed for my Flora."

"I don't need anyone else. I know Veronica Varano's face well. I can do it from memory. She has blond hair with just a touch of brown which I'll render completely golden to better match the other women you've conceived for the work. Her features and spirit will service your composition well. She's unique in Tuscany with her combination of intelligence, beauty, and purity. If I can capture that, I can think of myself as an artist."

"Yes, but how will the rest of the world think of you?"

"So, a challenge then," Bradan said. "Have a look. I've made a start already." He nodded toward a small rectangular portrait propped against the wall on a workbench behind the *Primavera*.

"You're turning to oil, too," Botticelli said. "Traitor. It seems the painters from the other side of the Alps are infecting us all." But he said this without rancor, acknowledging new realities in the competitive world of Italian art.

"It's coming even in Florence," Bradan said. "And it's easier to manipulate than tempera, ideal for fast work."

"Fast perhaps, but does it lend itself to refinement?"

"To that point, what do you think of my piece?" Bradan hardly dared ask the question. The maestro could be caustic about inferior work. Luca and Biagio sauntered over to watch Bradan squirm as he waited for the verdict.

Botticelli inspected the portrait, slowly drawing close, then pulling back. "This is a preparatory work for *Primavera*'s Flora, of course."

"You can see how I'm conceiving of her face before you agree to let me try my hand on such a grand work," Bradan said. He sensed that, out of apprehension, he was trying to explain his artwork. However, it should stand on its own needing no explanation.

Botticelli ignored him for a long while before finally saying, "Three things favor it. First, your subject is worthy. If I were in the habit of falling in love, I might be tempted with this woman. Second, I am behind on *Primavera*. As you have so astutely pointed out, half of it is little more than an idea in charcoal on a white background. It needs to be finished—and soon—to gain my commission. Third, you've competently executed your effort—very competently."

Bradan nodded thanks. This was as effusive as Botticelli's praise would get.

"As you see," Bradan said, "my memory will serve for the painting. Still, I would rather paint her from life to refine the preparatory draft—if that were possible—with details only my actual eye, not my mind's eye, can render."

"And how would that happen? Veronica is behind Medici walls, in a palace."

"In a prison," Bradan said.

Botticelli looked at him curiously. "How else should you guard the virtue and body of well-born innocents?"

"The times we live in."

"Certainly, the times we're in," the master artist said with exasperation. "What other times? You do say the strangest things. Florence is better than Rome or three dozen other cities in our fair land. You came from where before here? Venice, Padua? Those aren't exemplars of excellent behavior."

Bradan thought back over a thousand years and didn't remember better times; violence and rapine had been common during most of his life. Lindisfarne had been a place of tranquil contemplation—before the Vikings sacked it. The Caliphate of Córdoba many centuries ago on the far side of the Mediterranean had also been more serene than turbulent Florence. However, that Eden had eventually been subsumed in religious and dynastic strife. Regardless, it was best not to laud the Muslim Caliphate in Christian Florence as a paragon of learning and comity. Besides, Botticelli knew everything about shaping line and color to convey ethereal beauty and next to nothing about Italian, let alone world, politics. Bradan would stick to debates about aesthetics with the maestro.

"You have no reputation," the master artist continued. "Why would she know of you? Not even I, though on good terms with the family and having completed countless commissioned works for them, can get into their palazzo without special arrangement."

"But I do have a connection," Bradan said. "I helped save Lorenzo de' Medici five years back when the Pazzis and their allies in Rome moved to assassinate him in our cathedral. Unfortunately, I was not of much use to Lorenzo's brother.

However, I was in a group that escorted Clarice Orsini and her women friends including Veronica to safety in Pistoia. We spoke—I offered comfort under trying circumstances—so I'm not unknown to her."

Bradan debated adding the next bit, but couldn't restrain himself. "She helped me storm the Palazzo della Signoria and rescue the lord mayor and city council from Lorenzo's would-be assassins. That's her spirit that I mentioned earlier."

Botticelli stood flabbergasted. "How did this come to pass?"

"A long story for another time. Check with the family if you doubt me."

"You have unsuspected depths. So it seems they may think well of you after all. Had I known, I should have used your good offices to get more commissions from them. Well, that makes you less of a threat from the family's point of view, but what of the woman herself, this Veronica? She's a widow. Will she worry of her reputation and her chances of remarriage if she's seen in the company of a brave, but otherwise unsuitable, fellow?"

"What if we are never in the same room together?"

"Then you might as well use your imagination for her likeness."

"I've heard of the interior layout. There is a three-story court-yard in Lord Medici's palace. I sit on one side by an open upper-story window and she sits on the other side also by an open window opposite me. The household can post as many chaperones as they want. I'm more than close enough to add nuance and texture to my draft while keeping an appropriate distance. We can even talk if she chooses to. A relaxed subject allows the painter better insight into their personality."

"Using her as a model won't flatter her into your bed."

"That's not the idea," Bradan said.

"How uncharacteristic of you. You're usually all too happy to enjoy the pleasures of women."

"This painting demonstrates my skill to myself, at least, if no one else. That's what I'm after."

"All right, Flora is yours." The master artist laughed. "Unless you botch it, in which case I'll complete the face. Have Biagio and Luca take over the remaining plants and other background details. Tell them what needs to happen. You've mostly finished the incidentals, anyway. Also, Bradan, I need one additional figure detailed: Zephyrus."

"I'm flattered, maestro. I had thought you would keep that one for yourself since the March wind initiates all other action in the work. I can model it on anyone. One of Lord Medici's sons?"

"They've modeled for many other works where I render them as ideals of youth and vitality. More flattery would be pointless. What about yourself as the model?"

Bradan bowed again, he hoped without obvious irony. "I'm honored. So I'll be the heretic elemental bent on seizing the maiden."

"There is that quality in you I can't completely express, but I sense. It does not come from this world. Put that into the pagan god of the spring wind. Do you know your own features and soul well enough to reflect them in the work?"

* * *

"Will the painting look like me?"

"As much as I can make it," Bradan called over to Veronica. He easily made himself heard across the small interior courtyard. As he'd requested, they both sat in excellent lighting beside open, top-story windows of the Palazzo Medici.

"But I must lighten your hair to suit the other figures in the composition. Don't take offense."

She seemed irritated. "I want my hair as it is, but if you must, make your alterations. We all need to compromise for the allegorical purity of Master Sandro Botticelli's work."

Her voice was harder than he remembered from five years back. Then she'd seemed demure and naïve to the world. Maybe half a decade of Florence's tumultuous political scene—even sequestered behind the palazzo's high walls—had sharpened her opinions. Or seeing an archbishop hung from the civic center window and his minions torn limb from limb had opened her eyes to the possibilities of the world.

The passing years had rendered the woman more striking, and the hardness in her voice hadn't crept into her features.

Veronica faced him full frontal for this painting, allowing him to vividly capture her face down to transient expressions wafting across it.

"You're free to critique it as I go along," he said. He needed her kind feelings toward the work. Despite his good name with the family, he was here on her sufferance—though, oddly, she seemed eager to meet him, and he'd gotten no resistance to his formal petition for an audience.

"This modest effort"—he gestured at the portrait—"will be used to convey your likeness back to the workshop, where I'll transfer it to the main painting. You'll have admirers when the finished work is shown."

"You're one of Sandro's pupils," Veronica said. "That should give me confidence, though I've seen more of your martial prowess than skill with a brush."

The noblewoman paused suddenly; a thought had occurred to her. "It's not a nude, is it?"

"You're fully clothed now," Bradan replied. "And my imagination isn't good enough to portray you any differently so you'll be clothed in the painting, too."

"I think your imagination is excellent," Veronica said. She pulled up her dress's neckline. Any hint of cleavage vanished.

"You have my word, but see for yourself," he said.

Bradan nodded for one of the palazzo's guards to come over and help him lift the heavy wood painting and turn it to Veronica. While he had two liveried Medici soldiers to keep him from wandering idly around the enormous residence among his betters, she was accompanied by an elderly maidservant in a cinnamon-colored gown dourly observing her mistress while fingering a cross to remind one and all that the Almighty would judge transgressions against propriety harshly.

"Oh, but you have made me very knowing and self-amused," Veronica said. "Why am I smiling so inscrutably to the viewer?"

It *was* a sphinxlike smile and Veronica's eyes were watchful. Her features were as Bradan remembered them, classically Roman with full lips, and with shoulder-length hair framing her face. She wore a cream-colored, summer-weight dress, Florentine clothing at its most sophisticated.

"You tell me what you smiled at," he said. "I simply captured what you showed the world, but now that I've got it, I want to emphasize it. It sets you apart from the work's other figures."

"I don't want to be the unique figure. I'm happy without undue attention unless it's from the right quarters."

"I paint what I see," he said simply. "So what was your smile about?"

"I'm sure I was thinking secret thoughts and that tiptoed unintended into my expression. Do you have any secrets,

Bradan? You seem the least open of men compared to other Florentines. And that's saying something."

Bradan, in the process of repositioning the portrait with a guard so he could resume working, stopped dead.

What does she know of me? he wondered.

"I'm not mysterious," he said. "I've lead a life beyond reproach. The one piece of excitement for me was that savagery in the cathedral. Before that, I was in Padua quietly studying at their illustrious libraries. Call me studious if you want, but not mysterious."

"I heard you warded off two knife-wielding assassins with your bare hands in the cathedral. You were useful to the family—and to me—a few years ago in fending off the rabble that attacked us with Pope Sixtus's connivance."

"One needs a few martial skills to get by in Florence."

Bradan looked across the courtyard at the noblewoman and put down his brush. She appeared about to burst with a revelation.

"You were preoccupied with a thought and I caught it. Come. Tell me. The paintbrush doesn't lie."

Veronica nodded toward her maidservant.

"She's been with me since I was a child. She disapproves of many things about my circumstances, but reports nothing. Still, if we want to talk frankly, let's try a tongue neither she nor the guards will recognize."

What does she want to tell me? Bradan thought.

"Classical Latin," he said. "I suspect you know it? We can speak privately."

Veronica shifted easily into Latin. "The benefits of a good tutor. Even the most scholarly boys did not love the classics like me. Livy was a favorite of mine, Ovid even more so as he wrote of love. How comes it that you know Latin better than Tuscan Italian?"

"Latin was my mother tongue and you might say I also received a classical education." He remembered Merlin's endless drills on Latin declensions.

"More mysteries from you, Master Bradan, but we'll let that rest for the moment and look to my circumstances since there is urgency. First, I must apologize for agreeing to sit for you under a falsehood. Even with all the precautions you proposed to spare my name and reputation, I wouldn't be here for a painting unless I needed your help—it was little short of a miracle that your request came when it did, so I determined to endure the gossip about me, a widow intended for remarriage, sitting for a painting to be seen by thousands since it obscures my real motive in talking to you."

"I'm baffled. How can I assist you?"

"You know of the Pope's man in Florence."

Bradan couldn't imagine what she meant. "No doubt, we are all the Pope's men and women in the sense that he is the Lord's representative in this profane place."

"It wasn't a symbolic description," she said. "I referred to an actual individual and his henchmen. By reputation and my own experience, he is as bad as they come. He's a papal agent doing political and criminal things in Florence—they are one and the same to this person—and I've come to his attention, why I cannot think. He saw me briefly five years ago in your company at the Palazzo della Signoria during the conspiracy. Or he has seen me at a recent public function or at Sunday mass. Anyway, he wants to meet me. Alone. Without the family knowing about it."

"Ignore the request," Bradan said with asperity. "It took me much effort to meet you today accompanied by a detachment of guards and servants even with Lorenzo himself to vouch for me. So, turning aside unwanted interest from this 'Pope's man' should be nothing for you."

"Typically, yes."

"Alert the household and have Lord Lorenzo set his retainers on this freebooter. The fact that he's in Sixtus's employ will only fuel the animus the Medicis will certainly feel toward him."

Veronica's composure suddenly crumbled. Just a moment earlier, she'd projected the imperturbability of one whose options in life, if not exciting, are at least predictable.

"I think I'm adding to your troubles," Bradan said. "Forgive my inept efforts to aid you. Take time to collect yourself and tell me more. Let's start with why proper authority is not the way to address your circumstances."

"To do that, I'll need to give you more of my history. I hope my Latin suffices. If I become vague in places, please don't press for details. As you'll see, this is obviously not information I'd planned to divulge to you or anyone at all, but I don't see a choice."

Bradan nodded for Veronica to proceed.

"I'll start with the smaller of my two secrets: My father was Cardinal Pugliesi."

She paused for effect, but Bradan sat unsurprised.

"I've heard worse," he said. "I suppose your Pope's man proposes to use this intelligence to force you into bed with him? But half the dukes and prelates in Italy are the offspring of high-church officials, popes included. It could surely cause you difficulty, but all in all, this seems a paltry weapon. However, you had a second secret?"

"My mother was a Jew."

Bradan thought he'd misheard the Latin. She saw his uncertain expression and nodded affirmation.

"I see." Bradan considered for a minute. "Whatever your own religious inclinations are, this makes you a Jew in the eyes of many. If it's not too much to ask, just how did a cardinal happen to have relations with your mother?"

"'Have relations,' how delicately you put it. My grandfather Yanoach was a superb goldsmith from Siena who was hired by the cardinal—even now, I can't call him Father—to do craftwork for his palace in Rome. As he was widowed, Yanoach brought his only daughter, Rebecca, with him, not trusting relatives to care for her. Well, my grandfather did the required work for the cardinal and, while leaving Rome, he and his daughter were set upon by bandits—who knows, hired by the cardinal to recover his commission. He was murdered. His daughter escaped back to the palace, the only place she knew in Rome. It can only have been my mother's youth and beauty that gained her entry into the household and then inevitably into the cardinal's bed despite threat of exposure, expulsion from the Curia, and both of them being burned at the stake. I was the result—awkward for everyone. My mother died of plague shortly after my birth, so I was alone. What saved me from a life in the servants' quarters or worse was that I was the same age as Clarice Orsini, who needed a play companion. The cardinal and the Orsini family were relatives so there was a blood bond and, with the cardinal's acquiescence—blessing is too strong a word—I was baptized and discreetly adopted into the Orsini household. No one thought to probe my background and I grew up with Clarice and came to Florence with her when she married Lorenzo de' Medici. In turn I was married off to a wealthy dotard in a marriage planned to produce advantageous offspring for the greater glory of my adopted family."

"Thus can stains on the family lineage be quietly expunged and even turned to advantage," Bradan observed.

"It seems you understand such things. However, though he did try manfully, the dotard died before getting me with child."

"The Pope's man knows about your parentage?" Bradan asked.

Veronica nodded. "Besides forcing me into his bed, I think he enjoys debasing a woman of good family."

"So much impropriety in such a proper woman," Bradan observed. "If this fellow works for Pope Sixtus, his knowledge about you is powerful persuasion. Sixtus is a supporter of the Inquisition in Spain and would have emphatic views about a high churchman lying with your mother. Any offspring of that union would be at risk."

"I have lived as a good daughter of the Church."

"I'm sure that will be a helpful defense," Bradan said dryly. "The very inconceivability of your parentage rendered you safe until now."

"Nothing about my coming into existence followed the proper rules."

She sat across from him, drained and defeated by the threat to her position. However, she also seemed relieved to confide to a trusted individual. Veronica's maid stared angrily at him, not understanding the dialogue's content, but guessing from its tone that it had distressed her mistress. He suspected she'd like to hurl her crucifix at him.

"This will not make you feel better," Bradan said. "But, besides your physical appeal, there is another, stronger purpose for the papal agent to compromise you. He'll now have a source of information inside the Palazzo about the Medicis' doings. That's useful to Sixtus."

"And I'd flattered myself this was about me, but I'm just a small piece in a big game."

"A pretty piece," he said. "And we're all part of one game or other."

"Can you advise me?" she asked.

"Advise? The only option is to quietly confront your persecutor. And that's why you're seeing me."

"Or I could retire to a convent and not ask you to risk yourself on my behalf."

"Retire to a life of pious tedium?" Bradan asked. "Even our maker wouldn't want that much from you because of the caprices of your birth."

"But you speaking to him will not send him away," she said.

"Does he have a name besides being the Pope's man in Florence?"

"He doesn't hide it. Why bother? His name is Marco. It was another name before, but he changed it after spending time in Italy. Besides a brief look across a plaza five years ago, I've never set eyes on him, but evidently he is physically imposing, huge even, and prone to extreme violence. He led the free company that took part in the failed rebellion five years ago."

"We've met," Bradan said flatly. "I knew him as Medraut. He fled the city before he could be strung up or torn to pieces by the mob like his co-conspirators. I'd hoped he'd vanished for good, but now he's come back, it seems. He profits from troubled times and Florence is ever troubled. How does he communicate his demands to you?"

"I get written messages in out-of-the-way corners of my suite of rooms in this palace. He must have suborned a servant. I'm under someone's eyes and I don't know who."

Bradan picked up his brush and retouched the color of Veronica's eyes.

"I'll see the fellow," he said.

My infatuation with Veronica must have sucked the sense from me, he thought.

"This is an errand of chivalry," Veronica said.

"My paintbrush will be my lance."

She laughed. "You'll want a favor in return from the rescued damsel?"

"Actually, it's self-love. Whatever he does or doesn't get from you, sooner or later he'll come after me. We have a quarrel from times gone by. I face him now, or I do it later."

Her eyes were now perfect, one sky blue, the other a sort of violet-amber, both with black pupils deep enough to fall into.

"So this is what I propose: Get a message to Marco, you'll meet him near the Palazzo at the street of Santa Maria tonight. Anxious as he is to get at you, he'll still suspect a trap and bring along hired thugs—perhaps his old mercenary companions. They're a tough outfit. He'll be ready for anything. If he's really cautious, he'll try to bribe the city watch to ignore any disturbances. However, mostly he'll count on his own strength and swordplay to carry the day."

"With such a formidable opponent, how will you win?" she asked.

"The Florentine way: low cunning, unexpected allies, and fast work with a blade."

* * *

Bradan's blade slapped Marco's weapon. This was experimental. He wanted to see how good the other man was with a sword since they'd last met. Marco was Medraut, of course, every bit as vicious as ever. Passing years refined some personalities, but passing centuries only made Bradan's nemesis a more adept killer and amplified his appetites.

Marco's riposte came lightning fast and almost skewered Bradan, who swatted the strike aside at the last instant with his sword hilt. Marco pressed the advantage and came on, but with too much momentum, allowing Bradan to dodge. The big man slammed into a wall on the narrow street, righted himself, whirled around with his sword pointed at Bradan's throat, and edged toward him again. Moonlight flickered on the steel.

Watch his eyes, not his sword point.

They'd both made mistakes; Bradan had been too tentative in assessing his opponent and Marco shouldn't have been baited into a wild-boar lunge at Bradan. Duels often didn't take long. One participant made a mistake and the other contender simply ran him through.

"I should have put my blade in your back," Bradan said. "That was a big target."

"A life of art and scholarship made you hesitate."

"I did well enough against your companions earlier tonight." Bradan advanced on the big man.

"You killed two," Marco admitted. It was an observation. He didn't seem angered by the loss of comrades.

"I got one," Bradan said. "My wolf got another. He made good eating."

"Your animal can't protect you. He's down by the river chasing others in my party. There are enough of them to run the beast to ground."

"Better men have tried. And I don't need his help. You're not such a good swordsman."

"Better men than you discovered what I do with a blade," Medraut said.

"Arthur was old. How did it feel to kill your father?"

"Like killing anyone else."

Marco crossed himself and breathed a brief prayer in Latin over his sword. They dueled by the cathedral on a cramped side street confined by three-story, red-tile-roofed buildings. An open sewer ran down the middle of the street. Bradan tried not to think what he stepped in. The street reeked. Distractions would kill him; he needed utter focus on Medraut.

Their swords whirred and collided concussively. It was midnight and moonlight splashed on the steel. Bradan's blade was lighter than his opponent's and his dueling style correspondingly relied more on agility and his weapon's point. Marco, with a heavier blade, meant to hammer him to destruction with his sword's edge, but, though lighter, Bradan's blade was Toledo steel and proof against almost any strike. However, Bradan wondered if his arm would hold up under the bone-rattling blows. Nonetheless, Marco soon seemed winded. His heavy weapon didn't do him any favors.

"It's no surprise Veronica would send another in her place," Marco gasped out. "So I was ready with a whole squad of mercenaries, but I hadn't expected it would be you as the lone knight errant. I'd thought I'd seen the last of you after our insurrection failed. You had a role in that. Well played, I give it to you."

Bradan circled Marco, his point aimed at the man's middle, the biggest target.

"Florence inspires the art I make," he said.

"A waste—" Marco lunged forward, suddenly energized. Bradan had expected the big man's show of fatigue to be a ruse, but Marco's speed was nonetheless breathtaking.

Don't think. Extend your weapon.

Bradan's sword transfixed Marco's reaching arm. His blade was almost wrenched from his grasp as his opponent crashed past him. Bradan knew he'd hit a bone. Marco crumpled to the dirty street with a thud, his sword clanging to the street. Even with this wound, the big man kept his fighting instincts and clambered upright. Bradan realized he'd been injured too, on his thigh. It hurt badly and it bled, but it wasn't deep. And it wouldn't keep him from killing crippled and disarmed Marco. He had no compunctions. However, now there was a lot of company, as a half dozen of Marco's henchmen arrived, surging down the street toward Bradan. All had swords and two carried daggers, as well. Three of them rushed forward to support Marco while the other three dodged around them and came at Bradan. But the street's narrowness constrained the group, so only two could attack him at once and leave enough room to freely move their weapons.

Where's the city watch?

Despite the sounds of violence and tumult, the shuttered windows along the street stayed closed. No one was going to raise the alarm for official intervention.

Stall until Tintagel arrives. Or other help.

Bradan backed away from the approaching gang. He could kill or disable them all piecemeal. The street's confines worked against them, but gave a lone man—smart with a sword—just enough room to maneuver. He feinted at them and the two leading assailants danced back out of range, but not before Bradan's blade stabbed the leading fellow's calf below a dagger that had been lowered too late to block the injury. The man collapsed to the street, to be replaced by another. Marco's angry shouts goaded them forward again.

Beautifully plucked lute music wafted down from a rooftop three stories above. Everyone looked up at music coming from the night sky. Briefly, the tune was meditative, then the cadence accelerated. This was a brief prelude to—

A shower of eggs flew down from above, aimed with precision at the oncoming mercenaries and struck all of them including Marco leaning on a wall. The fusillade was endless. An entire Tuscan poultry farm had been stripped of eggs to be turned into projectiles. In moments, the street, Marco, and his crew were covered in gooey, slippery yolk and struggled to stand up.

Bradan heard Biagio's and Luca's derisive shouts above raining insults down on Marco's thugs along with eggs. Voices Bradan recognized as other apprentices joined in the cacophony. Biagio and Luca had mobilized the entire studio to join the fray. Earlier, Bradan had explained to the youths that he had an assignation with a lovely woman that night, but she had a jealous lover who would set hired criminals on him if he carried out the tryst. Could they distract the henchmen? In return, he promised them a demonstration of deadly swordplay. The story appealed to the adventurous romantic in the boys and they'd agreed to shadow him as he set out to meet Marco. Bradan wondered if they'd told Botticelli.

Now his young allies hurled heavy paving stones down on the thugs. Besides screaming abuse upward, Marco's men could do nothing now that the hail had turned deadly.

With shouts and light from lanterns, the city watch finally arrived, at first uncertain what they saw in the dim light, but Marco and his heavily armed men were obviously up to murderous activities, so the guardsmen gingerly moved forward in a mass, pikes and swords extended. Bradan discreetly set his sword aside. In the bad light, no one noticed. It was a good sword so he'd be back to retrieve it in the early morning, assuming the watch didn't determine he'd instigated the fracas and throw him in a cell. However, they moved past him, seeing only a lone unarmed man whom they could return to question if need be. The guardsmen worked to avoid sliding on the yolk covering the street. Marco and his thugs moved in the opposite direction as quickly as poor traction would allow, leaving the man Bradan had injured behind on the street. The two groups shouted taunts at each other, but neither side seemed anxious to press the issue; given the number of watchmen, the outcome would be inevitable so Marco's mercenaries retreated. The big man was distinctive and clearly recognizable as the leader of the gang of cutthroats. The guard would remember him and search Florence even if he escaped tonight, but Bradan surmised that Marco counted on his papal connections to keep him out of a dungeon.

So Veronica's reprieve would be temporary. Marco would recover from his wound and come after her again to exploit her secrets by denouncing her lineage. Bradan would have gained nothing by tonight's fight. He recited eight stanzas. A nimbus of orange light sprang up around Marco, enveloping him in a cocoon of eerie illumination. At first his men gaped, then they pushed frantically away from the big man. The closest guardsmen also sprang back, shouting in alarm.

"Bring a priest," Bradan said weakly over the confusion. The spell was medium-sized and drained his energy, but he didn't need to maintain the magic. Just long enough to terrify the watch and any citizenry who happened to be observing and generate suspicions of deviltry Marco couldn't refute and would undermine his ability to stay in the city. Further, any accusations he made against Veronica would carry less weight if he were suspected of sorcery. Window shutters along the street popped open to show candlelit faces, little rectangles of wavering illumination and shadow. Under different circumstances, Bradan would have captured the scene in an oil painting. "He's possessed by demons," he told the nearest guardsmen. "They performed occult rituals and unholy ceremonies with animals on a public street."

With impeccable timing, Tintagel howled, his vocalizations echoing among the stone housing. What must at first have looked to the watch commander like a deadly brawl, a threat to civic order, but nothing unusual in nighttime Florence, had morphed into a macabre, magical rite.

"Get no closer," the commander shouted. "Find an archer and shoot the demon. And do find a priest as this fellow suggests."

But there was no one to shoot or exorcise. Away from the yolk, with better traction, Marco and his men sprinted away, pelting down alleys. Bradan smiled, noting that the cutthroats headed away from Marco who still trailed a fading aura of unearthly orange. Spectators murmured prayers anxiously in the windows as they slammed shut.

"Your role in this?" the watch commander asked Bradan. He hadn't put away his sword, clearly uncertain how Bradan fit into the confusing and unnatural circumstances. Other guardsman formed a circle about him, not getting too close.

"No role at all besides praying for salvation. I returned home from maestro Botticelli's studio and came across an unholy ritual performed by the men who just fled. Besides that, a creature stalks these streets. The men may have called him from the pit."

"Captain, you can question this fellow's painting technique, but not his piety."

Botticelli, accompanied by the studio's apprentices, approached the cluster of guards interrogating Bradan. They made way respectfully for him, which signaled Bradan that the artist must be known to them as an affiliate of the Medicis.

"He was set upon by those odd fellows," the maestro said. "It seems none of us is safe from demonic threats on our streets."

Botticelli didn't volunteer information about casting eggs down on Marco and his thugs.

"Your work honors Florence," the captain said. "But how comes it that you and your entire studio roam about at Matins?"

"To remind me of my virtue," Bradan cut in. "I had an assignation with a woman. Master Botticelli suspected this and followed me to remind me not to stray, since the pleasures of the flesh forever draw me away from painting sacred themes."

The maestro picked up the cue. "What the fellow says is true. He is gaining capability as an artist, but still he's addicted to vices."

"There are peculiarities here from every quarter," the captain said. "The sorcerers and villains that just fled promised us any number of florins to look the other way whatever commotion we heard."

"Of course, you disregarded this transparent effort at bribery," Bradan said.

"Of course," the guardsman said. "Bribes aren't unusual, though here is the truly odd thing. A dark-haired woman who spoke passible Tuscan, but seemed foreign, offered us still more gold to disregard the original bribe and ensure we came posthaste if we detected anything amiss. She was a real beauty. We took her gold—as evidence only—and moved to bring her before a magistrate. However, she eluded us and disappeared."

"A counterbribe?" Bradan said. "In all events, you did your duty and chased off demons and took no inappropriate sums to do so."

"Running afoul of those armed men partaking in devil's rituals surely should teach me better behavior," he continued. "Ah, finally, here comes a priest. Let him purify the street."

Tintagel a block away let loose a growling bark. The guardsmen melted away in the direction they'd come and the priest hastily made the sign of the cross, uttered a short supplication in Latin, and moved after them accompanied by the watch captain calling out the Lord's Prayer.

Botticelli crossed himself. "If the priest flees, we should, too. I won't hear more about this adventure."

They all walked quickly back toward the studio through Florence's nighttime streets, looking behind themselves frequently. Would an evil creature stalk them?

"This is a city of sinners and beauties," Luca said.

"You're learning fast," Bradan said.

"It's Lauds," Botticelli said to Bradan. "Resume your work on Flora. We remain behind on *Primavera*. Your painting of la Veronica is ready to be transferred to the main work?"

"After one more sitting with the lady later this morning."

* * *

Veronica Varano sat in the same position as he'd painted her yesterday. Bradan added the final touches, details only he would know existed in her portrait, but were all the more important because of this.

"I met Marco," he said from behind the portrait. "Unfortunately, he'll live, but he'll hurt for a while. He ran into my sword."

"Natalia tells me of an unholy confrontation near the river." Veronica nodded toward her maidservant, who hadn't altered her forbidding expression one iota since yesterday.

"Servants are the eyes and ears of the city," Bradan said. "Often in surprising ways."

For privacy they spoke in Latin again, and it came easily as if they'd grown up with it playing as children at the height of the Roman Empire in a villa overlooking the Mediterranean. Indeed, the language felt at once comfortable and evocative of a different time and place.

"I believe you were one of my unexpected allies last night," he said. "An unknown person offered the city watch enough florins to ignore Marco's bribe. The watch intervened at a timely moment."

"You helped me," Veronica said. "I wanted to help you, but, as it happens, I was unable to have any of Lord Lorenzo's retainers approach the city watch's captain. Lorenzo ordered everyone to shelter behind our walls due to concern about civic unrest. So someone else outbid Marco. It seems you have any number of unexpected allies in Florence."

Bradan looked away from the portrait, startled. "I've lived here long enough to have many friends in the city, but none of them would have known to approach the watch with gold last night."

"Yet another tale to add to your legend. You are indeed mysterious." She sat forward. "Tell me what happened during the fight."

Bradan described his duel including enlisting Botticelli's apprentices to distract Marco's mercenaries with eggs. He only became vague about his spell-craft.

"You may have heard the last of him, but I haven't," he concluded. "He'll survive despite his wound, but he can't stay in the city. He's now suspected of witchcraft and bestiality. Whether he'll pass his information about you on to others or the Pope himself to force you to spy on the Medici household, I don't know, but perhaps not. There is endless fighting between the Papal States and Naples, between Florence and Venice, between everyone and the Turks. Sixtus simply has a lot to oversee."

"Swordplay, witchcraft, flying eggs—against this pageant, I'm hardly worth considering," she said.

"In Florence, it's complicated," he said. "Here's another complication: Marco found out about your mixed parentage. Who would know that about you? Probably the same individual with access to your rooms to deliver his threats. A personal servant long in your employ would be ideal on both counts."

Veronica looked disconcerted, then thoughtful. At last she said, "When I started getting notes, I suspected her yet she's served me well for years, so it didn't seem possible. I didn't want to believe it."

"You're still vulnerable on this issue. Consider parting ways to protect yourself."

"Or I should push a knife through her eye while she sleeps." Her Latin had transitioned from literate to flat and hard. "If this plot had succeeded, it would have brought me untold misery."

"Well, a knife in the eye would be in the long tradition of Florentine solutions to trust issues, but try a less permanent solution first."

"For an apprentice painter, you see a lot."

"Observation is art's foundation," Bradan said. "And after *Primavera* is done, my days as an apprentice are finished. I'll depart Botticelli's studio. I've developed a following of my own, and between that and my business and diplomatic activities on behalf of the Medicis, I've become prosperous."

Bradan set down his paintbrush. Done.

"Can I look at the finished portrait?"

186 PETER W. BLAISDELL

"Why not come over to this room to look at it closely?" he said. "We've made a show of observing social rules, but my work is finished, so there doesn't seem much harm to your closely inspecting it."

Veronica nodded and, without a glance or a word to her elderly maidservant, strode from the sitting room she'd occupied. In a moment she stood next to him before the painting.

"Ah, Bradan, I sat for you under false pretenses. I was desperate and the art masked my true reason to meet you, but seeing your work, you've flattered me with a beautiful representation."

Bradan nodded thanks.

"I had your complete attention only until it was finished," she said. "I suppose that's the nature of things between a painter and subject."

"I'm not that inconsistent. Whenever I see it, I'll remember you. It gives you immortality of a sort."

"Of a sort," she said wistfully.

"It captures not just how you looked when it was painted, but, for me, the memory of how it was to paint it." He laughed and added, "And you're clothed as I promised."

She laughed too. "Yes, as you promised. Thinking about it, I should have asked you to portray me showing off more of my form. That might secure me better marriage proposals if the artwork caught a rich merchant's eye. The family wants to get me off their books."

"Since this is your second marriage, can you choose a man you like—and who is suitable, too, of course?"

Veronica appeared surprised.

"What did you learn in Padua's libraries? Of course, it would be good to like him, but it's more important his family has wealth and a good lineage. That enhances the stature of both

my and his families and the children will have the benefit of
the reputations of both. Given my own unfit parentage that I
must keep a secret, that's particularly important to me. However, for the next suitor they propose, I'll insist on having a say
in selecting him. I can't do worse than they did in choosing my
first husband."

"So we'll entertain no delusions of passionate love," he said.
"The painting is a practical way to display your charms to Florentine society."

"This may find me admirers if they know I was the model; do
you believe anyone will look at it a generation from now?"

"This face *should* catch anyone's attention who sees the work
now or whenever. Your Flora anchors the whole piece and it will
be an astounding work. The features are entirely different from
the other figures."

After a pause he added, "Regarding whether anyone *will*
actually see the finished *Primavera*, it's probably going to hang
in a forgotten gallery in a country palazzo with only dust for
company. However, the creative effort matters more than its
fame on completion."

"I pray obscurity isn't its fate," Veronica said.

"I'll also pray it isn't forgotten," he said. "The work is too good
for that. So is the model. This woman has seen a great deal, but
doesn't let it lower her. And she knows more about the viewer
than the viewer knows about her."

CHAPTER 7

Politics as Usual

February 1967, San Francisco

Killing always felt the same, though there were infinite ways to slaughter someone, gut his father with a sword, shoot a crossbow bolt through the neck of a fleeing citizen during a melee in Renaissance Florence, or quickly loop piano wire around the neck of a young woman, adroitly pushing her long blond hair out of the way so as not to impede the wire's progress as it sliced through her windpipe and carotid arteries while he wore thick gloves to avoid cutting his hands with the garrote.

Van reflected that in the past, the distinction between butchery in battle and murder in peacetime wasn't precise; violence was common to both, and a Roman-Celtic warlord, or a fifteenth-century mercenary captain in Florence, could determine whether a person lived or didn't on a whim. However, modern "civilized" expectations forced him to be more circumspect. These days peacetime killing was murder, and murderous necessity was created by this woman, one of his congressional staff, getting pregnant—he assumed the kid was his—and threatening to wreck his political career, alert the press, go to his wife, and inflame the vox populi. That couldn't happen, and the solution was to remove the threat.

Moderns had trouble thinking in such terms, but a sixth-century Briton like himself only considered practical issues: Did she belong to a tribe that would exact vengeance? Was she valuable enough to live despite the trouble she presented? Could her body be disposed of unobtrusively? Merlin, meddling as he was, would have counseled tamer choices, or gotten Arthur to intervene, but the wizard and Arthur were so long gone Van barely remembered them.

There was a lot of blood, but only a little noise, just the girl's surprised chirp and then a sigh as he yanked the garrote tight, almost decapitating her. He wondered if Gwyn would stop by to collect the woman's stray soul, but hers was probably too inconsequential to notice. He looked up at the night sky—no airborne pack of the damned loitered about, just stars and a moon mostly blotted out by the marine layer that touched the East Bay's marinas where he'd motored from an hour ago. It was dark and coldly breezy, and the Bay Bridge lurked indistinctly south of him like a fantastically large Roman aqueduct with arches that spanned leagues.

Van returned to more prosaic considerations. Doing the deed on the boat was a pragmatic choice. The corpse could be disposed of easily into the nighttime San Francisco Bay. He could clean his thirty-two-foot Pearson Vanguard with seawater and bleach without drawing attention to the ablutions that any well-cared-for boat would get upon returning to the dock after a jaunt on the Bay. And there weren't many other craft out at this time of the evening to notice unusual activities.

Fifteen centuries of living made Van confident he could predict anyone's behavior, including what would entice Barbara to join him tonight, so he'd suggested they share a joint and wine under the stars on his boat and plan ahead for when he'd divorce his wife—shortly—and propel his political career on an ascendant trajectory with lissome, blond Barbara at his side. Van didn't think aspiring to the presidency was aiming too high. They'd shared other sojourns on the craft, *Camelot*, so Barbara was comfortable on the sailboat and helped him cast off with the assurance of a seasoned mariner. She wore sneakers for the slippery fiberglass deck and a windbreaker over a less practical beige miniskirt.

Van hadn't raised the sails since he planned a short trip and *Camelot* made good speed with only its motor. Modern boats were a wonder compared to the watercraft he'd sailed on over the centuries, many powered by oars with their clumsy, thick-timbered hulls rotten with worms. The Pearson was fast, nimble, dainty, a little like Barbara.

To mask any sounds of violence, a transistor radio loudly serenaded them with KMPX's psychedelic anthems to love and peace. As it transpired, the killing went so quietly, the radio's background noise was superfluous.

Looking down at the body, he regretted not screwing her before the murder and considered having sex with the corpse. However, he had a late-night interview to tape for tomorrow's early commuters; so, it was over the side with Barbara after tying a length of thick wire around her ankles and securing the other end to a portable power generator. The generator weighed a ton, but he lifted it easily and heaved it overboard, standing clear as the corpse also went over the side and splashed after the generator, down many fathoms to the seafloor below.

He knew she had relatives, but none lived in California and the woman only sporadically contacted them. She had wanted a clean break from her Midwestern roots. Conveniently, she was alone in the world and uncared for—like many moderns.

The last time Van visited her local apartment for a tryst, he'd surreptitiously looked for any signs of their affair. He'd pocketed these including a small framed picture of them together at Stinson Beach. Barbara looked spectacular bursting out of a yellow bikini. She had casual, local friends—a few on his staff— but none had any notion of their relationship and it would be a day or two before they even wondered why she hadn't turned up at the office. She had the reputation of a free spirit untroubled by disciplined work schedules. Of course he'd be as baffled and alarmed as any of them at her absence.

With no Gwyn and his hellhounds to see her off, Van stared at the choppy water and said a few words of a Dark Ages Christian burial rite, threw the Stinson Beach picture into the Bay, then walked aft to steer *Camelot* back to Emeryville's marina. He'd name his next boat *Barbara*.

* * *

Interviewer: "The honorable Van Newman, three-term congressman from a district that spans parts of Contra Costa, Lake, Solano and Sonoma counties, has joined us for a chat about his vision for California and to share his plans for next year's election. Welcome, Congressman. Let's start out with the obvious question: You've got an accent. Where's that from?"

Van (laughing): "Thanks for having me aboard, Paul. I get that question a lot. What brought me and my family to California was the promise of a better life, and I think we've achieved that, so I've made it my mission—my passion, actually—to share that opportunity with everyone from my district and across the state."

Interviewer: "But the accent?"

Van (still laughing): "You won't give up, will you, Paul? I lived outside the States as a kid, in Britain and all over, actually. If anything, it makes me feel more Californian and I also have a real appreciation of history thanks to living abroad."

Interviewer: "Okay. What are the biggest challenges facing California?"

Van: "First, crime. Violent crime is on the rise with murderers roaming free. They literally have no fear of being caught. It's shameful. So I'd propose stiffening sentencing guidelines and providing more funding for prison construction. Second—and this relates to my first point—drugs. Marijuana use is rampant. Let's boost penalties for those caught with even a single joint. Drugs and criminality go together. And third, as Governor Reagan says, 'Let's clean up the mess on university campuses across our state. Berkeley is the worst, but they're all fundamentally the same, including southern California institutions. We see nothing but demonstrations. You have to wonder what they're teaching in classrooms or even if they're teaching at all, but there's no wonder whatsoever about who's paying for it. We, the taxpayers, are. There needs to be accountability."

Interviewer: "You've won all your congressional elections by wide margins. Next election is more than a year off, but can you lay out your strategy for our listeners?"

Van: "Last year, it was a surprise my opponent died suddenly in the middle of the campaign—I'm not sure they ever found out what happened to him—and there was a scramble to nominate a replacement and confusion among voters as a result, so

I can't take full credit for my decisive victory (chuckles modestly), but I'm sure the other party will be better prepared in '68. And so will I. Voters like my direct approach to resolving problems. 'Newman, a new man for troubled times.' One of my young staffers came up with that slogan, but the message resonates with voters of every age."

Interviewer: "Thinking beyond the next congressional race, I'd love to hear your thoughts about running for higher office."

Van: "I'm glad you asked, Dan. I'll play coy on this one and I'll only say that I'm keeping every option open. It's been so much fun serving my district, but doing that on a bigger scale would be a way of giving back to a country that's given me so much."

Interviewer: "So a run for the presidency isn't out of the question?"

Van: "Everything's on the table, but of course my congressional district has my undivided attention at the moment."

Interviewer: "Congressman, I think that's a wrap. Thanks very much for your insights."

Van: "Always a pleasure, Dan!"

Interviewer: "My name's Paul."

Van: "Oh, sorry, Paul! Well, then a pleasure, Paul! The mic is off? It is? Good. I parked by a hydrant in front of the station. I was running late because of an earlier commitment. I'm sure it's been ticketed by now. I'll leave that with your station to pay off. I'm in a rush. I've got one more meeting tonight."

* * *

Bradan saw the big man shove his way through the Fillmore's patrons milling about in the jammed lobby waiting to go upstairs to the music. The man stood a head higher than the crowd and was as broad as a barn door. His size was his weapon; he bulldozed through them, leaving a swath of angry and stunned concertgoers in his wake. Along the way he bodily lifted a skinny, long-haired usher who tried to intercept him and threw the young man out of the way into the press of kids. Gallant boyfriends seemed ready to challenge the juggernaut after they and their girlfriends were roughly pushed aside or stepped on, but then they assessed the big man, decided against valor, and, instead, satisfied honor by shouting vulgarities after him.

The man's thuggish behavior didn't match his expensive camel hair topcoat over a tailored black suit and blue tie. He was clean shaven, with a strong chin, and he combed his brown hair straight back to just brush his ears—this was an individual concerned with appearance and grooming in contrast to the crowd of disheveled kids he plowed through like a tractor rolling across a wheat field.

Now the intruder was on top of Bradan, Taryn, and Gail.

He means no good, Bradan thought, stepping forward to meet the interloper, expecting violence.

"Medraut," he said. Recognition came in an instant and years dropped away. He remembered their brutal fight in Corvalle Mesa's prison.

Now he expected savagery.

"That's not my name any more," Van said.

"It's your name. Shit stinks whatever it's called."

How'd he find me? Bradan thought.

"Fighting didn't work for you last time we met," Bradan said.

The big man swung a fist at Bradan's face. The blow came out of nowhere and was thrown hard by someone who'd hit many people, but Bradan ducked instinctively then straightened and counterpunched, catching Van's shoulder—a clumsy blow, but it pushed Van stumbling backward into the crowd, knocking over people like bowling pins. By then everyone around realized this was serious and scrambled to get out of the way, but the press hemmed them in, creating a tangled mess centered about the fight. Bradan prepared to swing again. Gail yelled at them to stop and Taryn looked stunned, but then recovered her poise and coolly pulled Gail away from the struggle.

"You're better than you used to be," Van said, thrusting his way back through the onlookers to get at Bradan.

"Better than when? Corvalle Mesa? Córdoba? Paris? Or how about Florence?"

"Better than Cadbury."

"Too long ago to matter," Bradan said.

"Take it outside," the promoter screamed at them. He'd jumped down the stairs through the crush of concertgoers to burst into the brawl, still carrying his clipboard. "I'll call the police on you assholes. No one busts up my hall."

"Call them and they'll shut your place down," Van shouted.

"You're threatening me." The promoter turned red, then white.

"The police will take my word over yours. Your ballroom is a public nuisance with the noise from the music and these kids pissing in the street and smoking dope. You've got no friends in the SFPD or the local unions, but those groups love me."

"You can't touch me or this place of business. I've got permits."

"I'm a congressman, Van Newman."

Insane, Bradan thought. *How could a sixth-century relic flourish as a modern congressman? Maybe not so insane. Van has the amorality needed to propel his political career as far as he wants to go.*

"What happens if I bring your operation to the attention of the IRS?" Van asked. "Or California's tax authorities? You're not giving out tickets, just collecting cash from everyone heading upstairs. But what about record keeping and how much income from the gate you're collecting and the sales tax you pay—or don't pay—on the receipts?"

Bradan saw a police car roll up just outside the front entrance on Geary Street. This had to be a coincidence, since he didn't think Van had made good on this threat to summon them, but their arrival would make his bullying more real to the promoter. It might also inhibit Van from further violence.

"Please just leave," the promoter said. Now he talked quietly. "You have a beef with Bradan, but you can't fix it at the Fillmore." He looked out at the arriving cops and up at Van. "Let me know when you're here next time and I'll waive your ticket price."

"I save three dollars," Van said. "Generous. We'll talk about what your take is for these shows. I'd like to share. Peace, love, and sharing, that's the age we live in."

The promoter glared at him, but didn't talk back.

"For now, I'm going," Van said. "I'll return."

He grabbed Bradan's arm and tried to drag him toward the front entrance.

Bradan shook loose. "Outside," he said. The crowd cleared a path to let them exit. "How about we talk right next to the cop car?"

"You too, Morgana," Van said. "I've also got things to say to you. You've avoided me to be with him. He's just a target." He nodded at Bradan.

"You look better than ever," Van told Taryn. "You change your appearance when you ride with us, dear aunt. It's the clothing. When you hunt, you don't wear any." He laughed raucously.

"I'm Taryn."

"Pretty name," Van said. "We all adapt to the times, but you're still Morgana."

Bradan watched Taryn. *Which one of the colliding, incompatible impressions I have is real? Is it Taryn creating a melody at a pool party; or sending a searing guitar solo out to the Fillmore concert crowd; or sitting across a kitchen table writing lyrics with me? Or is it Morgana riding a motorcycle like a fiend and joining the Wild Hunt stalking lost souls—apparently just for kicks. I've seen the parts of her that I wanted to see and discounted everything else, but now that's impossible.*

I'll talk to Taryn/Morgana later. Meantime, the police are here. Taryn can hold her own, but Gail needs protection from Van. How about me? Can I hold my own?

Gail had followed them outside to Geary. "You told us you're Congressman Newman," she said.

Van glanced at her for the first time since he'd surged into the scene.

"Leave," Van said. "Watch the music." He moved to push her away, but Bradan stepped between them.

"Chivalrous," Van said. "Not your style. You've run over the years. Merlin would be proud tonight."

"He's long gone," Bradan said. "He'd be in the way."

"I always thought so, too," Van said. "So, then, it's the two of us—and Morgana, Taryn, the witch, whoever she wants to be tonight. Work us a spell, aunt, Morgana, Taryn, witch with a magic pussy."

Taryn nodded at Gail. "She's an outsider."

"I'm to be quiet, then?" Van said. "Or what happens? Suppose I hit her?"

Gail's mouth firmed to a thin line. Bradan thought the borrowed shades worked in her favor, giving her an uncharacteristically hard look.

"You know," she said, "I always thought your politics were shit, but that was from a distance. Now I see you up close and you're exactly the jerk I thought you'd be."

"Oh, you want to be part of this, too?" Van said. "You have a name?"

"Gail. I'm not giving you my last name."

"Well, Gail with-no-last-name, since you know about my politics, I've just had a spot on my staff open up. I'll hire you."

"Won't happen," Gail said. "I teach history and political science at a college in the Los Angeles area. I'm not leaving."

"You're part of the problem, then," Van said.

"How did you find me?" Bradan asked.

"A young member of my staff—she was a big music fan, but is unfortunately no longer with us—mentioned that a talented band was playing the Fillmore tonight. She showed me a news article that had your picture in it. I'm sure you play no better now than in my father's court from days gone by, but Morgana was in the picture, too, so it was too good a chance to pass up."

A second police car rolled up, flanking the first vehicle.

The more the better, Bradan thought. *The cops will see Van's the psycho aggressor in this situation. They'll even take him in to their station.*

A shirtless man, waiflike and thin with ribs showing clearly, stumbled past, oblivious to the growing police presence and the crowd of concertgoers spilling out of the ballroom, then he threw up on the sidewalk, splattering the nearest cop car and kids. An aging, potbellied sergeant slowly pushed open the passenger door and stepped out of the car, being careful to avoid the vomit. He looked angry and disgusted at the out-of-control shirtless man. He pulled out his nightstick and prodded the vagrant's flank, but then noticed Van.

"You're Congressman Van Newman? What are you doing in these parts?"

"I'm asking myself that same question, officer. My constituents let me know things are out of control in the Fillmore neighborhood, so I guess I'm seeing for myself. My district is a little ways from here, but they're still worried."

"I'm worried, too. Wouldn't let my own kids come down here to this filth. The Haight's worse."

"I'm working with SFPD leadership to clean it up," Van said. "I met your chief at a conference in D.C. last month. He's a good man, sees the problems."

"You know," the sergeant said. "I saw you speak last summer at a police union meeting with a bunch of other Bay Area politicos. You were the only one who made sense. You said, 'Be honest about our problems and direct about solving them.'"

His partner had now joined him along with the two cops from the other car.

"Guys, this is Congressman Van Newman," the sergeant said. "He's one of our few friends in high places in these crazy times. He should run for president. Police would support you."

Bradan saw there'd be no chance of taking Van in on assault charges with this crew.

"Hearing from folks like you on the front lines is a perk of being in my position," Van said. "And it's crossed my mind to consider higher office. I could do so much more good if I had more authority. But don't let me stop you from getting on with your work. This ragged fellow would be better off in a holding cell. You could use your club to encourage him to hang out in in another city."

"Yes, sir. You caught my thoughts exactly."

The sergeant prodded the homeless man with his nightstick to get into the backseat of his cruiser, being careful not to directly touch him. Progress was slow and the fellow was disoriented and looked sick. The sergeant's younger partner jabbed the transient repeatedly with his truncheon before finally getting him completely into the cruiser. The policeman kicked the door shut.

One task accomplished, but with a cop's instinct for tension, the sergeant now focused on Bradan, Taryn, and Gail confronting Van.

"Anything more we can help you with, sir?" he asked Van.

"Thanks, officer. Don't trouble yourself." Van pointed at Bradan. "There's an old complaint between us, but I'll take care of it myself."

The police stared at Bradan, letting everyone know that if the congressman had a conflict with him, they did, too. Bradan's long hair made him particularly suspicious. The situation froze. After a moment the cops slowly got into their squad cars. The shirtless man, hands pressed against the window, peered out of the police car at Bradan. Tonight it wasn't the Wild Hunt that had snared an abandoned soul, but the SFPD.

"Later," Van said to Bradan in British Celtic. "We crossed paths before. I wanted to set eyes on you tonight. I will find you again."

Bradan hadn't heard his mother tongue in more than a millennium, and it took a moment for him to translate the big man's malign promise and to comprehend its meaning.

Still in Celtic, Van addressed Taryn, "There's nothing better than hunting with you, Morgana. It keeps me in touch with the times we came from. Today is pale compared to then."

Van walked onto Geary and hailed a cab parked a little beyond the police cars. He departed without a backward glance.

"What now?" Taryn asked in English.

"I go back upstairs and get my guitar," Bradan said. He exhaled, emptying his lungs in a whoosh. He concentrated on keeping his voice controlled. He needed to focus on the mundane aspects of his musical career that had nothing to do with sixth-century magic and murder.

"The headliner's set must be done. I hope the virtuoso hasn't broken my Gibson. Also, let's find the guy from ATCO or Elektra if he's still around. There's a deal to be done. And, tomorrow, I'll go bail out the guy with no shirt. He won't do well in lockup. He can crash at the house if needs a warm place to stay."

CHAPTER 8

The House in the Haight

No huge figure materialized out of the night and fog to snap Bradan's neck. It was just him and Taryn sitting on the porch steps. The wolf had come out to sniff at them earlier, but decided he'd steer clear of this conversation and padded back inside. Bradan felt comforted that he kept vigil somewhere.

Van would come after him, but Bradan didn't think it would be tonight. The son of a bitch would stretch it out to prolong the fun. However, Bradan didn't intend to go anywhere. He had a life balanced fruitfully between academics and music. Though he'd run before, this time he'd be the hunter and pursue the ass-hole. He should have punched his pen through Van's eye socket three years ago at Corvalle Mesa. It was personal for Van; it was personal for Bradan; and it would be face to face. Who would Taryn ally herself with?

"Let's talk," he said to her. "Start with what your name is—what it really is."

"I like 'Taryn.' It fits where my head's at now."

"So, Taryn, where *is* your head at?" Sarcasm drenched his question.

"Until earlier tonight, I thought it was in a good place."

"You keep yourself smiling by the occasional midnight jaunt with the Wild Hunt looking for isolated innocents to grab," he said.

More anger than he'd intended crept into his voice. He'd meant to keep this conversation nonchalant, like he didn't give a shit one way or the other about being stalked by specters and witches, but he remembered it vividly, racing along the Pacific coast a few years back with no hope of outrunning the mad pack capering at his heels.

He wondered if the .45 now stuffed into his jeans in the small of his back would punch holes in sky-borne demons. The gun was on short-term loan from a hash dealer living in his basement.

"You're not so innocent," Taryn said. "You've had centuries to get dirty."

Heavy, cold mist swaddled them and the rest of the Haight in an uncomfortable blanket. He felt moisture seeping into his clothing. This night had gone on forever, but Bradan reckoned it was near dawn, though he couldn't discern even a trace of light amid the elemental fog; the invisible houses on their block could have existed in a different county. They shared a bottle of Jack Daniel's for warmth and to take the edge off a tense evening. His senses felt dulled by the whiskey, but he couldn't detect its effect on Taryn. The enchantress was her usual icy, unflappable self. However, she too paused to periodically scan their surroundings and look up at the night sky. Even the witch seemed uncertain about threats.

"And you're sitting here, so you made it through that night safe and sound, right?" She talked quietly. "No one caught you."

"I rode a fast bike."

"You believe that saved you?"

"That and Tintagel."

"Your wolf is formidable," she agreed. "But you had inside assistance."

"You're going to say you helped me?" he said disdainfully.

"We'll get back to that after deciding what language to talk in."

"I've used dozens over the generations," Taryn said. "Tuscan Italian when I was in Florence about five hundred years back, Old Brythonic or British Celtic, Latin, Old English, Arabic. An eon ago, I spoke to Faerie's residents in their tongue. I still use it when needed. But modern English works for the here and now."

He nodded. "Old as I am—as old as *we* are—it's good to match a language to the setting. Anyway, no one's awake to listen in and they wouldn't believe it even if they heard us."

Gail slept on Jeff Dorsey's bed. The bass player had split for the Castro neighborhood with his boyfriend after the show. Bradan would sort out more-permanent arrangements in the morning, assuming Gail still wanted any part of him now that she'd had a taste of the San Francisco side of his life. He'd pulled covers over her as she drifted off.

His Victorian row house, dark gray with black trim, sat at 31¾ Belvedere near its intersection with Haight Street in the heart of the scene and a few blocks from where the Grateful Dead lived, played, and occasionally got busted. So far Belvedere hadn't been raided despite dusk-to-dawn bacchanals that spilled into the street and copious quantities of narcotics and psychedelics consumed with gusto by a strolling cast of minstrels, hippies, and petty criminals who visited and crashed on available couches, beds, and open spots on the hardwood floor. Jim Morrison, up from LA for the weekend, felt right at home when he'd slept there last year as The Doors were just getting hot. Bradan mused that it was a miracle the SFPD hadn't kicked in the front entrance yet. However, he wondered whether Van would sic the police on his home now that he'd located Bradan.

The "¾" in his home address confused mail carriers new to the neighborhood and must have been the whimsical inspiration of a loopy city planner when street addresses were assigned two generations ago. At the moment the fraction perfectly suited the inclinations of the building's inhabitants: not really fitting into the structured grid of city planning. It gave things an outlaw feel. Certainly, the electricity bill went way up the day the Pillars had moved in, plugged in, and started playing together. Noise complaints went up, too, from the neighborhood's few remaining middle-class families. Nerves were further jangled when Tintagel perched in the house's third-floor garret and randomly howled at the moon in its various phases according to a celestial schedule known only to the beast.

"Give yourself credit for leading us in a merry chase on the equinox," she said. "But the Hunters would have caught you when you were gassing up if I hadn't complicated things. In the redwoods, you *do* remember me riding between you and the rest of the crew, Medraut particularly? He would have hammered you to pulp."

Bradan looked at Taryn. She'd retrieved her aviators from Gail and wore them despite the gloom, but now she took them off. Her mocha-colored eyes glowed, faintly backlit. It was like a small pilot flame burned just behind her irises.

"So, you're the spear-woman," he said. "But you couldn't distract all of them by yourself. That's taking too much credit."

"Will this convince you?" Taryn held up her wrist, showing faint runes indented in the flesh. They matched his own.

"Courtesy of our mutual mentor." She laughed with a dash of mockery, but also affection for Merlin, or did he misread her sentiments entirely?

"He taught me quite a bit, spell-wise," she said. "Even the hunters don't usually cross me. Merlin should have warned you about girls like me."

"Actually, *I* warned *Merlin* about girls like you. He didn't listen." Bradan peered into the opaque, opalesque night again and reached behind himself to pat the .45 for reassurance.

"Different moods, different looks," she said. "When I hunt, I'll change clothes—or I don't wear clothes—I change the hair, but I never vary my eyes. Those are hallowed." She still had her shades off and, for the briefest instant, Bradan saw their muted glow change into a red-orange inferno. The pilot flame had ignited a blast furnace. Then they were soft mocha again.

"On hunts, I shift things besides the eyes a little, just a bit, but it's still me." She put the shades back on and smiled benignly at him.

Did he need the gun to defend himself against the enchantress? Maybe that was true, but the weapon seemed a paltry defense against the witch's arts. He remembered trying to retrieve Roman coins fifteen centuries ago in Cadbury while fleeing Medraut and the Wild Hunt. The witch's ambiguous role then worried him now.

"I like your bangs better when you're not hunting," he said.

"Really?"

Taryn recited six rhyming lines and a small mirror appeared in her hand. She regarded herself from several angles and touched her hair. The mirror vanished.

"You're right," she said. "I'll keep this look the next time I ride."

"And Van, Medraut, the shit, what's your situation with him?" he asked.

"My 'situation,'" she drawled his words extending the vowels. "My situation is, I'm his permanent aunt, his occasional lover, and his sporadic hunting companion. The hunting bit I do for myself. It's fun. Your blood really flows when you're riding through the sky, hell for leather, at midnight, it's killingly cold, but you're unstoppable. Does any of that bother you?"

"Just about all of it."

He reflected a moment. "Except for the fun bit."

"You've flown in wars, too."

"I was with the good guys. And it wasn't fun."

His guitar case was propped against the front stoop's banister. He'd gotten the Les Paul back with only the D-string broken. He leaned across her to unsnap the case and pulled the guitar out. It wasn't plugged in, so the chords he strummed were tinny. He threaded a replacement D-string into the instrument and tightened the tuning peg with his ear against the wood body, seeking perfect pitch for the new string. Everything that was happening to him belonged in a song or an album of songs—assuming he survived to compose the music. Listeners would figure he'd been tripping when he wrote the stuff.

"So why hang out with me?" he asked.

"I'm lonely. You've been around a while, so you know how that goes. Our paths have crossed from time to time, but I got a kick out of keeping who I was secret. I wanted to see what you were up to. This setting seemed right to reveal myself—all this creative weirdness going on in a pretty place."

"So you found me. When were you going to have told me who you are?"

"Sooner or later. I want to confide experiences, sensations, sharing adventures from across fifteen centuries, but I can't do that with a person who's just lived a few decades like regular folks." She gestured expansively, encompassing the mundane, mortal world.

"Who but you would believe the places I've seen?" she asked.

"And I like talking about spells," the witch added. "Sharing trade craft, what cadences work, but more than that, the part where it all comes together and you make something irrational and mad happen that could never have occurred without enchantment, sort of like great sex."

"You could confide in Van, your loving—and evidently fuckable—nephew."

"He's not reflective, no fun to talk to, a creature of urges and vices."

"No better than an animal," Bradan said.

"But that doesn't make him a simple animal, so don't think he's not a threat."

"I agree. This animal is a threat. He's got no rules except what he can get away with."

"Why's he so focused on you?" Taryn asked. "C'mon, share. I'm showing you my baggage."

"For starters, I embarrassed him in front of Arthur's court. You were there. Then I stopped him from getting a pile of gold coins in Cadbury. You were there too because you wanted the pile. Were you working together? Anyway, circumstances went downhill from there. After he killed your brother, Arthur, I told the Roman-Celtic tribes. They respected Arthur, so Medraut was hunted."

"I didn't instigate that feud," Taryn said. "But I didn't cry when Arthur died. I had complicated feelings toward him, I bathed his body as he expired—everyone should be presentable when they cross over and that responsibility comes with who I am, what I am."

"You have rules?"

"There has to be order."

She draped the chic scarf over her shoulders, tugging at it to arrange the silk just so. It seemed too diaphanous for warmth, only a fashion statement. The enchantress reclined back on the steps stretching out long legs, reminiscing about times long bygone.

"I didn't praise Arthur when the tribes lauded his life and lamented his passing," she said. "I couldn't bring myself to do it."

"I could," Bradan said. "As you say, there needs to be order. We had a good thing and then it was gone. Britain was invaded and fought over like a stag that a pack of hounds had got after. Medraut was on one side, I was on the other. Our histories have crossed like a double helix ever since, Andalusia when the Arabs ruled, Florence under the Medicis, he led a free company of mercenaries when I worked in Botticelli's workshop. We fought and he got the worst of it. I missed running him through with a sword and only gored his arm. Fighting's been a constant over the centuries even if I've preferred libraries and art." He paused then added, "And then there was a woman."

"Isn't there always? Was she like me?"

"No one's like you."

"I hope that's a compliment. Was she like Gail?"

"She was a cardinal's daughter."

"Interesting parentage! I've known any number of churchmen with offspring. Many of them were even up for bedding a witch as long as word didn't get around. It's all the praying and fancy vestments that drive them to it."

"You were in Florence while I was there?"

"Don't think I was chasing you! You flatter yourself. I arrived from France fleeing witchcraft charges. A composer admired me and wrote wonderful, romantic chansons about me. It was gratifying, but it caught the attention of the archbishop of Paris. He saw me, liked what he saw, and tried to seduce me. I rebuffed him and was declared a witch."

"Let's turn that into a Pillars song," Bradan said.

"Let's. And what about your Florentine woman? Is she worth a song?"

"I've already put her in a painting. Her name was Veronica."

"La Veronica." She rolled the vowels with Latinate inflections. "You wanted her. Did Van want her, too?"

"He did, but he didn't get her. I had something to do with that."

"And Veronica?"

Bradan thought back a long time, pulling forth buried memories, blowing dust off an old volume in a forgotten stack in a library.

"Don't talk about it if you don't want to," Taryn said.

"She died of cholera a little after the painting was done," he said. "She wanted children from a noble marriage, but that never happened. I should see the painting again, not in a picture book, but in person. I haven't been back to Florence in a while. It hangs in the Uffizi Gallery. It's Botticelli's work, of course, but the face of Flora is mine and I based that on Veronica. I suppose it was her shot at immortality. We joked about that when I painted her."

Bradan stopped and remembered how Florence had been. Taryn didn't interrupt.

Finally, he said, "They really don't live very long."

"True, but a few of them cram a lot into their short lives. The stained-glass picture in the front door?" She gestured over his shoulder at 31¾ Belvedere. "*Primavera?*"

"You know your art. I designed it and had a stained-glass craftsman make it. He does local churches. Of course, it's not as detailed as the original in the Uffizi, but it's my memory of her."

Taryn climbed up the steps to inspect the work.

"Did you ride with the Wild Hunt during the Black Death?" he asked. "There must have any number of souls to chase down."

"That would have been scavenging, not hunting."

"Another one of your rules?"

"Live prey is more fun."

"Gwyn collects souls," he said. "You collect them, too?"

"They're usually not worth the bother. Besides, where would I put them?"

"It's the hunt itself that entertains you."

Taryn nodded. She pulled the aviators off and favored him with a second glance into the furnace. Then she put the sunglasses back on.

"And now, what will you do about Van?" she asked.

"Most recently, I met him in 1964 in a prison cell, of all places. It was touch and go for me, but he got the worst of it again. I've waited for him to come back. He just wears a suit now instead of mail armor. No damn way I'm hiding, but, lord knows, I can't figure out his timing. I'm sure he knew he could find me anytime it was convenient for him. I thought he'd be after me sooner, except he's been busy pumping up his political career. That's worked based on the cops' respect for him. He seems to be thinking of a presidential campaign. Once a petty chieftain, always a petty chieftain—actually, he's not so petty anymore. I think he's gotten very comfortable in today's world, so he hasn't been in a hurry—but Gwyn's probably goading him to get on with it. So today he's gunning for me again and I go after him. I didn't kill him the times before. This time I do. I have to figure out how. Who will you help?"

"I didn't instigate this feud," she said. "And I'm nobody's girl but my own."

"It's wonderful you're sitting this one out."

"Sarcasm, I like that in you," she said.

Bradan looked over at Taryn. "You said you spoke Tuscan Italian? I remember my duel with Van in Florence. It was a night of odd events, but here's the oddest: Van put the fix in by bribing the city guard to give him and his thugs time to kill me, but someone counterbribed them to intervene rapidly. The guard captain said it was a dark-haired foreign woman. Know about that?"

"Lots of dark-haired women in Italy," she said.

"You were in Florence at the time."

"I've said I wasn't following you." Did he see the witch smirk ever so faintly?

"Still," he said. "It was convenient that someone interceded on my behalf or I might not be sitting here tonight."

"Let's hope you stay lucky that way," she said. "You packing?"

Bradan nodded. "Zorro's piece. It's loaded."

"Show me."

He pulled the Colt .45 out of his jeans and carefully handed it to her.

Taryn checked the thumb safety, racked the slide back ejecting a fat slug, dexterously caught the bullet, and pushed it back into the magazine before palming the magazine back into the handgrip and chambering a round.

"Keep it close," she said.

"For a witch, you know your handguns."

"Spells don't always work when you need them to. I've handled flintlock pistols back in the day—one of them saved me from being burned at the stake—and all sorts of stabbing and cutting weapons before guns arrived."

She passed the automatic back to him. "This won't be enough. Sure, my nephew's more of a princeling than a prince, but in modern times he's powerful because he fits in so well as a politician. He's adaptable and he's adjusted to circumstances wherever he's lived, and he's smoothed away the obvious rough edges. No one looks below the surface as long as he's agile enough not to be caught at whatever shit he gets into or glib enough to talk his way out of a jam if he is caught."

"He's intimidating, but I've got more than a borrowed gun."

Bradan pulled a knife out of his boot and threw it at the wooden banister by her foot. The blade hit hard and lodged with a thunk. He wrenched it free with an effort and put it back in his boot.

"You did that trick in Cadbury," she said. "It amused Arthur's guests as I recall."

"And there's more." Bradan spoke five rhyming couplets. A wash of flames burst off the sidewalk in front of the porch as if a five-gallon can of gas had been upended on the concrete and a lit match tossed onto the fluid. The inferno was big and bright enough to cut through the nearby fog and illuminate neighboring row houses and splash orange on their windows.

Taryn made a theatrical show of cowering in fear then approached the flames. She passed her hand back and forth through the fire and finally held it steadily in the center of the flames.

"Pretty," she said. "It'd be nice if it were real. Then we could warm up."

Scorned, the conflagration guttered out.

Fatigued, Bradan slumped back against the steps. "I'm refining the spells to make them more potent."

"You've always been good with images," the witch said. "But you have a ways to go."

"Sarcasm, I like that in you," he said. "I might improve if we shared notes on spell-lore—if that doesn't compromise your neutrality."

"Maybe. Any other thoughts about how you'll take him out?"

"The Florentine way: low cunning, unexpected allies, and fast work with a weapon."

"I know that way. It's your only chance."

"How's Van even here?" Bradan asked. "Merlin for sure didn't extend his life."

"Gwyn."

"There must be a quid pro quo," he said. "What does Van give back?"

"Souls. You could say he's a local representative for the Hunters in the modern world. There's certainly plenty of slaughter; humans love carnage even without gods egging them on, so there's no shortage of spirits to collect, but it's a confusing age for Welsh deities to figure out. Van helps direct business to them. And he's facilitated strife wherever he goes since that leads to a higher body count."

"Excellent."

"My nephew's an opportunist who gains from the relationship," the witch said. "I can't quite capture it in English, so let's try an older tongue."

"No need for modern terms. I'm no more modern than you."

Taryn switched to British Celtic and nodded to herself at the aptness of the linguistic transition. "Gwyn is Medraut's liege lord and Medraut is Gwyn's pledged man. A covenant joins them. Part of the covenant is delivering your soul to Gwyn. Your soul has value beyond most to Gwyn, as you were Merlin's protégé. Merlin is long gone, but gods have infinite memories and he hasn't forgotten you."

Bradan sighed and responded in English, "So by taking on Van, I'm tangling with a Welsh god of the Otherworld and his legion of the damned."

"That's pretty much it," Taryn said. She seemed amused by it all. "They chased us in Laurel Canyon, just the two of them. Next time they'll bring the entire Hunt with them."

Bradan said, "Just how is it that you ride with this outfit?"

"I'm a member of Faerie in good standing. That comes with privileges."

Bradan looked east and saw the fog beginning to lighten. He stood up to stretch and saw dawn's rays brushing distant tree-tops in Golden Gate Park a few blocks away. Bradan wondered if fairies romped and frolicked amid its nighttime glens with Taryn choreographing their dances. That would explain the surreal lyrics she was fond of inserting into songs. That or the LSD she took.

"It's morning," he said. "Let's go inside. I've got ideas for music full of images of fifteenth-century Italian paintings, and hunters, too, and fairy folk—now that we've established you're Morgana le Fey."

"Don't forget your guitar," Taryn said. "We share writing credit and royalties on this one."

"Sure. We'll crank the Marshalls and shake the neighbors out of bed. If Van's looking for me, he just has to listen."

CHAPTER 9

Pillow Talk With a Demon

"Let's ride," Bradan said.

He rarely saw the witch surprised, but she stared at him now.

"Just the two of us?" Taryn finally asked. She laughed at the craziness of it. "Why?"

"It looks like fun. Also, I've been chased by Van too often. To beat him, I need to understand him better and his sponsor, his liege lord, this Gwyn thing. It's been touch and go when Van and I have tangled so far; just luck got me out of sticky spots. He manipulated circumstances to get at me in Corvalle Mesa. That was a mess. I could lose next time, permanently lose, but that's not going to happen. I have lame spells, but we're going to compare notes and improve the magic. A hunt seems a good place to start."

"We'd be noticed by the wrong crowd."

"Gwyn? We ride right now, during the day. I don't understand the ins and outs of it, but I think the Wild Hunt can't happen in broad daylight so he won't even know. You like rules, at least when they suit you. Well, I bet there's no rule in this world or the Otherworld that keeps us from riding—just us—with the sun up, just for the hell in it."

Taryn considered, then nodded guardedly.

"We'd need mounts," she said. "These aren't petting zoo ponies. They're not even exactly real."

"Golden Gate Park. If we look hard, there might be a few there."

"You followed me?"

"Last night before we talked, you wandered over to the park about 2:00 a.m. Probably trying to blow off steam after the shit that went down outside the Fillmore. I followed you, just curious. As you once said in Cadbury, 'Don't be accusatory. You weren't being private.'"

"I didn't think I'd be tailed," the witch said. "What did you see?"

"Unreal horses—among other things."

"You move quietly when you want. Well, no matter, you're right. There's a local outpost of Faerie in the park complete with its own troop of equines."

"They're at your beck and call?" he asked. "Sort of a cosmic relay station for the weary Wild Hunter, snap your fingers and here are fresh mounts?"

"They'd never loan horses to Gwyn. The locals don't get on with him. When he brings his hunters out this way, he's poaching on their turf. It didn't go over well when he tried to run you to ground on Highway 1 in '64. Not that they care about you one way or another. It's a territory thing and there's friction. But I'm friendly with everyone, Gwyn, the Golden Gate crew, so we can work it out today. You ever ridden a destrier? They're bred for war and quite a handful."

"I rode them in times gone by." Bradan was irritated by Taryn's condescension. "I've been around a while like you."

"These horses aren't ground bound. And they're fast as thought," the witch said.

"If they aren't 'exactly real,' can they carry my 'real' weight?"

"They've carried beings far heavier than you. You *do* realize you're moving in three-dimensions though the air."

"Give me your tamest pony."

* * *

The underside of the Golden Gate Bridge swooshed overhead. The horse didn't give the girders and enormous I-beams of the bridge's understructure much clearance and Bradan was splattered with dripping, salty moisture off the metalwork that was already rusting since the last paint job. He heard traffic right overhead, but by the time Bradan ducked, they had long since cleared the Golden Gate and soared over the Marin Headlands. A dense marine layer blotted out the sun suddenly, and then they punched through this and into a true cloud cover further up. He felt cold raindrops turning to ice and hail.

Bradan's beast continued to climb, proving its capabilities. An inexperienced rider meant it had free rein to follow its own inclinations. Bradan needed to change that perception fast as the climb became vertical with the destrier whisking ever upward, heading to the stratosphere where there was nothing but thin air and space above. Velocity and altitude made the temperature plunge. The clouds fell away far below. The witch was nowhere in sight; he'd lost her in his mad climb for the heavens. Instinctively he wanted to check instruments, air speed, altimeter, fuel pressure. It felt like he was in a P-51 with the canopy open, but his unearthly mount flew faster than his fighter ever had and with no apparent effort except that its nostrils flared wider. The Wild Hunters had toyed with him sadistically three years ago as they'd chased him; anytime, they could have swooped down to snag him like an osprey clutching after a salmon.

Reins, but no saddle, he thought. *I'm holding on to its neck and mane, about to fall off. Everything is slippery with rain. Does it need oxygen? I do.*

He yanked back on its bit, equestrian etiquette be damned. Anyway, this was no show horse, but a charger bred for war. The animal snorted and glared back at him, but its trajectory flattened out and Bradan settled onto its back as they followed a flat flight path. He looked down, but the height was so great he wasn't certain what he saw below. Was he in the "death zone" above which humans couldn't survive for lack of oxygen? That was around twenty-six thousand feet up. He felt elated but woozy, so he was probably near that altitude. San Francisco and the whole Bay Area were an indistinct brown, green, and gray sprawl mostly obscured by clouds along the coast and brightened by sun inland over Berkeley and other East Bay communities. Huge blotches of the San Francisco Bay broke up the land masses and, past the marine layer, he saw the Pacific.

Stupidly, he'd just worn what he'd played in at the Fillmore last night, jeans, boots, and a T-shirt. He'd tossed on his leather motorcycle jacket, but it was now sodden and no source of warmth. He felt behind himself with one hand, cautious about not losing his grip on this uncertain steed. Miraculously, despite the gyrations, the pistol was still stuffed into his jeans. He'd use it if the chance arose. His charger was armed, too. Though it bore no saddle, there was a sheath holding a lance strapped to the beast. Bradan hadn't seen a lance in seven centuries except in a museum. Maybe Faerie riders jousted for sport on moonlit nights over Golden Gate Park.

He urged the horse lower toward breathable air and warmth. There was a reason demons and witches did better with this mode of transportation than humans.

How could he handle the beast? He remembered his experience flying interference for B-17 bombers over Germany years back. His P-51 was fast and nimble and more than a match for the Messerschmitts that rose to meet them if the American pilot was good. Bradan thought he'd been pretty good.

He banked right. This was an odd blend of riding and flying; he didn't get the jolts he would have if he'd ridden a stallion on a trail. Unreal or not, he felt the horse breathe and exert itself. He felt its sweat. Periodically it looked back at him to weigh just what it could get away with and whether it could buck him off entirely. Its eyes were an abyss and looked right through him searching for a soul.

You'll need to look a long time for that, he thought.

Old instincts kicked in. He wasn't alone. Bradan scanned the sky. Danger came from behind when he'd flown over France and Germany. Close and getting closer, a passenger jet surged overhead. He heard it now, deafening.

Dive.

His destrier responded and they plunged downward. The 707 jet's slipstream buffeted them, almost brushing him off the horse. A saddle would help, but that was too civilized for demons.

Don't overcorrect.

His horse leveled off and he banked away from the jetliner into the marine layer. Had the pilots seen him? And what would they say? That they'd met Pegasus cavorting above the Marin

Headlands with a thug in a motorcycle jacket hanging on for dear life? His sighting would be ascribed to too much caffeine before takeoff and lousy visibility in a low cloud ceiling. He wondered if magic chargers registered on radar.

Van's home.

The horse didn't respond.

Medraut's home.

The local Faerie crew might distain the big man as one of Gwyn's minions and a trespasser, but they knew where he lived. Like a ground-bound horse on the way back to a familiar stable after lugging overweight, greenhorn day-trippers for hours, Bradan's mount shifted course to head east. Its speed increased enormously and Bradan crouched over its neck to avoid being smashed off its back by wind resistance. He clung for his life. The bay swept by far under him and then they were over Tilden Park's hills bleached green and tan by morning sunlight. The stallion angled down and circled above a subdivision with expansive ranch houses spiraling lower toward one in particular. Two Cadillacs and a Ford station wagon were parked in a wide driveway.

The good life, but not for long.

Will he be there?

Bradan held the .45 in his hand. He didn't remember even grabbing it. Time to put to the test Taryn's estimate that the heavy pistol wouldn't be enough to put lethal holes in Van.

Let's stir up the wasp's nest.

He pulled off a motorcycle boot, after securing the knife in his belt, and tossed the boot downward in a cartwheeling path to smack into the roof of the home below and bounce into the backyard by a pool.

Holding pattern fifty strides up.

His mount took a lazy turn over the home. There was no evidence of a response, so Bradan yanked off the other boot and threw it at an angle toward the front of the home to smash through a splendid bay window. The noise was enough to wake the dead.

The big man emerged, a bear from its lair, looking surprised and angry at this assault on his home, and not yet getting who was attacking his suburban palace. Then he looked up and saw Bradan.

Lower, just above ground level, and hold.

Bradan shot at Van twice. No preliminaries, this was a straight-up ambush. One bullet banged into the Ford, the other blasted through the front door. The .45 cannon kicked hard, but Bradan knew the weapon and recentered it on Van's head. However, he had become a moving target, a trained warrior rolling and tumbling toward the cover of one of the Cadillacs. Bradan fired again, hitting Van in the shoulder, but, Bradan estimated, not mortally. Nonetheless, he saw blood erupt and splatter the driveway and cars.

Yes! He's wounded, weak and slow. Swing directly over him for the kill shot.

The home's front door popped open and a small woman stepped onto the front porch. She looked dumbfounded by the activity. Van paid her no attention and crouched behind the big car's front bumper, his right shoulder drenched in blood and his arm dangling. The woman called to Van, then ran over to him. She looked up, saw Bradan, and brought her hand up over her mouth. Van stood and embraced her, though Bradan was sure this wasn't affection, but a frantic effort to use her as a shield. Indeed, it would be poor shooting now with the woman beside

Van and Bradan couldn't get a good angle no matter how he maneuvered his mount unless he killed her, too.

How much collateral damage can I tolerate?

Bradan screamed Celtic curses at Van. He thought of hurling the lance, but hunting was over for now. He urgently wanted to finish the job. Instead he veered upward and away from the home.

Hunting was addictive. All life's problems should be solved so directly, he mused. He stared down at the dwindling image of Walnut Creek below with its rows and circles of vast lots. He wanted to flatten the entire subdivision to erase Van. He'd return. Next time, he'd bring petrol bombs.

* * *

"Your bangs look phenomenal when you fly," Bradan said.

"The wind blows them to hell. It's the one downside of hunting." Taryn looked at him. "Talking of hunting, you came close."

"I didn't kill him. His staff will spin this as him heroically defending the woman he was with from a felon or madman out to get him. I can see the campaign literature already. He hid behind her."

"Still, he's out of commission for a while. And he'll have to explain flying horses to whoever she was. I shadowed you, just curious, wanted to make sure you wouldn't fall off."

"Would you have caught me?"

"I hadn't made up my mind. It's always fun to see what happens when a body hits after a really long fall."

"Messy, I'd assume. I almost got pulverized by a jet. That also would have been amusing."

"The plane caught me by surprise, too." She jumped off her horse and patted it, sending it off into the surrounding trees. Then she looked back to Bradan, saying, "Can I make a suggestion about hunting? Even when you're on a steed that can put you anywhere you want to be, planning helps."

He noted the witch stayed carefully neutral, not taking sides, just a detached observer offering tips from someone who'd done it many times before.

"It won't be mindless savagery next time," he said. "I couldn't help it today. Emotion took over."

"That's Gwyn's way, lose yourself to rage or whatever passes for feelings in a Welsh god. Set the horde free and see what happens. Someone else picks up the pieces."

"I wasn't completely out of control," Bradan said. "I didn't keep shooting because of the woman, his wife probably. I came pretty close, though."

"You have rules."

"Merlin's influence. I'll use the Florentine approach next time and plan ahead."

"Now that your blood's up, how about another kind of sport?" she asked.

Bradan reached over and ran his fingers through Taryn's hair. It was midnight black, long and wildly tousled from her ride. Would a witch's hair feel different? Her hair felt wonderfully smooth. He pulled her into an embrace.

"Too cold to play?" She reached down to stroke him. "Oh, you're not that cold."

"I'd love to play," he said. "But your fingers are frozen. Kind of a passion killer."

The enchantress blew on her fingers and placed them on his cheek.

"Warm as sipping brandy by a smoky fire," he said.

"Then let's play with a purpose."

They sat among redwood needles in a small clearing at the top of Tamalpais with the mountain and surrounding park to themselves. The smells of the trees and their resin saturated the clearing. He spotted distant fire towers, and an almost inaudible hum of traffic and urbanity intruded even here, but they were in a world remote from surrounding society.

The fairy destriers had vanished, reveling in a new wilderness. Bradan was cold in a way he didn't remember feeling since his youth in bleak, frozen Britain more than a millennium ago. Riding through the early-morning sky amid patches of dank marine layer with just jeans and a leather jacket had chilled him to the bone. However, the witch didn't seem discomforted at all.

"Let's go over here by the redwood," she said. "It's more impressive than the oak and bay trees. It shouldn't grow this far up the slope—they normally need more moisture so they're down in the fog layer—but this one does fine. The local Fair Folk tend it and there are nighttime dances here at prescribed times during the lunar calendar."

Bradan stood and extended an arm to pull her to her feet. He looked up. The tree was gigantic, stretching upward to the limits of his vision. They'd used it as a landmark to locate a quiet spot to recuperate after his excursion to devastate suburbia.

"Probably at least a thousand years old," he said. "But it's not the oldest thing on this hilltop. We are."

She nodded. "All the more reason to keep it safe. We're stewards."

"You're a naturalist?" Bradan said.

"It's my nature to revere wild spaces, another one of the rules I live by."

"You don't abide by many rules."

"Just important ones." She rubbed the redwood's bark like an old friend and looked up the trunk to branches above. "We try to protect them, much good it does. Humans are just pests munching through what was here before they arrived."

She ran her hand over the tree again and seemed to consider a moment.

"No splinters," the enchantress said. "Here will do. Maybe."

"Maybe what?"

She faced him and leaned against the tree shifting her back about to test its surface texture. She still wore what she'd had on the night before at the Fillmore. Now she kicked off her boots, and untied her long paisley scarf, which she'd used as a gypsy-style belt, and retied it around her hair creating a ponytail, then pushed her jeans down and stepped out of them. She pulled off her leather vest and the T-shirt and tossed them on top of the jeans. Then she put the vest on again so it protected her back and shoved her sunglasses up her forehead into her hair, a lioness unsheathing her claws. The intensity in her eyes ramped up.

Bradan pushed her vest open.

"You want to see?"

"Absolutely."

She pushed her breasts toward him. He kissed each in turn then undressed and kneeled between her legs and nuzzled her.

"That's really nice," Taryn said. She pushed herself into his face and moved her hips while he licked.

"No hurry," she said.

He took his time, sensing her look down at him then up at the sky visible through the branches and dust motes drifting about like fairy dust.

"A little further up." A while later she said, "Now hurry more, a lot more, yes—press really hard right there and nowhere else." He heard her exhale, stand on tiptoes, and tense all her muscles, her back pressed hard against the redwood, holding that tension, then releasing it with a half dozen contractions. She relaxed completely and draped herself over him. Then, recovering gradually, she pulled him upright to stand face to face with her.

"Put yourself inside me." She looked down. "You're ready. Can you make this position work? You're doing the pushing standing up."

"Can *you* make it work? It's you against the tree. Seems rough, even keeping the vest on to protect your back."

"Only one way to find out. Amazingly, after fifteen centuries and trying every position in the manuals—and many that aren't—I've never done it this way."

"Back to nature," he said. "It's smoother in this part, less splinters. Let's settle into this spot."

"So considerate of you."

He put his hands under her butt and lifted. Taryn hopped up slightly and spread her legs to help him push into her. She pulled his face into her breasts and held on to his shoulders while wrapping her legs around his thighs. Bradan thought the position was awkward at first, but she felt incredible and this swept other considerations aside and he moved in and out of her smoothly. He kissed Taryn's aureole. After their shamelessly crazy ride through the morning sky above the Bay, he expected a mad spell of lovemaking with the witch, but instead things paced themselves languidly. Sensuality tempered the ferocity. Sunlight swept down through a tear in the overstory and his back felt warm. His fingers felt the tree's sap where he held her against the trunk. They had all morning.

She breathed out a poem, then kissed him.

"I'm ready," he said. "I can pull out."

"Not a good idea. Keep going."

And he did until release. Taryn's eyes flared orange briefly and she used her muscles to milk him inside her.

"That was plenty and to spare," she said. The enchantress lowered her long legs until her feet touched the ground.

"You clawed my back." Bradan worked to catch his breath.

"You coupled with a witch. That should be special. We're connected to the animal side of our natures."

"And that's a good thing?" he said, massaging scratches she'd left on him. "What did you say a minute ago?"

"An incantation. It's one reason you couldn't pull out. The magic needed your contribution. Also, it was good to feel you spend. Thanks to our efforts, the redwood is protected now, not perfect, but anyone trying to cut it down may well find themselves forgetful about their intentions and wandering off to do other stuff."

"Not to be poetic," he said. "I just made an offering in a soft temple."

"Be poetic if you want, especially if the metaphor is about me."

The enchantress continued in a meditative vein, "It wouldn't have worked with just anyone."

"So happy to be special," he said dryly. "Would a second contribution seal the deal, incantation-wise?"

They uncoupled, but kept holding each other. "Yes," she said. "But that's ambitious. I worked to get everything I could out of you during the first round."

"A different position?" He looked around the glade.

"We need to stay close to the redwood." She turned around, facing the tree, and extended her arms to support herself against it and spread her legs.

"Would a spell help?" she asked, looking over her shoulder at him. "Okay, no need for a spell."

"Ready for round two," Bradan said. He kissed the nape of her neck. Taryn reached back and guided him in.

* * *

They napped together, lying on top of their clothing. It was cool in the glade, but not uncomfortable. Bradan awoke to see their horses. They were now familiar enough with him to graze close by. One of them stamped impatiently. It was afternoon. The pieces of the day assembled themselves in his mind.

"You're getting on well with the beasts," Taryn said sleepily. "They've quite taken to you."

"Trying to murder a person gave me credibility. I'm glad you lent me a tame one." He looked about the trees. "I got the feeling we had an audience while we played against the redwood."

"Maybe we did. Usually, the Fair Folk only come out at night, but they're voyeuristic."

"I think we kept them entertained."

"What happened to Gail?" Taryn asked. "She was at the house and then she wasn't." The enchantress reached about for her clothing.

"Writing songs with the amps set to ten at dawn chased her off." He got up and stretched hugely, running his fingertips over his tender back. "The rest of the house sure got pissed."

"Poor sports. They're good songs. We have the core of another album."

"They *are* good," Bradan said. "And I'd rather talk about you than Gail."

"It's just pillow talk. I always talk about other lovers after sex."

"I'm sure that does wonders for the relationship."

The witch shrugged. "Depends on how secure they are."

"She's sleeping with her department head," Bradan blurted. Now it was just out there to be picked over with the last person in the world he needed romantic advice from.

Well, let's just eviscerate my love life for everyone's amusement, he thought. *Usually I'm better with my secrets.*

"That's what she came up here to tell me," he said. "I don't think watching the Pillars had much to do with it, although she took our first album along with her. She headed back to LA this morning after making the bed."

Bradan thought for a moment. "She *did* fly all the way up here. I suppose that's better than just springing it on me when we next met on campus."

"Good riddance," the witch said. "At least she only hid it from you for a while and now we don't have to decide where she sleeps tonight. You had an inkling?"

"She's a better actor than you'd think, but I guessed weeks ago. Just body language, the way she was with him, the way she was with me, intangibles. I think she genuinely dislikes him, but what do I know about her feelings? She seems contemptuous of him, but she's masking that because she's desperate for tenure. So am I. This chairman guy, Chaffee, controls tenure review completely. Sleeping with him is the price for her. She'll do what she has to, to get what she wants. I hope does she get tenure. What I've seen of her research is really solid."

"Suppose you slept with him? You entertained me this morning. Do the same to him."

For a moment Bradan teetered between fury and laughter. He settled in the middle in a meditative place as the stronger emotions dissipated.

"It's happened a thousand times with me and women," he said. "It's issues within the relationship that sink it, or external shit, or both. I haven't gotten toughened about it, try as I might. When the relationship is durable we can go the distance, but then the immortality bit gets in the way. I have to pretend to age. It's a mess, but the bond can be so strong, it's worth it. And maybe there are kids, too. Then I'm a parent. For shorter flings, the woman may leave me, or I leave them. I went through a phase a few centuries ago where I only allowed myself significant relationships. Now I see value in the trivial ones, too. I try not to be with several women at once."

"You needn't worry about that with me! I could care less. Is Gail why you haven't tried to get into my pants until now?"

"Maybe you wouldn't have been interested."

"Maybe I would, but it just needed a good setting for the first time between us. A redwood grove is better than wine and candles."

"This morning was brilliant," he said.

"Also, I wanted you to know who I was before fucking."

"Another rule of yours?"

"I'm nobody's consolation prize. You know that." She tugged boots on over her jeans and stood up and pulled out Gail's pair of cat-eyed glasses. "I kept these. I don't know why."

She dropped them on the forest floor and beckoned her horse over and pointed to the glasses. The creature reared back and stomped downward with its front hooves. The earth around them shook. When the horse backed away, there were indentations several inches deep in the ground and no sign of Gail's spectacles except a few infinitesimal glass shards glittering back at him in the sun.

"Subtle," he said. "The hard part will be going to campus Monday, seeing her, seeing Chaffee, but I love the teaching and research side of my work. I'll try to avoid them."

"Yeah—I don't get that," Taryn said. "Merlin made you soft. You'll never beat Van if you have scruples. About this Chaffee bastard, why not ride down real soon, around 2:00 a.m., and rip his heart out, physically pull it out of his chest cavity right through the ribs. Listen to the bones snap as you take his heart. I'll loan you the horse you rode today. He's always up for a little slaughter. Occasionally we allow freelance work, lone hunts."

"An unsanctioned hit?" he asked.

"I can approve this one on my own authority."

Now Bradan did laugh. A dam burst. And he teetered right on the edge of accepting her offer then and there. Why not? The destrier was standing ready to ride at his side.

"That's mighty tempting, but I doubt anyone would want his soul. I'll deal with Chaffee in a way that doesn't involve Gail, but there are other priorities now, Van top of that list."

He encircled her waist with his arms. "We also have a record contract offer. Let's do the band meeting thing and twist arms to get a deal. We'll have Evan look over the contract language, too. I've no interest in being screwed by the label."

"I want our next album to go gold," Taryn said. She pushed her Ray-Bans down over her eyes, claws sheathed for the time being.

"Let's see how big we can make the Pillars," he said. "There's a concert down in Monterey in June. It's going to be huge. Three days over a weekend. Nobody's tried something on this scale for pop music before. Derek Taylor and John Phillips called and wanted to know if we could do Friday. There's a slot. What we wrote this morning will work in front of fifty thousand people. Nothing like a bad breakup to spur creativity."

CHAPTER 10

Meadows and Sunsets

March 1967, West Hollywood

"**H**e killed a woman," Meadow said.

"Who killed who?" Bradan asked.

"Her name is Barbara," Meadow said. "Her name *was* Barbara. She's in the San Francisco Bay now, a long way down in the water. Her body is. Her soul is in the same place as mine: halfway to nowhere."

"Why are you telling me this?" Bradan asked. "First, who was Barbara? Do I know her? *Did* I know her? Why should I care? There are a lot of bodies around. I'll be lucky if I don't wind up dumped in the Bay myself."

They rolled down Sunset Boulevard just as the day was transitioning into smoggy, ashy, evening beauty and it was dark enough for the neon on the buildings to contrast with the ambient orange-purple light of the setting sun. Traffic snaked along this curvy stretch of the boulevard with a string of red brake lights ahead of him as far as his eye could see. Passing the Whisky nightclub, Bradan gave the Harley gas to blast around a slow

Lincoln packed with kids in the back seat pressing their faces against the windows, taking in the bell-bottomed boulevardiers strolling past. Two parents sat in the front seat. The father glanced with hostility at Bradan passing him then stared out the windshield as they headed toward Beverley Hills. Bradan smiled placidly.

You think I'm the young enemy storming the gates of propriety, but really, I'm older than you can conceive.

Bradan looked at the club. It advertised go-go dancers. He was down here to meet booking agents and venue owners and pitch The Pillars of Creation. Doors were opening that hadn't before. If the Pillars could play the Fillmore, and had a pending major label record contract, the industry was beginning to realize they could draw a crowd in LA, too. Buffalo Springfield and The Byrds were at the Whisky. Bradan wanted to see the Pillars up there on the playbill, too.

The vibe on the Strip was totally different from San Francisco's Haight, but both were becoming false to whatever zeitgeist had birthed them, with buses pulling up in the Haight to disgorge throngs of tourists looking to be appalled by the hippies, and this stretch of Sunset crammed with a cavalcade of suburban kids hoping for glimpses of debauchery and license. The drugs of choice in both locales were also transitioning from grass and acid to Secanol, speed, and heroin.

Why seek visions if one could achieve narcoleptic oblivion?

"You care about people," Meadow said.

"Much good it's done me."

"You take in down-and-outers at your home in San Francisco."

"This Barbara—?"

"She didn't do anything to deserve it. She met the wrong guy."

"I'm not a very good paladin, as we both know." He sighed. "But tell me more if it makes you feel better."

"Paladin?"

"It means a knight in shining armor. I've known real knights and they didn't fit that image. They were people to avoid, not get help from. I'm no knight, but I'll listen to you about Barbara."

"One of the things that tried to get you on Highway 1 a couple of years ago killed her."

"Van?" The connection was instantaneous.

"I don't know his name. I saw him through her eyes as she died. He was very big. He was one of those riders who chased us. He almost chopped her head off. Then he just threw her into the water."

"Van," he said, a flat statement. "He's trying to kill me. I'm trying to kill him, came close a few days back."

Bradan had packed Zorro's .45 in one of the Harley's saddle bags. He'd cleaned and reloaded it after his failed assassination attempt. The weapon still smelled of gun oil. At the moment he thought he was safe with Van convalescing in a Contra Costa County ICU under police protection; the big slug had done damage. Bradan felt elation. A modest spell had allowed him to access the congressman's stationery. He'd sent a taunting "Get Well" card to Van on his own official letterhead.

"How do you know Barbara?" he asked.

"Before our crash, I knew her a little when she came out to California. We went to parties together. She kind of drifted around before running into this guy. Of course, we lost touch after the bike went down with me on it."

"Shit." Bradan felt salt rubbed into his psyche. He relived his crash with Meadow riding along as a passenger. He cut through traffic and pulled the bike over to the edge of Sunset and got off on the sidewalk at the border between West Hollywood and Beverley Hills. Bradan bent over with his hands on his knees trying not to think about anything at all and avoid vomiting.

"Don't use vulgarity. It's not cool." The ghost sounded like she'd just smoked a whole joint and the notion of urgency was beyond her, but she was very capable of conveying grief and guilt.

"I'm not trying to remind you of what's past," she said. "We've been through all that. I just wanted to say how I came to know her. Souls, spirits that don't cross over kind of associate. We're all in limbo together. When this guy murdered her, I just knew about it, I don't know how, maybe because we already had a connection."

"I'm trying to kill him. What else can I do?"

"That won't be easy. He's got powerful friends in this world and the next."

"Everyone tells me that. Shouldn't people be giving me support?"

"They should. I might be able to help."

"Moral support is appreciated." Bradan tried and failed to keep the irony out of his voice. Getting help from mild, sad, reflective Meadow was preposterous.

"You don't believe me." There was a pause. Bradan had an eerie sense Meadow conferred with others as insubstantial as herself. He heard whispers that could have come from a Gothic cathedral after the day's last mass had left the vast space to empty pews and shadows.

"There are a lot of them," she finally said. "But there are a lot of us, too. I can show you."

"Sure. Show me." This time, he didn't even try to keep dryness from his voice.

In the blink of an eye, he wasn't alone. Apparitions of every age, race, and description surrounded him as he stood next to the "Beverly Hills" sign flanking Sunset. They seemed to embody current generations and generations long gone, but all caught when they'd died. They flowed in masses off across the streets and jumbled up against buildings, at once heterogeneous and homogenous. Traffic passed through them unheeding and hip pedestrians sauntered obliviously through the shades. Though no one else sensed anything unusual, Bradan saw them clearly as washed-out images like a photograph left for years on a sunny windowsill.

A slender, young, blond woman in a windbreaker and mini-skirt, whom he intuited to be the recently deceased Barbara, stood closest to him. He could touch her if he'd wanted. She smiled a distressed smile that had once held the confidence of youth and drew a line across her throat with a forefinger.

Bradan saw Meadow next to Barbara. She also wore the clothes she'd died in.

"Do you want to talk to them?" Meadow asked. "They all have stories."

"Too many to hear with the attention they deserve," he said. "Please, stop this. What am I to do?"

"It's not just you against Van," Meadow said. "It would be prideful of you to think that."

"How does it work?" he asked. "Bad situations when they died, murder, crashes, violent ends? They all died around this area over the years?"

"They're all bound to this place because they died here, but they can go anywhere. None of them came to a peaceful finish surrounded by family and friends."

"They want to get even?"

"That's not possible. However they passed, it's way too late to change those circumstances."

"So it's not about personal vengeance, but I hit Van and Gwyn and that helps them?"

"Without their help, you won't succeed. Accept their offer." Bradan now heard uncharacteristic urgency in her tone. "Everyone deserves to pass on untroubled by things that want their spirits."

Bradan surveyed the spectral assemblage. "With all respect, this collection of lost souls doesn't look ready to tangle with Wild Hunters. They're just ordinary folks who died badly."

"They know who they will meet. I showed them who chased you down Highway 1."

A Pacific wind swept past him and the ghosts were gone. Barbara lingered a heartbeat after the rest to give Meadow an ephemeral wave. Bradan leaned against the bike.

"I'll take all the help I can get, but I'm not sure they'll be much use," he said finally.

"Hold your judgments." Meadow's image had vanished with the rest, but he heard her perfectly as always. "I'm owed that, don't you think?"

"Yes, you are. How is it I see them, but no one else does?"

"You have a young body, but with an ancient soul, so you see beneath the surface sometimes. Tonight I helped cut through your skepticism so you could take a peek."

"An ancient soul only gets you lots of bad dreams," he said.

"And you don't sleep through the night," she said.

"Nothing sleeping pills and Scotch can't fix."

Bradan got back on the Harley and jumped on the starter, cautious about moving away from the curb, worried he'd hit one of Meadow's kindred spirits who had been tardy about departing, but Sunset was clear and only occasional cars motored past.

"There is one thing I might be able to do for Barbara," he said. "It may help me, too, but no guarantees it works and I'd need information from you."

"What are you thinking?"

"If you know where your friend's body was tossed in the Bay because of your connection with her, I'll alert the police. They won't do much, because I'll have to make it an anonymous tip and it's a lot of work to send divers down to search in deep water without a solid lead to get the wheels of criminal justice turning. But there must be a missing person's report filed for her so there's official awareness that may make my tip more actionable. Also, I'll anonymously tell the papers. The *Chron* hates Newman, so they may be inclined to poke around themselves if I can give them enough background on Barbara to make it a reasonable lead. Media interest may goad the cops into searching."

"I know where her body is," Meadow said. "Will they arrest the congressman?"

"People like Van are almost always untouchable and there's probably nothing that links him with Barbara besides working in the same congressional office, but we can at least stir up questions. More important, your friend gets a proper burial assuming they actually look for and find her."

"That's respect, anyway," Meadow said. "One other thing."

"What?"

"Park me in the garage at night. It's cold and lonesome sitting on the street."

CHAPTER 11

All Tomorrow's Parties

March 1967, Claremont and San Francisco, California

elightful. I'll see both Gail and Chaffee at this bloody departmental party, Bradan thought. *Will they hold hands? Gail will be discreet, but maybe Chaffee will flaunt it.*

Don't be bitter. Jealousy is for losers. And purity is passé. Tough it out. Make nice with these cretins ahead of my tenure hearing.

Is that Chaffee's wife in a brown shift chatting up the dean and glaring over at Chaffee?

Jesus, this wine is horrible; I need Jack Daniel's to power through this get-together.

"Professor Bradan Badon—that name just rolls off the tongue—I'm so looking forward to your tenure presentation next Thursday," said Tobias Hackett. "The undergrads like you from what I hear and your research is getting attention. Folklore is out of my wheelhouse, but I've seen the reprints you sent around. They look strong. You even pulled in a grant from the National Endowment for the Humanities, better than most of this crowd."

Bradan wondered if Hackett would be an ally next Thursday. He was a pal of Chaffee and one of the oldest members of the department. Bradan understood that at one time, he'd done seminal work. No longer. His last significant contribution Bradan knew of had come out a decade back. Nonetheless, Bradan made it a point to flatter the full professor whenever he had a chance.

"Thanks, sir," Bradan said. "It's such an inspiration to hobnob with individuals who shaped their field of study."

"Please, Bradan, no need for 'sirs' among friends. I'm 'Toby' to you."

Did Bradan detect just a tad of condescension from Hackett? The fellow had a fireplug's build with little arms extending from a plump center. An image came to Bradan of a poodle urinating on the hydrant. Huge white muttonchop sideburns flanked Hackett's petulant mouth and pug nose. His nose had purplish veins, a real drinker's snout. He held a glass of wine in both hands.

"Good stuff, no?" Hackett said.

Bradan thought it was swill, but he clinked his glass convivially with both of Hackett's and sipped.

"To successful tenure hearings," Hackett toasted.

"Amen," Bradan said.

Keeping it casual, Bradan continued, "Toby, I've got a draft submission to a big history journal. It's about the presence of historical imagery in modern folklore. With the history angle, I wonder if you might consider joining me as a co-author?"

If all the professional ambition had leached out of Hackett to be replaced by gouty vanity and corpulence, then Bradan's offer would be swatted away as an impertinent effort to curry favor from a member of the tenure committee. But Bradan didn't think the old boar had quite given up on wanting to promote his name among academics actively doing research.

"An amusing thought," the old professor said. "It would be interesting to jump back into the game. I'd need to see your manuscript, of course. I might propose edits to improve it, just thoughts for you to consider."

"I'll get in touch with the journal editors right away to make sure I can add your name. It's slated for publication soon, but I think there's time. We'll both need to sign a letter to the journal indicating you contributed materially to the work. I'll drop the manuscript off at your office later this evening. Your name carries weight, so this is helpful to me."

That was a bald-faced lie. Hackett's name was unknown in academic folklore circles and, even in history, he was a fading luminary, but praise never hurt and Bradan needed all the good will he could mobilize ahead of his Thursday hearing.

I can't screw my way to tenure like Gail.

"And here's Harvey Kleiner to join the fun," Hackett said. "A chap of coruscating intellect if ever there was one."

Another man as squat as Hackett pushed through the gray-haired crowd to join them. It was no small feat making headway, as History was the largest department on campus and there were a hundred-odd faculty, staff, departmental administrators, and assorted grandees from the university attending. Graduate students were sprinkled in among the older faculty crowd in a calculated gesture toward inclusion by letting the next generation of budding academics consort with their betters. Several undergrad history majors circulated with trays of inedible mini sandwiches. Bradan noticed Amy among them. She smiled over at him, waved, and rolled her eyes.

Staying up with the times as he understood them, Kleiner affected long, brown-streaked gray hair covering his ears and wide-lapeled collar. A paisley-patterned shirt flowed over his tummy and he wore a belt as wide as a pirate's. He ignored Bradan and addressed himself to Hackett.

"Christ, there's a real spring in Gav's step these days. I think he's bedding—what's her name?—Halpern? Lord, what a cutie. She needs to think about her hair, but she's got a great rack, they're straining to get out of her shirt, a gift from God. I wish I had Chaffee's way with the ladies."

"Gentlemen, I'll help myself to more wine," Bradan said. He needed to get away from these two. "Back in a sec."

"Bring the bottle over and freshen my glasses up, Bradan," Hackett said. "Yes, Bradan, the whole bottle. It's quite all right. Everyone expects it of me." He chortled. "Harv, join us. You've got nothing except coffee. What a dullard. You dance on the table after one glass? Make a scene if you want, keep things hopping. Nothing ever happens at Gav's bashes except that he kisses up to the dean."

"I can't keep up with you, Toby, but all right, Bradan, bring over whatever red they're plying us with tonight. Can you drop off my coffee cup while you're at it? Thanks. Is it next Thursday? That's your big day?"

Bradan nodded.

"You're the one with the dog and the motorcycle?" Kleiner asked.

"Word gets around."

Hackett drained his glasses sequentially. "I had an undergrad want to commandeer my upper-div postwar American culture seminar to talk about the 'raw voice of the streets.' Jesus, nothing raw about these kids here. They're all trust-fund brats. No one's going to draft them. Daddy will get them off the hook with a good lawyer and some deferment or another."

Bradan threaded his way through the crowd toward the wine and canapés. Van, a Dark Ages Welsh specter, and an army of the damned was preferable to this lot, but the allure of his research meant he needed to stay on History's good side.

Away from Hackett and Kleiner, he inhaled deeply and smelled primrose and nightshade from the college's gardens and exhaled his ennui and ambivalence. How many gatherings had he attended over the centuries where interpersonal politics far outweighed whatever enjoyment was to be had? At least they could have served good liquor. He scanned the crowd. They stood outside on the Faculty Club's porch among a bustling herd of the history department's best and brightest. A string quartet from the music department sawed away in one corner, and trees shaded the evening gathering with birds perching or flying overhead like cherubs gazing down beatifically from a rococo painting.

Chaffee had placed himself dead center, holding court among the group as people eddied about him, the raconteur in his element and the nexus of this little galaxy. Bradan saw Gail at his side chatting away amiably and laughing at the chairman's jokes. She wore a new pair of glasses.

Bradan looked over at the table of appetizers and miscellaneous bottles, seeking high-proof spirits.

No hard liquor. I'll check the alcoholic content of the wine and go with the strongest.

At the table Bradan heard a knife chime against a glass. Slowly the chatter died down and the quartet came to a disjointed stop.

Chaffee rapped his glass again.

"Toby, that means you, too. Pipe down for a moment, then you can get back to serious drinking."

The crowd laughed indulgently and the old professor bowed theatrically, still holding both glasses.

Now Chaffee got into it. "What a pleasure to introduce my friend, Dean Jackson Palmer. He's not just my friend, but a friend of History. In an era of tightened budgets and outright hostility in many quarters—don't think I mean Sacramento—well, actually, I do mean Sacramento's abysmal state government"—rumbles of approval swept through the gathering—"it's important to have well-placed friends in administration at this institution. And he's the real deal, the ne plus ultra for both leadership and pedagogy at our august institution."

Bradan kept his expression bland and attentive. It didn't matter the era or the organization, sycophancy sounded the same.

Is there anything deadening to pour into myself? he wondered.

Chaffee's remarks eventually ground to a predictable climax of flattery and Palmer took over. He was smoother than Chaffee, with reflexive jabs at Reagan at the state level and American policy globally. The applause lines built on one another with practiced rhythm.

Brave talk, but no one from this crowd will storm any Bastilles.

"But that's all by the way," Palmer swept on. "My real point is that under Gav's leadership, History has a well-earned reputation in research and the utmost focus on pedagogical support for our undergraduates."

Bradan took a slug of dreadful but potent red and noticed that Chaffee, standing slightly behind Palmer, looked every bit as bored as Bradan felt. He was about to muster a smidgen of sympathy for the chairman when he saw him, with a discreet hand gesture, motion to Amy to come over. Another nearby student from the catering staff moved to approach with a tray, but the chairman shook his head and again motioned to Amy. She got the message and swept over, carrying her tray aloft like a Parisian waiter. She wore a miniskirt and looked unaffectedly cute. Arriving at Chaffee's side, he made a show of inspecting the sandwiches while conferring quietly with the undergraduate, all the while putting a hand on her skirt to stroke her bottom.

Bradan looked on sardonically. It must seem to Chaffee too good to be true: two young women in his bed and at his beck and call at the soiree, Gail on one elbow and Amy on the other. The chairman appeared to be daring the world to notice. Bradan felt fury wash over him. And this smug prick would decide his fate in a few days.

Looking away, Bradan spotted an older, gray-haired woman he recognized as History's department administrator and book-keeper push uninvited into the conversation. If anything, her bouffant hair had grown since Bradan had last been on a com-mittee with her. Chaffee seemed irritated at the intrusion and let his hand drop from Amy's butt. The admin ignored the under-graduate and charged ahead. It seemed to be a confrontation.

Bradan couldn't begin to guess the gist of it, but, out of curi-osity, he turned away and recited a six-line spell. This one was no real drain, but he still gasped with exertion immediately after the last line fell into place. He now heard their quiet dia-logue with perfect clarity through the ear of a sparrow sitting above them.

"Professor Chaffee, I'm not going to be brushed off again. If you won't see me anywhere else, then we do it here. We need to review the quarterly departmental budget. Your discretionary fund is overdrawn—really overdrawn—and the expenditures are mostly in the form of disbursements to you. We're heading into a college-wide audit and I can't explain those expenditures. Can *you*?"

"Clara, we can't do this here," Chaffee said softly.

Amy looked utterly baffled, but stayed in attendance and gamely held the sandwich tray. Clara grabbed an appetizer and bit into to it carnivorously.

Chaffee continued, "After the shindig is over, I'll ditch Melinda and this bunch of windbags and we'll go over to my office. Palmer will finish eventually, God willing. There's no impropriety whatsoever."

"Then what happened to the funds?" Clara asked. She kept her voice down, but spoke intensely. "It's not me you need to convince; it's the college's internal auditors. Did any of the missing money, by chance, go for presents to your stable of floozies?"

Chaffee's face whitened. "You're accusing me of siphoning off funds?"

"There's a receipt for a platinum necklace stuffed in with other bills," Clara said. "Forget to shred that one? Maybe it's not for the girls, you wear platinum?"

Bradan turned away from the crowd again and pretended to sip from his glass to mask intoning a spell. This one would be bigger, but exhaustion would be a small price. Instantly, amplified fivefold, Chaffee's pledges of financial rectitude made privately to Clara wafted out to the whole crowd. It sounded like it came over a PA system, but none had been set up. Chaffee might have been bellowing his financial improprieties for all to hear. The word *embezzlement* was easily discernible. He sounded guilty as hell.

Drowned out and dumbfounded, Palmer stopped mid-paean and listened. People might not know who Clara was, but one and all they recognized Chaffee's voice. Palmer looked about for the department chair and spotted him arguing with the admin. Everything hung suspended.

Then several things occurred together: Chaffee stopped talking, realizing something was horribly wrong; Clara's face reddened and, with a tattletale smirk, she pushed determinedly through the crowd toward the dean; the woman in the brown shift snarled and launched herself at Chaffee to throw a full glass of red wine at him, leaving a stain on his blue shirt that looked like a dagger had been plunged into his chest. Then she exited, passed Gail and Amy, paused to confront the two younger women, but instead decided not to say anything, and marched out of the party without a word; and Palmer, thinking on his feet, motioned urgently to the string quartet to begin playing. The musicians lurched into a piece by Debussy just as Clara grabbed the dean's arm to unload her story.

Pandemonium broke out.

Amy strode toward the faculty building still holding her tray.

"What just happened?" Hackett asked. He moved next to Bradan. "You look pretty sick, young man. It *is* pretty sickening, gross financial irregularities using History's money. What would make Gav just shout it out to the four winds? He's quite loud, by the way. Half the campus must have heard. Probably too much to drink, and he was just fondling those two women and taking no pains to hide it. He was being really grabby. Melinda saw it all—who didn't? Gav's wife is a good person. The poor woman will have suspected Gavin's infidelities—lord above, we all knew—but she'll take this badly nonetheless. Tossing wine at Gav is just the opening volley. It's one thing to have liaisons with junior faculty and students—I'd like to, myself—but don't make a public spectacle of it. That's quite shabby."

The old professor grabbed Bradan's bicep. "Steady on there, lad. Too much wine, I'd say."

"Too much excitement," Bradan managed to gasp out. He leaned on the table for support.

"That, too. It will be interesting to see how Palmer responds. There's enough other stuff bouncing around campus administration without having this blow up. Gav really stepped in it. This will put the auditors on his scent. Worse than embezzlement, he called the dean tedious."

"That *was* nasty," Bradan said.

Hackett drained yet another glass. "Still, Palmer may just try to ride it out and tell Chaffee to keep a low profile until it quiets down. Then again, the dean may suspend Gavin or ease him into early retirement, in which case they'll need a new chair for History. They'll do a national search, of course, but they'll want an interim chair in the meantime. I may put my name forward— sort of a consensus candidate, a known and reliable individual. And I've been friendly with Jackson for years."

"Just the man for it," Bradan said. "I've got to dash."

"Wherever to? The fun's just starting."

"To find Amy."

"What are you raving about, man?" the old professor asked. "That kid Gav was spooning over? Why worry? She'll be fine. They're resilient at that age."

"Chaffee's wife looked ready to slit the kid's throat," Bradan said. "Amy may need a shoulder to lean on after this shit especially if lawyers are about to drag her affair with Chaffee into the public arena."

Strength returning, Bradan walked in the direction he'd seen Amy take through an open double door into the faculty building. She might have already fled to her sorority or she could be taking a moment to gather her wits in a quiet corner of the building.

A dimly lit lounge was just to his left with leather chairs and bookcases built into the walls stuffed with volumes up to the ceiling that no one read. It reminded him of London's Athenaeum club from a century gone by. Normally this was off-limits to anyone except tenured faculty and guarded to keep out the uninitiated, but the building's staff was currently occupied on the porch outside tending to History's disintegrating party. They hadn't allowed women into the lounge, faculty or otherwise, until a few years back, but Amy sat legs extended in the biggest chair. In the wan light, she looked stunned, but otherwise intact, the sandwich tray in her lap.

"You're underage, but here's a glass, not very good. Drink it if you want. Hide the wine if anyone comes in."

"Hi, Professor Badon. Thanks." Amy reached out and took the glass. He sat down on a couch opposite her.

"You'll be the talk of the town—for about five seconds," he said. "This will blow over. No undergrad pays any attention to department get-togethers. And none of the faculty has a clue about who you are—or cares, either. They'll all be more interested in what Chaffee did with the missing money."

"I'm not worried about it too much," Amy said. "I *do* still need a passing grade in Chaffee's idiotic course."

Gail walked in and sat down. Aside from Amy's chair and the couch, there wasn't anywhere else to sit close by, so she eased herself onto the couch, drawing her skirt under herself, and edged as far from Bradan as possible.

"So what happens now?" Amy asked matter-of-factly.

"Just my two cents," Bradan said. "Make sure you tell your side of things to your sorority sisters right away. From my experience, whoever gets a story out first tends to be believed. You live with them, so presenting a solid front to the rest of campus will be helpful. Also, I'm not sure how significant this Todd guy is to you, but if he is important, talk to him fast and say Chaffee is a lech and a liar—whatever you did or didn't do with Gav behind closed doors doesn't matter. Stick to that story. In a week no one will remember. Finals are coming up so people are thinking of grades more than campus gossip."

Amy gulped the wine. "Truthfully, I don't deserve to pass."

"Maybe not, but you didn't deserve this stink either, so make it work in your favor," Bradan said. "Definitely take Chaffee's final. You may not want to set foot in his classroom or ever see him again—I can empathize with wanting to avoid a person where circumstances keep pushing you together."

He saw Gail glance over at him from her side of the couch.

"But don't give anyone an excuse to mark you down because you skipped the exam," he said. "Is this for Gav's 'The Notion of Europe in a Post-Leninist World'? Damn, who dreams these courses up? Anyway, study hard and, for the essays, throw in phrases like 'imperial overreach' and 'Marxist dialectics' and you'll do fine."

After a moment he added, "And for your final grade, petition the department to have someone—not Chaffee—review your work and give you a grade. I suspect they may pass you no matter how badly you've done. You could need a faculty signature to get the wheels turning. I'm happy to do that."

"Or I can do it," Gail said. "I'm the adviser for History undergrads."

"All the better," Bradan said. He turned back to Amy. "Keep it civil. But if you get resistance from the department, threaten to bring your parents and their lawyer into things."

"My family has given money to this place," Amy said.

"Well, hallelujah," Bradan said. "Time to exploit those connections and make them work in your favor. If your family knows a campus trustee, now's the time to call in favors. Have them speak to the chancellor. He'll lean on Palmer to help you."

Amy drained her glass. "So I could come out of this okay?"

Bradan nodded. "Life is all about unfair advantages." He smiled and added, "And we all try to create those for ourselves."

"Chaffee seems on great terms with the dean," Gail said.

"From their point of view, Chaffee's misuse of funds trumps everything else, so he's deserving of no loyalty from them," Bradan said. "Sure, normally they'd paint Amy as manipulating a distinguished faculty member with her sexual wiles to give her an undeserved grade, but in this case, I'm guessing they won't. Palmer has other shit to deal with and doesn't need this blowing up in his face more than it already has; senior members of the department would be all too happy to step in as chair if Chaffee is eased aside; and then they've got Chaffee's wife who won't let things settle quietly back to status quo ante. I'd guess she's on the phone to a divorce lawyer right now talking huge alimony settlement. No one wants her attorney asking around among the faculty about allegations that Gavin's behavior has been going on since forever, trying to build a case for a pattern of adultery to get a big payday."

Bradan leaned back. "How do you feel?"

"Not bad after your pep talk," Amy said. "I'll head back to my sorority now. I think you're right about getting the girls together and letting them know. They'll laugh behind my back, but they'll sympathize, too. It's happened to some of them. I'll also study like you said."

"Talk with me anytime if you need," Gail said. She reached out and held Amy's hand for a moment before the young woman left.

"Think Melinda will sic her lawyer on members of the department to build up a case he's a philanderer?" Gail asked.

"Sure, but the old boys in the department won't spill the beans. That would be breaking ranks. That works in your favor because it may get crazy if Chaffee's wife is out for blood—and she seems to suspect Amy and you—so if her attorney comes in your direction, you're the soul of propriety and have no idea how ugly rumors got started. In fact, you find the allegations hurtful. Any relationships in the department you've had are purely professional and your only focus is on getting your next paper submitted, peer reviewed, and published. That's your story."

"You see it all so clearly," she said coolly. "And then there's that edge never too far beneath your surface."

"Yeah, I need to get better at stifling my feelings."

"About me and Chaffee." She said as a statement.

He nodded. "Among other things. I haven't got the hang of just letting things go after all the years. Actually, I'm getting worse as time goes by." Bradan picked up Amy's wineglass, saw it was empty, and set it aside regretfully. He'd pour himself a large glass of Rémy Martin once he got to his apartment.

"I'm guessing tenure review for both of us will be postponed," he said.

* * *

"Bullets can't keep me down."

"Congressman Newman, do the police have any idea who tried to kill you? And how did your attackers get away with no apparent trace? They vanished into thin air?"

"That's a bunch of questions rolled into one," Van said. "First, no, the authorities don't have any leads or witnesses, but they're looking hard, interviewing neighbors, combing through their records of known nutcases who might have it in for me—have I got that right, Al?" Van looked at a ranking uniformed policeman with a gold star on his shirt lapel standing near him at the podium. The cop nodded agreement.

Van continued, "Second, yep, the perpetrator got clean away. I didn't really see him—too busy dodging gunfire." The media crowd laughed sympathetically. Now anger overwhelmed Van. "But if I can personally hunt him down, I'll do just that. And then none of you want to see what happens to the guy that did this to me."

He smoothed his tone for the journalists. Manipulating and flattering the media was one of the foundations of modern political power.

"Of course, there's no need for vigilantism. Al and his colleagues will have whoever did this in prison soon."

"Congressman, you just said 'him,'" another TV anchor called out. "So there was only one, male attacker?"

"I chose my words badly," Van said. "I didn't see who shot at me and my wife."

"Congressman, first, congratulations on a remarkable recovery. Anything you want to share about possible presidential campaign plans?"

"I keep getting those questions," Van said. "And I'm flattered, truly touched, by the interest. Let me just say that, at the moment, I'm focused on my congressional district, but you'll be the first to know if I think I can serve on the national level."

A woman newscaster stepped forward. "Congressman, I'll echo the rest of us and wish you a continued speedy recovery. You spent little time in the ICU. Also, can you comment on the retrieval yesterday of the body of Barbara Renaldi from the Bay?"

Van paused, stunned.

"She was on your staff," the journalist pressed.

Van gathered himself. "I know who the hell she was. Al, can you help out here? I understand it's a missing person investigation at the moment. The entire staff, myself included, has been worried sick that she was in trouble, but until this minute, I didn't know about a body. Al, any words?"

The uniformed cop stepped to the mic. "I don't know much more than you all. I was going to brief Congressman Newman about this after the press conference, but the little I'm aware of is that it's being handled by Alameda County sheriff's department since the body was recovered off Oakland. Like the congressman said, so far we've been coordinating with other local authorities on this as a missing person case—she lived in this county, in Danville. I'm not even sure if it was believed to be accidental—"

"Murder," the journalist filled in. "Sources tell us she had her neck almost sliced off. Then her body was weighted down and tossed in the Bay. It was an execution."

The media types below Van's podium came alive, sensing blood, not yet sure whose.

Van let aggrieved shock wash over his face. It wasn't hard to manufacture the emotion under the circumstances. What else did they know about Barbara's death?

"This has turned the happy day of my hospital release into a tragedy," he said. "I and my office wish to express our heartfelt condolences to the poor young woman's family. Barbara was just about the friendliest soul you could ever have the pleasure of meeting. We'll work tirelessly with the police and sheriff to find and prosecute the perpetrator. This horrible event reinforces the need for strong efforts to combat violent crime."

Edging away from the podium—he needed time to digest Barbara's discovery—Van gave the crowd of newspeople, TV journalists, congressional staffers, doctors who'd treated him, and assorted citizenry a good-bye wave from the steps of the John Muir Health Center where his staff had set up the informal press conference. A big chocolate cake with "Welcome Back" inscribed in white icing melted on a folding table flanking the podium.

Until the revelation about Barbara's discovery, Van had inhaled the attention of the roughly two hundred audience members standing before him. This would get national attention thanks to the TV crews. Oddly, the scene recalled tribal councils in Arthur's hall at Cadbury. The goal was the same: to show strength while winning over any skeptics to his cause. Then, it had been tattooed tribal chieftains; now, it was the predatory media.

"Congressman, a few more questions."

"I'm not going to tarry, folks. This has hit me pretty hard."

Had he scrubbed Barbara's apartment of every trace connecting him to her? He should have burned the picture of the two of them together on Stinson Beach rather than throwing it in the Bay as a final tribute to their extinct relationship. How long could a photo last in salt water? Had anyone found it? He'd done the respectful thing by saying words and casting a memento of their affair into the water after her body. It was sad that his gesture might link him to Barbara. And how did they locate her body? Bradan?

Divert the press down a different line of questioning. "I'll close out by saying I can't take credit for my speedy recovery from the gunshot. Without my wife, Ellen, and our three kids at my side, I wouldn't be out of this medical institution so soon." He reached over to give his wife a huge kiss.

"And without Drs. Cary Lord and Jonah Lieberman, I wouldn't have a functioning right arm—or I wouldn't be alive." The congressman nodded at two white-coated medical staff nearby. "Both of you, step up to the podium and be recognized for your wonderful work on me."

Lord took the mic. "Thanks, Congressman Newman. I wish we *could* actually take credit for your recovery, but neither I nor my colleague, Jonah, have ever seen a patient shrug off so much damage, so quickly. The bullet tumbled when it hit you and partially shattered the clavicle and scapula and caused extensive soft-tissue trauma. It nicked a lung, too. That all mostly healed incredibly quickly including the bone damage. You'll have your arm in a sling for another two weeks, but after that you'll be tossing the first pitch at local baseball games. Jonah and I are considering writing this up as a case for *The New England Journal of Medicine*."

Van laughed. "Well, if voters read this journal I'm all for it." He gently eased the physicians aside and resumed his central spot behind the podium.

"Last, and, a little strangely, I'd like to thank whoever shot me. I wouldn't be as motivated to keep up our fight to beat crime and drugs without being reminded of just why I do that. I'll carry that into next year's election. And now there are important battles to be fought and enemies to be vanquished, and, it appears, Barbara's killer to be located, so save your inquiries for another time."

The crowd clapped tepidly, but Van thought the last bit would play well if they put it on evening newscasts. It would go a little way toward rescuing a disastrous day.

Time to fuck up Bradan but good.

* * *

"Are you at the right party?" Bradan asked.

"You teach about Marxist dialectics?" the tall kid asked.

"I teach folklore, not Marxism."

"Is there grass? Reds work, too. Or acid. Beer and cigarettes ain't doing it for me." The kid fidgeted with a beer can while holding a cigarette that he hadn't gotten around to lighting.

"I get high on life," Bradan said sardonically.

The young guy addressing him was tall, long-haired, and wore a leather headband stamped with peace signs. At first Bradan pegged him for a Berkeley student who'd found out about the Belvedere's vaunted house parties and strayed across the Bay Bridge looking to get laid and trip on whatever was being ingested among the Haight's free spirits, but he seemed too dumb for serious academics even if he spouted arbitrary intro-political-science-class jargon. He was also too earnest, without the ironic, superior detachment a Berkeley student would have affected at a Haight party. In fact, the man looked like an actor that someone with no knowledge of the local scene had called up from Central Casting to fill the role of "hippie" for a background crowd shot.

Everyone else had blazed up and a pall of dope smoke gathered about the big room's high ceiling like cloud cover. The patchouli and incense Bradan had lit didn't cover the marijuana, but it did make for a wild phantasmagoria of smells that the slowly turning ceiling fan distributed equitably above the crowd of partiers as the old structure inhaled the fragrances of dreamy, young humanity into its wooden floors and wallpaper.

Bradan had determined to stay sober, whatever decadence the rest of tonight's blowout attendees might indulge in. Van was at large, though evidently with his arm still in a sling, so the only question was when the showdown might occur. His antagonist would make no mistake this time and bring his entire temporal and profane armies along to waste Bradan body and soul.

Distracted by these thoughts, Bradan felt the reassuring weight of the pistol jammed into the small of his back under an untucked T-shirt and sport coat. A knife was also sheathed in his boot. These were now regular features of his wardrobe. He'd considered fleeing, but that would just postpone the inevitable, so why not do the fight right here, right now? He'd hurt Van before and he'd fuck him up permanently when they met next.

However, to do that, Bradan needed to mobilize allies. Tintagel kept watch from the roof where the sightlines as far as Golden Gate Park were excellent. Besides guard duty, the wolf wasn't a fan of noisy, pot-fueled revelries, so he'd retreated as far up in the house as possible. However, Bradan would need more than Tintagel to tackle Van and Gwyn's specters. He might be able to recruit some of them at this very party.

"You high?" The tall kid tried to reignite their chat.

Bradan shook his head. "Far from it. Just a little tense."

"Yeah, you can feel it. It's mellow, but then again, it ain't. The foxy woman over by the fireplace said you teach intellectual stuff at a university in LA. I'm not sure what that means, but it sounds neat. You must do your best thinking at the beach."

"With my toes in the sand."

Bradan abruptly stepped around the kid and forced his way through the crowd to the front bay window to push aside velvet curtains and peer outside. Nothing seemed untoward on the street.

Turning, he scoped out the room and saw Taryn dead center among a flock of musicians, street artists, neighbors, and miscellaneous residents of 31¾ Belvedere—he never knew how many individuals crashed here on any given night. The witch had turfed the tall kid off to Bradan to be rid of a nuisance. That would be typical of the enchantress. Well, he owed her after borrowing a flying horse from Faerie for a Dark Ages hit.

Taryn deftly evaded the bass player from a San Francisco band trying to encircle her waist with his arm. Everyone laughed at the clumsy gesture of lustful affection and took deep tokes of their joints to cover any awkwardness. Pretending not to be perturbed by unwanted advances, Taryn theatrically kissed the fellow's cheek, staying the best of friends, keeping the party vibe flowing.

It was past 11:00 and there were already over two hundred attendees and the number climbed by the minute to cascade out of Belvedere's living room, into halls, eddy about in upstairs bedrooms, and down the front stoop and into the street. Bradan saw and heard a cavalcade of Harleys announce their presence outside with engine noise that must have echoed from there to the Tenderloin, drowning out Kenny Salazar with a young, redheaded woman sitting on his lap as he idly played chords on a battered upright piano and tried to engage musically with Jeff Dorsey, who sat in an overstuffed chair nearby strumming Bradan's twelve-string. Bradan had let the word get out that the band would dry-run their new songs at the party, so folks hung around expectantly near the piano.

New material meant copyright issues, so Bradan had invited Evan Cohen, the band's manager and lawyer, to check out the songs. The attorney also dug a good gathering. Bradan hoped he wouldn't overly indulge tonight. Meantime, members of the Pillars mixed and mingled playing affable but self-absorbed hosts, leaving actual party management to Bradan.

I should go up to the roof to see if anything's coming.

Instead, he spotted a thin line of flame beginning to eat its way up the drapery flanking the bay window, sparked by a lit joint on the floor where the curtains touched hardwood.

He shoved his way back over to the kid.

"Your beer, please." Not waiting for slow, addled comprehension, Bradan grabbed the beer and threw liquid across the room at the flames, which hissed into submission.

"Plenty more cans in a tub in the kitchen," he said. "Help yourself."

Two of the Grateful Dead strolled past and nodded at him. The witch, looking ethereal in a long, red silk shirt over jeans, blew him a kiss above the multitude. She giggled at his efforts to disengage from the kid who wasn't so far gone he didn't catch the exchange.

"You know her?" he asked.

"Sure. We're in a band together. We'll play new stuff later tonight for you all."

"The music gear that's cluttered about." The kid's words came slowly. The fellow was clearly just now putting things together in his mind.

"Yep, those are our amps and instruments, The Pillars of Creation."

"She's sings in that band. I've heard them. Wow, I'd love to hear her tonight and bang her."

"As would so many others," Bradan said. "That's her call, but it could be a long wait. See if there are other women you could get together with instead. That's what parties are for: to meet new people and amaze them with what you know." Bradan swept his arm over the assemblage.

"Oh, yeah, sure, man. But what about dialectics?"

"I can't think of a better icebreaker," Bradan said. "What an opening line. Girls will fall all over themselves to jump into bed with you."

The fellow drifted off, looking about for targets to score with.

It was a party after all, so Bradan circulated now that he'd evaded a discussion of society's material contradictions and extinguished a fire. He spotted Paul Kantner of Jefferson Airplane.

"God, that kid is an idiot," Kantner said. "He's asking everyone for drugs. He's got to be a narc."

"Think so? Just what I don't need tonight."

"San Francisco is forty-nine square miles surrounded by reality," the guitarist said. "And the reality part is always attacking us. They'd love to bust everyone here."

Bradan looked about at familiar faces in the room. They were right at the cusp of something indefinable, but imaginative and artistic, as intimate as their little neighborhood and as expansive as new attitudes and ways of thinking filtering out across the world. And as prone to vanishing in the Pacific wind as fairy dust.

The city's burgeoning psychedelic musical community was still small enough to be a collective of talent Bradan mostly knew, and his Belvedere address had become a music salon with impromptu jam sessions populated with local performers. There were also occasional visits by the LA crowd or musicians from New York.

"Hey Nico, when'd you come out west from the big city?"

"I flew in yesterday," the singer said. "They should have warned me. It's colder here than New York or Europe."

"This passes for spring in San Francisco." Bradan pulled off his sport coat and draped it over her shoulders. He'd planned to wear it at his now postponed tenure hearing. God knew when that would be rescheduled.

"Take this. Not trendy, but it's warm."

"I've had enough of trendy." She smiled wanly and ran her hand through blond hair that hung down to the middle of her back, arranging it over the jacket's collar.

"Andy played me a couple of your songs a while back," she said. "They're intelligent, not the clichés people do these days. How did you write such material?"

"I'm inspired by life and life has been strange recently."

"It has indeed," she said. She talked the way she sang, with deadpan, Germanic-inflected intonation in a voice that had seen it all.

"I'll visit the Factory or your place next time I'm out east," Bradan said.

"It would be so incredible to compose together." She kissed him lightly on the cheek. "You're doing Monterey?"

He nodded.

"Their lineup keeps getting better, I hear. I'll be there. And now I must say hi to beautiful Taryn. Ciao." She threaded her way over to the witch.

Looking after the Velvet Underground's singer, Zorro sauntered up. To Bradan he resembled Che Guevara though he wore a cowboy hat instead of a beret. Despite hash consumption that must have eaten into the profits of his trade, Bradan had always found him sharp as a tack.

"Was my piece helpful?"

"Man, more than you know," Bradan responded. "Great balance for a .45. I had to fire it a couple of times, cleaned it afterward."

"Hit anything?"

Bradan debated a second before responding. "Don't worry; no one can trace it back to you."

"I'm not worried, Bradan. You always seem to land on your feet and take care of friends, but this situation, is someone leaning on you? You still strapped?"

Bradan nodded. "Yeah, and they're leaning hard." Time to broach the topic of allies. "You know people, right?"

Zorro paused, sizing him up. "Yeah, I know lots of people. Comes with my line of work. Reading between the lines, I think you mean people that can handle themselves, straighten stuff out."

"That's exactly who I need. I can throw money at them, too."

"How many friends you need?"

"How many you have?"

"Shit, what have you gotten yourself into?" Zorro asked.

"Long story. A congressman has it in for me. The police like him. He picks his friends well. He's got people that help him. Some of them, your group may be able to handle, others they won't be able to handle. Not to be mysterious, I'll need to figure out what to do about the second group myself, but I could use backup with the first group."

"Let's meet Zack. He's over by Taryn."

"I know him. He's my mechanic," Bradan said. "He works on the Panhead."

"No introductions needed, then. He rides with the baddest club around the area. They've got chapters most everywhere. I think a few of them just rolled up to join the party. We'll grab Zack and head outside."

A dozen motorcyclists massed around the front stoop. One of their number popped wheelies up and down Belvedere, getting the ungainly bike to stand on its back wheel like a bear lifting itself onto hind legs reaching for a beehive. The Harley's noise reverberated off Belvedere Street's row houses. Half the county must be able to hear tonight's bash.

Most of the bikers had long hair like the Haight's resident hippies and an affection for marijuana, but the resemblance ended there. The bikers moved as a unit, arrived together, clustered on the steps together, made a run for the beer in the kitchen's tub together, and now sipped from cans while straddling their bikes or sitting on the steps, for the moment mellow and chatting among themselves and with other partiers, but with enough latent menace so people gave them and their Harleys space.

To Bradan's amazement, two of the gang looked like younger, more muscular versions of Hackett and Kleiner complete with side whiskers. The resemblance was so uncanny Bradan had to restrain himself from asking what they thought of his papers on folklore's role in modern culture and his chances for making tenure. The rest of the gang members were twice their size. Bradan noticed many wore chains as belts, handy if a flail was needed. No doubt there were also various boot knives and pistols distributed among the group.

"I know you," a lean, bearded biker sitting on his motorcycle shouted at Bradan. The man was tatted up and down his muscled, bare arms, which were visible through a sleeveless T-shirt and denim jacket, arms ripped off. He'd stuffed gloves in the back pocket of his jeans. Bradan noted that he was fully patched. The rest of the bikers looked on curiously.

"Corvalle Mesa lockup, man," he shouted over the engines. "Remember, prison brotherhood, the hole. I saw them drag you in and then you tried to bust out with the rest of us."

"I *got* out," Bradan yelled back. "You take my advice and run before they organized a response?" He remembered the savagery of that day in the prison's confines three years back. He thought the guy's name was Eddie.

"Nah. Should have listened. I coulda made it out, but I was having too much fun pounding the shit out of the guards. I live for that."

Prison time together created immediate entrée beyond any vouching Zack or Zorro could have provided as Eddie regaled his brethren with an account of Bradan and his own incarceration and escape, prominently featuring himself dealing out murderous beatings to the hated guards. Eddie fingered a scar down one of his cheeks. Apparently the favor had been returned once the sheriffs regained control of the prison.

To solidify the bond with his new compadres, Bradan hoisted the garage door up and manhandled his Panhead out onto the street. It fit right in with the other iron parked curbside in front of the row houses. Silently he breathed apologies to Meadow for dragging her into low company, but tonight she kept her thoughts to herself.

"Eddie, remember that big dude you hammered on at Corvalle?" Bradan asked. "He's a congressman, believe it or not."

"I do believe it. Assholes always rise to the top."

"In this case, yes. He's after me just like he was back then. I'm fixing to go at him myself—I already have—but he'll have backup and it might be cool to have you guys in my corner. I'm thinking he'll use the cops as his storm troops."

"When might it get crazy?"

"Whenever. As early as tonight."

It was amazing how much fealty three hundred dollars and a dozen tabs of yellow sunshine could garner.

"Come on in," Bradan said. "We're about to play."

"We can hear you out here? If so, we'll kind of hang outside for a while doing guard duty."

"You can hear us out here," Bradan assured Eddie. "Or anywhere within a mile."

"My kind of tunes," the outlaw said.

Inside, the Pillars assembled, plugged in, but didn't get loud immediately, instead moving meditatively through the unamplified introduction to "Dawn's Faerie Dance." Bradan played his twelve-string acoustic guitar while Jeff played flute. The entire band contributed to five-part harmonies. The songs felt like a '50s-era folk quintet from New York's Village performing for the denizens of Faerie in a forest glade.

Then the mood changed abruptly and Bradan and Taryn's feedback-saturated electric guitars tore through the gentle melodies, cueing a thunderous rhythm section and surging keyboards that almost, but not quite, buried the Pillars' vocals. Jagged canyons of sound overlaying emerald waterfalls of tonality stretched the song's architecture beyond rock into jazz and avant-garde territory and then back to rock. Bradan's and Taryn's guitar lines caressed and clashed. By pushing the volume to extremes, Bradan worked to get otherworldly harmonics from his instrument's electronics, wresting sapphire notes to send out to the cosmos.

And there was enough rhythm for partiers to dance. In all the eras Bradan had lived, women were the most enthusiastic dancers, in touch with tribal rhythms men didn't respond to as eagerly.

Bradan couldn't hear Belvedere's invasion over the volume, but he saw bodies suddenly pushing themselves from the kitchen and back bedrooms into to the living room where the Pillars played. A panicked-looking couple crashed into Constantine and his drum kit, sending snares and cymbals tumbling about. Amplifiers fell over onto the floor and the band came to a ragged finish.

"Cops are coming in the back," a woman shouted. "They've got folks in choke holds."

People fled helter-skelter into the living room, meeting others flooding in through the front door. The living room turned into an eddying mass. Bradan unstrapped his Gibson and stuck it behind Kenny's organ to shield it from the crush of movement. He saw police, at least ten of them both in uniforms and plain clothes, corralling people in from the back of the house and attacking into the front room.

This must be a drug bust, Bradan thought, *not a simple noise complaint.*

No one mentioned a search warrant.

In front, things didn't seem to be going so well for the forces of law and order as a huge ruckus broke out and he heard motorcycle engines being revved to infinity and angry shouts and sirens. It sounded like two cars collided and then one of the sirens was abruptly silenced.

Judging that the confusion on the street offered the greatest chance of escape for the partiers, Bradan shouted, "Out the front."

Taking him too literally, a bare-chested young man somersaulted through the bay window in a shower of glass, dragging curtains behind him like Batman.

He'll be a bloody mess when he lands, Bradan thought.

Everyone else charged the front door, jamming into the foyer. He saw Taryn authoritatively herd the crowd in that direction, too. Sensing that she was a leader in this mob, a cop tried to grab her, but somehow missed completely and crashed head-long into the piano. Another plain-clothed cop in a suit leaped at her with cuffs, but a Persian carpet hanging on the wall to improve acoustics chose that moment to come tumbling down in an enveloping avalanche of silk weave that completely missed the hippies and covered him and two uniformed cops, turning them into a blindly thrashing shambles.

Knowing that the witch could see in darkness, Bradan snapped off the living room's lights to add confusion. She'd prod folks in the right direction. The kitchen lights had already been doused. Bradan heard a person fall into the tub with the ice cubes and beer.

There was no chance in hell for him to force his way out the front door until the mass of revelers cleared, but he wanted to see what mayhem unfolded outside—he'd let this genie out of the bottle and he needed to manage it—so he'd emulate the kid who'd burst through his bay window. Bradan ripped aside the curtain's remnants, gingerly kicked out remaining shards of glass embedded in the sill, and clambered outside, held on to the ledge, extended his body full length and dropped the remaining feet to the driveway below, having the presence of mind to tumble when he hit to avoid breaking an ankle. He felt glass cut his back and thighs as he rolled to a stop next to his Panhead.

"You can really host a bash," Meadow said. "Couldn't you have left me in the garage out of the way?"

"The fun's not over," he said getting up and looking about. "Not by half."

Belvedere Street was chaos. Cop cars, marked and unmarked, were stacked up in both directions between parked vehicles on the narrow street. Police lights flashed over everything. Veering between the cars, Eddie's biker outfit lashed the police and civilian vehicles with chains and lead pipes. They also swung at the cops themselves and indiscriminately at anyone else who came within reach. Eddie gave him a thumbs-up as he rode past on the sidewalk. People tumbled out of his row house and threaded their way toward relatively quiet Haight Street down the block. So far, so good. Bradan wanted to obstruct the police, but he didn't want a shootout.

Will that be my decision?

Some of his neighbors were every bit as violent as the bikers. A hippie kid stood atop a police car with a cinder block and dashed it down on the windshield.

Crowd momentum is hard to control and collateral damage is the way this could go.

Down the street, Bradan saw a command post with police officials clustered about the hood of a car. The tall, head-banded young man who'd interrogated Bradan about mumbo-jumbo Marxist tenets stood next to the cops.

So, Kantner was right: a narc.

Bradan didn't remember offering him any drugs when the guy had asked; there were advantages to staying sober at a party. However, inevitably there were narcotics by the fistful to be had at tonight's soiree. So if the police needed an excuse to barge in, it wouldn't have been hard to concoct one. Still, this operation seemed way too much effort for even a San Francisco Police Department drug bust on a notorious neighborhood nuisance and he wasn't surprised to see Van, arm ostentatiously in a sling, by the police brass with news teams in tow. Two bikers raced past them and one of the cops aimed a service revolver, but didn't fire at fast-moving targets in a crowded environment.

A bunch of disoriented guests tumbled out the front door, including Kenny and Jeff.

"Get them out of here down to Haight Street and then disperse everyone about the neighborhood," he told his band mates. "Lose any dope or pills you've got on you. They'll search anyone they can grab. Tell the rest of them. If they drove here, they're out of luck. No one's getting cars off this block for a couple of hours. They can get their shit in the morning."

But the police seemed too preoccupied with outlaw bikers at the moment to concentrate on their initial mission of shaking down partiers for illicit drugs. Cops exited Belvedere, several the worse for wear after stumbling about in the dark and unexpectedly tangling with various items of furniture or wall hangings. Trying to restore organization to their assault, uniformed cops began questioning people on the sidewalk, and they'd spread-eagled several guys against cars to frisk them. Bradan didn't see Zorro or Zack. With a final deafening cacophony of Harley engines, the bikers blasted off into the night, having created enough anarchic craziness to fully justify the money Bradan had given Eddie. Bradan wondered if they'd done the acid before the cops showed up and been inspired to new nadirs of vile behavior.

Evan wandered over. "Am I needed?"

"For sure," Bradan said. He sat down on his front steps, but didn't lean back. His back bled from a dozen cuts.

"I'd give it about a minute, then I'll get a lot of attention. Might be good to have a lawyer around. Join me on the steps. Thanks. I'll get you a backstage pass for Monterey."

He stretched long legs out on the stoop and waited. Taryn wandered out of the house and perched herself next to him on the banister. She looked distastefully at all the blood that covered his back.

"I can help with that," the witch said. She hopped down on the steps behind him and dabbed at the wounds with her scarf.

"Brilliant," he said to her appreciatively.

"They'll want to take me downtown," he told Evan. "I need to avoid that. Bad shit happens to me in prisons, really bad shit."

The lawyer surreptitiously took a long drag on a joint then extinguished it with dampened fingers and hid the remainder on a ledge under the stairs.

"This is a war zone," he said. "But I'm really not sure what they can pull you in on. You're the homeowner of record, all right, but I think I remember you working assiduously to keep the noise levels down when the band kicked in and recommending that everyone stick to soft drinks. The motorcyclists damaged the cops and their vehicles, but you didn't invite them to the party and can't be held accountable for their actions. If there were drugs found, that's on whoever possessed them, not you."

"Yep, that's exactly what happened."

As the commotion on the block subsided, Bradan watched a contingent of police move purposefully in his direction, including the long-haired, undercover cop. Two camera crews tagged along. Van held back, sitting on the hood of a police cruiser watching, cradling his injured arm.

Without preamble, a cop in a suit said, "We need to search you. Stand up, hands behind your head, face the house."

The gun! And the boot knife. Christ, I'm a walking armory.

"They have the right to ask if they think you're a danger," Evan advised. "You can refuse, but then they can restrain you and bring you in."

A loaded .45 makes me a danger. If they find the piece, they'll pull me in on a concealed weapons charge and throw away the key. I should have dumped it. Same with the knife.

As Bradan vacillated, two uniformed cops grabbed him and shoved him against the garage door. The detective briskly and thoroughly patted him down, running his hand over arms, legs, and the small of Bradan's back. The cop even had him pull off his boots to check for weapons or contraband, grunting distaste at all the blood. Then he swung Bradan around and checked his front pockets.

Where are my weapons? Did they fall out when I went out the window?

"Where'd the wounds come from?"

"Thanks for the concern. I tripped and fell in the excitement. I'll survive."

"You under the influence of anything?"

"Coca-Cola."

"It was his party," the young narc said. "He ran it."

"Damn straight I ran it," Bradan said to the older detective who'd frisked him. "Your colleague kept asked me about drugs—which we don't have at my parties—then he got distracted by scoring with chicks. He wasn't having much luck tonight."

Two of the uniformed cops couldn't suppress smiles.

The cops really wanted to know about the bikers, but Bradan looked baffled and said he'd never seen them before and certainly hadn't invited them. This was a private party to test drive a couple of the band's new songs. Having Evan Cohen right beside Bradan asking polite but firm questions back at the detectives kept the interrogation strained but civil.

A billion questions and an hour later, the police grudgingly left Belvedere, having issued him with an expensive set of citations for offenses too numerous for Bradan to remember, but not egregious enough to arrest him for. The lawyer gave the police his business card as they departed. Bradan gave them his homeowner's insurance information in case the city or neighbors decided to sue him for damage to nearby homes or vehicles, but none of the local renters would opt for this as they'd either attended the soiree themselves and partaken in all manner of narcotics or would be too terrified of biker gang reprisals to pursue the matter. Nonetheless, Bradan resolved to make the rounds tomorrow, up and down the block, to offer compensation to anyone who thought they'd suffered injuries. He'd also offer them free copies of the Pillars' album.

They questioned Taryn, too, but a winning smile, an apparent respect for authority figures, and the aviator sunglasses worn with panache dazzled her inquisitors into a forbearing attitude. No one demanded to search her.

Both news crews had filmed for a few moments, then drifted off when no further debauchery was in the offing. Bradan scanned the neighborhood. Van had vanished. As the last police car departed down the block, Taryn pulled the .45 from the small of her back where it had been stuffed into her jeans covered by her shirt. She twirled the weapon around her forefinger like a gunslinger.

"I didn't see that," Evan said. "Let me know when you get the final draft of the Elektra contract. We should bargain hard with them. I liked your new song, by the way." The lawyer strolled off toward Haight Street.

"What now?" Taryn asked.

"Round two," Bradan said. "We're not done yet. Next up has got to be a magical stunt. The SFPD's gone, so no difficult questions about apparitions in the sky."

Tintagel howled from the roof.

"And here it comes," Bradan said.

Bradan leaped up the porch steps and continued upward on the inside staircases. Taryn followed. Bursting through an attic door onto the roof, he saw the wolf staring out over the park.

Tintagel's howls either warned Bradan about uninvited party guests or welcomed old supernatural comrades.

Bradan looked north and observed the Wild Hunt in all its glory swirling directly toward 31¾ Belvedere's rooftop. They looked as spectral and vicious as ever. Dawn was hours off, so there'd be no relief. Van and Gwyn rode at the head of the gibbering pack. Both stared at him, Van with focused human savagery, and the god with unearthly purpose.

"Gun," Bradan yelled at Taryn.

"Useless. And no need."

As the mass of hunters streamed over Golden Gate Park, an airborne assemblage of a different sort rose to meet them, emanating from the trees below. The park exhaled a multicolored phantasmagoria of shapes, some humanlike, others animals, and still others in no comprehensible form whatsoever, diaphanous assemblages of light and shadow.

"The locals?" Bradan shouted.

"Yes, and they've got reinforcements from the Mount Tamalpais realm. Even together, they don't outnumber the Wild Hunt, but this is their home territory, and Gwyn's forces lose vigor as they move away from their old Celtic haunts. That gives the local outfits an advantage."

"Cosmically speaking," Bradan said.

Many of the Faerie folk flew of their own accord while others rode horses. It could have been his imagination, and there were infinite equines, but he saw the mount he'd ridden days ago when he'd tried to assassinate Van.

Among the Faerie army, a team of blue horses pulled a ponderous Conestoga covered wagon. It made directly for Gwyn's Huey gunships, which responded with long bursts of automatic fire sending strings of orange tracers through the night.

However, elfin figures clinging to the wagon used buckets to catch the bullets like construction laborers snagging hot rivets on steel I-beams atop a Depression-era skyscraper frame. They threw them back at the helicopters.

The rival hosts collided midair, or rather the fairy forces enveloped Gwyn's army of the damned in a hazy, desperate battle than sent clouds of interstellar dust towering into the night sky. Bradan couldn't see an advantage for either party. How could phantoms kill specters, elves kill ghosts? Then Gwyn's army seemed to reach a silent consensus that inconclusive savagery was draining enough of their energy to strand them far from Avalon. The Welsh god gestured mightily at his legions, pointing his sword heavenward. Acting to reinforce Gwyn's edict, an elfin woman with white-blond hair wearing copper-colored armor raced amid the battle corralling the hunters away from the fairies. The rival armies reluctantly disengaged and the sickly orange-colored horizon pulled Gwyn's forces back to their point of origin in an elongate vortex of tangled equines and specters, but not before Van materialized out of the tumult to hurl a double-bladed ax at Bradan. The big man tossed hard, but was hampered by his-still recovering arm. Then he disappeared with the rest of the specters like refuse sucked into a drain.

Bradan threw himself to the tar-paper roof, feeling the ax slice across his shoulder blades and rip into the roof before bursting out the far side to clatter three stories down to the street below. Tintagel sprinted after the weapon, a puppy chasing a ball.

Taryn had taken cover behind a chimney stack. She emerged and kneeled to examine Bradan's wound and blow on it. Her breath anesthetized the gash across his shoulders.

For several moments he lay on the roof recovering his wits. The rough surface felt softer than his bed. He breathed hoarsely as he pushed himself off the tar paper. He'd barely survived another fight. The ax had come near to chopping him in two despite Van's poor aim.

"Wonder what the neighbors noticed?" Taryn asked.

"It's late," he said. "The news crews and police are long gone. They're asleep, high, or hiding after our party. They'll compare notes in the morning and decide they were either tripping or the aurora borealis pushed south this spring."

Bradan looked skyward. "Those light effects on the horizon, the Wild Hunt came from there and left that way."

"It's a portal to the Otherworld," the enchantress said. "Gwyn and company can get back to Avalon instantly without bothering to fly all the way."

"They got sucked right into it, like a black hole."

"Even Gwyn doesn't control it totally," Taryn said. "Get too close and it pulls them in. He's old even by a god's standards. Trips through the portal are stressful. One of these times, it will be his one-way road to annihilation."

"Maybe I'll have a chance to help him down that road," Bradan said.

He looked over the neighborhood and distant park. Without Gwyn's forces to contend with, the fairy battalions had vanished, too. Bradan sat down tiredly on the rooftop and leaned against a vent stack, shifting to avoid hurting his many wounds. The part of him not covered in blood was soaked with sweat. An unopened beer can sat nearby. He was parched beyond belief and this was the elixir he desperately needed. He tried to open it, but his hands shook so hard he fumbled about before finally levering the pull tab open to drink deeply, getting foam in his lap. He offered the witch a sip.

"So gallant." She shook her head. "Mead, if that's available."

"At our next get-together," he said. "So, a question, the offering we made on Tamalpais?"

"Yes?" The witch's tone was neutral and her expression was as opaque and unknowable as ever.

"Was that just to preserve a redwood?"

"Saving an enormous tree is a real feat. Aside from relieving animal urges, what else did you think we were doing?"

"Requesting support from the locals."

"They don't need extra incentive to push out intruders— although they always appreciate respectful gestures."

Bradan gave up trying to find a comfortable spot to lean against. "Offerings in soft temples?"

Taryn stretched out full length on her back and looked straight up at the Milky Way.

"You're so inquisitive. Bedsides sarcasm, it's one of your better qualities, but too many questions messes things up. I'll answer as best I'm allowed. My request on Mount Tam was open-ended. Faerie could interpret my importuning as they saw fit. They showed up when they were needed. That's what matters."

"Not to get too inquisitive," he said. "But you didn't ride with either side tonight."

"Which side should I have chosen? That's too big a decision after smoking a whole joint and drinking a bottle of cheap wine at our party."

"Always ambiguous."

"That's my nature," Taryn said. She laughed. "Also, we passed the audition."

"They liked the song we played at the party?" Bradan asked. "They can sit in any time they want."

"You have new fans. They weren't going to let the Wild Hunt vaporize you in their backyard without objecting."

"Would they help me again?" Bradan asked. "We need both groups, Golden Gate and Mount Tam."

"Everyone hates Gwyn and his crew. They're the only ones that collect souls and that's not cool with the rest of Faerie. But Gwyn's group is also the strongest and most savage in the Otherworld and includes Van and that blond bitch who helped Gwyn lead his forces. She's sort of his enforcer and no friend of mine. It would be a big ask to get the locals to assist you a second time against that outfit. So if you want Faerie's favors, I'd recommend offering up a gift in return."

"Could we make another contribution as I did on Tamalpais? That was fun. Actually, we could make two offerings—assuming I'm up for it and you agree."

"That kind of offering is much appreciated by the Mount Tamalpais crew. They're voyeurs; they enjoyed our show by the redwood, particularly the part where I clawed you. But the Golden Gate Gang are prudes. They'd be offended by that sort of thing, so Victorian. We'll need to make a different sort of gift that appeals to everyone."

"They all liked our song tonight," Bradan said. "Suppose we play everything off of our new album at a premier party just for them?"

"That might just buy you a lot of good will. How about in the park at night?"

"That's what I'm proposing. It's good to have friends. Speaking of which, thanks for hiding the gun and knife. I'd forgotten I had them on me. I don't even notice them anymore. You got them when you cleaned my glass cuts on the porch? Suppose they'd searched you?"

"I would have thrown a tantrum and demanded that a woman cop frisk me. It would have been too much of a nuisance. They were after a big drug bust thanks to that idiot kid they'd planted. Searching everyone for a joint or two wasn't the plan."

"Van set the dogs loose on me," Bradan said. "We've had endless parties here and the police never crashed one until tonight."

"Another skirmish," he continued. "The worst is yet to come."

"Yeah, but they aren't coming back tonight," Taryn said. "They need time to lick their wounds and plan for the next crossing of swords. Meantime, there's space in my bed for two. Join me. It needn't be any sort of offering; just screwing for the fun of it."

"I've got cuts everywhere," he said. "Don't rip up my back."

"That happens when you fuck a witch."

CHAPTER 12

Be Sure to Wear Flowers

March 1967, Front Porch
31¾ Belvedere Street, San Francisco

Bradan and Taryn picked up beer bottles and party debris from the stretch of Belvedere in front of the house. He noticed hypodermic needles in the gutter, which he lifted gingerly to toss in a trash bag. Even with work gloves on, and the immunity of a near immortal, he'd rather not stab himself. He was thankful none of the cops who'd taken down last night's bash noticed the syringes.

The rest of the band and a dozen house guests had promised vaguely to help with cleanup, but at 11:00 a.m., it was just the two of them working away methodically. Even reliable Scarlet Zorro lay passed out in his room next to a woman Bradan didn't recognize, but didn't think was his regular girlfriend, and a calico cat slept on his pillow. Tintagel usually, but not always, ignored cats.

Bradan looked over at Taryn to verify the reality of doing this mundane chore with a fifteen-century-old Celtic witch. She

looked good in the morning after a night of sex. However, contrasting with her usual tight, trendy clothing, today she wore
a long-sleeved flannel shirt under white, painter's bib overalls
with no more shape than a spacesuit. Like Bradan, Taryn protected herself with gloves as she got down on hands and knees
to reach under parked cars and retrieve rubbish as naturally as
if she were crafting an intricate spell.

They'd already filled several bags with garbage, but, needles
aside, in the light of late morning with the sun having ushered
the fog out to sea, 31¾ Belvedere appeared remarkably tranquil.
He'd expected a battlefield when he woke up, but things looked
normal except for a neighbor's Cadillac hearse, repurposed into
their daily driver, down the street with a smashed windshield.
Bradan guessed this was either defiance of mortality or simple
vandalism caused by an out-of-control partier. Bradan made a
mental note to check in with the hearse's owner even if it meant
coughing up cash to cover repairs.

His Martin twelve-string acoustic guitar sat in its case on the
porch swing ready to be strummed whenever he took a break
from cleaning up. Taryn would join him and they harmonized.
After a little impromptu music making, she got into it and went
inside to retrieve her own guitar and rejoined him so they could
improvise together. The energy picked up. Whenever they came
up with a worthy idea, Bradan jotted down the lyrics and music.
Good melodies were inspired by strange times. Neighbors
strolled past on the sidewalk, threading their way between the
trash bags and stopped to talk about last night's party, and listen
and offer thoughts on the nascent piece, making it a collective
creative effort.

Light shone through the Renaissance stained-glass design in
his front door and dappled the porch with pretty colors. The

aromas of flowers from nearby houses and quiet traffic noises from Haight Street reflected a nice balance between nature and city, and, though summer wasn't here yet, the summery, late-morning feeling of warmth and musical fellowship felt like it would go on forever, floating on a cloud of marijuana smoke and idealism.

But not for Bradan.

"Are you throwing in your lot with me?" he asked Taryn. "The odds aren't promising." They'd paused in their cleanup efforts standing beside his Harley parked in front the house.

"I keep my options open," the witch said. "That's worked over the centuries."

"Playing the park to mobilize support from the Otherworld gets you noticed by Van, and Gwyn's outfit. They'll think that's a step too far in consorting with their prey."

"I'm just recruiting for you," Taryn said. "Not taking sides. It gives you a sporting chance against overwhelming odds."

"I like sporting chances, too, but will Van and Gwyn appreciate your effort? They prefer overwhelming odds in their favor. To them I'm a soul long overdue for collecting, about fifteen centuries overdue."

"I don't answer to them," she said firmly. "I'll place my bets where I want."

"Watch your back."

She nodded. "Caution never hurts with that lot. They're brutal. Even combined, the Golden Gate and Tamalpais crews will have trouble against the Wild Hunt especially now that Van and Gwyn know you've petitioned two of Faerie's tribes to support you. They'll be better prepared in the future."

"I have unexpected allies of my own that may even up the odds. But I need to get them to partner with Faerie."

"How many?" Taryn asked.

"Numberless."

* * *

"Are ghosts friendly with fairies?"

Bradan popped the question out of the blue, but Meadow's mellow, brooding response didn't register any surprise.

"Why do you ask? Our paths don't cross."

"I'm doing a thing in Golden Gate Park tonight and I'm trying to figure out the seating arrangements, who sits next to who."

"What does this have to do with me or anyone like me?" Anger colored her tone. Meadow never got mad, but he'd succeeded in provoking her this afternoon with his flip attitude. She thought she was being played with.

"I'm not being hurtful," he said gently. "You made me an offer in LA a few weeks back. I need your help."

"You doubted my offer."

He needed to make amends or Meadow and the ghostly legion wouldn't help him.

How do I apologize to shades?

"By yourselves, I don't think you could do much, but if you joined with the Fair Folk, maybe. We'll get Barbara's killer and save me, too. However, your associates"—he knew how false *associates* sounded, but couldn't think of another descriptor for the myriad of specters in Meadow's world—"your associates need allies to match the Wild Hunters. The hunters collect lost souls and you all *are* lost souls. It won't go well for you unless we can find help, and I've got just the group."

"The creatures that live in the park, these fairies?"

"Yes, and from Mount Tamalpais, too, the Fair Folk, fairies, denizens of Faerie, whatever they're called. You saw them last night?"

"They seem neat, but they're really different, from a strange place."

"Yes, 'different,' but if they're on our side and if they're effective, who cares how different they are?"

"They're strong," the ghost agreed. "You parked me outside to impress the bikers so I saw what happened after the police left and a huge fight broke out over the park. They drove off the hunters including that thing that killed Barbara."

"That thing, Van, came close to chopping me in two with an ax before they left, but he and his pack will come back tougher than ever, so I want to enlist your friends"—*friends* had a better ring to it than *associates*—"to partner with Faerie. Without everyone working together, we'll lose. I'll do music in the park to make introductions, break the ice. I'll serenade the tribes."

"Invite them personally," Meadow said. "Without that they'll never agree since you rejected our first proposal. You'll have to make a strong case."

"Invite them? I'd be speaking to the wind. How do I invite them?"

"Don't go anywhere," she said.

Bradan sat down on the porch's top step. As on Sunset Boulevard, he sensed an invisible consultation occurring just beyond his perception. And then they were all around him again in their faded multitudes, up and down the street and into buildings and cars, heedless of physical structures, as insubstantial as pipe smoke, spreading all the way out to the ocean and throughout the city's neighborhoods. Among them were spirits from just yesterday and eras long bygone, shades of hippies consorted with Native Americans from millennia back. They all faced him. He recognized none of them except Barbara Renaldi, and Meadow, as before, standing directly in front of him, acting as the bridge between Bradan's "real" world and whatever came after violent, unnatural death. He remembered her from life and it lacerated his emotions to see her now close enough to touch. Would she be his translator for those who hadn't known English during their truncated earthly lives? Or was language meaningless after passing over? Though their collective gaze wasn't hostile, it was skeptical, and he felt an enormous psychic weight from their concentrated attention like his own soul was being scrutinized and found wanting.

Bradan realized he didn't know how to pitch his proposed alliance between Faerie and the spirits against the Wild Hunt, but his guitar sat conveniently close, so he picked it up and sang the half-formed piece he'd crafted with Taryn that morning. The lyrics hadn't been whipped into shape yet, but they alluded to struggle followed by tranquility. He didn't know whether it had the potential to evolve into a hit, but its mood matched his audience today. The piece started in a sad minor key, but transitioned to a major key at its climax before puttering to a half-hearted finish.

To any neighbor walking by, he played to himself on the front porch next to his motorcycle. However, when he looked about, he saw countless shades regarding him impassively, the spirits' plane of existence abutting Bradan's physical world.

God, that's unimpressive, Bradan thought. *It could be very good, but it needs work. What would his silent spectators make of it?*

I could be addressing my undergraduate folklore class. The lack of response is the same.

"I'll make it better before you hear it again," he promised them.

Should I say more about what I was trying to do with that song? Maybe play them another?

Knowing he was being presumptuous about realms that he knew nothing about, he said, "You may feel forgotten by life. This is a chance to participate again."

He watched Meadow to gauge what effect—if any—his plea was having.

Finally she gave him a thumbs-up and the spectral cloud clapped their approval as muted as owl's wings in an evening redwood grove.

They're being polite, he thought. *Does death do that?*

"Woman Who Sees Storms suggests extending the song with another chorus and changing the wording in your opening line," Meadow said, nodded to a young Native American standing beside her.

"Her instincts are good," Bradan said, jotting down this compositional advice.

"We'll play more songs like that tonight in the park," he added. "But the songs will be better because they're finished. Please join me along with my band. I don't know whether you'll get along with the Fair Folk, but I think you might, and you can't fight together against the hunters unless you know each other."

In an eyeblink they vanished, leaving him sitting on the sunny porch with his twelve-string guitar. Light passing through Botticelli's painting in stained glass touched him with variegated patterns.

* * *

Finally the house began to show signs of life. He heard dishes clattering about in the kitchen. Constantine ambled through the front door and plopped down on the porch swing next to Bradan. He lifted a wine bottle to his lips, looked at it with repugnance, belched loudly, and set the bottle on the banister.

"Good afternoon," Bradan said.

"It's that late?" the drummer asked.

"Sure is. Thanks for helping pick up."

Constantine looked blearily about the street like he saw it for the first time in his life. "Someone did a real good job making the neighborhood pretty again. 'Cept for the Caddy down the way. You should have left it for me to clean up. I would have taken care of it in a jiffy."

"No doubt," Bradan said sarcastically.

"What's in your hair?"

"Flowers. Daisies. They grow in the backyard."

"Didn't think flowers were your scene. You said it was a tired cliché."

"I'm writing a song," Bradan said. "Pretty petals seemed to fit the mood. It's about the modern world, all the wonderful stuff that's happening, spaceships to the moon, people just hanging out in parks digging being alive."

"Nothing dark?" the drummer asked.

"It's all light." Bradan considered for a moment how to describe the piece.

"The lyrics are pastel," he said.

"Run through the changes on your twelve-string. Let's hear a 'pastel' song." The drummer pulled out sticks from his back pocket. Bradan never saw him without them.

Bradan glanced at a piece of paper in his lap with notes and lyrics and played the song. Halfway through, Constantine began adding percussion, hitting the bench's armrest with his drumsticks.

"I like it," the drummer said. "There's more to it than you let on. We should get the Pillars together and flesh it out. Too bad you didn't have it ready for our second album."

"We can still use it for our gig tonight in Golden Gate," Bradan said.

Constantine looked away from him. "I'm not a fan of that park idea. It's cold and creepy after dark."

"We're an acid rock band," Bradan said. "We can do anything we want. Let's get everyone together and talk about it later in the afternoon."

* * *

"They're like musicians," the witch said. "The Fair Folk sleep during the day. They dream of magic and rapine."

"Rapine?" Bradan asked. "Excepting Gwyn's outfit, I thought they floated around on butterfly wings smelling roses and daisies."

"Fairies can be the sweetest of beings, but there's also a malevolent aspect of their personalities. That part isn't mentioned much in children's tales. No need to give kids nightmares."

"If they can go psycho, I guess that makes them good allies against the Wild Hunt," he said.

Taryn had ditched the overalls and flannel shirt in favor of figure-hugging jeans and a chic, pearl-gray, high-necked sweater with a silver necklace. Bradan saw a pendant configured as a Druid symbol hanging from the necklace. In the shifting shadows and sunlight, he saw iridescent flares of light from it. Remembering a long-ago lesson of Merlin's, he recalled that the Celtic icon defended its wearer from malign enchantment. She didn't usually wear it. If the supremely self-sufficient witch needed protection, what had they gotten themselves into on this stroll in the park?

"But they'll wake up for me?" he asked. "It's midafternoon."

"Well, that's the tricky part. Midafternoon is early for them. If they're grumpy at being disturbed, they'll attack whoever woke them. That doesn't usually end well. It's a bit messy, actually. So I'm wearing this pendant."

"What about me? Am I protected?"

Taryn shook her head. "Only one pendant—the Druids didn't make many—so you're on your own. Just you and your guitar. Best be entertaining, although I'm happy to join in on harmony vocals as needed."

"So don't let them get up on the wrong side of bed?"

"In a manner of speaking, yes."

"A gig for the ages," Bradan said acerbically. "Let's hope I live to tell the tale."

He carried the Martin with him in its case. That would have to be his protective talisman. To his knowledge, Druids hadn't played guitars.

Tintagel loped along by their side, clearly disdainful of Golden Gate Park's tame, manicured foliage flanking the path. Passersby, speaking in a babel of languages and enjoying an afternoon stroll in the park, gave the animal a wide berth.

The most overgrown part of the park was Strawberry Hill, a little island surrounded by Stow Lake, which was really a pond. Even this patch of water and dense trees was a pale imitation of the places Bradan had known as a child. He shared the wolf's contempt for this token patch of wilderness amid a densely populated city, remembering Britain reverting to true forest in the days when Arthur warred with Medraut, and invading barbarians from the continent fought one another and the Celts. Was it this memory that transmuted his perception of the park today? The trees on the island appeared larger and less well tended than usual and soared upward toward the heavens, blotting out the sun. The three of them moved in deep shadow up the hillside toward the top. They had the glade to themselves; nature around them had cleared itself of tourists.

"If they're in the park at all today, this is where they'd be," the witch said quietly. Did she not want to be overheard? he wondered.

Tintagel stopped being frisky and looked about inquisitively, but he was subdued, too. Even the beast was intimidated by circumstances.

"It's as good a place as any," Bradan said, keeping his voice low. He sat down on a tree stump and pulled the twelve-string out of its case. He was so tense, he had trouble tuning the instrument and his notes sounded small in the glade.

"Change in costume?" he asked. Taryn paced among the nearby trees in a long olive-green dress covered with a brown cloak. She wore a tiara of mistletoe, and the Ray-Bans were gone. However, the pendant stayed. He hadn't seen her change clothing.

The witch's eyes blazed. "I have to look the part, don't you think?"

"To preside over human sacrifice?"

"Don't be so pessimistic. You play a mean guitar and you've got a superb tenor. You'll do fine."

"Then let's wake up Faerie," Bradan said, though he wished he was far away from rapacious Fair Folk.

In the moment, he couldn't remember a single song's words or music. Nothing from the Pillars' repertoire, nothing from the scores of other songs he'd learned over fifteen centuries. His brain had simply frozen. The witch looked at him encouragingly and the wolf wagged its tail, but nothing came forth.

Quiet rustlings began among the trees and underbrush. A faint, carnivorous giggle floated out from the trunks and a splash like a sea serpent surfacing in Stow Lake sounded from below.

Anything, just play, he thought.

Bradan opened his mouth and out came the song he and Taryn had improvised on a porch swing this morning. He'd performed it for the host of shades earlier today. They'd seemed underwhelmed despite their clapping. However, Bradan had made the changes suggested by Woman Who Sees Storms. The first line became infinitely better with her suggested wording and a second chorus deepened the song's texture and allowed him to double back on the work's themes. On the fly, Bradan added a run up the fretboard to the tinkly high notes the Martin could make when coaxed. Thank God for the twelve-string's shimmering textures. He'd played it in a hundred smoky bars, and the instrument's wood had soaked up that emotion and energy. He tapped into that. If there was a guitar to make magic on, this was it.

Taryn's mezzo-soprano joined him on the choruses. Rather than letting the song dribble away inconclusively as he had earlier, they stopped it with Bradan's concluding E-major chord to give it a clean finish.

As he played, Bradan became aware of a growing ensemble of creatures large and small, ground bound and floating, clustering about him. He didn't make eye contact yet.

They'll either eat me or they'll want more.

The cosmos paused.

"You caught their attention," Taryn said. "They liked the song a lot, but they had suggestions about the wording in the first line. I told them to join us here tonight at midnight for an encore and I hinted that you'd bring visitors. That intrigued them. Seeing the same folks for eternity gets stale. It seems the Fair Folk wouldn't mind going on dates with new partners."

"Who knows how they'll get on with ghosts," Bradan said. A practical thought occurred to him. "We'll need power if we go electric. I guess we could bring a portable generator."

"No need. Look around."

Bradan surveyed the glade. He recognized the creatures encircling him from last night's battle royal over Golden Gate Park. Up close they appeared even more insubstantially peculiar, as much creatures of pure light and energy as entities of material and matter. Indeed, these were citizens of the Otherworld. He also saw dozens of electrical outlets embedded in tree trunks. Power for amplifiers wouldn't be a problem.

"Rock and roll," Bradan said.

"One other thing," Taryn said. "The Golden Gate crew is apparently not as prudish as I'd thought. If you live as long as they do, you have to spend your time doing something. Sex is a big part of pleasurably whiling away the millennia. Word travels fast in this community and they heard about our tryst on Mount Tamalpais, and they'd like to see a performance, too. Is that possible? It would be a drag if I exhausted you last night."

Bradan's long life had prepared him for almost any surprise. "I'm not exhausted," he said.

"Super! How exhibitionistic are you feeling?"

"Let's find out. Do we need to worry about splinters?"

The denizens of Faerie clustered closer for a front-row seat. Tintagel modestly departed the glade.

* * *

Bradan thought the best place for band meetings was 31¾ Belvedere's front porch. Cold, damp fog rolling in from the ocean encouraged short discussions due to the chill discomfort for the participants sitting on the wooden steps. Conversely, if the weather was beautiful, the meetings were short because everyone wanted to play in the sun. Today Bradan needed this meeting to be productive—however long that took. A performance would enlist supernatural support for his bid to eradicate Van, no easy task with the Wild Hunt led by a Welsh god in the congressman's corner. The spirits and Faerie anticipated a concert, so the next step was to persuade his band mates to help out. In making his case to the Pillars, he'd leave out a homicidal congressman, assorted ghosts, Faerie, the Wild Hunt, and a Welsh god of the Otherworld for the time being. Even without that, only a deft touch would sway the Pillars to do a midnight gig in the park.

They'll think I'm tripping.

Bradan looked around the porch. They were all here. Taryn had just sashayed over from Haight Street to join the rest of the Pillars in a tight-fitting denim jacket picked up from a secondhand store, playing the temperamental diva by being late to the meeting, but then making amends by rolling a joint and passing it around to the rest of the band.

"The Fair Folk were impressed by our performance in the park," she told Bradan too quietly for the rest to hear.

"The music or the sex?"

"Both."

She kissed Bradan with sensual warmth and caressed his crotch. Then she was back to prim and proper with a coy smile for the rest of the Pillars. The band clapped sardonically at the public affection.

Bradan breathed deeply to collect himself after the witch's carnal overture.

"Nothing in the world is more threatening than a wanton woman who wants sex just for its own sake," she said.

"Good to hear your priorities," Bradan said quietly. "Mine is survival."

Taryn seated herself languidly on the sidewalk next to his Harley. Bradan didn't know whether the witch recognized his bike was haunted, but she was always respectful of the machine.

He addressed himself to the Pillars. "The Golden Gate thing we talked about—"

"We already played the park. Why do it again?" Constantine interrupted. He sprawled on a middle step, wine bottle in hand. "And at night. Who sees us? Who pays us?" After taking a long drink, he set the bottle down and twirled a drumstick in each hand. This was his nervous tic during band meetings. The sticks spun so quickly they looked like airplane propellers.

"I don't usually agree with Tine," Jeff said. The bass player pronounced the last syllable of Constantine's name as "tiny" just to goad the drummer.

"But, yeah, why *are* we wanting to play in an empty park at midnight?" Jeff continued. He lay full length on the front stoop and ran his fingers through his goatee. He fancied it gave him a sinister, piratical look. "Probably colder than shit what with fog and such."

"This will be good public relations for the Pillars," Bradan said. He leaned nonchalantly against the porch's wooden banister, trying to keep things light, but also trying to drive the discussions to a conclusion, no easy feat with an ensemble as temperamental as the Pillars.

If I push them too hard, any consensus collapses like a house of cards, he thought. *Play to their vanity.*

"You guys are good, real good," he said. "We just proved it at the Fillmore. And we've got a bunch of LA gigs lined up, and this June thing in Monterey, so our reputation is growing, but we need a real splash to push the second album and convince the new label we have a following, that anyone out there has heard of us. And we don't have a lot of cash. This will be guerrilla marketing."

"You mean like guerrilla warfare?" Jeff asked.

"Sort of except no one dies," Bradan answered, exasperated. He hoped that was true at the midnight gig he was trying to sell them on. "I've got a contact at the *San Francisco Chronicle*. I'll tell them about our performance. If he brings along a photographer, we get an entertainment page story with all of our pictures featured."

"Man, we do *not* need media hacks to hype the Pillars," Constantine said.

"We're making the system work for us," Bradan said. "Also, there are a couple of underground music presses over in the East Bay that would cover a stunt like this if we told them. We'll get a small crowd together to watch if we spread the word in the house. They'll tell friends. We only got through one of our songs last night before the police showed, so this is part two of our roll-out party for *An Emerald Boat on the Euphrates*."

"Who came up with that title?" Constantine demanded between swigs of wine. "Bradan, you always get your way on band stuff."

"Jesus. Our band's a democracy." Bradan worked hard not to shout at them. "We all voted on it. Kenny, help me out. You're usually up for anything if it spreads word about the band."

"Can I do a tab of windowpane before we play?" the keyboard player wondered. This afternoon he affected a black top hat like a nineteenth-century British toff. "Maybe a couple of tabs. I need it to fortify my soul. That park is spooky at night. I'm being watched when I take a walk there after sundown. Last night, after the party, and the cops and all that negativity, me and my girlfriend, Yolanda, we were getting it on near Stow Lake and things were checking us out. We pulled on our clothes and ran, literally ran all the way back here to the house. Man, we were chased, not sure by what, but something we couldn't see too well, but they was all around us in the trees."

"Chased by things you couldn't see?" Constantine said. "Man, I'm chased by things I can see: my ex-girlfriends. I'll take invisible pursuers any day."

Bradan cut in before the conversation spun wildly off course. "Ladies and gents, can we do this park gig?"

"I've always wanted to serenade the stars and fog," Taryn said. The witch had an instinctive sense of group dynamics. She was the Pillars' newest member, so she'd deferred to the musicians with more band history and let them say their piece before interjecting her own thoughts.

Meadow, a sixth unheard participant in the band meeting, must be observing the discussion bemused by contending band egos, Bradan thought.

"I'm in," Kenny said. He doffed his top hat theatrically to the rest of the band. "If it helps get our name out, we gotta do it, but how do we get my Hammond over to the park? It weighs a ton. And, if anything weird happens over there, I'm leaving."

"Constantine?" Bradan said. "We can't do this without drums."

"I been thinking." His sticks stopped spinning. "The single off the new album, we all should get a songwriting credit for that. If radio picks it up, we could all make bucks. Kind of spreads the wealth around."

The rest of the band now paid rapt attention.

"Why's that?" Bradan asked casually.

"Well, you and Taryn wrote the lyrics to 'A Waltz in Faerie' after an insane all-nighter with a bottle of Jack Daniel's right here on this porch. Hell, you woke up the whole neighborhood when you sprinted into the house to put the melody together in the living room. You had the amps set as high as they would go. Guess you couldn't contain all that creative energy, but without my drum fills, it's nothing much except existential words and a great guitar riff—I'll give you credit for the guitar part and the chorus. Good job. But the piece still needed excellent percussion."

"Right on, man," Jeff said. "Wow, I'm agreeing with Tine twice in one day. History is made. We all deserve royalties. It's a tripping song, but without a solid bass line, it's a limp noddle, just a regular pop song. It's way better because I changed the turnaround during the middle measures."

"Let's put it to a vote," Kenny said. "Taryn, you got strong feelings one way or the other?"

The witch shrugged. "You guys all contributed."

Bradan could see how the wind blew. "Don't vote. You're right. We all share writing credit on this one. Everyone deserves royalties."

Bradan stretched hugely. *This is herding cats, but they agreed to play Golden Gate.*

"The gig in the park is at midnight," he said. "Let's get together inside now and run through the set list. I've got a new thing that I played for Constantine. I'll run it past you. See if the rest of you think it will work tonight. We'll make enough noise to literally raise the dead."

* * *

"Power?" Jeff said.

The bass player asked as if he thought no one had stumbled on the performance's fatal flaw until just now.

"That's covered," Bradan said.

"We're in the middle of a giant park," Constantine said. "What, like there are outlets in the trees?"

"Yep," Bradan said. "Parks and Rec thinks of everything."

"Cops?" Kenny asked.

"We play until they show up," Bradan said. "Or they never notice. The fog's so thick no one can see much. The music will be muffled, too. The mist only gets worse as the night goes on."

Constantine looked at him like he'd missed the obvious "'Raise the dead,' you said. Everything's turned way up. They'll notice. The whole Haight will notice. We're doing the entire second album. The police will show up just like at last night's party."

"Then they show up. We'll distract them. Tintagel's good at that, especially in a forest with bad visibility. I can't see the hand in front of my face."

"Man, in this fog, I'm getting that feeling of being watched again," Kenny said. "We're not the only beings here."

"You're high," Jeff said. "Let me take a hit of whatever you're doing."

They'd driven in vans and assorted cars from the Belvedere house to Stow Lake. Zorro lugged Bradan's guitars and amps in the back of the dealer's '57 Cadillac. Even in foggy, clammy conditions, it turned out to be quite a crowd with friends, sleeping companions, various hangers-on, and whoever in their neighborhood had happened to hear about the quickly organized midnight concert in the park. What would they make of the myriad of ghosts and Fair Folk they were about to confront? For that matter, what would supernatural beings make of all the hippies about to descend on their heretofore quiet nighttime park environs?

He'd ridden the Harley over from the house. He needed Meadow's mediation with the spirits and he already knew the bike could go cross-country from his experience in Laurel Canyon, so he rolled slowly over the little bridge crossing the lake and gunned the big bike up a narrow hiking trail to the top of Strawberry Hill. It was so murky and misty he could only just make out the path. He parked the Harley under a tree near where they set up.

"This lake, it's not fast-flowing water," he told Meadow. "It's not moving at all."

"I'm fine. Thanks for being considerate. None of my friends will be troubled, either. You'll have a big audience. They're already gathering. A few of them know this place already. One of them killed himself right where you're standing."

What a party, he thought.

"No stage," Bradan said. "It's too much effort to construct and everyone should be at the same level, the Pillars and whoever's in the audience. The musicians aren't elevated over anyone."

"Groovy," Taryn said caustically. "That's egalitarian of you." She threw her guitar's strap over her shoulder.

"Ever the aristocrat," he said.

Despite crappy visibility, she had her Ray-Bans on. "Is the *Chron* guy here?" she asked.

"Yeah, but that could be a problem."

"Press is good for us," she said.

"But pictures of ghosts and fairies aren't. He brought a staff photographer along like I asked him to, but I wonder, do the Fair Folk show up on film?"

"No one's tried taking their pictures since Victorian times. Didn't work then, won't work now. What about your spirits?"

He'd told the witch about Meadow and her legion of ghosts. Taryn seemed impressed and showed sudden interest in taking the Harley for a ride. He supposed connections with the afterlife gained him credibility with a Celtic enchantress.

"They're gray-tone even in perfect light," he said, remembering the faded figures he'd played for earlier. "Tonight they'll be well nigh invisible. Can I borrow your scarf?"

Vaguely curious, the witch handed it to him. Bradan tied it around his hair in a headband. Then he plugged in his instrument and gently strummed chord changes from the piece he'd played for Faerie and the spirits earlier. If he was going to meld the Otherworld and the afterlife into a cohesive unit capable of contending with the Wild Hunt and—not incidentally—save his own ass, he needed excellent sound despite their wilderness environment, so Zorro sat on a log behind a folding table with a mixing board and headphones to balance the Pillars' sound. The hash dealer had unexpected talents in high-fidelity audio reproduction. And Faerie had unexpected awareness of the electrical needs of an acid rock band; pure AC power flowed effortlessly from the many outlets Bradan had seen earlier into the band's speakers about to render their songs live and loud. From what ultimate source of energy the power emanated, Bradan didn't care to guess.

He looked about the glade. The Pillars had set up a couple of portable spotlights that illuminated the band, spectators, and trees, creating deep pools of shadow contrasting with blinding glare that bleached out the vegetation and people. Adding to the mélange, Zorro's girlfriend held up colored gels and flowing emulsions in front of the lights, crafting an informal light show. Her preferred color palette tended toward the red end of the spectrum and dipped the scene in bloody hues.

The lights' illumination bounced about surreally and the fog eddied in big puddles amid the trees. It had a tactile quality, caressing Bradan's skin as wetly as an erotic touch. At ground level it was dense, but if he looked directly up, he saw the moon though the milky darkness. And stars.

The band and its supporters had set up the musical equipment in remarkably short order, and now about 250 people huddled under blankets and ponchos amid the performers. In fact, there were no formal seating arrangements and their audience sat amid the Pillars, on top of their amplifiers and by the mic stands, and with their backs against tree trunks. Wine and beer made the rounds as well as the obligatory dope. A young couple sat on Bradan's Harley clutching each other for warmth. Meadow would appreciate their cuddly body heat on a cold night.

Are my supernatural guests in attendance? Bradan wondered.

It's hard to distinguish specters from spectators.

He took a long pull from a cognac bottle.

The stage was set.

"Buckle up," he said. "We're under way."

Beside him Constantine sent an eruption of percussive sounds up to the stratosphere, hammering his drums into submission. Bradan answered with a squall of chords from the Les Paul, and The Pillars of Creation slammed into the first cut from their new album. And now he saw Meadow and her innumerable fellow shades, many so faint they were one with the mist. Swirling among them, every imaginable resident of Faerie capered or flew about accompanied by a bestiary of peculiar creatures that even Bradan's background in folklore left him hard pressed to identify. Regardless, he hoped they all would join him against the hunters and not set upon one another.

I don't need to mediate a supernatural civil war.

Focusing on the intricacies of his music, Bradan still glimpsed the reactions of the human audience, but they seemed more bemused than terrified by their sudden eerie company. Likely all the intoxicants and hallucinogens they'd taken onboard along with the murky visibility made them unsure just what they saw. Would any of them share these strange dreams with others? Who cared? They were all doped up and no one would believe a bunch of hippies, anyway. Even the *Chron* journalist would doubt his senses.

The band's vocals blended with the guitars and keyboards. Elves, fairies, and other magic creatures danced about the glade. Bradan saw the destrier he'd ridden during his failed assassination attempt gallop by with a herd of similar equines. With phenomenal agility, they avoid trampling the Pillars, their equipment, or human spectators. At first Meadow's spirits hung back, but then tentatively they began interacting with the Fair Folk, for the moment shrugging off the memories of tragic death in favor of dancing with one another and the fairies.

A dam burst and it became a party and spilled down Strawberry Hill out across Stow Lake and into the greater reaches of Golden Gate Park, everything enveloped by dense fog and unconstrained by gravity or any law of nature.

The Pillars' music glued the festivities together and the band was in fine voice, despite the insane distractions, pushing through the new material from their second album—if the corporate record label execs could only see them now.

Bradan glanced about. Thank heavens none of his fellow musicians had freaked out at the jarring sights and fled the concert. Bradan felt tempted to add his own magical images to the light show, but that would drain him of the vitality he needed to vault his solos into the crowd's consciousness.

They must believe this is all a bizarre hallucination.

He traded leads with the witch, both of them feeding off of each other's energy and the crowd dynamics. They were on fire tonight as the Pillars provided a soundtrack to a phantasmagorical party.

With all the energy floating past in the ether, Bradan felt he could do anything; whatever images his imagination conceived, he could make real by tapping into this vitality without paying the usual price of exhaustion commensurate with the ambition of the vision. In the middle of the new song framing his reaction to the circus of current national events, he inserted four rhyming couplets. His band mates don't know or care what he was about, just Bradan doing vocal improvisations over the main riff. However, Taryn looked over at him. Even though her eyes were concealed by the sunglasses, he sensed the witch's suspicions as her normally fluid playing became more staccato.

Images formed among the human and supernatural revelers. They became a canvas for the song's themes. Bradan had intended to present pretty, surreal pictures, but—unbidden—rockets flying men to the moon turned into space capsules engulfed in flames that never left the launchpad; love-ins amid city parks transformed into pitched street battles with flung bottles and tear gas against a backdrop of flaming neighborhoods; puffy clouds and sweet vistas mutated into mushroom clouds and warfare. None of it was peace and love.

Bradan was shocked that the song's pastel lyrics invoked frightful pictures, but he'd written it inspired by current events and its graceful, lyrical poetry couldn't disguise its fractured foundations. It was as light and airy as an era's aspirations and as bleak as the world's reality. Bradan now saw elements in his creation that he didn't realize were integral to the piece. He watched as Fair Folk fought with one another and the ghosts with violent energy like atoms colliding in a cyclotron. Some of the ghosts weren't victims, but perpetrators who'd done awful violence to themselves or others before they died, and this facet of their personalities revealed itself. The electrical outlets in the trees sparked, sending blue flame out to scorch the trunks and the couple fondling each other on his Harley abruptly jumped off, screamed curses at each other's faces, and ran into the trees in opposite directions.

Bradan had fomented the civil war he'd hoped to avoid instead of cementing an alliance between vastly different tribes whose synchrony he desperately needed; and once again, as in prison, he'd set loose forces as savage as the Wild Hunt with his careless, arrogant images thrown up in a fit of creative hubris that had set latent fuel afire. And now he paid the penalty for casting the spell as exhaustion hit him. He stopped playing and leaned drunkenly against a speaker cabinet.

Fix this, he thought. *Somehow.*

The album's final song was an uplifting anthem without a desolate subtext. If anything would erase the malevolent shit he'd just materialized, this was it. Wearily, Bradan hit its opening chords. However, he'd inserted the song out of sequence on tonight's set list and none of the other Pillars realized the direction they must go to shift the party's hellish vibe back to fun. For several moments there was cacophonous musical chaos as each of the Pillars charged about doing their own thing, uncertain which song they should play, aural anarchy. They looked ready to join in the general strife and physically attack one another, but Taryn saw what he was trying to do and locked in with his melody. Their two guitars plowed through the opening bars of the anthem, dragging along the other three instruments. Hours of cohesive instincts developed during practice finally kicked in and all five of them coalesced into harmony to send the song soaring over the crowd.

Bradan's dark images collapsed and vanished. The fractious partiers forgot what they were fighting over and returned to a mellow plane of being. Hippies embraced and spirits and fairies once again locked arms to dance. The couple who'd rushed off separately into the woods sheepishly returned to the glade and held each other for warmth on a cold night. Accord restored, the Pillars played through the rest of their material and the night spun merrily along.

Then all the songs finished.

"Good night," Bradan said. "See you in Monterey."

* * *

"What the hell?" Constantine said as they loaded gear into a van. "You see all that shit in the mist as we played?"

"It was too misty," Bradan said deadpan. "I wasn't paying attention. I was into the music. How high are you?"

"Man, I wasn't so high that I imagined what I just saw."

"Super-good drumming. You kept all us all together tonight. You okay to drive our stuff to Belvedere? Tintagel, hop in with Constantine. Ride shotgun. Make sure he gets home."

It was 3:30 a.m. Bradan watched neighbors and housemates filter through the trees and down to the roads heading into the Haight. He walked back up the hill to the glade at the top. He still wore Taryn's silk scarf as a headband. If he listened hard, he heard the Pillars songs echoing through the park and across the Milky Way—or it was the amplifiers' residual tones bouncing among the trunks? Everyone and every being had disappeared, returning to whatever real or unreal place they called home except for the young couple sitting on his Harley. The bike sat where he'd parked it with the girl and boy asleep upright in the saddle leaning against each other. He nudged them back to life.

"What did you do?" Meadow asked when they'd wandered off into the trees holding hands.

The glade was empty. He didn't know whether the emptiness was hostile, friendly, or indifferent. The magical outlets had vanished, leaving only scorched patches on trunks. He guessed these would heal in time.

"I played guitar," Bradan said. "Sang a little, too."

"You know what I'm asking."

"I thought my images would add magic to the evening. Turned out I was wrong."

"You brought out the worst in them. Spirits attacked each other and attacked the fairies, too. I didn't think they could do that. We always stick together. We're all in the same limbo."

"I bring out the best in folks. But it *did* all come back together by the concert's end. Will everyone work together when we need them to?"

"I don't know," Meadow said. She sounded tired and dispirited.

"Want to dance?" he asked gently. "Just you and me? Like when you were alive. It would be magic."

"It wouldn't be good magic."

Time to go home. He jumped on the starter. It took many tries and several backfires to get the bike to cooperate, probably because of the night's dampness.

CHAPTER 13

Tenure Track

May 1967, Claremont, California

"Professor Badon! You're in The Pillars of Creation."
Bradan looked around to see Kay Liu from his
undergraduate folklore class striding toward him
across the campus commons.

"I just got your second album," she gushed. "That's so trippy,
having a professor who plays in a band. One of the songs was on
the radio. Do you write the material?"

"Thanks, Kay. We can talk about music later."

He'd almost gotten to the faculty lounge walking in uncomfortable silence with Harv Kleiner, one of the full professors on
his tenure review committee who normally wouldn't have been
caught dead with Bradan, but this afternoon they'd accidently
met en route to the lounge, so separating would have been
awkward and they'd tacitly chosen the lesser evil and marched
along together. Bradan tried small talk, but gave up after meeting chilly monosyllables.

Kay had chosen that moment to shout out Bradan's musical
accomplishments. However, she was smart and saw this was bad

timing for a collegial chat with her folklore professor. She nodded respectfully at Kleiner and waved enthusiastically at Bradan before veering off to join friends sitting on the lawn in front of the library.

"Love your class," she said in parting.

The older man broke his silence. "You're in a band?" Everything Kleiner said was clipped like he'd bitten the sentence off before speaking it.

Just what Bradan didn't need: an interrogation about his Jekyll and Hyde life a few minutes before the tenure hearing. Whatever he said would be incomprehensible to Kleiner and erode his tenuous academic credibility.

"A string quartet?" the senior academic persisted. "Is that what she meant by band? I never can understand what undergrads are trying to say."

"Sort of," Bradan hedged. "There are five of us. We're a quintet."

"We have a love of music in common. I play violin. Not professionally, but I enjoy it. Bartók and Shostakovich are favorites."

"I'd like to hear you perform."

"You won't. I don't have the time to keep at it with my research and the teaching load they saddle us with here. Tedious. The students get stupider every year. I might have gone down a different path and made a career of violin, but life closes one road so you must take another. Here we are. I'd wish you good luck in the hearing, but I don't play favorites."

True to his word, Kleiner made no effort to shake his hand; he simply strode into the dim faculty lounge.

Abandoned by the senior academic, Bradan stood before the lounge repurposed today for his and Gail's tenure hearings. He remembered chatting with Amy in its stygian depths. The normal meeting room used for History's tenure hearings off the chairman's office had been commandeered by Toby Hackett in his new capacity as History's interim chair while Chaffee clung tenaciously to his current office, refusing eviction despite scandal.

Bradan sighed and sat down on a chair in the hall outside the lounge. He'd never gotten his sport coat back from Nico that he'd intended to wear to this hearing. So he'd bought another using royalty money from the Pillars' first album. He was sure there was cosmic significance to this, synergy between the two parts of his life. He also wore a tie and dress slacks and had cut his hair to general criticism from the Pillars, particularly Taryn, who liked a long wild mane on him.

Gail stepped through the club's front door, glanced into the lounge, then superstitiously turned away to look for a chair. She saw Bradan and hesitated between a seat near him and one at the far end of the hall.

Bradan reflected that this was a day for awkward moments.

Finally she smiled tightly at him and sat in the closer chair. Studiously avoiding eye contact, she consulted a file folder with notes and her publication reprints. Though he knew his own material by heart, Bradan also thumbed through his papers to duck making conversation.

Tobias Hackett burst through the club's doors accompanied by two other senior History faculty, welcomed both Bradan and Gail effusively as if he hadn't seen them in months, and sauntered into the lounge shouting a greeting at Kleiner.

A moment later Gavin Chaffee entered the building, nodded slightly at Bradan, but didn't acknowledge Gail. Bradan thought he looked diminished, but just before reaching the door into the lounge, the former department chair straightened himself, gained stature, and strode inside. Bradan heard no welcome from the other four committee members.

"Didn't think Chaffee would be on this thing," Bradan said to Gail.

"He's still a tenured, full professor, so they're stuck with him," she replied.

"We're stuck with him," Bradan said.

"For what it's worth, I'm not seeing him anymore," she said.

"Good to know," he said sardonically. "How's Amy doing? Landed on her feet?"

Gail nodded.

Hackett reappeared at the faculty lounge's double doors. "The gang's all here," he said brightly. "It probably seems a trifle strange, but we're doing both of you today, killing two birds with one stone, so to speak." He chuckled. "Actually, that's not the best metaphor."

"So I'll flip a coin," he continued. "Gail, you call the toss and the winner sees us first. The other one waits patiently and we'll invite them in after we've finished with the first."

Gail won the flip and Hackett ushered her into the lounge. Bradan couldn't bring himself to wish her good luck as she passed, but the old professor didn't appear to notice any tension between them. The doors closed.

The committee review of Gail's performance went on interminably. It was a sadistic refinement of torture to ask that he wait for her fate to be determined. Of course they wouldn't tell Gail to her face until they'd deliberated and privately voted. Bradan wondered whether they'd decide her fate before interviewing him or call him in right after her and then confer about both of them together. Which option favored his prospects? He paced up and down the hall.

He heard a radio playing from a food service kitchen across from the lounge. It was a Pillars' song. He'd be thrilled in other circumstances.

Finally the lounge doors opened and Gail walked out. She'd gone into the hearing in her usual rumpled, self-confident persona, but came out looking like a steamroller had crushed her. Her bouncy curls hung limply against her head and neck, sweat sticking the hair to her skin. Bradan wondered what he'd look like upon emerging from the hearing.

"You're next," she said flatly and sat down in the nearest chair. "They've asked me to stay here while they interview you. Then they'll tell us both together what they've decided."

"Seems a stupid way to do it," Bradan said.

He entered the lounge. It looked more intimidating then when he'd sat here with Amy two months ago. There was still too much leather furniture, an impressive collection of books, and not enough sunlight. The room smelled of sweat and tension. The walk into the chamber was endless as they stared at him like otherworldly gods.

The committee sat five abreast at a table on the far end. With them all lined up, Bradan noticed their hair—what there was of it—in shades of gray or white. He should give them his recently shorn locks to make up for the deficit.

A veritable geriatric ward, Bradan thought.

Big overstuffed chairs had been shoved to the room's perimeter except for one sitting dead center before the inquisitors. This chair was much lower than the committee's seats, so Bradan had to look up at them. At least it felt comfortable. He carefully settled in, clutching his folder of material like a sixth-century warrior's shield, his entire academic output and intellectual worth contained in a few sheets of paper.

"You know the format for these things?" Hackett opened.

Bradan nodded. The newly minted chairman was as amiable as ever. Kleiner looked impassive. Chaffee regarded Bradan disdainfully and seemed impatient to get on with it. The other two didn't look up from perusing the pre-reading material Bradan had given the committee. Plainly they hadn't examined it until just now.

"It's simple, really," said Hackett. "No boring opening statements from candidates in *my* department."

Hackett was marking his territory to remind the others—Chaffee particularly—how the department's power balance had shifted.

Exploit their differences, Bradan thought. *If I'm to come out of this alive, then I take control.*

"We already know your work—or we should know your work, Dan, Jonas." Hackett pouted at two committee members beside him examining the pre-reading. Abashed, they closed their folders and contritely looked at Bradan.

These buffoons haven't made the slightest effort to understand what I've spent years of my life studying.

"Each of us gets to ask as many questions as we'd like," Hackett said. "And you can rebut as you deem appropriate. Let's get going. I'll ask the first—"

Chaffee interrupted. "Toby, if it's all the same to you, let's get to the central issue here as I see it."

"As the chairman, it's *my* prerogative—"

Chaffee cut Hackett off again. "Bradan, just what role do you see folklore as having in a history department? A nationally recognized history department? It's an odd fit, you'll agree."

Steer them toward the paper I'm co-authoring with Hackett and watch the fur fly.

"I expected that question and it's legitimate," Bradan said.

Of course he expected Chaffee's question. The former chairman had previewed it on the day he sat in on Bradan's class and patted Gail's ass. Bradan remembered that quite well.

"What's wrong with your eyes?" Kleiner asked. "They looked orange for a second."

"Nothing," Bradan said. "I need eye drops. Much of my work fits squarely into modern historical research. The first three publications in your packet of pre-reads are in leading history journals. If you'd care to glance at them—"

"Why Toby, I see you're an author on one of these with Bradan," Chaffee said.

"Yes, Gav, it's called publishing significant research. You should try it sometime."

Kleiner broke in to head off intracommittee acrimony and preserve the proceeding's stodgy dignity.

"Professor Badon, review that work with us, please. I read it, but it's been a while and it's a rather complex topic."

Steer them toward grants. That's how this damned institution funds itself. I pull in more money than the rest of them combined. Appeal to their greed. In 1,500 years, that's never gone out of fashion.

"Certainly. The work you're referring to was funded by the National Endowment for the Humanities with a matching grant from the Leitmonter Family Foundation." Bradan outlined the focus of the research on historical imagery in modern tribal folklore. To him it sounded impressively arcane and reflected well on the institution's prestige.

"A colleague at UCLA wanted my advice on how to generate funding," he added. "The family foundation was very generous in supporting the work you see before you."

*Get them worried I can jump ship and take my grantsman-
ship skills to UCLA or any other university.*

They plowed through the rest of Bradan's publications with
what seemed to be genuine interest from everyone except Chaffee, who yawned repeatedly.

"Research is fine, but we always give teaching short shrift in
these tenure discussions." This came from one of the full professors who hadn't said much so far, Dan Farthing. "I, for one,
am struggling to stay relevant to my students in these shifting
times, wars, protests, love-ins, crazy music. We're supposed to
look at history and connect it to the world around us, but I don't
get what's happening now at all. History stopped for me years
ago, decades ago. Professor Badon, as a younger member of our
staff—"

Young? If you only knew, Bradan thought.

"—how do you keep the kids engaged?"

Kleiner broke in, "Well, I heard an unsolicited endorse-
ment on the campus commons a moment ago from a student
about Bradan's efforts to stay connected to today's zeitgeist. She
seemed pretty impressed."

"We do surveys of student satisfaction with their professors,"
Hackett said. "Professor Badon scores well, quite well. One respon-
dent even said they liked the pyrotechnics in his visual aids."

"Oh, what a load of shit," Chaffee burst out. "You're such
hypocrites. Who the hell cares about teaching?"

Ah, the elephant in the room, Bradan thought.

"I kind of agree with Gavin on this one." This interjection
came from Jonas Russo, the other professor who'd said little
and hadn't read any of Bradan's papers. "I really don't think the
students are fit to pass judgment on our teaching abilities, so I
never worry much about those survey results."

Bradan sat quietly as the committee volleyed back and forth about the relative importance of research versus teaching. This went on for forty-five minutes before grinding to a halt.

They've exhausted themselves and need to go to the bathroom.

"Bradan, you're excused," Hackett said peremptorily. "Grab a seat outside with Gail and I'll come out when we're done in here."

Outside the lounge, Bradan was tempted to put his ear to the door, but he didn't have to. Any sort of decorum was buried under rancor and he clearly heard an acrimonious discussion inside that carried on forever. For a while Hackett's and Chaffee's voices dominated with only occasional interludes from Kleiner, Russo, and Farthing. However, Hackett held his own and over time shouted down opposing opinions.

Gail looked at Bradan unhappily.

Kleiner was the first to emerge. Thin-lipped, he shook hands with first Gail, then Bradan. Chaffee erupted through the lounge doors and barreled out of the building without looking at anyone. Finally Hackett sauntered out accompanied by the remainder of the committee.

"Congratulations to both of you, Associate Professors Badon and Halpern," Hackett said. "Sounds a lot better than assistant professor, no? Welcome to the permanent faculty of our august institution. I'll have Clara talk to you about your new salaries next Monday—assuming Gav hasn't absconded with departmental funds for promotions."

The rotund senior faculty member's eyes sparkled merrily as he bestowed largess like a Celtic chieftain. Bradan wanted to collapse in relief. In the grand scheme of things, this was a paltry victory, but he'd take whatever came his way. He hoped he'd survive to savor it, given the Wild Hunt's ongoing interest in him.

"I'm not supposed to say this, but Gav Chaffee voted against both of you. Not very supportive of younger faculty if you were to ask me. Anyway, since that debacle at the Faculty Club, he doesn't have veto power on these matters and he's less persuasive than he used to be, seems to be coming apart at the seams, actually. And he hasn't made any friends in History with his ex-wife's damned lawyer hectoring us all about patterns of infidelity and such like. Now Chaffee's got his own attorney to make our lives doubly miserable. We're all caught in the cross fire. But back to both of you, your hearing was decided by a simple majority. And he's no longer the chair. I am. And by the power vested in me, I say let's see if we can get wine served up to celebrate. Bradan, you flatter yourself that you know vino, so I'll let you choose."

"Too much responsibility," Bradan demurred. "I'll defer to seniority."

"So be it," Hackett said enthusiastically. "I'll order. By the way, on a related note: Bradan, keep those grants coming in. As I'm sure you're more than well aware, the university gets a cut of everything you pull in."

"Administrative overhead." Bradan nodded.

"A cut of the spoils." Hackett chortled. "But it keeps us solvent in troubled times, eh?"

* * *

"So what now?" Bradan asked Gail.

He loosened his tie, wondering how long it would take for his hair to grow back. He yanked the tie off completely.

"I like your haircut," Gail said. "Where do you want it to go?"

"We had a good thing. Now we don't, but we both got what we wanted."

"You took the high road and won on your research and teaching."

They sat in the faculty lounge talking quietly while staff rearranged the room and shoved chairs back into place. Toby Hackett had made obligatory, congratulatory toasts then departed, sensing the two had things to thrash out and he had new bottles of wine to conquer elsewhere. A half-finished carafe of execrable cabernet sat on a coffee table in front of them. A completely empty bottle sat next to it, which Tobias Hackett had polished off by himself. A plate of inedible hors d'oeuvres flanked the bottles.

Dan Farthing lingered a little, chatting about the importance of passing on knowledge to the next generation. To Bradan he sounded sincere—and a bit like Merlin. Also, perhaps, the older professor was conscious of needing to observe academic rituals that stretched back to medieval Oxford and Padua: A successful tenure hearing should be acknowledged. Bradan stood to shake his hand and so did Gail. Then Farthing split.

Windows were opened and the room reverted from inquisitorial chamber to staid faculty lounge. Odors of anger and anxiety made way for aromas of pine and eucalyptus from trees outside. Professors filtered in and baritone murmurs from important conversations drifted over to them. Bradan had to remind himself that he was now permitted to sit in their company.

"The road I took to tenure wasn't all that moral," Bradan said. "Hackett's name is on one of my papers, which he had nothing whatsoever to do with. And I've been pretty good at pulling in grants. The department frankly could care less about the academic value of my research, but they love the dollars I earn. I flatter myself that I do important, original work, and I put my heart into teaching, but that's all a sideshow as far as they're concerned."

He paused, realizing he was as tired as if he'd cast a complex spell. Idealism was fatiguing, and the effort was only occasionally worthwhile. Merlin would have told him not to be disheartened.

So what becomes of me and Gail?

"At least you told me about your thing with Chaffee when you came up to San Francisco," he said. "Instead of stringing me along while you hid it."

"You suspected?" She slumped back in a chair and patted her curls to give them more body. They were still damp with sweat. She'd wasn't wearing glasses and her features were better for it.

He nodded. "The signs were there if I wanted to see them."

As in Sproul Hall three years ago, Bradan glanced at the curve of her breasts beneath her shirt, but today physical attraction didn't align with anything else he felt. He wondered if she'd seen his look and hoped she hadn't; this wasn't the time or place to recapture a long-ago moment of spontaneous passion. They were different people then.

"I guess I wasn't revealing much to you when I visited," she said. "Is Taryn still in the picture?"

"Good question. She plays by her own rules and nothing with her is all that predictable. I'm not sure where I fit in. She plays great guitar and has quite a voice. We write imaginative material together, too. She has a gift with rhyme. It must come from all the places she's lived. She has the soul of a Celt."

"She's pretty and talented, but strange. Does she even like you?"

"Perceptive question. I don't know. I've lived in a lot of places, too, so we talk of things we don't talk to anyone else about."

"Music stuff?" Gail asked.

"Sure. And other things."

Bradan decided to change the topic away from the murky intersection of lust and career advancement. "My San Francisco band adventure turned out to be more helpful than I'd thought in the halls of academe." He laughed and told her about meeting Kay before the hearing.

"To my amazement, I scored points with Kleiner by fronting an acid rock band."

"Maybe I was wrong," she said. "You don't have to make a choice between music and being a professor."

"The jury's still out," he said.

"Speaking about choices, I don't quite want to let this go," Gail said.

"Our thing? Let's pause until the dust settles, see what happens after that. That's the high road for 'our thing.' There's stuff up in air with me right now, but I have a spare ticket to a concert we're doing in Monterey. The Pillars are on Friday evening mid-June. It's a pretty big deal. Come up and see us if you want."

"Thanks. I'll think about it."

She's keeping it noncommittal, he thought. *So am I.*

CHAPTER 14

Feed Your Head

June 1967, Monterey, California

B radan felt in his bones that now—this very moment—
was the last time the era would be so innocent and no sin
had consequences. It was like going down a roller coaster's first big drop when every loop and twist thereafter was a
pale thrill compared to the first adrenaline descent.

He didn't have to be prescient to see the transience of their
age. He recalled his experiences with other times when he'd had
the same sensation of an important moment passing, impossible
to seize and keep. He remembered debating art with Botticelli
amid the paint and clutter of the master's studio as Florence
burst with creative passion on their doorstep. He also remembered painting Veronica and capturing everything that could be
captured of her soul with a brush. Like today's moment, that era
had passed in an eyeblink.

Or maybe those moments weren't so ideal and righteous.
Maybe it wasn't prescience about the future that needed sharp-
ening, but perception about the present. Bradan thought of

today's wars and civil strife. He also remembered bodies in Florentine alleys near Botticelli's studio. Scratch away an era's fabled veneer and hypocrisy and latent violence bubbled through, leaving no reason to mourn the era's demise.

Bradan felt the weight of his pistol jammed into the small of his back. Obsessively he touched it, then stretched down to check that his boot knife was accessible. Van hadn't attacked him since his house party, but Bradan guessed the congressman would decide that a huge open-air concert presented chances to isolate and eliminate him. Bradan had determined to face Van and his otherworldly patron and he had his allies lined up.

Looking across the Monterey concert grounds coming together with casual, magical efficiency before his eyes, Bradan heard wind chimes in the ocean breeze. They hung from a nearby concession stand. Young, long-haired laborers filled the vast, empty fairgrounds with chairs and set up concert-scale lighting and PA systems. Ten thousand spectators would soon sit in front of them with thousands more standing beyond or reclining in campgrounds, maybe fifty thousand total. Though Friday night's bands weren't scheduled to perform for hours, handheld camera crews already circulated among the growing number of attendees, focusing on the most hippie-looking folks for their establishing crowd shots, face paint, flowy dresses, headbands, and eccentric hats. Conventionally dressed music fans were ignored. Already the historical narrative was being shaped to suit expectations.

They were making the myth of an ideal moment to define this era.

Still, it was good that this was being documented. Bradan hadn't appreciated the scale of the effort until just now standing onstage. Unlike at his recent house party, even the cops were mellow and appeared more entertained by the pageant than ready to bust heads.

The concert organizers were trying to bottle lightning. The next three days would determine whether they'd succeeded, but, so far, the vibe was good with a super-well-curated spectrum of old and new acts. Bradan hoped The Beatles would make a surprise appearance. And Cream and The Doors, where were they? Not here. However, almost everyone else who mattered was.

Bradan watched David Crosby happily react to the high-quality sound that floated over the grounds during The Byrds' sound check. The Pillars were on deck to do their own check in a few minutes. Meanwhile, Tintagel stretched out full length dead center on the stage. The sound and lighting crews stayed well away from him. Periodically the animal roused himself to howl in harmony with the music when one of the acts caught his fancy.

Taryn sat at the front of the stage with her legs dangling over the edge next to Jeff, Kenny, and Kenny's girlfriend. They were like high school kids sitting poolside except their legs hung over a big banner emblazoned with "Music, Love, and Flowers" fronting the stage. The witch glanced over at Bradan, giving him a thumbs-up.

As yet the chairs were sparsely populated, making it easy to pick out Gail sitting before the stage. She came early to everything. She waved up at him and nodded politely to Taryn. So, Bradan thought, she'd used the ticket he'd given her. He'd also given her a backstage pass allowing her to hobnob with rock aristocracy. The newly minted associate history professor wouldn't know their music, but he wondered if she sensed modern history in the making and a time on the cusp of change. Bradan would try to introduce her to performers when the opportunity arose. Hell, most of the luminaries barely knew him. However, he was determined to change obscurity into recognition with the power of the Pillars' songs.

"Hey Bradan, can you sign this for my girlfriend?" One of the sound staff approached him with the Pillars' second album extended before him and a pen.

"Wow, you couldn't have timed that better," Bradan told the man, trying to hide how much he was flattered. He said, "Who should I make this out to? Also, can you make sure there's plenty of echo on my mic? Cheers, mate."

"And give me real volume on the kick drum mic," Constantine said.

"Can do," the man said. "It's not just for my girlfriend. I dig your second album, too, *An Emerald Boat on the Euphrates.* Your first was good, but this one is really strong."

The man hustled off to resume assembling a speaker tower for the PA system.

"He didn't even ask me to sign," Constantine said pouting. "Still can't believe we're doing this for no money."

They stood side-stage waiting their turn at the sound check.

"Just go with it," Bradan said. "It's a good feeling being here and thousands of people, tens of thousands, will listen to our music. There was a time when we wouldn't have accepted money for our shows, give back to the community and all that."

"Grass is expensive and getting more so," the drummer said. "Got to pay the rent."

"You don't pay a dime for your Belvedere space. I cover everyone's room including for band members."

"You know what I mean."

* * *

"Remember this moment," Bradan said. "It doesn't get better."

The Pillars filed onstage. They'd been slotted into the middle of a hodgepodge of acts on Friday evening. If there was a musical theme, it seemed to be showcasing established, mid-tier pop performers who wouldn't challenge the crowd's expectations. Simon and Garfunkel would close things out later in the evening. Edgier performers, Hendrix, Joplin, The Who, would seize the stage on Saturday and Sunday.

Wherever the Pillars were in the lineup, Bradan was happy to be here before a sea of spectators. As they hit the stage, they were bathed in lights. Because the band was lit to the point of incandescence, he couldn't see the audience, but he noticed little orange arcs as cigarettes moved about off into the distance, giving him a sense of the scale of the affair: limitless. And the crowd was in fine spirits, mellow from the first acts. Well, the Pillars would jar them awake.

To his amazement, there was a ripple of recognition and applause. Folks had heard their albums! Their new record company's corporate PR machinery had actually gotten the word out.

Other acts had a musical eminence to introduce them, but in the confusion of getting the preceding performers offstage, no one came forward to announce the Pillars. Bradan would happily have settled for Frank Zappa, but he didn't think Zappa was at Monterey. Instead, from side-stage, John Phillips motioned Bradan to just get on with it, introduce himself and the Pillars. Constantine shrugged and the rest of his band looked impatient to get into their set, so Bradan stepped up to the mic.

"Ladies and gentlemen, it's about to get a little louder and a lot heavier. Any visions you have as we play are entirely your own affair and should be collected at the gate as you exit. We take no responsibility for them. We have our own visions to present. Ladies and gentlemen, The Pillars of Creation."

They slammed into the opening track of *An Emerald Boat on the Euphrates*. The band sounded super tight and Bradan knew they were making creative magic . . .

* * *

Far above, Gwyn mused over the festival with macabre, god-like detachment. The specter sat on an immense destrier. Rider and steed had paused midair amid the marine layer's nighttime mist, supported as firmly as if they stood on granite.

At Gwyn's side, Van, also mounted, stared down at the tiny stage with a predator's focus.

They both were invisible to the concertgoers, dark figures on black horses against a charcoal sky.

Tonight Van felt more like his Dark Ages Medraut incarnation. The twentieth-century veneer peeled away. What he wouldn't give for his cavalry troop from Cadbury or his Florentine mercenaries to lead in a charge down onto the unsuspecting crowd below, ripe for his ax and lance, and cut a path to Bradan, but that would be Gwyn's approach: unleash the Wild Hunt, oversee mass slaughter, and collect the resulting tattered souls. However, subtlety was a better strategy to isolate and kill Bradan with minimal fuss. Other denizens of Faerie wouldn't tolerate Gwyn's Wild Hunters on their turf without a savage fight. The confrontation over Golden Gate Park had proven that. Keep things low-key.

Did Welsh gods understand subtlety?

Van wondered what Gwyn saw below: probably a scene at once trivial, alien, and fanciful that made even a Welsh Faerie realm appear sane and sensible. What Van saw were cute hippie chicks, though none of them held a candle to Taryn. Bradan stood clearly visible center stage fronting his band. Van heard music and crowd roars so loud they easily carried to his elevation. The five Pillars preened and postured like sixth-century Celtic bards. Contemptible. What could give Bradan sway over these multitudes with simple songs? What could make the witch associate herself with this rabble? And why was she Bradan's lover? There was always a sexual angle if the witch took an interest in someone.

Taryn hadn't ridden with the Wild Hunt since joining Bradan's band of minstrels months ago. Not coincidentally, she hadn't ridden Van lately, milking him for every last drop he could produce while sitting astride him with that satisfied smirk of hers. The witch was her own person, as she insisted on telling him and anyone else in Faerie who would listen, but this long-term thing she and Bradan had was fraternization of the worst sort. Did she still feel the wild call of earlier times? Van and the witch had broken many beds together, but no longer.

He didn't want to admit to jealousy, but there it was. Van gripped his mount's reins hard enough to make the beast whinny.

Gwyn roused himself from godly contemplation to look over at him.

"The witch left you for him."

Van didn't respond. As ever, he didn't hear the god speak human words, but he understood the deity's meaning.

"How does the boy still live?"

How indeed. Van couldn't argue that eliminating Bradan was the one part of his bargain with Gwyn made in Avalon long ago that he hadn't kept, though he had scars to show he'd tried.

His nemesis had proven more elusive than he'd imagined, and a better opponent when cornered than he'd expected, peculiar considering Bradan seemed to hold to basic rules of decency while Van allowed only expediency and satisfying his wants to guide his life. Shouldn't this have been an advantage?

Yet enemies made life worth living. And Bradan had proven a durable rival. However, he now needed to die. Van had a rifle in his saddle holster. A military contact had given him an M16, part of an army consignment destined for Vietnam and not legal for civilian possession, but being a congressman had privileges. It wouldn't be gallant to shoot Bradan from a distance with a machine gun, but gallantry was for losers and not even Arthur had been gallant, despite fifteen centuries of mythmaking to the contrary. The reality was, one did whatever one had to in order to win. Close combat hadn't worked in Florence or in a prison cell at Corvalle Mesa, so he'd create circumstances that brought his rival within range of the assault rifle.

In his experience, *clever* didn't win fights as often as *effective* did.

"He's no boy," Van said. "Hasn't been for a thousand years."

"Once he dies, what needs doing is done. I can go."

"Go where?" Van asked.

"Away."

Van intuited that this was all that would be disclosed. He remembered Merlin who was in Cadbury for eons and then one day he wasn't. Maybe entities like Merlin and Gwyn departed to their own peculiar heaven or hell based on a cosmic clock ticking away the eras that only they heard.

"You're retiring," Van said.

He didn't sense comprehension from the god. Van barely understood the notion himself. One simply played the role one had been born into as grandly as possible and died doing so. For all of Van's near-immortal life, his role had allowed him to slake every desire, so exiting it while alive was preposterous.

This is somebody's twilight, but not mine, he thought.

And with Gwyn departing, who would vacuum up all the spare souls produced by mankind's battles? There was more warfare now than ever. And did the Wild Hunters democratically elect a new regent or simply become stardust? He'd put his own name forward to lead them, but he was having too much fun in congress.

Regardless, it was a personal vendetta between him and Bradan and whether Gwyn was in Avalon or the ninth circle of hell was irrelevant; Van *would* slaughter Bradan.

"*When the boy goes, I go.*" The god's thoughts reverberated in Van's brain.

"I'll kill him soon," Van said.

"*Now. I need it now.*"

"There are too many people watching."

"*Kill them all. Many souls for the taking.*"

Van and the Welsh god of the Otherworld had scouted ahead of the Wild Hunt's main body. The Hunters would be called forth when annihilation was needed. The sun had set hours ago, but thanks to Gwyn's presence, a sliver of hellish illumination lingered on the western horizon, ruddy colored and sinister. This was the crack between worlds through which the rest of the Hunt would emerge in due course.

Keep the mindless horde at bay, Van thought. *Eradicating Bradan shouldn't take an army.*

Dealing with Gwyn hadn't gotten easier over the centuries. Tonight the lord of the Otherworld was proving as intransigent as a congressional subcommittee. Just like on Highway 1 and over Laurel Canyon, Gwyn was inserting himself with fire and maul into Van's personal fight to crush Bradan. But this was *his* fight. After Bradan's death at Van's hand, Gwyn could take Bradan's soul and hang it in whatever trophy case Otherworld deities kept such things. Personally Van didn't think souls were worth the effort; he knew he didn't have one.

"If it comes to that, we kill them all," Van said.

He lied to placate the god. Now it was time to try reason—if that was even possible with Gwyn.

"It's less trouble to find Bradan alone or with a small number of others. If you annihilate thousands, and are recognized to have done so, you bring this world and your world into direct conflict."

"In other times, we freely visited this world. It wasn't meddling."

"Not anymore. Nowadays let them kill each other. They're very good at it. They do the work, you collect the souls."

Van let that logic sink in. He didn't know what would happen if this world and the Otherworld collided on the scale that Gwyn contemplated, but he didn't want to find out. Much as he desired to murder Bradan, he liked his current circumstances. He had power and respect that he'd never achieved in Celtic Britain and he wouldn't jeopardize that with a frontal assault on humanity. He appreciated modern luxuries and couldn't conceive of returning to the mud and squalor of earlier times, especially since 1967 encouraged him to indulge his animal urges as long as he didn't get caught.

Gwyn hadn't left all of his hunters behind. Van saw a Praetorian Guard of a half dozen beings hovering near the god.

Probably Gwyn knew he hunted on territory under the suzerainty of other parts of Faerie and took precautions. Even gods weren't invulnerable.

One of these bodyguards yowled at Van. He'd ridden too close to Gwyn. The sound was sinister and familiar, too. Van remembered hearing it in Avalon fifteen centuries ago as Arthur was prepared for burial. As before, a young woman flitted toward him and hovered in the nighttime mist. She was impossibly beautiful, hard and perfect. Pointed ears poked through her hair. The festival's lights suffused the maiden's white-blond mane, creating an angelic halo contrasting with her salacious expression. He expected to see fangs as she grinned, but, no, she had even white teeth appropriate for a fruit sorbet. He saw her lambent milky, green eyes, cloudy portals into the netherworld, ready to gather spiritual sustenance from an unfortunate's soul.

Don't look, he thought.

Too late.

He felt himself slipping into those pools, moving down a greasy slope to eternity.

Gwyn snapped his fingers and Van returned to 1967 above Monterey. He was massively tempted to unsheathe the M16 and empty it into the elf maiden for her effrontery in attacking him, but he needed her talents, and he didn't know if bullets would hurt her, anyway.

Tonight the demon didn't wear elegant armor. Instead she'd donned bell-bottomed jeans and a white, cottony shirt with a British Union Jack flag design on the front. The shirt was thin and no protection from the cold, but the elements didn't bother her. The thorns in her tiara of white roses didn't bother her, either. Of course she was barefoot. Van had to stifle laughter at this parody of flower-power high fashion. It was a mockery of everything below—Van was sure she intended this scorn. No doubt the pretty demon wanted to wrest innocent, transcendental souls from concertgoers as she'd just tried to snatch his; and she was welcome to Bradan's, but after Van had butchered his mortal body. The demon was the ideal agent to catalyze Bradan's demise. Besides a soul-destroying gaze, she was brilliantly fast and her slender build belied immense strength.

"Pull the plug," Van said.

She understood but didn't obey, pending Gwyn's assent.

"Create confusion with darkness," Van said patiently. "Then we can separate Bradan from the rest. We don't want a war on two fronts with half of Faerie and all of humanity. Quietly, bring him here."

Gwyn finally nodded to the demon and she leaped downward toward the festival stage moving so rapidly she blurred into a streak of magenta light.

* * *

Mid-song, the Pillars' sound went stone-cold dead except for Constantine's powerful drumming. Every amplified, electric instrument simultaneously fell silent, and without the song's melody as a musical guide, the percussion ground to a halt, too. The stage and building lights also went out, leaving the crowd in darkness.

Only the orange glow of cigarettes and joints moved about like fireflies.

Bradan heard confusion in the crowd and among the staff and musicians waiting side-stage. This swelled to laughter and jumbled chatter. He heard Tintagel snarl.

A simple power outage or something more? Bradan wondered. *The wolf is worried. The hell with it. We're here. I ain't running. We're going ahead.*

"Play acoustically," he yelled at his band mates. He couldn't see any of them, but he knew roughly where they were onstage. "The songs don't have to be loud to be good. We composed them without amps. They'll get the power back up in a minute. Meantime, we play on. Taryn, you see better than a cat. Grab our acoustic guitars. We left them backstage. I have two. One goes to Jeff. I'll use my Martin twelve-string. You've got yours? Good. Kenny, I don't have another guitar for you, so, without your keys, just focus on vocals. You're in great voice tonight."

Tell the crowd what I'm doing, Bradan thought. *I can't shout loudly enough for anyone to hear me, but I'll use the same magic that made Chaffee's unintended confessions resonate across campus. And I hoped I'd get through the day without a spell! Brace for exhaustion; I can only get this thing to last for a few moments before it fatigues the hell out of me, so make it count.*

He intoned a spell.

"Hey folks, sorry for the disruption," Bradan said. The enchantment picked up his voice and sent it whooshing out to the far reaches of the fairgrounds with crystalline clarity. "It'll get fixed. Meantime, we're playing our set unplugged. You'll have to listen carefully, so just think of this as an intimate little club 'round midnight with fifty thousand of your close friends and the Pillars are the house band. We'd appreciate your help keeping the visions flowing. If you know our songs, sing along. If you don't, pretend you do and hum along with your neighbors."

Bradan slumped against the mic stand holding on to it for support while recovering from the spell's effects. No one could see his weakness—except the witch.

"Cute spell." Taryn's eyes blazed orange in front of him and he felt the twelve-string thrust into his hands.

"Play your ass off, sweetheart," he told her. "Can you show our lyrics on the front of the stage illuminated so they're readable? It's the crowd's cue sheet. Don't tire yourself. Just long enough to get them singing."

"On it, boss," came the mocking response.

"Constantine, can you play in the dark? Count us in to 'Dawn's Faerie Dance.'"

Amazingly, Bradan got no argument from the Pillars' temperamental percussionist. Instead there was an experimental drum roll on his snare as he oriented himself to his unseen kit, then a perfect count in. And instead of the usual volcanic explosion of sound when the band's amplifiers and the concert PA system kicked their music up to 115 decibels, there was warm, muted melody from three acoustic guitars, light, jazzy drumming, and incandescent harmonies swirling over everything.

"Nice going," he heard Phillips yell from side-stage. "Carry us until we can fix this shitty power. You sound great, kinda folky."

Scattered voices picked up the Pillars' song, some knew it, others read the huge lettering that Taryn had created on the front of the stage. More joined in. People held aloft cigarette lighters, creating a sea of fire. And it became a giant summer camp sing-along.

Magic, Bradan thought, elated.

Adding to their song's otherworldly timber, an extra soprano joined the mix, harmonizing as the Pillars sang. Bradan couldn't see the voice's origin, but it soon morphed into a demon's wail in a strange accent and then further mutated into taunting laughter.

Here it comes, he thought.

"We have company," Taryn hissed at him from across the stage. "The wrong kind."

"Bradan, look out!" Gail Halpern shouted from side-stage. "She's a psycho!"

In the light of the crowd's lighters and flashlights the production crew used to trace the source of the power outage, Bradan saw a blond woman dart onto stage, moving right at him. Showing more spirit for physical confrontation than he expected, Gail reached out to grab the demon, but was punched for her efforts and stumbled into a stack of Marshalls. Two of the sound men also grabbed at her, but she swatted them away. It happened fast, but to Bradan it seemed she put no more energy into the movement than a slap, yet both men missed getting a grip on her and were propelled off the stage into the press corps below. Then she was on him, grabbing his arm with a supernaturally strong grip and pulling him upward off the stage en route to God knew where. However, Gail and the sound staff's intercession had given him a chance to formulate a countermove and begin reciting a spell. He still held on to his precious guitar with the hand the elf maiden hadn't grabbed. With both hands occupied, he couldn't reach for his .45, but Tintagel sprinted after him and made an enormous bound upward to grab Bradan's shoe. The wolf's weight momentarily halted the demon's efforts to pull Bradan skyward.

I'm being ripped apart by a pretty fiend and my pet. Van and Gwyn sent this thing. I need an image just for this demon. No one else can see it. Say the words fast. A simple image—

Red-bearded Gwyn appeared on his horse suspended before the stage as if seizing a front-row seat to their set. He stared at Bradan and the demon, and gestured forcefully with his sword toward the heavens. The image was perfect, in every way complete including a wind from the Otherworld fanning the god's red mane. For an instant the elf maiden ignored the summons and held tight to Bradan.

Will my spell do it?

With a squall of fury, she released Bradan, sending him crashing down to the stage in an ungainly heap. Responding to the peremptory summons, the elf maiden flew heavenward. Tintagel agilely dodged aside, letting Bradan hit the stage hard. He cradled his guitar and took the shock of landing on his tailbone. Unlike the blond demon, the wolf paid no attention to Gwyn's image and with a final snarl in her direction, he trotted backstage with one of Bradan's shoes gripped in his fangs. Gwyn's illusion faded.

With the elf maiden gone, the festival lighting sprang back to life. Bradan picked himself up off the stage. He lacked one shoe, but the wolf would return it eventually. The concert's production staff let out a cheer at the resumption of electricity, and Bradan saw Phillips give him a thumbs-up and shout, "Five minutes to wrap it up."

"Deftly done," Taryn said.

"You saw?" Bradan asked.

"No. You hid whatever drove off the fairy bitch, probably Gwyn's image, but I heard the spell. Clever rhymes."

"Thanks. Van will come back with or without the elf. And Gwyn, too. The god's taken a personal interest in my demise, but they'd get a lot of attention if they attacked again with the lights and sound back on. So they'll make their next move in a quieter time."

"Van wants discretion," the witch said. "He has a stake in keeping what he has here, but Gwyn won't care. This isn't his world."

"Then I hope our friends are on call when I need them."
Bradan tapped his mic.

"We're live again," he told the crowd. His voice quavered from his brawl with Gwyn's minion and fatigue from his spell. Hopefully the crowd would think it was emotion from the Pillars' set. "It was fun doing quieter stuff," he said. "But now we'll plug back in and close out the set with acid madness. Hang on to your seats."

And off the Pillars went. Bradan tried to focus on his guitar work and singing, but he scanned the night sky above the crowd for nameless terrors, so his solos sucked. Taryn's guitar work covered for his weak effort.

As they walked offstage slapping backs and congratulating one another about adapting so nimbly to an unplanned acoustic interlude and playing a strong set to a receptive crowd, John Phillips approached Bradan.

"Great harmonies, five-part, very sophisticated, even your drummer sings. You've been listening to Mamas and Papas records for tips? And who was the babe that went after you? Couldn't see much with no light, but she seemed about the prettiest girl in the world."

"Not really of this world," Bradan said.

"She tackled you. Then she just disappeared."

"Crazy fan," Bradan said. "The downside of fame."

"Your dog attacked you, too."

"He does that if he doesn't like our set list," Bradan said.

Gail came up and hugged him tightly. "Thanks for getting me up here. I'll never pass for hip, but I wouldn't have missed this."

"You fit right in with the crowd. Thanks for helping with the girl."

"That was no fan," Gail said. "First she just kind of appeared backstage out of nowhere. Then she tossed me aside like I was a doll. She had the weirdest eyes."

"What else could she have been?" Bradan asked keeping his tone nonchalant. "An escapee from an institution probably. You hanging around for the rest of the weekend? I'll introduce you to the acts."

Gail's face fell. "Can't. I'm heading for the airport now. Conference all day Saturday and Sunday in Anaheim."

"See you Tuesday night for dinner at the faculty lounge," Bradan said.

* * *

Chaos.

Bradan watched side-stage as The Who's Peter Townshend raised his guitar like a battle ax and smashed it into the stage, snapping the neck and eliciting howls of feedback-drenched agony from the speakers. It was like pressing an ear to Hell's front door. Then the guitarist attacked his amplifiers with the remnants of his instrument as smoke bombs erupted, swaddling the band in dense smog illuminated surreally by stage lights. It looked like a sixth-century clash between Celts and Saxons. Keith Moon kicked over his drums to complete the mayhem. "My Generation," indeed. If the Wild Hunt waited over the horizon, this would catch their attention. And they'd have a hard time topping the band's lunacy.

Bradan dodged a flying drumstick and watched as the Grateful Dead prepared to take their turn. Jerry Garcia passed him and said, "Man, how are we supposed to follow this crazy shit? The stage is a war zone."

Jimi Hendrix took over after the Dead. The guitar maestro flew through a half dozen songs to finish with "Wild Thing," an elemental, three-chord rocker that he embellished with phenomenal visionary solos. Mid-song, Hendrix the musician shifted to Jimi the shaman who produced a can of lighter fluid and laid his battered guitar onstage before soaking it with flammable liquid and throwing a lit match onto the instrument, setting it afire, an offering to strange deities. Bradan hoped the Wild Hunt didn't take this as an invitation. However, aside from the crowd sitting stunned at the performance, no army of the damned materialized.

Give them time, Bradan thought.

After The Who's and Hendrix's competitive mayhem, everything was anticlimax and the Mamas and Papas used their set to bring the festival to a soft landing. In cool times, Bradan knew, music could make the moment even cooler. He watched people stream for the exits, lingering to preserve the positive feelings, but these would fade to memories soon.

"You're on your own," Mama Cass told the crowd, closing the festival and the moment.

* * *

It was supposed to be a friendly, private little chat, just straighten a few issues out, let's not bring the lawyers into it, but the label rep insisted it couldn't wait. Thus Bradan and the rep negotiated on a couple of folding chairs as the music festival reverted to a vacant, nighttime fairground. It wasn't a friendly chat. Discussions were intense and protracted. Bradan wished he had Evan Cohen in his corner. With tens of thousands of dollars on the table, he lost track of time. Hours passed before the rep finally departed for LA, so it was just Bradan, Tintagel, the Harley, empty concession stands, and heaps of trash. Litter blew through the dark grounds. A few production staff worked by the stage dismantling vestiges of the party, but they were specks in the distance. Bradan had the joint to himself.

He needed to leave. Perhaps Van would attack another time—or he would get to Van first.

And then they were there. All of them.

Bradan looked upward. His blood froze. This time it wasn't just the elf maiden. Gwyn had set his entire legion on him. Leading the charge, Van peeled away from the specters, phantoms, and naked warriors, and pushed aside other hunters to carve a path right at him.

Van wins this race, Bradan thought. *He's firing an assault rifle.*

Fifteen hundred years of riding allowed the big man to guide his horse with his knees, leaving both hands free to level and aim his cannon at Bradan. Van had his M16 on full auto and Bradan saw the weapon blink at him, muzzle flashes.

Bradan remembered German Messerschmitt fighters from his World War II experience over Europe. At a distance they looked innocent enough, friendly even, as their wings lit up in greeting with flickering lights—until one realized that those flashes meant floods of bullets coming at him.

The dirt and pine needles on the ground and a plywood stand next to him exploded as Van emptied his gun at him. Closing fast, the big man tossed the empty magazine aside and grabbed a replacement.

Flee on the bike? Bradan thought. *Too slow. Run on foot.*

Bradan felt a sudden punch in the middle of his back almost knocking him off his feet, accompanied by an impatient snort.

Whirling, he saw the destrier from Golden Gate Park's fairy troop he'd borrowed for his attack on Van. With no points for grace, he leaped on, clinging to its mane.

"My friends are here," Meadow said. "As promised."

"I need everyone I can get," Bradan yelled.

The local fairy armies from Golden Gate and Mount Tamalpais had also risen to the challenge, along with Meadow's collective of ghosts. They coordinated their activities with military precision and surged upward out of Monterey's pine forests surrounding the concert grounds to meet the invading Wild Hunters. The Pillars' March gig in the park to introduce the groups had worked. Unexpected allies, indeed. Now he just needed low cunning and fast work with weapons to stand a chance. With no prompting, his horse leaped aloft, dodging another long burst of Van's rifle fire.

He's burning tons of ammunition. He rides well, but can he aim at a dodging target when he's mounted? The rifle is well balanced, but the barrel climbs if you go machine-gun mode. Also, M16s are supposed to jam a lot.

From past experience, Bradan knew his charger could really climb. His whispered instruction shot him skyward. He spotted Van way below him. The big man's mount made slow going because of its rider's weight.

What was happening? Just as for other battles in his long life, Bradan was fearful, but he needed situational awareness to survive the night. At his vantage point two thousand feet above the ground, he saw the collision of hosts in the night sky with savagery exceeding anything from three months before over Golden Gate Park. The rivals used every kind of weapon to hack, stab, and shoot at one another though Bradan saw that physical implements appeared to have little effect on supernatural beings, resulting in them clawing, punching, and strangling one another in hand-to-hand combat.

All about, puffs of rainbow-colored light exploded soundlessly. He guessed these were the final extinction of members of one side or the other.

Is this how creatures who were already dead meet their terminus?

The scale of the battle was immense and extended beyond the coast and out over the Pacific. Among his hunters, Gwyn and the blond elf maiden worked to orchestrate their forces.

Bradan saw Taryn. She was dead center in the midst of the slaughter sitting immobile, mounted on a brown stallion as the fight swirled about her like a snag in a fast-flowing river buffeted by the tumult, but ultimately apart from it. Bradan sensed uncertainty about which side to choose. The fairy maiden angled toward Taryn. This wouldn't be a friendly encounter.

The witch will have to pick a side. Enemies define you.

Bradan pulled out his .45. Van enormously outgunned him, but it was better than nothing. Amid the aerial war, Bradan banked his horse down toward Van below still struggling to gain altitude. He dusted off instincts from a quarter century back when he'd flown P-51s against Me 109 fighters over Germany. Coming from a much higher position, he was in a good spot to take the fight to Van. His equine bucked, objecting to this rash move, but if Bradan was to stand a chance, he needed to quickly get within pistol range of the big man and take as many shots as he could during the first pass.

He was scared, but not panicked. Years back, in a fighter, he'd been good at deflection shooting. Tonight, on a stallion, he needed to use those principles to lead his target.

Van saw Bradan diving at him and leveled his rifle. Bradan heard its reports and sensed bullets zipping past him. The big man was shooting high. Bradan aimed his pistol and fired. He only had eight shots and one spare magazine. He couldn't be profligate; he needed to hit the bastard. Instead he hit the big man's horse. Midair, the animal lurched, but seemed unhurt. However, the jump made Van lose his grip on a magazine he was trying to jam into his rifle. The magazine fell downward.

My chance.

Elated, Bradan fired, but adrenaline turned his arm into a noodle. He lost count of how many shots he'd taken, and he hit nothing and needed to reload. He passed Van close, seeing his opponent's calm, focused expression, composed for killing. Bradan didn't waste breath screaming at him. He palmed his last magazine into the .45. Even with a pistol, he shouldn't miss at this range, but he was dizzy from the fast maneuvering. They circled each other in an aerial minuet close enough for their mounts to kick at each other. Bradan felt the concussive hits of Van's charger on his mount and likewise felt his destrier lash back with its rear hooves, nearly throwing him off.

Check your six.

Bradan looked directly behind him and saw the blond demon closing fast. Uniquely in the turbulent dogfight, she didn't ride a flying horse but raced about with insane speed through the air on her own. Now he'd have to divide his attention between the demon and Van. The big man urgently waved off the maiden, planning to kill Bradan without interference, but she ignored him and lunged for Bradan, only to be dragged backward as Taryn grabbed her. The momentum pulled the witch off her horse and the two tumbled away heading earthward fast. Bradan didn't watch the struggling pair, as he'd gotten his pistol reloaded and blasted away at Van, but instead of hitting the big man, his bullets struck Van's rifle, shattering metal and plastic and spinning it out of the big man's hands. Bradan slowed his madly careening stallion and lined up his pistol on Van's chest. With his enemy disarmed, he'd finish this now.

Empty gun.

He hurled the .45 at Van, who dodged easily.

Bradan pulled a lance out of the sheath strapped to his mount. Van did the same. As if firearms weren't lethal enough, this fight would now revert to cruder weaponry, giving the big man an advantage since he'd been a warrior all his life while Bradan had been an artist and academic. Still, Bradan had also used weapons and he could improvise. After all, he had wounded Van with a plastic pen. Bradan struggled to remember what he'd learned in Dark Ages England about fighting with lances. This wasn't two paladins jousting under rules of conduct and honorable intent. Neither he nor Van had a shield or armor. Any hits his opponent landed would rend flesh, shatter bone, and be bloody and fatal, nothing chivalric about it. So he had to land the first hit.

They'd drifted a little apart. Bradan looked down at the fairgrounds a long way below. He was conscious of the utter unreality of charging through thin air, but, if he fell, the impact would be real enough. Bradan lined up his horse and leveled the lance, bracing it under his arm. It was heavy and clumsy. The wooden shaft was also slippery with his sweat. If he thought about it further, he'd lose his nerve. He charged. Van was already coming at him. He had greater reach, so Bradan leaned far forward over his destrier's neck, feeling its mane blowing back in his face. He extended his weapon as far ahead of him as he could, trying to get its point into his opponent before he was struck himself.

Even if he hit Van first, he had no stirrups to allow his body to absorb the impact's shock and could be catapulted off the horse. *No time for reflection.*

Their lances collided. Van's weapon survived, but Bradan's splintered into a million pieces. Bradan remembered seeing this occasionally in medieval tournaments leaving one combatant unarmed. Then, a replacement lance would be chivalrously brought forth so that both combatants could fight on equal terms. Now, Van circled back to run defenseless Bradan through.

He's toying with me.

Bradan still reeled from the impact of the hit. He'd clung to his horse's mane to keep from being pitched off. His best course was to flee, but without thinking Bradan drew his boot knife, a useless weapon against a lance. He could do campfire tricks with it but nothing more. And for campfire tricks, he needed to be closer to his opponent. Van launched himself full gallop at him. In turn Bradan raced his horse at the big man and closed rapidly. Van must have thought he was mad.

Deploying every instinct he could muster about leading his target from his days in a fighter, Bradan ignored the steel-tipped lance aimed at his chest, growing closer by the instant, and veered his horse away at the last second while casting his knife at Van, keeping his forefinger along the top of the handle to steady the blade as it left his hand. *Focus on the target*—Van's neck. *Control the blade and follow through with the arm.*

It's an art.

Van's lance grazed his side, tearing through skin, and almost pushed him off his mount, but his destrier was smart and slowed to get under him and let him clamber back on.

"Sugar cubes for you if I get out of this alive," he said.

His mount snorted approval.

Where is Van?

Bradan wheeled around to see Van's riderless mount nearby, circling aimlessly. He didn't see the big man until he looked downward. A body curled in a fetal position hurtled toward the ground to be lost against the dark earth. Bradan pushed his horse into a steep dive along the descent path.

Is he dead? This can't end ambiguously. I'm not looking over my shoulder for the next thousand years.

Bradan heard a heavy, broken thud as his opponent hit the ground.

Kick him. Make sure I killed him.

Bradan landed his destrier near Van to find Tintagel already there. The wolf nosed the body and sauntered over to him. Tintagel's unconcerned demeanor told him everything: Van was dead. Out of perverse curiosity, he moved close enough to see his knife transfixing Van's neck and reached down to wrench it free, wipe the blade on the grass, and shove it back into his boot. He kicked the corpse, anyway.

Bradan leaped upward, punching at the night sky, and let out an animal yell that echoed through surrounding trees. The wolf backed away from him, hackles raised.

Bradan thought he was defined by his enemies, but only partly. Without Van around every corner ready to pounce, he'd define himself purely by his creative endeavors.

The police would be alerted about the body in due time when the festival's cleanup crew stumbled on it. Or Bradan might place an anonymous call to the cops himself. With Van a congressman, there would be an enormous investigation, but without a murder weapon, just the peculiar circumstances of a badly wrecked body near the county fairgrounds with no sign of how he'd fallen to his death, forensic puzzlement would soon give way to bureaucratic lassitude, a special election would be called to fill the vacant congressional seat, and that would be that. Bradan would also alert Meadow to Van's demise so Barbara would hear of it. He didn't know if this would bring relief, elation, or closure.

Taryn walked through the empty concession stands toward him. She was splattered with blood but appeared otherwise unhurt. She'd survived the fall and there was no sign of the blond demon. The witch squatted down by Van's broken body. She didn't wear her sunglasses and Bradan saw her eyes blaze. However, it wasn't anger. The emotion was sadness. He'd never seen that in her.

"It was going to happen," she said to Bradan.

They both looked skyward. The battle carried on unabated.

"I'm not done," Bradan said. "To stop this, we remove Gwyn."

"He's hanging on to this world by his fingernails," Taryn said. "You're his final task before he can depart. Why are you so important?"

"I'm the legacy of a feud with Merlin. A long time ago, Gwyn missed getting me because Merlin faced him down. In whatever ledger book these things are counted, that's something Gwyn must correct. However, before he can do that, I'll nudge him into whatever dimension comes next for a god, but I need your help. You're hurt?"

He hadn't seen it before. The witch dabbed at a deep gash across her thigh. Her jeans were shredded near the wound and she limped.

"I'll survive. You're hurt, too."

Bradan looked at his left side with blood seeping through his T-shirt. "Chivalry. I'm okay if my ribs get a while to heal. He got the worst of it." Bradan nodded toward Van's body.

"We need an illusion for a god," he said. "A delusion for a god that draws him back where he belongs. Let's get our guitars."

"I'm up for anything," the witch said. "But what good will music do?"

"Usually Gwyn brings the chaos. Tonight we'll send it back to him. I had to struggle to rein in the bad images at that park gig that went out of control. Tonight we're not putting it back in a box. We're setting our own madness loose to join the insanity happening up there."

"The truck's nearby," she said. "All we've got is acoustic guitars. Constantine took the other van with the rest of the instruments."

"Acoustics work. It's not the volume; it's the song. We showed that Friday night."

"Do we need the Pillars?"

"The two of us can create just enough chaos to distract a god."

Bradan and Taryn sat on the floor of the Pillars' pickup and started playing his song with pastel lyrics that masked nihilistic commentary about the current moment. Even without the full band and a mountain of amplifiers, he felt the song's undercurrents encourage arrogant visions and tap into a riptide pulling him into deep waters. He would pitch over the continental shelf into the abyss, just where he wanted to go.

"Gwyn," Taryn shouted.

Lost in the music, Bradan paused to look up and saw the enormous figure with blunt features and disordered red hair. If Van was big, the Welsh god was otherworldly in scale and rode a charger proportionately enormous. Bradan knew the deity had no human feelings—his rainbow eyes were beautiful and vacant—and Gwyn would kill him with the same elemental unconcern as a lightning bolt struck someone on an open field.

"We need one more thing," he yelled. "Bait."

"What bait?"

"Me. Keep the music going."

Bradan sang out a spell using the song's meter. As in Golden Gate Park, the song's bleak energy catapulted his magic to soaring power. An image formed in his mind of himself on a horse and a gory sunset acting as a portal to the Otherworld. The image wavered, then sharpened to crystalline clarity, and covered the nighttime western horizon.

His image on horseback flew upward right at Gwyn then nimbly sidestepped to dodge around his opponent midair. God or not, Gwyn braked his mount ponderously to slow his downward momentum before lurching after Bradan's phantom image streaking toward the hellish crack in the horizon. Gwyn, Bradan's image, and the orange horizon merged.

"Hold it a fraction of a second more," Bradan said. "One more verse."

Then both he and the witch slumped over their instruments and the portal slammed shut. It was soundless, but Bradan reeled from the psychic concussion and fell over backward on the truck's metal bed.

"A moment passing," Bradan said, staring up at the night sky blurred by a marine layer. The phantom entities that crowded the mists to fight viciously drifted apart, overtaken with lassitude as if realizing the futility of their quarrel. Then they faded away, Meadow's ghostly companions, the Wild Hunters, and the Fair Folk.

A man with a handheld film camera pointed it upward. As the eerie airborne company dissipated, he tilted the camera down and noticed Bradan and Taryn. He pushed headphones off his ears and approached them.

"You guys see that?"

"The festival promoters closed out with fireworks," Bradan said. "Too bad no one was here to watch them except us and a few other stragglers."

"That wasn't fireworks," the filmmaker said. "It was like a French movie thing except it was all over the clouds, a fairy tale writ large."

"Visionary, like Jean Cocteau," the witch said. Bradan caught the dry-as-dust sarcasm in the witch's voice. "You got it on camera?"

"Damn straight I got it," the filmmaker said. "Probably a bizarre meteorological phenomenon. I'll splice it into the footage with the musical acts. Magic onstage, magic in the skies. It all tells a story that no one would believe otherwise."

"Sure your camera was loaded?" Bradan asked. "You're D. A. Pennebaker. I've seen your documentaries, so I know you're on top of the equipment, but check to make sure."

Pennebaker examined his camera and swore. "I ran out of film stock, don't know when. I'll check when we develop it. God, I want whatever just happened up there." He nodded at the night and mist.

"You get the Pillars?" Bradan asked.

"I wanted to," the filmmaker said. "But the lights went down. I heard it all, but it was too dark to film. Your acoustic set was phenomenal. I was side-stage when that girl rushed out to grab you. She either wanted to fuck you or tear you to pieces."

"I'll never know which," Bradan said.

"Regardless, what a rock-and-roll moment."

* * *

"They voted," the witch said.

"All of them, the whole Wild Hunt?" Bradan asked.

Taryn nodded. "I'm elected to take Gwyn's role."

"Like a tenure hearing?" Bradan asked deadpan.

"More than you know."

"No one objected to you flying on my side last night?"

"I'm on my own side, always and forever. And last night I wanted to ride with you, so I did. Besides, with Gwyn gone, they were frantic to replace him with someone they've known since the Dark Ages."

Monday morning they held hands, looking out at the empty festival grounds from the center of the deserted stage. The sound system and lighting had already been disassembled and trucked away. Hammering noises and the shearing whine of a power saw came from backstage. Tintagel snoozed at their feet, and a few kids on the production crew picked up the detritus of fifty thousand concertgoers. It was lonely work after the magic had gone elsewhere.

"To the Wild Hunt's new regent." Bradan bowed to Taryn. "But I thought you didn't like collecting souls, found it boring. Also, there was the problem of where to put them."

"Now I've got staff to handle that." Taryn wiped blood off her hands and thigh with her paisley silk scarf.

She regarded the once pretty garment and let it fall to the plywood stage.

"It was ruined, anyway. The blond elf bled a lot before she died. I was happy to collect her soul. It's pretty on the outside, ugly inside. There's a cosmic rule about that for demons' souls— and some humans.'"

The witch pocketed the Ray-Bans and her eyes blazed orange. Now she flew her true colors. Why not? There was no one except him to see her.

"Don't tell me," Bradan said. "You've got a whole new vision for the outfit, blow up Gwyn's mindless strategy and take the Wild Hunt in a new direction? Why not go after the bad guys instead of the nobodies?"

"There's that mockery again. Actually, it *is* boring chasing down poor unfortunates' souls, so we're not doing that anymore. Instead we're going after spirits that deserve an eternity of darkness. I'm thinking of warlords, business jackals, hypocritical religious leaders."

"More sporting?"

"Sure. I want really nasty foxes for my hounds to run to ground."

They embraced warmly. It was partly sensual, partly mutual exhaustion from last night. Holding on to each other seemed natural, essential even, after surviving the concert.

"Come join us hunting," she said.

"That sounds like opium," he said. "It'll get addictive."

"Let it!"

"I'll make you a deal: Keep on playing with the Pillars, collaborate on writing songs with me, and I'm at your beck and call to go hunting every full moon. Give me my favorite pony, the one I rode last night."

"The tame one?"

"Yeah, that one."

* * *

A beautiful sunset illuminated fat clouds that looked like pillows in the twilight sky for a reclining celestial giant, dreaming cosmic dreams, to snooze on. And, high up, the evening's first stars were beacons guiding a traveler's safe passage.

Bradan rode his Harley south, not pushing the pace. There was no hurry and he didn't want a battering from the bike's Stone Age suspension. Instead he rode at modest speed and the miles passed easily. Highway 1's pavement was bone dry and he moved smoothly through its sweeping curves past pines and the Pacific.

He had no LSD onboard; however, the ghost was argumentative.

"You didn't get either of them," Meadow said. "They're cool women, very different, but I liked them both. You should have tried to make it permanent with one of them."

"I like them both, too. Which one should I settle down with?"

The ghost didn't answer.

"Sure, I didn't 'get' them," he said. "And they didn't 'get' me. But neither Taryn nor Gail is a happily-ever-after kind of gal. They both have their goals in life; I have mine. And they got what they wanted. I did, too. We'll still see each other. A lot, I hope. Isn't that a good outcome? Besides, I have you."

There was a long pause. He sensed Meadow mulling over his flattery. Finally she said, "Thanks for the kind thoughts. Occasionally you say something nice."

"Occasionally," he said wryly.

"But it's not nice to leave things up in the air with them like you did," Meadow challenged him.

"I'll see Gail tomorrow night at dinner in the Faculty Club," he said. "She still has the key to my apartment. I haven't changed the locks—though I nearly did when I heard about her with Chaffee. After dinner she can stay overnight if she likes. I want her to. Also, I'm writing a research paper with her. It's significant work, really novel."

He gave the Harley more gas and speed increased, blowing back his hair. He felt the exhilaration of an open road to nowhere in particular.

"For Taryn, the two of us are taking the Pillars to surprising places creatively, blending in musical influences from all over the world."

Bradan decided not to share with Meadow that he and Taryn would also be tearing up the night skies at the head of the Wild Hunt every full moon. Well, Bradan would ride with Taryn's outfit for the adrenaline thrill of it, but leave whatever blood sport ensued to the witch and her specters. And they *were* after really bad actors instead of the innocents Gwyn had chased.

"And I'm trying to be more open to ideas from the rest of the band, too. Being fifteen hundred years old should make me more mature and generous. We'll see."

After some miles, he asked, "How's Barbara doing?"

"See for yourself," Meadow answered. "Pull off the highway at the next overlook."

Barbara waited for them sitting on a roadside guard rail with a view of the sea covered in platinum moonlight. Beyond the rail there was a steep drop-off down to rocks and surf below. She still wore her windbreaker and miniskirt and, except for a grayish pallor visible in the moon's illumination, she might have been a stranded young motorist waiting for a tow truck to arrive and repair her car. However, she cradled a round object in her lap which, at first, incongruously, Bradan thought was a basketball. But as he rolled his bike closer, it turned out to be Van's head. Shocked, he jerked to a sudden stop in front of her. Barbara stood up, nodded at him, and smiled wistfully, then her expression hardened, and she hurled the head with both hands far out over the cliff's edge. She turned back to Bradan and the bike, waved, and vanished.

"A head for a head," he said. "Biblical Judith disposing of an evildoer. Can she rest now?"

"Yes. She needed witnesses before she could go."

"And what about you, Meadow? Can I help you go to a better place?"

"I'm here for a while," the ghost said. "It's not so bad, out riding when the weather's nice. You never listen to my advice, but I like our talks. They pass the time."

"Then let's get back on the highway. We have a ways to go before LA. We'll talk on the way."

Many hours later, sunrise shouldered its way above the California coastal mountain ranges, and, high up, an amiable dawn lightened his road weariness and inspired him to dream new songs.

California Dreaming
Amid the Avatars

The Present, Indio, California

Bradan saw multitudes of avatars.

He reflexively tried to avoid colliding with the diaphanous images, but everyone else physically present just walked through them. It was tough enough avoiding flesh-and-blood humans in the congested festival grounds. Why worry about virtual manifestations of someone's ego?

They came in every shape and size, the incorporeal designees of remote fans worldwide who wanted the open-air concert experience without the desert heat, insane concession prices, and crushing press of humanity—and the fountains of dust stirred up by the crowd. Also, people could virtually present themselves to fellow concertgoers in any self-aggrandizing and fanciful form they chose.

Bradan was startled when he spotted an image of Gwyn, complete with massive size, long red hair, and saturnine visage. Breaking his habit, Bradan made it a point to stroll right through him. Of course he felt nothing tactile, just a psychic sensation of cold fingers caressing his mind. Credit his nightmares for that.

Bradan saw ghosts, too.

There weren't many. However, they had a deeper backstory than the avatars. These were souls for whom the festival grounds held significance strong enough to keep them here and included everyone from shades in modern dress to Native Americans who had been here long before it was a polo grounds or concert setting. Bradan saw Meadow in the distance and moved toward her, but, getting closer, he realized it wasn't his motorcycle's spirit. She'd left years back, he hoped for a better place.

I outlive even phantoms, he thought.

The Harley was parked in his North Beach San Francisco garage, just a piece of metal now without soul, so he didn't ride it anymore. However, the bike was an echo of another time, another place, and important for that, so he kept it. His current mode of transport—a state-of-the-art car—had acquired a new spirit, an altogether more boisterous personality than Meadow. He wondered how they would have gotten along.

Bradan planted himself in front of the main stage among an assembling multitude. Unlike concerts of yore, most of the action was now virtual, as homebound audiences experienced it with better sound, better visuals than the in-person experience, so attendance by flesh-and-blood fans was shrinking. The avatars outnumbered real people. Changing times.

In the quiet between acts, Bradan heard wind chimes. He wouldn't have noticed unless he'd come in person. In Monterey 1967, the chimes had been hung with sincerity and innocence; today they were an ironic comment, a smug wink to the crowd.

He didn't know who would play next, didn't care. At the moment, life had nothing to do with professional music. He was just here to dig the scene. Like in 1967's Summer of Love, today was both a good and bad time, and an energizing time that inspired his creative instincts. He'd love to compose music, write and paint. However, he'd done little of that. Life had gotten in the way. Not bad life, just busy life as quotidian activities chewed away at the time needed to realize what his imagination conceived.

When he chose to strum it, his Martin twelve-string had retained its incandescent tone from times gone by. If anything, passing years had infused its wood with more stories to tell and melodies to play. And he still disturbed the neighbors occasionally when he plugged his Les Paul into a Marshall stack. However, these days, what little composing he did was in a home studio using programs to render ideas into music without touching a physical instrument.

At Bradan's side, Tintagel sat on his haunches, alertly observing the crowd. Bradan had gotten him past skeptical security by claiming the wolf was a service animal. The beast's primeval menace made this a tough sell, but he was reluctantly waved into the concert after Bradan threatened to contact his attorney. Just as in long-ago classrooms, most folks gave the wolf a wide berth. Occasionally Tintagel snapped at one of the more objectionable avatars, but this was done in sport since the creature wasn't fooled by illusions. Nonetheless, seeing these atavistic demonstrations, only the ditsiest fans wanted to pat the wolf.

A singer strode onto the stage. "To the real and unreal among you, hello, everyone!"

On cue, spotlights washed her in icy white light. Backing musicians filed after her and picked up instruments. They stayed in the shadows. It wasn't a band; she was the star.

"I'm doing a ton of my own stuff for you tonight," the singer said. "But first I've got to share a song that we're going to drop in a few days. You hear it here first tonight. Credit where it's due, I didn't write it. It's by—" She paused to let her bass player lean forward and say something to her.

"Ah yes. It's by The Pillars of Creation and the song is called 'An Emerald Boat on the Euphrates.' I think it's from an album of the same name. See what ya think."

Bradan stood shocked. History traveled in circles. It was the Pillars' song, but the performers threw a cool, loping baseline under jazzy percussion and strong instrumental work. The singer inserted a scat interlude into the song's middle section that took it to a different place. Bradan had heard a million covers of the Pillars' material, good, bad, mostly indifferent, but this was inventive as hell. When it finished, he clapped enthusiastically along with the avatars and real festivalgoers.

"Fun, huh? We cannot forget these old masterpieces, but we must also add our own take on them. Shit, it's hot up here, worse than Senegal, my home. Can I get water? God, thanks!"

They moved into the rest of their set.

Bradan messaged Taryn about what he'd just heard and got an instant reply. Technology was magic.

Taryn: We aren't forgotten. Want 2 ride?

Bradan: Creative juices flowing right here, not that I have time to make art or song.

Taryn: Come on ride. Not hunting, just mindless fun.

Bradan: Desert views?

Taryn: Spectacular.

Bradan: Ur on. C u at midnight. Bring spare pony. Lance not needed.

Now he wanted to reach out in a different direction. He called Gail. She was no fan of messaging's terse semaphore, so he went old-school and phoned her after disabling his device's visual image of him. She looked like the eighty-year-old she was; he looked as youthful as the young concertgoers around him. He could use makeup to add lines, wrinkles, and decades, but that took time, or he could magically remake his image to be a geriatric, but that took energy. He'd do neither and blame a technology failure for blocking sight of him tonight. They'd simply talk.

After the pleasantries, he asked how her dialysis was going.

"Therapy goes as it always goes." She never called her treatment for kidney failure "dialysis," instead referring to it as "therapy." He guessed that made it seem more manageable. As she'd aged, her intonations had reverted to her Brooklyn youth. No point in masking her origins to satisfy a tenure committee's biases. She could be exactly who she was.

"Where are you? It's noisy."

"Catching live music," he said.

"Your music thing. Aren't you a bit old for that?"

"Yeah, my 'music thing.'"

This was covering timeworn and not altogether agreeable ground between them. They'd never gotten married, but their relationship did have a good run of years and produced a son before it crashed and burned when he'd decamped to Miami and she'd gotten a full history professorship at Tulane. These days, communicating at a distance, their rapport had blossomed anew and now they talked frequently. Their son had fathered two daughters, one of whom, Rebecca, attended UC Berkeley majoring in political science. He'd never gotten his granddaughter interested in folklore. However, she did like music and had minored in composition. In fact, she might be at this festival with friends though she'd never recognize him looking as young as he did. He only visited her after spending an hour making himself up. He also changed his gait and posture to mimic bad joints.

"I saw Rebecca last week," he said. "She was at a protest on Telegraph." Bradan left out the part where their granddaughter had been teargased. "She's as full of ideals as you once were."

"As *we* once were. It was your idea to march into Sproul during Free Speech."

"I was cynical about people's motives then. I'm only more so now." This was another sore topic best left unplumbed. "But the idealism is there, too, as strong as ever and I'm feeling super inventive when I can find a moment away from scrambling after dollars. Crazy times, but inspiring; it's the gist for imagination."

They talked for a long while about current times and then signed off with pledges to call again soon. She was getting fatigued.

The façade with Gail was unsustainable. Only Taryn, the wolf, and the ghosts understood. Soon he'd abandon staying in touch with her, their son, their grandchildren, and this whole branch of his family. No amount of makeup and acting would forever mask the fact that he didn't age; he'd still look thirty in the next century, and the next, so gently severing ties was the appropriate step. He'd pretend to die of old age, assume another name, and quietly proceed with his long, well-lived life. The process was more complicated nowadays with government bureaucracy tracking a citizen's status, but nothing that a clever spell or two couldn't enable. It had happened dozens of times before. He remembered all of his families over more than a millennium.

"Yo, bro, you in trouble?" An avatar who looked like Jerry Garcia complete with a Grateful Dead T-shirt stood beside him. "You're crying."

"Dust," Bradan said.

"I'd offer you water, but—" The avatar shrugged.

"Yeah, I understand. I've got my own and a bandana, too." Bradan chugged water out of a bottle to mask the tears.

"Why you even there in person? Avoid dust, heat, thirst, firestorm smoke. Come as you aren't, like me. I work in systems design in Amsterdam. I'm with a friend from Cameroon." He gestured at a Tupac Shakur avatar.

"I'll go virtual next year," Bradan said. "Have a good concert."

Jerry and Tupac ambled off toward the stage, passing through the dense crowd as easily as vapor.

Merlin had been right: near immortality, even coupled with the vitality of youth, was a curse, but the curse could be leavened by pouring all the good, bad, and strange things from the eras he'd lived into the witch's cauldron of his imagination.

And every era had a signature. It was hard to see through the gauzy scrim of memory and realize what had really happened, but if one succeeded, the prize was raw material for the creative process.

At midnight he looked up and saw Taryn circling down toward him on her stallion with his charger in tow. She landed close to the main stage, but no one paid the slightest attention, assuming they were simply inventively designed avatars. Bradan mounted up and soon they circled far over the stunning panorama of the nighttime desert valley and the luridly lit concert grounds it surrounded.

There was more, much more to do. It was time to write songs again.

AUTHOR'S NOTES

A Note on Laurel Canyon's Creek

The novel describes a fast-flowing creek through Laurel Canyon in Los Angeles that plays a crucial role in saving the main character, Bradan, and the witch, Taryn. To the author's knowledge, no such creek exists today, but evidently it once did before the area was developed. It would make a scenic—though probably inconvenient—addition to modern Laurel Canyon, and it's too bad it's gone.

A Note on the Primavera Painting

Botticelli's *Primavera* painting plays a central part in a chapter providing backstory for the main character and one of the villains. There is no indication that the face of the picture's goddess of flowers, Flora, was painted by anyone other than Botticelli himself despite the proposed role of the novel's protagonist, Bradan. But who knows with absolute certainty?

A Note on Timelines

The timelines for recording, mixing, and distributing of The Pillars of Creation's major-label album have been shortened to align with other activities in the novel. For the same reason, timelines have also been shortened for the publication of the main character's academic research in peer-reviewed journals.

ACKNOWLEDGMENTS
AND BACKGROUND

L iterate entertainment is my goal. *The Lords of the Summer Season* blends fantasy, action, historical fiction, and a dash of romance. There are themes and motifs aplenty, but I've tried to use the plot to propel the story along at a fast pace. To this end, I've imported Robert E. Howard's headlong momentum into the action scenes, and Hunter S. Thompson influenced the motorcycle chases.

We've seen Bradan, *The Lords of the Summer Season*'s hero, before in *The Lords of Oblivion* and *The Lords of Powder*. Each of the three books can be read on its own or together as a series. All of them use extensive flashback and flashforward, but, if there is a chronological order to the novels, it would be: *The Lords of the Summer Season*, which takes place mostly in 1967, followed by *The Lords of Powder* occurring mostly in 1978, followed by *The Lords of Oblivion* set primarily in the present. Oddly, I've written them in reverse order to that sequence.

In *The Lords of the Summer Season*, Bradan remains as sarcastic and disenchanted as he was in the previous two novels, unsurprised by humanity's self-serving actions, but willing to be persuaded of their better nature. He's near immortal, so he's seen a lot including his own less-than-stellar behavior and he therefore reserves some mockery for himself. His redeeming qualities include an interest in helping unfortunates. He also has cultivated a sense of aesthetics and a robust creative spirit, both of which are showcased in this novel where he's a guitarist in a psychedelic-era, acid rock band in San Francisco and Los Angeles and a painter in Florence, as well as a lute-playing bard in Arthur and Merlin's sixth-century Britain.

The Lords of the Summer Season is mostly set during 1967's "Summer of Love." This period is too expansive and amorphous to be more than touched on by any one book, and, indeed, there is now a growing body of fiction set during this period with the requisite name checks for prominent musicians and pop cultural luminaries. For purists, this era centered in San Francisco's Haight-Ashbury neighborhood. However, I've expanded the geographic scope of my novel to include the Los Angeles music scene on Sunset Strip and in Laurel Canyon backyards. It all fits within the mid-'60s countercultural zeitgeist even though the respective groups of musicians in San Fran and LA didn't always see eye to eye.

Why focus on the Summer of Love? It's an intriguing period to explore in a fantasy, a genre that relies on magic as a key story element. The actual era may have been enchanted, having being mythologized to the point where its larger-than-life personages and their actions are bigger and bolder than prosaic reality. As noted in film director John Ford's westerns, when legend becomes fact, print the legend. Further, that distant summer provides an interesting commentary on present times, sharing elements including vibrant music, political ferment, and civic polarization. If one had to pick the exact moment when it all peaked flower-power-wise, a strong argument can be made for the Monterey Pop festival in June of 1967 when the tribes gathered to hear three days of sometimes spectacular pop/rock music. Hence, *The Lords of the Summer Season*'s climax occurs there.

Readers interested in this period need do no more than search the Internet for sounds and images contemporary to that period; but, additionally, books including *The Haight, Love, Rock and Revolution, The Photography of Jim Marshall*, by Joel Selvin, Bill Kreutzmann's *Deal*, Joel Selvin's *Summer of Love*, Michael Walker's *Laurel Canyon*, and John Glatt's *Live at the Fillmore East and West* are interesting introductions to the mid-'60s music scene as well as the broader "vibe" of that time.

I've also included flashback chapters set in sixth-century Britain, Renaissance Florence, and on the University of California's Berkeley campus during the Free Speech Movement in 1964 to provide backstories for the main characters. These are vivid memories for both the heroes and villains. In addition, the fifteenth-century Florentine artistic flowering provided a thought-provoking counterpoint to the Summer of Love. Obviously there are massive differences, not the least of which is that Florence's artistic rebirth lasted over a hundred years while the Summer of Love lasted a few months (or a few years if the late 1960s/early 1970s pop cultural scene is included in its entirety). Nonetheless, I like to think that Jerry Garcia would have gotten on well with Da Vinci. Both periods shared an energetic political and cultural environment—not always positive—that fostered creative responses from resident artists. In fact, this novel considers how creative inspiration is ignited by setting.

Granted, it's a stretch to juxtapose the Summer of Love and the Florentine Renaissance, but *The Lords of the Summer Season* is modern fantasy, so a writer in this genre should occasionally attempt outré flights of storytelling fancy. As best-selling writer Tad Williams states, a fantasy author can get away with anything as long as something tries to eat the hero every few pages. In *The Lords of the Summer Season*, plenty of dangers real and supernatural confront Bradan, starting on the first page. However, you, the gentle reader, can judge whether the approach works here.

Besides trying to make it by fronting an acid rock band, Bradan assiduously pursues tenure as a professor of folklore at a small southern California liberal arts university, giving him a bird's-eye view of the academic circus. A great deal of the '60s upheaval occurred on college campuses, and the novel takes a jaundiced look at academia. These institutions are certainly ripe for mockery with their pretensions, hierarchy, and inflated egos. As one of the novel's characters notes, almost no other large organizations except churches have such a gap between their stated mission and their actual behavior; self-interest happily thrives beneath an idealistic veneer. That was true five decades ago and it is today.

No fantasy story is complete without a vengeful villain or, in this case, two vengeful villains without morality. They oppose the (somewhat) moral Bradan at every turn. In *The Lords of the Summer Season*, the main antagonist, Van Newman, is a modern incarnation of Mordred, or, using the Welsh spelling as I do in the novel, Medraut. He's variously described as Arthur's bastard son and his killer at the battle of Camlann, but there are as many descriptions of him as there are Arthurian stories in the Early and High Medieval periods. To me, he seemed to have the amorality, ability to manipulate, and drive that would serve him well in the modern political arena and that's how he appears in *The Lords of the Summer Season*. Readers interested in learning more about Arthurian legends are encouraged to start with Christopher Hibbert's *King Arthur*. And for a wonderful travelogue visiting important British Dark Ages sites, Max Adams's *In the Land of Giants* is recommended.

The story's second villain is Gwyn ap Nudd, Welsh king of the Otherworld, Medraut's sponsor, and leader of the Wild Hunt.

Like Medraut, his role and character are variously described by sources, but he definitely wasn't someone to get on the wrong side of since he wrenched out the souls of individuals who fell afoul of him. His henchmen, the Wild Hunt, were atavistic savagery incarnate, vision colliding with reality. Peter Nicolai Arbo's painting *The Wild Hunt of Odin*, portrays the hunt luridly. Though Odin leads it in Arbo's image, other legends say this is Gwyn's pack. In my novel, the Wild Hunt is led by Gwyn and, among other things, serves as a metaphor for unbounded creativity run amok.

Of course, romance belongs in a fantasy about the Summer of Love, and Bradan has two contrasting women to cuddle and clash with. Taryn is the modern incarnation of Morgana le Fey, legendary enchantress in Arthur's Dark Ages court, as well as Merlin's paramour. Like Bradan, she's almost immortal, a bit immoral, and unashamedly ambiguous about her intentions toward Bradan. Gail Halpern, while not supernatural, is unashamedly clear and direct about her goals, essential for a woman forging her way through a thicket of academic politics in the mid-'60s. And let's not forget Veronica from fifteenth-century Florence, Bradan's muse and the model for one of the Renaissance's great allegorical paintings. She's based on historical figures during this era. Had she lived longer, who knows where her relationship with Bradan might have gone? These three characters help the novel consider the nature of romantic attraction.

Regarding the tone of *The Lords of the Summer Season*, I've followed George R. R. Martin's dictum to take actual events and crank things up to eleven. That seemed appropriate for a story about an acid rock band.

Many thanks to Anne, Shikha, Steve F., Steve L., John B., and Carolyn for insightful input. Of course, any errors, omissions, or purple prose are my fault.

ABOUT THE AUTHOR

Peter Blaisdell lives in the LA area. He has a Ph.D. in Biochemistry and has conducted postdoctoral research in microbiology. He has published peer-reviewed research papers as well as articles on business management. On the literary side of his life, he is an active reviewer of general fiction, fantasy, science fiction, and magical realism.

The Lords of the Summer Season is the third work in this series, which includes the previously published *The Lords of Oblivion* and *The Lords of Powder*. Each book can be read as a stand-alone novel or together as part of an ongoing series. All of them use extensive flashback and flashforward, but, if there is a chronological order to the novels, it would be: *The Lords of the Summer Season*, which takes place mostly in 1967, followed by *The Lords of Powder* occurring mostly in 1978, followed by *The Lords of Oblivion* set primarily in the present. Oddly, I've written them in reverse order to that sequence.

Contact the author at blaisdellliteraryenterprises.com.

CPSIA information can be obtained
at www.ICGtesting.com
Printed in the USA
JSHW050803170222
22951JS00001BA/22

9 780999 220504